ALEXANDER ZVYAGINTSEV

THE NUREMBERG TRIALS

Translated from the Russian by Christopher Culver

Published with the support of the Institute
for Literary Translation, Russia

GLAGOSLAV PUBLICATIONS

THE NUREMBERG TRIALS
by Alexander Zvyagintsev

Translated from the Russian by Christopher Culver

Published with the support of the Institute
for Literary Translation, Russia

Publishers Maxim Hodak & Max Mendor

© 2019, Alexander Zvyagintsev

© 2019, Glagoslav Publications

www.glagoslav.com

ISBN: 978-1-78437-986-5

ALEXANDER ZVYAGINTSEV

THE NUREMBERG TRIALS

Translated from the Russian by Christopher Culver

ИНСТИТУТ ПЕРЕВОДА

AD VERBUM

Published with the support of the Institute
for Literary Translation, Russia

CONTENTS

AND IT WILL BE GIVEN TO YOU

PART II. TOWARDS FATE

AN ENCOUNTER WITH
A TINGE OF PARTING

CHAPTER I. AND REMEMBER ME!

All the newspapers in the USA were buzzing about the events in the newly defeated Germany, about the throngs of prisoners who no longer knew where to go, about the search for Hitler and the other high-ranking Nazis who were either in hiding or had taken their own lives. Nazi Germany was finished; all that was left was to deal with its rotten remains and decide what could and should be put in its place. There was no shortage now of heroic types ready to take the most extreme measures: "Kill them all! If you leave even a single one, they'll start breeding again like rabbits and you'll have to start all over again," such were the words of one irate statesman on the Germans, though in the past his view had been quite moderate. The more cunning and cold-blooded preferred like always to leave it in the hands of others: "Let the Russians do the dirty work. We won't have anything to do with it."

A man, around 30 years of age, put his newspaper aside and sat deep in thought. Outside his New York apartment the whole city was teeming, overjoyed at a triumphant victory. No one, whether in New York or anywhere else, was aware that this man who had been studying the American press was a deeply embedded Soviet agent, known by the code name "Hector". Even in Moscow only a handful of people knew of this.

As he had often done in recent days, Hector was thinking about his father, who had died before the war even began.

Hector had grown up like any ordinary American: high school, football, college, a free and independent life on campus with all that came with it. His mother had died in a car accident when he was only 12. His father was always busy with work; a State Department employee, he was always being called to Washington and rarely seen at their suburban home. Hector had therefore come to feel himself a lonely hunter, who could only rely on himself.

Yet he loved and respected his father, sensing in him a serious and tense inner world and a firm belief in the existence of certain values that must be preserved, whatever they might be. What these values were exactly, Hector could guess during the infrequent times that the two of them talked seriously. His father never appealed to him to believe in something or lectured him, he spoke only of his views on some event or another, letting his son make his own conclusions. Thus Hector learned that his father despised distinctions of class, the division of people into rich and poor, that he had little love for extreme competition where people would do anything to excel above the others and push them down. He considered the American love for business to be a rat race, where, if you didn't succeed, you could end up in the dump. The eternal pursuit of money, his father thought, left little time for other things, even the pleasure of spending it. Some of these talks were soon forgotten, but something was yet firmly lodged in Hector's thinking.

His father was especially troubled by everything that was happening in Germany since Hitler came to power. He believed that this man was the devil himself and capable of leading the world into a horrific catastrophe, and he had to be stopped at any cost. From some of what his father said, Hector could conclude that in America there were people who had not only helped Hitler seize power, they even helped to arm him, to create the most advanced and well-equipped of armies.

In the late Thirties, after he graduated from college, Hector left for Europe to see the Old World, the native land of his ancestors. A telegram unexpectedly arrived with news that his father was gravely ill and Hector had to return. Upon arrival he could hardly recognize his father: liver cancer had eaten away at him. When they were left alone, his father said with labored breathing, "I want to tell you something that might be too much if you heard it from others… I've been collaborating with the Russians for several years now… I've been passing on information that might help them in the fight against Hitler."

Hector was stunned and could only sit there silently. There was a ringing emptiness in his head. His father saw what he felt and also remained silent for some time, breathing heavily. Then he said, "You know that I consider Germany in Hitler's grasp to be the gravest danger for the entire world. But it's not just that. I am convinced that only the Russians can stop him. There is no one else. The French simply do not want to fight, the British are obsessed with the idea of foisting him on the Russians and don't want any more to do with it. We Americans believe that we're completely safe and so we're sitting out, hoping it'll be left to others. Many people in this country are waiting to enjoy the spectacle of the Russians and Germans bleeding each other dry. But the way I see it, that's mistaken and mean-spirited..."

Hector continued to stay silent and look at his father.

"That's why I decided that we've got to help the Russians... I know that they're no angels and I don't like a lot of what Stalin's doing, but... Only he can smash Hitler, only Russia with its huge forces. After they beat Hitler, surely they'll change..."

His father gasped for air. Large drops of sweat could be seen on his jaundiced forehead with its prominent blue veins.

"That's all. Now you know... I hope you'll understand my decision. I don't care about money. I just did what I thought was necessary. There's a piece of paper on the table, it'll tell you how to get in touch with the Russians, if you... Do whatever you see fit."

His father died the same evening. For the next six months Hector was wracked with doubt. Yet the world constantly pointed to how his father had been right. The West maintained its cold stance towards the war, counting on the fact that Germany and the Soviet Union would destroy each other. All of Russia's attempts to build a coalition against Hitler coolly and methodically came to naught. In these days, the United States had already taken a large number of refugees from Germany, and Hector learned firsthand what Hitler's system was really like. It was clear that Europe could not hold out against Hitler's forces, that the Germans would simply parade through the continent. The Russians were the last hope. It was nearly by accident that he found out then that Ford and General Motors were, through their German branches, actively participating in building up the motorized forces of Hitler's army. The Soviet Union was doomed to a terrible fight. By now his mind was firmly made up, and he used his father's note to contact the Russians...

Now, several years since his father's death, and when Hitler had been defeated at the cost of so many lives, chiefly Russian ones, he thought that his father had been right. He had made the right choice when he decided to help them. But what now, when the war was over? Should he become a spy, disclosing the secrets of his own country?

Outside his window, New York continued to celebrate.

Notes

As reported by TASS, on April 27, 1942 the USSR presented a note to all foreign embassies entitled "On the monstrous atrocities and violence of the German fascist invaders in occupied Soviet areas and on the responsibility of the German government and high command for these crimes."

On November 2, 1942 the Presidium of the Supreme Soviet of the USSR adopted the decree "On the formation of an Extraordinary State Committee to establish and investigate the atrocities of the fascist invaders and their accomplices and the damage they have brought against citizens, collective farms, public organizations, state enterprises and institutions of the USSR."

CHAPTER II. THE LABYRINTH OF HELL

"What are we looking for here?"

"The truth. We're looking for the truth. What else?"

"I mean specifically."

"Well, if you mean specifically, we're looking for truth that Hitler really committed suicide, and didn't just flee in a submarine to Australia…"

"They've already found two bodies!"

"That's the problem. There should be just one! One, but the real one! The man himself! We don't need any doubles…"

Their minds were weary from their long trawl through the musty catacombs of Hitler's underground bunker and their tired eyes were visibly sore. The endless corridors that resembled a labyrinth, the dark crannies and secret rooms, there seemed no end to them. Here and there lights shone and a fetid mist hung in the air.

Everywhere there were traces of a hurried flight: the floors were strewn with papers, overturned books, photographs and postcards marked with the prints of soles, an officer's uniform carelessly thrown down in haste, boots in non-matching sizes, foppish dress uniforms with swastikas and caps… In one room they found a number of red velvet boxes containing Iron Cross medals, while another room held a mountain of copies of *Mein Kampf.* On top of them was a first-aid kit in fine leather and a white metal box that, after they had carefully opened it, proved to be a device for measuring air quality – the inhabitants of the bunker, so far under the earth, worried that they would be smoked out like animals.

"The smell here," Captain Karpovich grimaced.

"It's the ordinary smell of the underworld," Major Rebrov grinned back at him. "It's the den of the Nazi beast, after all. Did you think it would smell like roses here?"

Major Denis Rebrov and Captain Mikhail Karpovich were members of the same search team founded at Moscow's order right after Soviet forces had entered Germany, with the express goal of finding and capturing high-ranking Nazis. When they stormed into Berlin, their team, reporting directly to General Filin, turned their search directly to Hitler himself or his body in the underground bunker under the Reich Chancellery.

Rebrov and Karpovich were still young, but the years of war, missions and the most demanding intelligence work weighed heavily on their shoulders. They made a good team. Rebrov always led, but this didn't bother the good-natured and hardworking Karpovich at all. Rebrov had managed to graduate from the university literally the same day that the war broke out. He spoke German fluently and his superiors appreciated him for his English skills, his ability to think quickly and make independent decisions on the fly. Everyone knew that the head of the intelligence division, Gen. Filin, had an especial sympathy for him. And for good reason, Karpovich thought, men like Rebrov were sorely needed. He ought to be a general. Karpovich himself could hardly wait to return to civilian life – before the war he had studied car repair in a technical school and got engaged to a girl.

Karpovich kicked down yet another door and peered into a small room. He recoiled.

A table stood in the middle of the room, covered with a white tablecloth. Right on the tablecloth lay the body of a dead man in the black dress uniform of an SS officer. His polished shoes shone with a deathly gleam.

"Don't touch him," Rebrov warned as he peered into the room over Karpovich's shoulder. "He might be booby-trapped. He looks too enticing…"

They carefully walked around the corpse.

"He's got a bullet hole in his temple," noted Karpovich.

"I can see that. I don't know who the hell this is, but it's not Hitler… Let's mark the door and warn the sappers."

"Yeah, no one wants to die after the war's over," Karpovich muttered as he marked a large cross on the door with chalk.

"When are they going to let us go home, eh?" Karpovich asked yet again, kicking the dress uniform jacket of some Nazi bigwig to the side. "Do we really have to hang around here until we've caught every Himmler?"

"You did spend the whole war dreaming of getting your hands on them…"

"I did, but I feel like something is drawing me home!"

Karpovich suddenly perked up. "Listen, what would you do to him if we found him? Just imagine, we open that door there and Hitler's just sitting there, alive. The man himself! What would you do to him, huh? Honestly?"

"We'll find him, you'll see." Rebrov gestured, "Open it."

As with so many doors before, Karpovich knocked this one down with a kick and in the light of their lantern they glimpsed a man in a German uniform sitting on the floor. With his hands he was shielding his face from the blinding rays.

"Hands up!" Karpovich barked, pointing his gun at the German.

The German, without rising up from the floor, docilely raised his hands. He was clearly mortified with fear. Then he clumsily moved to all fours and got up on his knees. He froze in that position, on his knees with his hands up.

"Don't shoot! I'm unarmed. Please, don't shoot!"

Rebrov quickly looked around the room and couldn't help but frown.

"What a smell! Have you been sitting here long?"

"I don't know, a few days…"

"Mikhail, move him to another room before we suffocate in here…"

After Karpovich led the man into a room where several tables and chairs had been preserved, he ordered the German to sit on a chair in the middle of the room. Karpovich himself sat authoritatively at the head of the table, swept several papers and photographs from it in disgust, set his rifle in front of him, and stared hard at the prisoner. Rebrov casually perched on a chair near the door. Their actions followed a clearly defined logic; they had already carried out dozens of interrogations before.

"Who are you?" Karpovich asked.

"Private Joachim Fisch, sir."

"From what unit?"

"SS Begleitkommando Adolf Hitler…"

Karpovich and Rebrov exchanged a meaningful glance

"So, you were Hitler's bodyguard?" ascertained Rebrov.

Fisch turned towards him. His face, dirty and overgrown with stubble, showed a desire to answer questions clearly and in as much detail as possible. "I dealt with communications – I passed on dispatches, letters, newspapers. I carried out some personal assignments. Lately I was working as a telephone operator, I worked at the switchboard…"

Karpovich cut him off, "Where is Hitler? Where did he run off to? How? Who helped him?"

"Hitler shot himself, sir!"

"You're lying! Everyone knows that there was a body double of Hitler in the bunker, and the real Hitler fled Berlin. Where did he go? We got his personal pilot, he said you knew everything! Hans Baur, Hitler's pilot. You know the guy?"

"Of course I know Hans Baur, but…."

"No buts! Either you spill your guts or we'll shoot you! Right here and now! How did Hitler get out of Berlin? Who helped him? Who was with him?"

The German, still keeping his hands visible on his knees, trembled. The men could hear how he breathed air into his dry throat in small gasps.

Rebrov stood up and moved towards the German, who shrank from him and closed his eyes.

"What about the body lying in the room next to the fire extinguisher?" Rebrov asked him softly.

"That's Truschke, sir. He shot himself."

"From fear? Or was he too dedicated to the cause, he couldn't handle the fall of the Thousand-Year Reich?"

"No, because of his wife."

"What?!" Karpovich couldn't contain his surprise.

"Because of his wife. She was pregnant, she was going to give birth soon, but then he suddenly found out the child wasn't his. His wife had cheated on him. He put his dress uniform on and…"

"The life of an SS man," Karpovich shook his head. "It's a real love story."

"Let's go," Rebrov ordered the German, who then tried to stand up but couldn't.

"Are you going to shoot me?"

"Us? No," Rebrov shrugged.

"We're going to cook you and eat you," Karpovich laughed. "Listen, Rebrov, let's go back up, we can interrogate him there. I don't want to stay here another minute. I feel like I'm going to vomit!"

They had gone out into the hallway and managed to take only a few steps before the sound of a rifle hit them. The reverberation of shots in the narrow corridor hurt their ears.

Fisch, who had been walking in front, grabbed his shoulders and fell to the floor. Rebrov and Karpovich dropped alongside him. The hallway shook with another series of shots. Then, silence descended.

From around a corner a figure appeared, half-crouched and holding a German rifle. Keeping low to the ground, it moved toward them. When it was only a few steps from Fisch, shots rang out. It was Rebrov who was shooting, after he had rolled over on his back and gripped his pistol with both hands.

The figure jerked, fell to the side and remained frozen on the floor"

Without turning around, Rebrov asked, "Karpovich! Mikhail, you OK?"

Karpovich could only give a nearly inaudible moan in reply.

Rebrov, continuing to fire, turned over on his belly and then stood up, as he put one bullet after another into the man who had fallen. When his rounds had finished, he rushed to Karpovich. The captain was lying on his back, his lifeless eyes staring at the ceiling and bloody foam bubbling on his lips.

"You got him, you bastard, and after the war was already over." he whispered with his mouth clenched, lacking the strength to even part his lips. "I won't get to see…"

Staggering and squinting at the sudden daylight, Fisch emerged from a cellar window in the courtyard of the Reich Chancellery, which had been completely leveled. He stood there for some time, taking deep breaths. Rebrov's stoic face appeared in the window behind him. When Fisch saw him, he rushed to Rebrov and held out his hand to help him climb out. "I'm here, sir," he quickly muttered. "I'm not trying to run away! I don't know who that man with the rifle was. Don't kill me! I've got a wife and little girl!"

Rebrov looked around at the bombed courtyard, still burning, and the ruins of the walls. He seemed to hardly know where he was.

A dust-covered jeep approach them and a man, no longer young, jumped out. His officer's uniform could not hide his slight, awkward, and completely civilian figure. His stern face, cut with deep wrinkles, and his mysterious gray eyes clashed with his awkward external appearance.

"Denis!"

Rebrov turned to look. His lips twitched. "Mikhail. Karpovich… They killed him," he could barely manage to get the words out.

"Who did?"

"In the Reich Chancellery cellar. Some idiot suddenly jumped out at us."

"This guy?" Filin turned his gaze to Fisch.

The German shrank with fear and raised his hands, frantically shaking his head.

"No," Rebrov shook his head. "This one surrendered. He had been just sitting there for days, afraid to poke his head out. He's from the Begleitkommando, he was with Hitler to the end."

"Well then, we've got some matters to discuss…"

Rebrov shrugged his shoulders

"Comrade general, we've got to get Mikhail out of here. I'm going back for him…"

"Wait! I'll give you some men to help," Filin shouted after him.

Rebrov seemed not to hear him and without speaking crawled back into the cellar window.

"Quickly, follow him," Filin ordered the two machine gunners that accompanied him. "And watch out down there!"

Notes

The War Cabinet still saw objections to a formal state trial of war criminals for the most notorious Nazis whose crimes had no geographic location. If, however, their two great Allies definitely wanted a judicial trial of such men, the British were willing to bow to them in the matter. … [Eden] stated that the British understood that the normal military courts of the four Allies would be used to take care of the ordinary war crimes committed inside Germany.

From the memorandum of
a conversation on the investigation
of war crimes, held at the Fairmont Hotel
in San Francisco on May 3, 1945.

CHAPTER III. THE DEVIL'S SOLITAIRE

Fisch, who was used to standing at attention, was devouring Filin, seated at a desk, with his eyes, just as a few days before he had done with Hitler, Goebbels, and Himmler.

Filin, looking up at him with his clear eyes, asked in an unexpectedly gentle tone, "What year were you born in?"

"1920!" Fisch answered sprightly.

"1920! You're still young. Why should you die, soldier? You've got your whole life ahead of you. You ought to be grateful you're still alive in the midst of all this carnage. Do you have a family?"

"A wife and daughter, general."

"A wife and daughter. You ought to feel some responsibility for them."

"That's right, general, I do. I'd do anything to see them again!"

"That's good. So, you were with Hitler until the end, and you are ready to swear that it was Adolf Hitler himself and not his body double?"

"That's right, general. He had lost a lot of weight recently, of course, but it was him."

"How many years did you serve him?"

"Since May 1940."

"Well, that's certainly long enough to be able to tell Hitler from his double, isn't it?"

"That's right!"

"So, you wouldn't be mistaken? And if it suddenly turned out that Hitler had fled nonetheless and was in hiding, and you're lying and covering for him, do you understand what's going to happen to you?"

"I do."

"And…"

"He killed himself. It was on April 30. I ran into him in the hallway. He walked past without saying anything. Some time later he and

Eva Braun took their leave of the people closest to them and retired to their room. In the hallway I heard a cry, "Linge, I think that will be all!"

"Who's Linge?"

"Hitler's valet."

"Did you hear the gunshots yourself?"

"No."

"Where were you at that time?"

"In the switchroom."

"Alone?"

"With Hentschel and Retzlaff."

"Who are they?"

"Civilian employees in the bunker. Then there was a deathly silence. I couldn't stand it any longer, I looked out into the hallway and saw Linge and Günsche, Hitler's adjutant, go into the room that the Führer was in. Hitler was sitting on a sofa next to a table with his head slumped on his chest. Eva Braun was next to him, with her legs folded and he head slumped all the way down on her knees. She was wearing a dark blue dress with a white collar in the shape of little flowers…"

"Little flowers. Did you go into the room?"

"No?"

"How far were you standing from Hitler's body."

"About six meters."

"What happened next?"

"I felt uneasy, I wanted to leave, but then I came back. Now Hitler's body had been laid out on the floor. People from his security detail were standing next to him. They lifted him up and wrapped him in a gray blanket. Then they carried him out the emergency exit. His boots were sticking out of the blanket… Then Retzlaff ran up to me and said 'They're burning the boss! Come on, let's go up and watch!' He was in a very excited state, completely crazy. We were all in that state…"

"And then?"

"I totally refused to go."

"Why?"

"I… I didn't want to see it. And then… All of us there were simply frozen with fear. We didn't understand anything of what happened. I just remember being afraid that 'Gestapo Müller', as we called him, would shoot us all on the spot so that there wouldn't be any witnesses left."

"So the Gestapo chief Heinrich Müller was there at the time? In the bunker?"

"Yes. I had seen him shortly before all of this happened… I'm telling you, we in the bunker were terrified that the secret police would kill us all to wipe out any and all traces."

Filin sat for a moment deep in thought.

"Goebbels was still in the bunker after his death…"

"Yes, general, he lived there with his wife and children. He had six kids and they would run around the bunker laughing and playing. It was creepy. On April 26 – I remember the date well – Hanna Reitsch, she's an aviator, managed to land a light plane right at the Brandenburg Gate on Unter den Linden street…"

"Yes, that's why they removed the streetlights from there…"

"I heard Reitsch trying to persuade Goebbels' wife to leave the children with her. 'Well, if you want to remain here, so be it' she said, 'But why the kids?' But Magda said that her and her husband had already decided everything, they had their own ideas about the children's future. While they were talking, the children were playing in the next room…"

"When did you see Goebbels for the last time? In what circumstances?"

"We knew that he had decided to kill himself in the bunker along with his wife and kids."

"After killing their own children."

"Yes, you're probably right. His children were aged four to twelve and they still didn't understand anything of what was going on. I'm telling you, they spent the whole time playing. On May 1, Magda came out of their room and walked past me as I was sitting at the switchboard with the door open. I saw tears in her eyes. She sat down and started playing solitaire, and then Goebbels came out of their room. He stood there watching his wife. He asked her, 'What are you doing?' Without looking at him, she said, 'I'm playing solitaire.'"

"Before that she had poisoned her own children. All six of them…"

"Yes, sir. I can't imagine how a person could do such a thing! And then Artur Axmann, the leader of the Hitler Youth, came in and just started talking, reminiscing about the past. Magda made some coffee. But the children…"

"The children were laying in the next room, poisoned by their own mother."

"Yes. That's when I decided to leave. Goebbels came to me and I told him that. He said it was all over and shook my hand. It was the first time ever, he had never done such a thing before."

"I wouldn't be proud of that."

"I just want you to believe me, general, I'm not hiding anything and I'm only telling you the truth. I didn't say anything as he took his leave. I was the last soldier to leave this kingdom of death."

"So, when Goebbels killed himself, you weren't present and you didn't see his body?"

"No."

"What about Bormann? He also stayed to the very end."

"Yes. He gathered a group of people, they decided to try to break out of Berlin and head west. Several officers were in that group, but I didn't go with them. I wasn't anyone to them anyway, a soldier like me. General, believe me, I just relayed dispatches, passed on letters and newspapers, and worked the telephones. My duties were to always be at hand, but without anyone noticing me. I wasn't a member of the Nazi Party, I didn't join the Hitler Youth. I just did my duty as a soldier. I did it honestly."

"And if they had asked you to kill someone?" Filin smiled. "Shoot them?"

"They wouldn't have ordered me to do that. There were other people for that. I carried out other duties. For example, I passed on presents that Hitler sent famous people on their birthdays, like the boxer Max Schmeling or the actress Olga Chekhova. She's an amazingly beautiful woman, Hitler really admired her…"

"Where does she live?"

"In Kladow, it's a suburb of Berlin. She's got a house there…"

He could hardly be lying, Filin thought wearily. He's too scared, he really wants to stay alive. And he's not smart enough to lie. He talks about what he saw. But he didn't see everything. Who knows what happened in Hitler's room, and whose shoes were sticking out from under the blanket…

After trawling through the smoking ruins of Berlin, Gen. Filin's jeep broke free of the city and hit the highway. It soon stopped in front of a group of Soviet soldiers who were lazily smoking in the sunshine. Several steps away from them, a middle-aged German man in civilian clothes was sitting on the ground with his head down.

Filin and Rebrov got out of the car and walked towards them. When the soldiers saw the officers, they threw their cigarettes down.

"What's going on here?" Filin asked impatiently.

"Comrade general, allow me to report," a young, mustached sergeant, clearly hailing from the Caucasus, rushed up. "We've detained this kraut. We noticed that he's been hanging around here for a few days now. He's clearly on the lookout for something. It's very suspicious. Obviously he's former military…"

Filin turned to Rebrov. "You talk to him, Denis."

While Rebrov was interrogating the German, Filin absentmindedly looked around, thinking his own thoughts.

"Comrade General!" The sergeant from the Caucasus came up to him. "May I speak with you?"

"Sure, sergeant. What is it?" Filin sighed.

"Tell me, did Hitler really shoot himself? Or take poison? People are saying that he flew off somewhere and his guards shot his body double and burned the corpse…"

Filin wearily nodded. "That's what people are saying."

The other soldiers were listening keenly to their conversation.

"They're also saying that he headed for the sea, that a submarine was waiting for him there that would take him to Antarctica, where a secret lair had been prepared…"

"What, to Antarctica?" Filin laughed. "He went to join the penguins?"

"That's what people are saying, comrade general."

"I know what people are saying. I've heard it, too. Some bodies have been found in the meantime, and one of them should be Hitler's. They're trying to establish which one is his."

"I understand, comrade general. I hope to God the bastard didn't get away!"

"He shouldn't have…"

Rebrov came up to them.

"Well?" Filin raised his brows.

"The devil knows! He says that an acquaintance of his called him here and said he had something important to tell him, but then he never showed up. He doesn't know what the guy wanted to tell him." Rebrov looked around.

"It's a strange place to meet someone, right next to the road. What's that thing there?"

Rebrov stepped aside and kicked at a metal lever sticking out of the ground among the ruins of a small building. "It's some kind of lever," he said. He tugged at it several times, first with one hand and then with two.

"Careful, Denis!" Filin stopped him. "What if it's mined?"

But it was already too late. Behind them a screeching was heard that gradually grew louder, and part of the asphalt surface of the road began to slowly shift, revealing a dark tunnel leading underground. The soldiers stared slack-jawed in amazement. Rebrov jumped up and rushed to the German.

"What's down there? What's down there, I'm asking you?"

"I don't know! I don't know. Heinrich told me nothing about it," the German frantically sought to defend himself. "I don't know!"

"Well, let's have a look," Filin said calmly. "It might be an underground hangar. Yesterday some of Hitler's guards said something about that during the interrogation. And not only Hitler's men… Just be careful, we've had enough running into idiots with rifles…"

As they made their way down the tunnel, descending at an incline, they reached an enormous underground hangar containing three light aircraft.

"It must have been prepared for Hitler himself," one of the soldiers gasped.

"They would have taken off right from the highway, using it as a runway," Filin suggested.

The soldiers continued to argue about Hitler.

"Exactly, Hitler could have flown off from here!"

"And how could he have gotten here from his bunker? You think he crawled here?"

"Through an underground pathway! There are such things there. I was there, I know…"

Filin, interrupting their conversation, called the sergeant over and calmly said,

"So, sergeant, you'll stay in charge here. Don't allow anyone to enter. A team from SMERSH will come with sappers, they'll inspect everything. Let them look for any underground pathways. As for this guy," he pointed to the German, "hand him over to them."

"Yes, sir, comrade general!"

"Let's go, Denis. There's no one still alive here. The others can manage without us."

Notes

According to the intelligence received by our reconnaissance, the servicemen at the Travemünde air base were ordered in the last weeks of the war to continually maintain a four-engine plane

in a state of readiness which would be able to
carry a large amount of fuel. The plane may have
been intended to allow Hitler to escape to Japan.
It could accommodate only three passengers,
apparently Hitler and Eva Braun along with one
other person close to him. Besides this plane,
three hydroplanes were also kept at this secret
air base in a state of full readiness…

CHAPTER IV. CHEAP TRICKS

Several soldiers from the 110th American Airborne Division commanded by an officer with a Clark Gable mustache and the same appearance of a southern gentlemen, slowly proceeded in two jeeps up along a winding mountain road in the Bavarian Alps. An elderly German in a Tyrolean hat was showing them the way. He sat with his hands on his knees in the back between two soldiers. The Bavarian was exaggeratedly polite and courteous, but it didn't bother the Americans. They had already grown used to Germans behaving that way.

"We're almost there, Herr Officer," the Bavarian said. "The house is around that bend."

"Is he alone there?" the American officer asked.

"I cannot say, Herr Officer. I didn't go in."

"What about weapons? Are there any weapons?"

"Forgive me, Herr Officer, but I do not know about that either."

The road finally ended at a one-story wooden house. The soldiers jumped out of the jeeps, spoke a few words in a low voice, and surrounded the house with their rifles ready.

No sounds came from the house. The officer made a sign and two soldiers knocked the door down and burst into the house. In the half-lit room a man lay on a wooden bed, bearded and dressed in civilian clothes. He was staring at the ceiling with dull eyes.

"Hands up! Drop weapons! Do you have any weapons?"

The bearded man rose with some difficulty and, struck with fear, held his hands up. Then he shook his head desperately. He was either afflicted by a nervous tick or suffering from a terrible hangover – the table and floor were covered with empty bottles.

"Did you manage all this yourself?" the officer smirked, distrustful of the man.

The bearded man continued to stare at him slack-jawed and with empty eyes. He seemed to simply not understand what the officer had asked.

"Is this him?" the American asked their Bavarian guide, nodding towards the bearded man.

"*Jawohl*, Herr Officer," the guide said. "It is the man himself."

The American officer turned towards the bearded figure. The hands of the man, who seemed to no longer be in command of his body, flopped down tiredly.

"Fine, you don't have to keep your hands up," the author pitied him. "Are you Dr. Robert Ley?"

The bearded man drunkenly shook his head.

"You have made some mistake."

"Some mistake? Who are you, then?"

"I am… Dr. Ernst Distelmeyer. You have made a mistake. I do not know any Dr. Ley!"

The officer turned to the guide. He straightened as if standing at attention.

"Don't trust him, Herr Officer! It's him, Dr. Ley! The same man… Aren't you ashamed of yourself, Dr. Ley? Show some courage!"

But the German only stupidly shook his head. "I am Dr. Distelmeyer. I have proof."

"OK, then," the American cut the pointless argument short. "You're a doctor. Come with us!"

"You have made a mistake, officer," the bearded man complained.

"Fine, we'll talk about it when you've sobered up."

At the headquarters of the American division, another officer now listened to the somewhat more sober but still insistent bearded man.

"You have made a mistake," he went on. "I have got proof. I am Dr. Distelmeyer. Why do you not believe me?"

"Because you're lying!" the American roared. "We've got every reason to believe that you are Robert Ley, head of the German Labor Front, director of the Central Inspectorate for Foreign Workers. One of the closest men to Hitler. The Führer had an especial trust in you!"

"There must be some horrible mistake. Horrible…"

"God," the American couldn't control himself, "and people like you had the whole world by the throat. You worm, you think you can trick us just like that? Your friend Himmler also had fake documents in the name of some Heinrich Hitzinger… The only difference between you two is that you decided to grow a beard and Himmler shaved off his ugly little mustache and wore a black eye patch. Do you really think such cheap tricks would save you from being found?"

"It is a mistake, a mistake." Ley muttered, rocking back and forth. "It's a very big mistake. A very big mistake."

"Oh well," the American said. He got up and opened the door to admit a neatly dressed elderly German who was holding his hat in his hand. Ley gaped at him and then turned away.

"Dr. Ley, you're here!" the old man cried. "What are you doing here?"

"That's a good question," the American officer laughed. "Our Dr. Ley is playing the fool. Who knows what he's hoping for. Allow me, Dr. Ley, to present Franz Schwartz, the former treasurer of the Nazi Party and someone you've known for many years. And on the other side of that door is his son, who you used to work with…"

Ley, muttering something, put his hand into his hands.

"Well, are you going to go on acting like this? Or should we end this farce? You're a general, you should act like it."

"Enough," Ley let out his breath. "Enough already. I'm really Dr. Ley…"

"That's better," the American said with contempt. "You're under arrest, Dr. Ley. US command will decide what to do with you. I'll give you some advice as I say goodbye, and when you finally sober up in prison, you should think very carefully about it. Soon you're going to be asked a lot of questions. Answer them honestly, those questions. Every single one. Stop fooling around and remember that your life is in our hands. We're the ones who decide what to do with it. You just have to answer our questions."

Notes

As Hector, a Soviet intelligence agent in the United States reports, a special team of doctors and scientists has been sent from the USA to Germany. Their task is to record carefully (without revealing their interests to the other Allies) and in detail everything related to SS and Gestapo doctors' experiments with mescaline, an extract from the peyote cactus. Experiments were conducted on prisoners, mainly Russians, in the Dachau concentration camp. The goal was to find a way of sapping willpower and paralyzing the human mind in order to shift thinking in the right direction.

A dedicated Unit 19 was created in the United States which was to use the results obtained by the Germans to create various drugs that highly secret American agents could use outside the US. This meant special-purpose weapons: chemical, biological, and psychological means of influence.

CHAPTER V. A QUEEN COMES ON STAGE

Rebrov got out of a big black Horch which had until recently belonged to some Nazi bigwig, and he looked at the nice two-story home that loomed over a small and neat garden. The house had remained untouched through the bombings and the Soviet assault and looked absurdly peaceful and respectable among the rubble and dust of Berlin. In Kladow, on the distant outskirts of the German capital, a number of such homes had survived.

He was surprised only by a rather deep trench, three meters long, that had been dug in the garden next to the low fence. Rebrov stared at it with some astonishment and then headed for the home. The door was open for some reason, but just in case Rebrov knocked before resolving to step inside.

In the large room a tall and slender lady with blond hair was standing facing away from the window and hugging her shoulders. The light coming through the window gave an air of artificiality, as if the woman was upon a stage and Rebrov watched in wonder from the darkness of the theatre.

The woman remained silent for some time, as if she was allowing herself to be admired. And there was indeed something to admire. Rebrov suddenly felt not so much a shyness as a kind of embarrassment, and he was angry at himself for it. Not in this time and place! She had clearly already rehearsed the whole scene and had chosen the most convincing take on it.

"Good afternoon," he said in a rough, dry voice. "I'm Maj. Rebrov…"

"It's a pleasure to meet you. I'm…"

"I know who you are."

"Is that so?"

"You're Olga Chekhova, the actress."

Chekhova smiled and gave a curt nod.

"Do you always keep the door open?" Rebrov asked, maintaining his adversarial tone. "You're not afraid?"

"I am. I'm very afraid. You can't imagine how terrible things have been in Germany recently. But I saw your car drive up and so I prepared for your arrival."

Rebrov looked around. His gaze suddenly fell upon several Russian icons prominently placed on the bookshelves.

"Have you always had these so prominently displayed? Even under Hitler?"

"To tell you the truth, no, not under Hitler," Chekhova confessed. "When I set them there, I was thinking, 'The Russians are coming, and they won't shoot me right away if they see these.'"

"What about the ditch dug in the garden, was that also done with the Russians in mind? Were you thinking about shooting back at them?"

Chekhova shook her head. "Some crazy people from the Volkssturm dug it, they had been going around here over the last several days looking for cowards, traitors, and deserters. They were really intending to fire on Russian tanks from that ditch."

Rebrov grimaced. "Hitler clearly had a knack for making people insane."

"Perhaps," Chekhova agreed. "Imagine, a few days ago everyone in Berlin believed that General Wenck's army was close at hand, and that he'd save us all with some kind of miracle weapon. The Russians would be immediately put to flight! Now it's strange to even look back at that. Those were strange times, unreal."

"I just can't understand what you Germans saw in Hitler… Maybe you, Hitler's favorite actress, can explain that to me? They say you were close to him. He sent you gifts."

"Why do you think that?"

"In the situation we're in right now, I'd usually say, 'I ask the questions here.'"

"Well, as you wish," Chekhova acquiesced. "As far as Hitler is concerned… When I saw him for the first time, he complimented me for my role in the film *Burning Border*. I played a Polish revolutionary in it. My first impression of him? Well, he was shy, awkward, although he maintained a ceremonious Austrian courtesy with the ladies. That same impression was shared by many people who encountered Hitler in his narrow circle."

"But how did he attract crowds of people with tears in their eyes and dreaming to kiss his hands? Who were ready to give their lives for him? Ready to commit any atrocity at his order?"

"And that's the thing, I too have often thought about it," Chekhova admitted. "It was amazing, almost incomprehensible, his transformation from a ranting bore into a fanatical leader whenever he would stand up in front of people and begin to speak. Something, some madness was burning inside him that cannot simply be explained. He quite literally set the people on fire."

"The Germans. I saw him in newsreels, he struck me as only ridiculous and repulsive. Was he acting at those times? Just pretending?"

"No, no one would have believed him, a person couldn't just pretend. I'm telling you that as an actress. Some dark power came upon him in those moments. Where it came from, I don't know. But he seemed to me like he was in some kind of trance…"

"Could he have shot himself? Committed suicide?"

"I don't know… I don't know what's happened with him lately. They say that he had changed drastically."

"I see." Rebrov drummed his fingers on the table.

"And now, Mrs. Chekhova, I suggest you ride with us for a bit…"

"From what I understand, I cannot refuse. I won't even ask where you're taking me. After all, here in my home, it is you who is asking the questions."

"You understand things quite well."

"I am not, unlike many other actresses, a silly woman."

"And that's what troubles me," Rebrov admitted.

Chekhova walked past him to the door. The light but dizzying smell of her perfume enveloped him like a fresh sea breeze.

Notes

From a letter by an American lawyer in Germany: "Under their exterior facade of humility and submission, especially when there was no reason to demonstrate it, the Germans that we met in the streets behaved not just impudently towards the victors, but often even audaciously. When the Americans ask them how to find a certain address, often you hear an answer like 'It's somewhere over there, behind the ruins…'"

CHAPTER VI.
MYSTERIOUS CIRCUMSTANCES

Filin sat at his desk in his spacious office in the Berlin suburb of Karlhorst, where the Soviet command had based itself. He was reading *Pravda*. Rather, he was re-reading for yet another time an article that was already known to him.

"Yesterday German command disseminated a message from the so-called Führer's General Staff that Hitler had died on the afternoon of May 1… This communication from German radio is clearly yet another fascist trick: by spreading news of Hitler's death, the German fascists clearly hope to give Hitler a chance to flee from the scene and evade the law."

Well, sure, see that as you will… It was clear that this article had been written following orders from the very top and dictated by ingenious political considerations. Filin knew that Stalin had been informed of Hitler's suicide at 4 a.m. on May 1… It was Marshal Zhukov who told him of it, and Stalin said, "It's all over, the scoundrel! A pity we didn't manage to get him alive. Where is Hitler's body?" He had been informed that the corpse had been burnt.

That is to say, both Stalin and Zhukov were convinced that Hitler was dead and now the only thing that remained was to find the body. But now such an announcement appeared in *Pravda*… And several days later, when he answered an American journalist's questions about what happened to Hitler, Zhukov said, "These circumstances are simply mysterious. We still haven't identified Hitler's body. We haven't found it. So, I can't tell you anything definitive about his fate. He might have flown away from Berlin at the last moment, as the runways would have allowed him to do so." Then the Berlin commandant Berzarin added, "We've found all kinds of bodies, among them perhaps that of Hitler. But we cannot say for sure whether he is dead or not…"

Over the last several days, Filin had seen dozens of men from Hitler's circle brought before him, from senior officers and doctors to couriers and chauffeurs. Filin was convinced that Hitler was dead and cremated. He was completely sure that Hitler had recently been in such a state that he simply could not have left his underground bunker, let alone when it was surrounded by Soviet forces and the area engulfed in flames. As one of the interrogated prisoners had said, even if a road to freedom was laid before him, he didn't have the strength left to use it. The man just couldn't go on living any more.

Filin understood one more thing, however: Hitler was a figure of such enormous magnitude that he couldn't help but be surrounded by the most fantastic rumors. And Moscow couldn't help but demand a "thorough and rigorous investigation of all claims of Hitler's fate". On the other hand, Moscow could not give up the political games played around the Führer's death. It had to see what parties might act on Hitler's possible flight, how the Allies, with their clever and complex games, might behave in this situation.

Judging by the reports from Soviet agents embedded in the American and British governments and military, there were many people opposing any trial of the German generals and industrialists; they placed all the blame on the dead Hitler. These men called for a "humane" and "merciful" settlement and for abandoning any "revenge" on their defeated enemies… Of course, these men needed only a dead Hitler. The case of Himmler, whom the Americans had allowed to take poison after they had caught him, sparked many reflections. The Americans had searched him, stripped him of his clothes, and found a cyanide capsule. But they had never guessed to look in his mouth! Everyone had long since known that the Nazi leaders kept their cyanide capsules hidden in a hole in a tooth. Perhaps they simply didn't want Himmler to talk openly about the secret negotiations at the end of the war…

The door opened and Denis Rebrov came in. "You called me, comrade general?"

"Sit down, we need to talk."

Filin had a special attitude towards Rebrov. First of all, he had been aware of Rebrov since the latter was studying at Leningrad University. The state constantly searched for men with the skills it took to work in intelligence, and Filin in his day had found a considerable number of capable young men who then went on to intelligence training. Secondly, Filin thought that Rebrov's generation, born just after the October Revolution, was a special and outstanding generation. They were young people with hearts aflame, firmly convinced that no one in this wide world could laugh and love better than them, and truly prepared for heroism and effort, faithful to the highest values. Filin himself, born two decades before the revolution, had seen too many things and experienced too much to ever be like them, but in this generation he saw a justification for the blood and horror brought by the revolution and civil war. These people are indeed capable of building a new life, he thought. That is why he despaired at seeing these young and magnificent men, people on whom he had hung all his hopes, be the first to perish in the carnage of war. Even his own son had died near Moscow, after enlisting as a volunteer in the first days of the war.

His thoughts were interrupted by Rebrov saying, "Sergei Ivanovich, I'd like to visit Leningrad. For a few days, at least…"

Filin set his papers aside and exhaled. "You want to find your parents' graves?"

"I do."

"It might be hard. Such terrible things happened during the Leningrad blockade…"

"I know. But I should at least try. Otherwise how can I live with myself?"

"You should," Filin agreed. "Of course you should. Tomorrow you just need to carry out one delicate assignment that I received from Moscow, and then I'll try to help you with Leningrad."

"Why me? Could someone else maybe do it?"

"Tomorrow you'll understand why I need you in particular. The job requires a special approach, one that you know just how to provide."

Notes

From the *New York Post*: "We want to know the American line on war criminals — what we are waiting for to shoot Hermann Goering and turn German generals over to Allied judges. <…> Is Ambassador Robert Murphy trying to save German industrialists, German generals and German clericals — as he saved his disreputable French friends?"

Edgar Ansel Mowrer, May 29, 1945

CHAPTER VII. AN OBLIGATORY VISIT

In June 1945, Moscow seemed to be enveloped in pure, bright greenery. It hid the wounds it had suffered in the war and looked more beautiful than ever before. The city had been adorned with decorations for the Victory Day parade that had taken place the day before.

Rebrov, who was sitting in the front seat of a car next to the driver and put completely at ease by all this beauty, cast his attentive gaze over the girls in light summer dresses and involuntarily thought that this visit to Moscow had a strong tinge of farewell to it.

Gen. Filin, sitting in the back, was lost in his own thoughts. His new assignment, which had been sent down from the very top, had turned out to be quite unexpected, and it meant he would have no rest anytime soon. But you can't argue with orders…

The driver stopped the car outside a house on Bolshaya Polyanka street. "We're here, comrade general."

As he got out of the car, Filin took several deep breaths, drunk with the air that suggested spring and, most importantly, peacetime. Suddenly the odd idea came into his head that he wasn't so old yet after all and probably still had quite a lot of life to look forward to.

Standing next to him was Rebrov, who was looking glumly at his legs. They were both dressed in civilian clothes, but Rebrov in his brand-new suit looked like a character from a prewar American comic book, while Filin reminded one of the awkward scientist Paganel who the actor Cherkasov portrayed in *The Children of Captain Grant*, only without any quality of being weird or forgetful. Filin, unlike his cinematic doppelganger, never forgot anything. He never even mixed things up.

"Well, Maj. Rebrov, are you ready to meet Hitler's favorite actress?" Filin asked in an unexpectedly cheerful tone. "Your knees aren't shaking? You don't have sweaty palms?"

"I would have preferred Marlene Dietrich, comrade general," Rebrov joked.

"Geez, look at how picky this guy is," Filin shook his head. "He wants Marlene Dietrich instead! How could I get her for you? She's not anywhere in our occupation zone… And what is it about her as a woman that you like especially?"

"It's just that Marlene Dietrich didn't want to be a favorite of Hitler. She spurned him and his attempts to woo her."

"By the way, I haven't invited you here on a date, comrade major," Filin said. "We're here for an extremely important mission. And Olga Chekhova is a lot more useful to us than your dear Marlene Dietrich, who, I might remind you, isn't working for us but the Americans."

"I understand."

"I hope you do. And this woman, Olga Konstantinovna Chekhova herself, is just as stunning. Yeah, yeah, don't look at me like that! I know a few things or two about all this."

The door to the two-room apartment was opened by a young officer. He saluted, ushered them in, and immediately left.

Olga Chekhova was standing by the window in the very same pose as in Berlin, when Rebrov had visited her. A table next to her held a dish with fruit and a chessboard with the pieces set out.

Chekhova slowly turned. The actress allowed a theatrical pause, as if allowing them to admire her.

"Hello, general. You haven't come alone today."

"No, Olga Konstantinovna. This is your old acquaintance Maj. Rebrov," Filin gestured towards him.

"Yes, I see. The man who brought me here, to Moscow…"

Denis, remaining at the entrance, nodded dryly. Chekhova observed him carefully, then shrugged, as if to say, well, it's your choice to be so gloomy. She turned to Filin. "What are we going to gossip about today, Sergei Ivanovich? Or who?"

"Well, to start with, I've got something to make you happy. They've made a decision about you going back to Berlin. Perhaps you were afraid of being sent off to Siberia?" Filin smiled.

Chekhova froze with surprise. When she regained control of herself, she asked, "When?"

"In a few days you'll be flown there. Maj. Rebrov will accompany you, your old friend," Filin said with a mild irony.

Chekhova, smiling, turned towards Rebrov, but he demonstratively looked away.

"Berlin, Berlin. What awaits me there? I fear it's not an audience's applause," Chekhova said pensively as she sat down at the table.

Filin sat across from her. He understood that Chekhova needed time to process the news and he began studying the position of the pieces on the chessboard. He even tried a move with the queen...

"Tell me, Sergei Ivanovich, will they not allow me to meet with anyone in Moscow? I haven't seen anyone here, neither my aunt or my brother..."

"Sadly, such meetings have not been authorized yet."

"How odd."

"There's nothing I can do about that, Olga Konstantinovna," Filin said in a soft and soothing tone. "You should ask about it when you meet comrades Beria and Abakumov."

"I already have. They promised..."

Sergei Ivanovich threw up his hands. After a silence, he went on in the same soft tone, "Apparently, something didn't work out as planned. In the meantime I'd like to talk about something else. Olga Konstantinovna, in your opinion, how do you think the German leaders will act during their trial?"

"Their trial?" Chekhova was genuinely taken aback. "Are they going to be put on trial?"

"Yes, a decision has already been made to convene an international tribunal. The initial preparations have already started."

"How strange... You're trying monsters for being monsters?"

"They are to be tried not for being monsters but for the crimes they have committed," Filin explained.

"Very well, then... I wonder what things are like there today, in Berlin."

Judging by things, Chekhova was not up to discussing the tribunal and how the Nazi higher-ups might behave there. Her thoughts were elsewhere.

"You'll see for yourself soon," Filin reassured her. "It could have hardly changed much since you waited out the bombing in your basement. So, it's not a place for the fainthearted, but I have no doubt that you, Olga Konstantinovna, can do it"

"Have you studied me so well?" Chekhova asked, slightly coquettishly.

"It didn't take much investigation to determine that you are a strong woman. Our people will help you in Berlin, you're not going to die of hunger. But, Olga Konstantinovna, we are counting on your help in the future, if we ever need it."

Chekhova nodded. Her gaze again fell on Denis, whose features were impenetrable. "This officer of yours, general, is unlikely to have any sympathy for me."

"Nor would any other Soviet people!" Denis couldn't hold back. "You worked for the fascists! You were with Hitler and Goebbels…"

"Goebbels had a very peculiar way of relating to me. And Himmler dreamed of putting me behind bars, my young friend."

"I'm not your friend," Denis let out.

"Maj. Rebrov, get a hold of yourself!" Filin cut him short.

To no one in particular, Chekhova said, "I fear that even the Germans will hate me know. Oh, I know them! Now they will all turn out to be anti-fascists who always opposed Hitler, while I will be seen as his accomplice…"

"You don't need to exaggerate things, Olga Konstantinovna," Filin reassured her. "We won't let you be slandered."

Chekhova stood straighter and stubbornly raised her chin up. "Somehow, I'm ready for anything…"

"Let's get back to the matter we have to discuss, Olga Konstantinovna," Filin pushed the chessboard aside. "Hitler's men, what are they likely to do during the trial? How are they going to act? Will they stand together or will they start tearing into one another? Well, let's take Goering, for example. What can we expect from him?"

Notes

There is no doubt that Hitler has received substantial financial support from major industrialists. Lately there is a feeling that influential financial circles have been putting pressure on Chancellor Hindenburg to allow an experiment and let the Nazis take power… Just today word came in from sources that are usually well informed, that representatives of various American financial figures are showing great activity in this very direction.

From a cable sent by the US Embassyin Berlin to the State Department on September 23, 1930.

CHAPTER VIII. STANDING ON CEREMONY

After they got out of the car, Filin and Rebrov were in no hurry to go anywhere, so they walked through Red Square past the Kremlin towards the History Museum, which had been made even fancier with red flags hung for the coming Victory Day parade.

"Still, Sergei Ivanovich, I don't really understand why we need this trial anyway," Rebrov stated firmly, continuing some disagreement that had already begun. "After all they've done, to just stand on ceremony and try them! With lawyers and presumption of innocence! To have to prove anything! Just read out the verdict and that's that."

"You sound just like Churchill," Filin gave a weary smile.

"Why Churchill?"

"He also said, back in '42, that every Nazi above a certain rank should just be shot. Roosevelt even suggested a year ago that every German should be castrated…"

"Is that so? I had no idea."

"And yet…"

"Look at him!" Rebrov shook his head in a boyish fashion. "Brilliant idea!"

"You think so?"

Over the last several years, working under an assignment that came straight from the Kremlin, Gen. Filin had been tracking and organizing all information about the Allies' intentions for Germany and the Nazi higher-ups after the war.

The Soviet Union's intentions in this regard were clearly set out by Stalin: "Whatever might happen, there must be an appropriate court decision. Otherwise people will say that Churchill, Roosevelt, and Stalin simply took revenge on their political foes!" Furthermore, in October 1944 when Churchill stated at the Kremlin, "The problem was how to prevent Germany getting on her feet in the lifetime of our grandchildren," Stalin protested, "Too strict measures will lead to a desire for revenge."

Thus Stalin had to continually insist on the Soviet Union's position, for Churchill kept on about drawing up lists of figures to be killed and insisting that the Allies, after identifying them, simply shoot them on the spot without any investigation or trial. He even asked Stalin, when he was at the Kremlin, to sign a document to this effect, but Stalin resolutely refused. Churchill emphasized that he had already discussed the whole idea with President Roosevelt.

The English were so eager for revenge that the only thing they could talk about, a Soviet undercover agent relayed, was where to set up the gallows and the length of the rope to hang them with. Well, they also debated how much time should pass between when the criminal was identified and when he was executed, but it ought to be no more than six hours. Nonetheless, the commander of the firing squad should be under no obligation to get permission from his superiors. Churchill did express unease at this, stating that the British would be unable to deal with carrying out all these executions in practice, even if they were necessary the necessary time for it.

The Americans also did not want any great ceremony. In March 1942, the American Secretary of State Hull said at a dinner attended by the UK ambassador to the US, Lord Halifax, that he would like to "shoot and physically kill all the Nazi leaders down to quite low levels!" General Dwight Eisenhower believed it necessary to simply shoot representatives of the German leadership, and anyone sensitive to legal concerns should simply explain the shootings as "escape attempts". And in general, one shouldn't confuse retaliation with legal justice.

President Roosevelt's feelings were also complex. On August 19, 1944, he noted, "We have got to be tough with Germany and I mean the German people, not just the Nazis. You either have to castrate the German people or you have got to treat them in such a manner so they can't go on reproducing people who want to continue the way they have in the past."

Thus the idea of an international tribunal was slow to arise and gather support. Already in 1945, when the entire world press was talking about the terrible atrocities revealed after Germany's defeat, 67 percent of Americans favored quick and extrajudicial execution of Nazi criminals, essentially lynching. At the same time, the suggestion was made to destroy Germany as an industrial state. The US Treasury Secretary Henry Morgenthau, Jr. offered a plan to "prevent Germany from unleashing a third world war". Under this plan, Germany would be broken up and decentralized, all its heavy industry and aviation would be done away with, and it would be turned into an agrarian country under the firm control of the United States and Great Britain. As Morgenthau put it, Germany should now become "one large potato patch". Or a "ghost area", whichever idea had more appeal.

Among the Americans, however, there were some who thought differently. Secretary of War Stimson told some of his trusted men that the British were firmly against a court and they wanted to kill these men without ceremony or delay, an unprecedented position. By this time, there was already a new president; Roosevelt had died and Truman, who succeeded him, believed that a trial was needed. He was a rather simple American man and spoke straightforwardly: the Germans should be judged by a court of law, and then hung.

"You see, Denis, if Hitler's entire upper echelon were simply crushed like scorpions, then in no time people will begin saying that it was just the victors' revenge… They will say that the crimes were exaggerated, that the testimony was rigged, the documents were forged.

"After all that happened?!" Rebrov was incredulous.

"After all that happened," Filin reiterated calmly. "People who want to believe such things are easy to find. Already there's enough of them, and once some time has passed, everything will get turned upside down. They'll start saying that we attacked them…"

"We attacked the fascists? That's nonsense!"

"It's not nonsense, just political intrigues. That's why we need a trial. A legitimate, legally impeccable trial. And an international one. A trial that will issue a verdict that cannot be appealed or overturned, a verdict that is final and forever. So that our children don't have to prove everything again… So that they won't ever be forced to explain that they attacked us, and we don't have to issue any apologies.

"Are you serious? Or is this just a joke?"

Filin just squinted at the walls of the Kremlin, then said, "It might seem impossible for you today, but tomorrow provocateurs or outright enemies will appear, all kinds of 'truth-seekers' who will start accusing us of aggression or certain atrocities."

"We were choking on our own blood!"

Filin looked askew at Denis, who showed fury on his face. After pausing, he asked, "By the way, at Chekhova's home, did you really crack? Or did you simply decide to give her a hard time, play good cop, bad cop?"

"I cracked," Denis admitted, then muttered childishly, "She's too… Why are we fussing over her?"

"It's bad, bad that you cracked. Very bad. I hope that in the future you can maintain control of yourself. We've got a difficult task ahead of ourselves, and not a pleasant one. You will have to constantly watch over yourself, every step and every word. Do you understand me?"

Rebrov nodded guiltily.

"And when it comes to Chekhova…" Filin suddenly smiled. "She's an actress. In every fiber of her being. In every gesture, every step. Actors are completely different beings than you and me, you understand?"

"I don't know."

"If you don't know, then take my word for it."

Rebrov quickly glanced at Filin but said nothing. He only remembered that Filin's wife had been an actress. She couldn't take her son's death in the first battle outside Moscow and so she had died, withering away after a serious illness. It came as a terrible blow to Filin, one that he bore stoically but never talked about.

"Do you remember, by the way, what she said about Goering?" Filin interrupted his thoughts.

"She said that he is an actor, and that at the trial he will play the role of a great historic figure, but he can act like a simpleton, too."

"No, Denis, that's not at all what she said. She said that he's a bad actor, or rather a poser. He'll be dying from fright but still thinking the whole time about what pose to adopt. Nonetheless, he's still a fierce and devious animal, who will defend his own life to the end."

"She didn't say he was an animal."

"Well, that's on my part, for the sake of clarity… I can see that you're angry at me that I called you back from Leningrad early."

"No, it's just… I didn't have time to do anything there. I didn't learn anything about my parents… They called me back, to flirt with Mrs. Chekhova here."

"Not to flirt, but to do your job," Filin corrected him.

"And now we've got to fly to Berlin with her. Will it be for a long time?"

"We'll see."

Notes

"Working for Soviet intelligence was the film star Olga Chekhova, a friend of Eva Braun… She would spend days and nights in Hitler's home.

"I am not in the least bit surprised that neither
the USSR's state security services, nor those
of Russia today, could confirm that Chekhova was
involved in Soviet intelligence. There probably
were never any documents to that effect, and the
reason is simple: my father never disclosed it
then, in 1945, or after. It was a quite typical
affair.

Hundreds of names never passed through the files
of the state security services, I know that
for a fact. My father believes that "a real
deeply embedded agent can never be allowed to
be widely known by the authorities". This was a
generally adopted system in Soviet espionage,
which my father had headed for fifteen years…"

From the recollections
of Lavrentiy Beria's son Sergo.

CHAPTER IX.
TO GO OVER A COLLAPSING BRIDGE

General Filin was at work in his Moscow office, a place he had seldom seen recently, especially after Soviet forces entered Germany. He had preferred working closer to the front, it was more convenient and effective. On the rare occasions he came to Moscow, he practically lived in this office, sleeping on a sofa in one of the break rooms. Only when it was absolutely necessary did he look in at home, where everything only reminded him of his wife and son. His old friend and chief, Gen. Gres, took all this into account when he tasked Filin with the upcoming trial of the Nazi leaders. The trial would go on for a long while, and that meant Filin would have to spend a great deal of time in Germany.

From agents' reports and official bulletins, it was known that President Truman had made his choice and the US chief prosecutor at the trial would be Robert H. Jackson, who had already assembled a large team of lawyers, secretaries, and investigators. Everyone would be working under him.

Jackson was 53 years old. He had started out as a provincial lawyer in Pennsylvania, where he made a name for himself defending trade unionists. He was an ardent supporter of President Roosevelt's New Deal and he continued his impressive career in Washington, where he was made Attorney General. The newspapers even talked about him as a future president. He was a straightforward and honest man, who stuck to his guns even when the official line said differently. Many called him an idealist, but he was an idealist of the American sort, believing that American democracy was greater than all else and the whole world should conform to it and accept America's supremacy as a given. Like many small-town Americans, he was a man with rather limited horizons; he had practically never traveled outside the US. He had even failed to renew his passport a few years before, and now with his appointment as chief prosecutor and need to go abroad, he was forced to urgently apply for a new one.

Jackson believed in justice and sharply criticized those who believed that a war crimes tribunal should only be a smokescreen for doing away with one's enemies. "If we just want to shoot the Germans and that is to be our official policy, then so be it," he said. "But don't try to conceal such atrocities under the facade of carrying out justice." A militant idealist, Jackson saw the upcoming tribunal as the trial of an evil of a global scale, when he would personally stand before the whole world as a true American hero. At the same time, Jackson had a poor understanding of who he would be dealing with. When he wished for a real trial, he didn't stop to think that the accused might dare to argue with him. In this regard, agent Hector recalled that as Attorney General, Jackson had forbidden the FBI from wiretapping telephone lines and was very proud of this decision. However, the eavesdropping went on nonetheless. There was thus always a certain gap between Jackson's ideals and the real world…

Filin drummed his fingers on his desk. Idealists, especially militant ones, are not easy people to figure out. In dealing with them, one had to always be ready for surprises. An idealist might be capable of great feats, but at the same time he might not understand the most elementary things.

One had to admit that the Americans had undertaken great effort to find any documents relating to Hitler's regime. Each US army division was assigned specialized personnel who were to seize and guard any enemy archives. Hundreds of experts were involved. Such a concern for the enemy's paperwork lay not only in a desire to carefully prepare the case against the major war criminals, there was also, to a much greater extent, an aim of obtaining valuable information of a military, economic, or intelligence nature. Any documents that were found were taken, often immediately by the truckload, to specialized centers set up in each army division. Here these documents were sorted, cataloged, and organized.

In army headquarters, state buildings, and the homes of Nazi leaders huge troves of government, Nazi Party, military, and personal documents were found. They had been buried, hidden behind false walls, in salt mines, and other secret places. According to agents in Flensburg, the archive of the Supreme Command of the German Armed Forces had been seized, including plans for Operation Barbarossa, while in Marburg the Ministry of Foreign Affairs archive was found, and in Fechenheim they discovered the archive of the Wehrmacht High Command. In the Bavarian Alps they found documents relating to the German air force command, led by Goering. In eastern Bavaria, in one of the old fortresses and behind a false wall, they found Rosenberg's archive, including his diary and his correspondence on Nazi Party affairs. In the cellar of the Platerhof in the Obersalzberg, a collection of papers belonging to Hitler's adjutant Schmundt was discovered, including plans for Operation Grün, the aborted plan for the invasion of Czechoslovakia. In the basement of the State Bank in Cologne, among the papers of the banker von Schröder they found his letters sent to Himmler that show that German industrialists were complicit in war crimes…

Jackson's men, Hector reported, had already begun reviewing the documents collected in the various US Army headquarters. Special field teams had already been created and coordination officers assigned to them. The tons of German documents were sorted, after which those considered the most important were sent on to the US prosecution's office, then still based in Paris. There the documents were cataloged and passed on to analysts, where it was decided whether they would be submitted as evidence in the upcoming trial. The documents selected for that purpose were forwarded to the document center of the US prosecutors, where they were translated, described in detail, photocopied, and then the originals were kept locked in a safe.

The Americans worked diligently. But, Filin noted with a smile, one couldn't expect them to share their entire find. Rather, the documents would be released individually over time, whenever it was to their advantage or at least posed no harm to them…

Sounds could be heard in the hallway outside, then the door flew open wide and General Gres tumbled into the office. He was a heavy-set man, with a shiny bald head, a thunderous voice, and a heavy, intent gaze. He looked like the very picture of a typical general, while Filin was the most atypical. At the same time, Gres was a cautious and cunning counter-intelligence officer, able to lie in wait, construct clever strategies, and if necessary, calmly make compromises. Or even retreat.

Gres sat down heavily on the black faux leather sofa and continued a conversation that had been interrupted. "So, at the trial, you need Rebrov specifically? Tell me, why? Why him and no one else? Do you believe in him so much?"

"I've known him for many years. I trust in him completely. He speaks German like a real German. English, too. He's got training in law. He has served in SMERSH, identified saboteurs, and took part in capturing them, and he has worked in recruiting German agents. He knows hand-to-hand combat and he's a good shot."

"It's great that he's a good shot, of course, but that's not the most important thing to us. Can he think? Does he have powers of observation? Are his nerves good?"

"Well, after the war I think everyone's nerves are a bit shaken."

"Just a bit?"

"Just a bit. His parents died in the Leningrad blockade. His fiancée died in the bombing. He's all alone. There's nothing for him in the civilian world."

Gres glanced at Filin, whose face was impassive.

"I think he should stay with us," Filin went on. "A new era has begun, we need people just like him. For the Western public, who will be there in droves, he'll look perfect."

"Fine, but you know our rules."

"I shall bear my own personal responsibility for it."

"That's right."

The generals fell silent.

"Anyway, Sergei, you are to be dedicated to the trials," Gres slapped his hand on his knee. "Completely dedicated. The trials must take place, and at any price. It is a matter of the greatest importance. The current situation, you know yourself how it is…"

"As one English newspaper put it, 'The honeymoon of the coalition against Hitler is over.'"

"Was there even a honeymoon? That's another matter. One to realize that the West is full of people who don't need any international tribunal. They need German secrets, German resources, German agents, but not any revelations that such a tribunal might bring… What if it suddenly becomes known who brought Hitler to power? Who helped him arm, who forgave Germany's debts? They, these people, are still at the helm over there, by the way."

After a pause Gres went on, "In Germany, you know, this trial isn't being met with any great delight either. As far as former Nazis are concerned it's all clear: they'll do anything to stop the tribunal from happening. But those who weren't Nazis themselves are afraid of this tribunal becoming a trial of Germany and the German people, and if they are afraid of it, that means they are against it. Things like that. You'll have plenty of enemies over there. Just make sure you discover them in time."

"I think it's already too late to stop the tribunal from happening,"

Filin said. "The agreement has been signed at the highest levels, the engine has already been started. Plus, we've got public opinion on our side."

"Well, we should hope for public approval. It might be too late to cancel the tribunal, but it could be delayed, pushed aside, and quietly forgotten. One good provocation, and immediately there will be talk that we should wait for a while. And over there… We cannot allow it. So you've got a difficult task ahead of you."

"Has the place been chosen definitively?"

"Yes, Nuremberg. It's in the American occupation zone. They now have the full run of the place. You do realize that every intelligence agency in the world is going to be there, with their best people. Of course, they'll be on the lookout for opportunities to have eyes and ears among our delegation. There will be recruitment attempts. You will have to deal with this."

"I understand."

"And there's another thing. The decision has been made to attract our American agent Hector to Nuremberg on assignment. You know how much effort and resources have been put in him. He's a treasure, a real treasure! So, God forbid you expose him!"

Gres stood up. He walked over to the desk that Filin was sitting behind, placed his hands on it, and leaned over to say, in as convincing a tone as possible, "There's one other thing, Sergei. The boss is placing great importance on this tribunal, extraordinary importance. He will personally follow it and take action if necessary. You know yourself what that means. Furthermore, Vyshinsky himself will be supervising all of the work of our delegation from Moscow! He will report everything to the great leader. You understand me?"

"So, we'll have to walk on the edge of an abyss. Or over a bridge that could collapse at any moment."

"You're quite the philosopher."

"So, that means we have no specific assignment yet when it comes to Rebrov?"

"Your specific assignment is to ensure that work on the tribunal proceeds smoothly, to help our investigators and attorneys, identify any enemy, and prevent any undesirable turn of events. You will take such actions as the situation requires, and you'll decide yourselves what to do as things unfold. You're not children."

"What about our contacts with the Americans? The British?"

"They are to be very formal, businesslike. You and Rebrov are members of our delegation. Well, in informal situations, if you have to… But you're in foreign territory over there…"

"I haven't played the role of spy for a long time," Filin stretched and closed his eyes.

"You don't need to do any spying. You just need to think and be the boss. But your man Rebrov can try that on occasion. Do you think he can do it?"

"It's why I chose him. He's got a wide gamut of skills."

"Gamut, geez, what words you've picked up," Gres laughed. "Europeans, goodness!"

Notes

The Potsdam Conference lasted from July 17 to August 2, 1945. The leaders of the three major Allies attended. It was the third and final meeting of the "Big Three".

The conference discussed the political and economic principles that were to guide the initial period of dealing with defeated Germany. The basis of these principles were points aimed at demilitarization, democratization, and denazification of defeated Germany so that the German lands would never again pose a risk of aggression. It was decided that Germany would be completely disarmed and the entire German armaments industry would be eliminated. Along with this, the Nazi Party was to be abolished and all Nazi or militaristic propaganda was to be outlawed, all Nazi laws were to be abolished, and measures were to be adopted to punish war criminals.

At the insistence of the Soviet delegation to the Potsdam Conference, a measure was adopted to publish a list of Nazi war criminals and bring them to justice at an international tribunal.

CHAPTER X.
WHAT TO DO WITH
THE ENEMY'S CORPSE?

Stalin stood by the window in the Soviet delegation's office in the Ce-cilienhof palace, once home to the German Crown Prince, puffing his pipe and looking out at the flower garden that had been maintained with German precision. Yesterday he had been told that the American delegation was working in the former salon of the Crown Prince, while the Soviets had settled into his former office. Stalin grinned and said that was the way things should be assigned. He was joking, of course, but as always there was some serious intent behind the joke.

At last, without turning around, Stalin asked,

"Have you finished everything with regard to Hitler, comrade Aba-kumov?"

General Abakumov, who had been standing at attention by the desk and already weary of the great leader's protracted silence, report-ed, "That's right, comrade Stalin. The body was secretly buried after the necessary examinations to identify it were carried out... The pit that was dug is 1.7 meters deep and even with the ground. Several small pine trees were planted on the surface, 111 of them."

"So many?" Stalin was amazed.

"So that no one will come upon it by accident."

"Quite right. Well, then."

"Comrade Stalin," said Abakumov uncertainly. "if you think it nec-essary, you can see Hitler's body... It's not far from here."

"What for?" Stalin, puzzled, slowly turned his tiger-like eyes to him. "I believe you. I'm sure that everything is exactly as you report it."

Abakumov stood even straighter with pride. "But every day the newspapers are claiming that Hitler has fled or is in hiding. That we carried out the identification of the body incompetently and that we're hiding something..."

"Oh," Stalin waved his pipe. "Let them worry. What is more advantageous for us politically? For the Americans and British to know for sure that Hitler is dead? Or for them to be afraid that Hitler might pop up alive and well at any moment? Or for them to fear that he is in our hands and providing us with evidence? Especially now, when they are so happy to scare us with their atomic bomb…"

Abakumov remained silent, seeing that Stalin wasn't expecting an answer.

"As for seeing his body, why? We've got enough living enemies these days, and now you need to identify them. Let the Americans and British worry about Hitler if they must. But there's one more thing, comrade Abakumov… Here, in Potsdam, I've seen yet again how important the trial of the senior German criminals in Nuremberg is for us. We should do everything possible, bring in our best people, to make this trial go smoothly. To go the way we need it to go."

Notes

In the area of Hitler's Reich Chancellery, some 100 meters southeast of the building, on the site where the bodies of Goebbels and his wife had been found earlier, two dead dogs were discovered… The bodies of the dogs and the items found alongside them were photographed and are being stored at the SMERSH headquarters. The present memo has been drawn up to document these events.

Assistant Director
of Counterintelligence,
SMERSH

CHAPTER XI. THE CITY OF THE FALLEN

Defeated Berlin in the summer of 1945 resembled a medieval engraving depicting the plague. Starving figures with downcast eyes wandered aimlessly among the ruins of houses and twisted iron. Enormous lines stretched outside field kitchens or points to get water. Most of these people were women with children and elderly who now found themselves in a desperate situation; Germany's men were either buried in countless graves, scattered to the ends of the earth, held in prisoner-of-war camps with no idea what fate awaited them, or hiding in cellars and forests in the hope of saving their skin. Flea markets popped up on any bare patch of ground where people sold anything they could. The armed patrols of the victors drove past them in their fancy cars.

Olga Chekhova, her features frozen in amazement, looked out from the car window at this city that was now a ghost town. Once she had shone on the stage here and the city had been hung with movie posters with her likeness.

Rebrov sat next to her in the back seat with a stony face. The phantoms and shadows of the Reich's capital seemed to hardly affect him.

"The smell," Chekhova suddenly let out. "What a strange and awful smell…"

"It's the smell of dead bodies," came an explanation from their driver, who wore sergeant's stripes. "They haven't managed to bury everyone. They can't reach every cellar, the entrances are caved in, and there are so many dead bodies…"

"How horrible," Chekhova closed her eyes.

"You should have seen Stalingrad," the driver said in a slightly mocking fashion. "That was horrible, truly horrible."

"But these people," Chekhova nodded towards the women with children outside the car window. "They're not guilty."

"Were the people taken to Auschwitz guilty?" The driver angrily bit his lip. "When I saw those walking corpses there, I thought I was hallucinating. How could people still be alive in such a state? And the mountains of bones there of the people who had been burned in the ovens. Mountains, you understand?"

"How did you wind up in the camps, sergeant," Denis asked.

"It was us who liberated them, comrade major."

Chekhova closed her eyes.

"We heard things then that make you not want to go on living. What they did to people there. They drove whole crowds of people into the ovens. They threw children into the flames… But now, if you talk to a German, no one knows anything about it, they didn't see it, they didn't suspect anything… No one, nothing."

Rebrov glanced involuntarily at Chekhova. Her beautiful profile and exquisite features looked utterly out of place against the background of the ruined city.

Down from torn feathers drifted throughout the house and there was no way to deal with it. Small feathers were later found on the second floor and in the cellar. This vexed Chekhova terribly, as she sought to always keep things neat in the German fashion. She made pillows from the feathers with a niece and then they went to trade them for food. Instead of flowers, they planted cabbage and beets in their gardens, but how long would it take them to grow… The fact that they were famous saved them from truly starving — the soldiers and civilian employees of the occupation administration they had to deal with, knew what challenges they faced and sometimes helped with goods. The Russians would hand out vodka, sugar, or grain, while the Americans usually shared cigarettes. A package of cigarettes on the black market, where you could find almost anything, was worth more than gold. Rebrov had helped her with things in the first days, but then he had disappeared and she was forced to manage on her own.

The thought came into her head of putting together a small troupe of actors and touring the cities to put on plays…

She had just begun pondering who among Germany's actors were still alive and hadn't fled, and who might be willing to take a chance on that kind of work, when a foppish looking man entered her home, wearing a hat that he hadn't even thought to take off.

"Frazier," he introduced himself. "Just call me Mr. Frazier."

"And to what do I owe your visit?" Chekhova was amazed. In former days she would have hardly deigned to speak with a stranger or someone she found unpleasant, but now times were different and she was in a desperate situation where she simply had to find a way to survive. So, she would have to use every opportunity…

"Mrs. Chekhova, I represent Paramount Studios here in Germany," the man said emphatically. "Here are my credentials that show I am fully authorized to enter into negotiations with you." Frazier took some papers out and waved them. "They haven't forgotten you in Hollywood, Mrs. Chekhova. Paramount would like to contract you for several films…"

Chekhova was so stunned that she could not even answer right away. Good Lord, Hollywood! A place out of a fairy tale, a heaven on Earth. And starring in films…

"What are you thinking about, Mrs. Chekhova?" Frazier stared at her. "Do you still remember Hollywood? Or did the bombing and Russian soldiers destroy your memory? Look, no more ration cards, no more being hungry or looking for decent clothes to wear. No more ruins or occupying forces, no more patrols or banditry. No more shootings, searches, and threats. I've heard that you aim to put together some small theatre troupe. Why?"

"So that I won't die of starvation."

"Forget about starvation. You'll have everything you want!"

"But I have family here, friends, colleagues."

"Stop trying to convince yourself," an irritated Frazier waved her concerns away. "You know perfectly well that you can't stay in Germany?"

"Why can't I?"

"Because some people will hate you for your personal dealings with Hitler and Goebbels, and others will hate you for spying for the Russians. You'll be hated not just in Germany but all Europe."

"That's all lies! Lies! I have never been a spy!"

Frazier smiled graciously. "Yeah? But what difference does it make? You think anyone will understand?"

Chekhova closed her eyes. This unpleasant visitor was right, no one would understand.

"Listen, I can understand your hesitation about starring in more films. Age takes its toll, it's already getting harder for you to play femme fatales…"

"How rude!" Chekhova straightened.

"Come on," Frazier said. "It's just the honest truth. Moreover, you've forgotten English and American audiences aren't likely to care for a German accent. They see all Germans as Nazis now."

"Why are you offering me a contract, then?"

"We're ready to take the risk," Frazier smiled. "We Americans are broad-minded people and we know you can't do business, good business, without some level of risk. And we've got a plan B."

"Is that so? What is your plan B?"

Frazier strolled around the room as if he lived there. He stopped at the Russian icons and grinned. "In America, based on the experiences here that have caused you such troubles and worries, you can easily save up sufficient capital and be set for life. A life without any problems, Mrs. Chekohva!" He raised a finger. "I can assure you, without any problems…"

"I just don't understand what you mean," she said helplessly, and then became angry at herself for sounding so pitiful. She had to pull herself together. This man was going too far.

"Memoirs," Frazier snapped his fingers. "Your memoirs, Mrs. Chekhova. The studio is prepared to pay for the rights to publish them and the film rights. We're talking serious money!"

"You think that my memoirs would be so interesting to people?"

"I'm certain of it. Even if what really happened wasn't exciting enough to draw American readers, you could, with a clear conscience, look back on your intimate relationships with top officials of the Third Reich. Best of all with the ones who are already dead, so they won't be troubling us with any annoying refutations…"

"Have you gone mad?! I have no intentions of 'looking back' on anything like that!"

"Now, now, don't be so quick to refuse. What's the hurry? Just calm down. You need to approach this more levelheaded. I'll be leaving now, but I'll come again soon. You just think about it, think carefully. Especially since you don't have any other choice."

"Why not?"

"Because we won't take no for an answer," Frazier said with an obvious threat. "Remember that."

Notes

At Church House, Westminster the London Conference of victor nations continues. It intends to develop a charter for an International

Military Tribunal. This Tribunal promises to be a grandiose international spectacle, it will investigate crimes of an unprecedented scale. Newspapers and newsreels are full of documentation of Nazi crimes. The newspapers are reporting that this evidence of crimes, amounting to many volumes, astounds even the most experienced lawyers.

Nevertheless, the charter for the Tribunal currently being discussed will provide guarantees to the men being tried, particularly the right to defense either on their own part or with the aid of lawyers, the right to cross-examine witnesses, and the right to make final remarks to the judge…

CHAPTER XII. NO ENTRY

"No Entry to Germans" was carelessly painted in white right on the door under the sign "BAR". A young man, tall, light-haired, and wearing a modest civilian suit that was clearly not his size, involuntarily slowed his step and looked for some time at the text, as if trying to figure out where he was. He even looked around, as if unable to believe his own eyes.

Before him stretched an ordinary street of a postwar German town that had been subjected to massive bombardment by the Allies: ruins, heaps of bricks, and a few accidentally spared houses, one of which now hosted a bar for occupying forces as some people passed by on their way somewhere, dressed too warmly for this scorching summer day and holding suitcases and bundles.

The young man had light gray, almost transparent eyes. The stubble of several days on his face highlighted his thinness and fatigue, but unlike the people walking past him, he didn't look haggard and stupidly indifferent to everything that was happening.

A military jeep, packed with American soldiers who were chatting merrily about something, drove up to the bar. The soldiers got out, carelessly pushed past the man who blocked their way, and disappeared into the bar. He lowered his head and continued walking on, but in the unlit arch of the building he saw a young German girl and a dark-skinned American sergeant against the wall. The girl was smoothly fixing her skirt while the American, ashamed of nothing and in no hurry, was zipping up his pants.

Having squared himself away, the sergeant handed the girl a package with a grin. She immediately opened it to find one stocking. She looked at him, bewildered, and then said in broken English, "It is just one, John. One. I need two… Two." She held up two fingers.

"Tomorrow," the American shouted, awfully pleased with himself. "Tomorrow my friend here will give you the second one, and then you'll have two. But first…" The American showed with a gesture what would happen first. "And then the second stocking. From my friend. Understand?"

The German girl nodded submissively, though her eyes were filled with tears. The American caressed her cheek condescendingly, then he suddenly caught sight of the man who had stood watching the scene."

"Get out of here, you Nazi scum!" the American roared as he moved, fists clenched, towards the gray-eyed man in the tight suit.

But the man, whose features had not changed in the slightest, suddenly made a short strike with his fist and struck the American in the stomach. The American gasped, his eyes popped out, and he bent over. He struck a blow to the American's neck with the same short chopping motion and the American fell to the ground. He then turned towards the girl, grabbed her by the arm, and began dragging her down the street, away from the archway where the American was lying with his hands on his stomach.

"Let's get out of here." He walked in a hurry, dragging the girl with him. She kept looking back, and then she suddenly tore her arm away from his grip and stopped. The gray-eyed man also stopped and wanted to say something, but he didn't manage to.

"What have you done? Who asked you?" The girl was indignant, her features distorted by rage. "My sister and me are going to starve to death now! We'll have to run away from here! Where will we go? Should we just die?"

The gray-eyed man looked at her, failing to understand.

"He was a regular customer! He would bring his friends to us. He gave us cigarettes and we traded them for bread," the girl groaned. "And now we won't have any way to survive. If you kill him, the Americans will find us and shoot us. Do you understand what you've done, you idiot!"

"You're a German," the gray-eyed man murmured in a choked voice.

"Yes, I'm a German, and who are you? The SS? Or Gestapo? You got us into this, you bastards! It's all because of you! I'm going to call a patrol now, let them shoot you, you Nazi animal! I'll tell them that you attacked me and John!"

She clutched at the young man and began to yell, "Help! Patrol!"

The gray-eyed man looked for a moment at her pitiful and spiteful little face, still so young, and then with the same chopping blow to the neck he sent her tumbling to the ground. "You dirty creature," he muttered. "Filthy scum!"

The girl lay motionless for a while, then suddenly stirred and rose to her knees, shaking her head and grabbing his leg with both arms. She wheezed something and then bloody foam came to her lips.

The gray-eyed man slowly reached towards her, took her by the throat, and then squeezed slightly. Then he raised his hand a little, the girl's neck stretched and her chin became sharper… The man looked into her dead face and slightly shook her light body. The girl went immediately limp, her eyes rolled back. He then let go and the girl's body fell to the ground like a rag doll. He pushed it aside with his foot, disgusted, took out a wrinkled handkerchief, and carefully wiped his hands. Then he threw the handkerchief at the girl's face and quickly walked on without looking back.

Notes

Our driver, a German, immediately told us that he could introduce us this very same day to some young and completely decent girls, and that he would do this without any hidden interest 'out of respect for Russia's fine officers'.

"Top-quality freuleins, attractive girls!"

It wouldn't cost us much, and payment could be made not only in marks but also in food or other goods…

Boris Polevoy, Nuremberg Diary

CHAPTER XIII. A FIRING-SQUAD GIRL

Rebrov sat next to the driver with his eyes closed. He felt insanely tired.

Over the last several months, in prisons and camps, hundreds if not thousands of German prisoners had been brought before him, from ordinary soldiers and telephone operators to generals and state officials. Among them were some who were mere shadows, completely broken and mad with fear; fierce enemies who were hiding their rage and hate; psychopaths and calculating cynics; victims and punishers high on idealism. With all of them one had to try to figure out when they were lying, when they did not understand, and when they really did not know. And all this under extreme pressure from Moscow, demanding detailed reports of what had happened to Hitler's upper echelon, each particular individual…

Rebrov was only comforted by the thought that things were much harder on Gen. Filin, but the latter maintained calm and even gave Rebrov the opportunity to sometimes catch his breath.

They reached Kladow and stopped at Chekhova's house. The driver took a large cardboard box out of the trunk.

The door was opened by Chekhova herself. She looked at ease, though slightly thinner than before. She said, pleased, "Is it really you? Thank God, I thought that it was again…"

Rebrov wasn't listening to her, he told the driver, "Take that into the house, and then wait for me in the car."

"What's that? Chekhova asked, pointing at the box after they had been left alone.

"Food," Rebrov answered curtly. "Grain, bread, canned meat, sugar, and even vodka."

"Good Lord, these days that is an enormous bounty!"

"Well, it's not what Hitler sent you on your birthday, of course."

"You already know how things were then! Was I to throw his gifts back in his face and be sent to a concentration camp?"

"It was your choice. You'll have to pay the price."

"Why do you hate me so? I can see it."

"It just that I'm standing here chatting with you when…"

"When what?"

"When I should be searching for my parents' grave. Understand?"

The fatigue and tension of the last days had probably taken their toll, because Rebrov realized that he shouldn't be talking about these things at this place and time, but he couldn't stop himself.

"Searching for my parents while there's still a chance to find them. Because later it will already be too late."

"Were they killed?"

"Yes, they died in the Leningrad blockade from hunger and cold. When they had no more strength left they embraced each other and died together… Probably one died first and the other remained lying alongside because they didn't have the strength to get up. They were buried together, but I still don't know where. And I'm trying to find out where one snake was shot, where another might have disappeared to, and how a third is going to behave at his trial…"

"I'm not keeping you here," Chekhova said quietly.

"I understand that."

"Do you want to get revenge on every German?"

"No, not all of them. But there are some among them that have to be punished. No matter what. Sorry, I broke down, I'm just so tired. Forget it, I shouldn't have told you about that."

They fell silent for some time, and then Chekhova suddenly said, quite sincerely, "Strange things have been going on around me recently. In Moscow I felt certain that the Germans would now turn anti-Nazi and attack me for being seen with Hitler. But now it's not that that the Germans hate me for. They hate me for supposedly being a Soviet spy, and that I supposedly received a high Russian honor from Stalin himself at the Kremlin."

"They probably confused you with your aunt Olga Knipper-Chekhova. She really has received a state honor…"

"I thought about that too, but… I have been getting threatening letters, people are saying and writing all kinds of nonsense about me, things you would not believe. Like that I had a golden notebook that I entered my reports into, with a pencil set with diamonds. Can you imagine? A diamond-studded pencil! And that I gave these reports to my driver and he sent them on to Moscow! And then he was arrested by the Gestapo! But I have not had a driver for years now, because Goebbels took my car from me."

"Why?"

"So that the German people would see that in difficult times, famous people have to walk too."

Rebrov looked at Chekhova. He felt that his nervous collapse had passed and he was again back to normal.

"Tell me something, could you have ever imagined that Goebbels and his wife were capable of such a thing, poisoning their children with their own hands? By the way, he and his wife Magda were encouraged to send the children away from Berlin, but she refused. Was she such a fanatic? It's not even cannibalism…"

"Goebbels had completely suppressed his wife's own mind. He warped her to his image without a trace left. Like any paranoid individual, he could influence mentally unbalanced people. And Magda was the sort of person who looks for another to obey."

"But you managed to resist him…"

"What do you mean?"

"Well, he must have been attracted to a beautiful woman like you, Olga Konstantinovna."

"Ha, you appear to be capable of compliments after all."

Chekhova smiled to Rebrov in a feminine way and straightened her hair with the well-worked gesture of a lady.

"As for Goebbels, he always had an artificial suntan, which didn't help him much. He looked like he had just come up from hell, where he had warmed himself in hellfire. He was a cripple with the face of an insane extremist. At first he supported me as an actress, but then our relationship broke down… I may be an actress, but I could not hide how much he disgusted me."

She shrugged her shoulders. "You know, a month after the attack on Russia, Goebbels held a reception. They announced there that soon Moscow would be taken. Goebbels told everyone, "We've got a Russia expert here, Frau Chekhova. I think she will back up my firm belief that the war will be over by winter, and we'll be celebrating Christmas in the Kremlin. On Red Square. The Russian Revolution will help us. I'm certain that after our victories, the Russians will rise up against the Bolsheviks, and the Soviet Union will fall apart like the tsar's empire." Chekhova flashed a triumphant smile. "You know what I told him? 'There will not be any revolution, Herr Minister. Faced with any outside threat, the Russians would come together and fight to the end."

"And what did Herr Minister say then?"

"His face turned green, and then he hissed, 'Well, we'll give them an end, then.'"

Rebrov walked around the room. "That's all very intriguing, but…"

"But what?"

"I'm here on other business. Not to listen to your memories, intriguing they may be." Rebrov said this angrily, as if getting back at Chekhova for letting her lead the conversation the way she wanted. "Olga Konstantinovna, let's get back to the present. We've got proof that you are meeting with the Americans."

"Do you?! Are you following me?"

"We are watching over you," Rebrov corrected her. "For your own safety. Who are they, these people? What do they want from you?"

"The man who visited me is named Frazier, he's a representative of Paramount Studios. He offered me a contract and said I could go to America."

"Was that all?"

"That was all. And he promised that he would come again, and that he wouldn't take no for an answer. But I don't know who those people are."

"I must admit that I'd like to get a glimpse of Mr. Frazier. It may be that Paramount isn't very aware of his activities."

"You think so?"

"Berlin is swarming these days with all kinds of shady characters. When he comes to visit you again, draw the curtains on the window, as if you don't want anyone to see you. That will be the signal for us. And now I've got to go."

"I'll see you out, as is the Russian custom."

They went to the gate and then out into the street. Rebrov's car was parked some twenty meters away. The driver was waiting at the wheel.

"Is this goodbye?" Chekhova asked calmly.

"Goodbye. And be sure to signal to us when Frazier visits you."

"*Jawohl*," Chekhova laughed. "Don't worry, comrade major. Your orders will be followed." Rebrov smiled involuntarily and headed for the car. Chekhova, with a sad smile on her face, watched him go.

At that same moment a young and tall German woman walked towards her, coming as if out of nowhere. "Are you Olga Chekhova," she asked sharply.

"Yes. Why do you ask?"

"You dirty spy! Traitor!" As she shouted these curses she flung herself towards Chekhova as if wanting to bite her. "You betrayed the Führer and the whole German people! Take this!" She suddenly spat right into

Chekhova's face. Chekhova recoiled, but now the German drew a pistol from the bag she had been holding.

Rebrov turned when he heard their voices, but now he rushed towards Chekhova, drawing his pistol from its holster. "Drop the gun!" he barked, trying to draw the German's attention to himself. The German turned in his direction, squinted, and calmly, utterly professionally holding her gun in both hands she aimed at Rebrov, who was unable to shoot because he might have hit Chekhova instead.

The German woman, whose face showed a surprising calm, was already pressing the trigger when Chekhova knocked her down with all her might, the only thing that stopped her bullet from hitting Rebrov. Now enough distance lay between Chekhova and the German girl that Rebrov could open fire…

He downed her with his first shot.

When he reached them, he first took the gun from the German's hands. Then he bent over the girl: she wasn't breathing. Rebrov sighed heavily and turned towards Chekhova. "How are you?" Chekhova didn't answer. She only took out her handkerchief and carefully wiped her face, which had gone quite pale.

"Do you know her?" Rebrov asked.

Chekhova, waving her handkerchief with shaking fingers, shook her head. "I've never seen her before. She must have been some extreme supporter of Hitler."

Rebrov knelt down and turned the dead woman over on her back.

"She's so young," Chekhova whispered as she gazed upon the girl's body.

"Judging by how she handled her weapon, she must have been a *blitzmädchen*," Rebrov winced.

"A what?" Chekhova asked, surprised. "I don't now what those are."

"Young German girls that were specially taught quick shooting and who were used for executions."

"How terrible!"

"Living people were used to train them, so that they would get used to killing."

Rebrov stood up and looked at Chekhova. "You saved my life."

"And you saved mine. She would have just shot me. There was such hatred within her."

Notes

Olga Konstantinovna Chekhova has moved to East Berlin, Friedrichshagen. Her move was carried out with the help of SMERSH resources and counterintelligence measures. Chekhova expresses great satisfaction with our efforts and our concern.

> From a report sent to Moscow by
> a Soviet occupation forces
> counterintelligence chief

CHAPTER XIV. VAE VICTIS

A cozy German suburb in the American occupation zone, kept so clean it seemed unreal and with neat cottages among the flowers and gardens, was a pleasure for the eye and made one think about how simple and reasonable life could be if human beings did not turn it into a constant nightmare.

A military jeep was parked outside one of the houses. As usual, two American soldiers were lounging with their legs up like cats in the sun, laughing merrily from time to time at some stupid joke.

The gray-eyed man, hidden behind a big, sprawling tree, bit his lip as he listened to their chortling. He leaned back against the tree trunk and looked up. His eyes were fixed on the cloudless sky, his features painfully distorted.

After an American officer stepped out of the house and headed for the jeep, the gray-eyed man straightened and braced himself like a hunter. He did nothing, however, only waiting for the American jeep to drive off, and when he was sure that no one else was around, he headed for the house.

After knocking on the door, he smoothed his hair and tugged at his tight suit jacket. The door was opened by an elderly, hawk-nosed man with gray hair kept carefully parted.

"Olaf, my friend, finally!" He embraced the gray-eyed man and showed him into the house. "I must say, I was getting worried. I didn't know what had happened to you. Where did you disappear to? What kept you so long?"

"I'm OK, baron. I just had to wait for a while, I hid around the corner. I could show up when you've got these… new landlords."

The man called the baron looked at Olaf carefully. "Has something got you down?" he asked with concern.

"Something?" Olaf walked into the spacious office and sat comfortably in a huge leather armchair. He clearly felt at home in the baron's house. "You should ask! What has Germany become? What has happened to the German people? There are signs on restaurants that Germans are forbidden from entering. German girls are openly selling themselves for American cigarettes and stockings. They're lining up to do it…"

"*Vae victis*, my boy," the baron uttered tranquilly. "Woe to the vanquished. When defeat happens, the winners kill the men, the women are taken as concubines, and the holy places of the vanquished are turned into stables or brothels. It has always been so. The idiots who brought Germany to this state should have remembered that when they started all this mess."

The baron smiled and repeated, "*Vae victis*. You can't win, so you've just got to get down on your knees and hope for mercy from the victors. That's what I just heard from an American, you must have seen him." He walked across the room to Olaf. "But it's not just mercy that we can count on."

"What else can we count on? Their pity? Or that they have a bad memory?"

"On their good memory! They should remember that this is Germany, not Russia, a part of the Western world. It is Germany that can protect them from the Communist onslaught. And only Germany. They have already thought of this, and they are also very interested in our achievements. Germany is too great a power for the West to leave it to the Russians, and the West's disagreements with Russia are too fundamental. They understand that very well over there."

"If they understand that, then why have they agreed to hold the tribunal, which will make the Germans a cursed nation forever?"

"Because those idiots that are going on trial committed too many atrocities," the baron said. "Too many for anyone to simply close their eyes to them. Those fools weren't even strong enough to off themselves before they were exposed to the ridicule of the whole world. I have always despised Hitler, Goebbels, and Himmler, but at least they committed suicide."

"Are you sure about that?"

"I really hope so. That fat pig Goering, drunkard Ley, and crazy Hess, what can they hope for? That they might be able to escape the noose? That they can prove they were innocent when it comes to the death camps and gas chambers? Idiots!"

The baron chewed at his narrow, bloodless lips. "If I had my way, I'd drop a bomb on the prison where they're being kept, like cattle before the slaughter. You pledged your love to Germany the great, so you can die for her sake! But, as you see, I don't have any bombs at my disposal."

He went to Olaf and laid a hand on his shoulder. "Don't despair, my boy! Just twenty-five years ago Germany also lay in ruins, and many people thought it would never rise again. But soon she will rise up again to her full extent. Yes, thanks to Hitler, we must give him the credit here. But he was a paranoid mystic, obsessed with his hatred of the Jews and his theories of racial supremacy, carrying his Spear of Destiny that supposedly delivered him messages from the universe. I suspect that he went down into his bunker in Berlin certain that the owners of the Spear would come and save him…" The baron laughed caustically. "'I am like a sleepwalker, going wherever Providence commands me to come. I believe in the magic of the Spear. Enter the mystery and you will gain the whole world!' Those were his revelations, he had found something to brag about. A paranoid sleepwalker as head of state! Obviously that could have only ended in disaster."

"But millions of Germans believed him," Olaf reminded him.

"Yes, and now they have to pay for that. But that doesn't mean that you and I have to get down on our knees in front of the Americans and wait for their mercy."

"What do we have to do, then?"

"We must do everything so that Germany doesn't have to pay too much for its defeat, so that it does not destroy the spirit of the German people and weigh on German youth like a great shame. Above all, we've got to destroy this shameful tribunal, and at any price. I would hope for your assistance in this matter. That's why I called you here. I've got great plans and big hopes for you."

Olaf looked at the baron, bewildered. "What do I have to do?"

"First you have to make everything legal. Real papers will be prepared for you, including certification from the American commandant's office. You will be completely safe with them."

"You can do that?"

"Soon you will see that we can do very many things, you cannot even imagine how many. You must simply understand clearly what you have to do. You should forget that you ever served in a special task force to carry out reconnaissance and sabotage behind enemy lines. That your commander was Otto Skorzeny himself. Everything concerning Operation Oak, Long Jump, or Panzerfaust should be left in the past. Now you're working on Operation Tribunal, where you won't have to do any shooting or blowing things up. But who knows…"

Notes

At the London conference, the chief prosecutors from the four victor countries came together for the first joint meeting to agree on the list of accused. It was proposed that 10-12 people from various parts of the Nazi regime be tried. The USSR demanded that the industrialists who had armed Hitler should stand among the accused, but the other Allies did not agree.

After much debate, the list was approved. The court would try 24 war criminals from all divisions of the regime.

CHAPTER XV. IF I HAD MY WAY!

A barrel organ, played by a ragged old man in a ridiculous hat, sadly wheezed on. Several steps away from him people squatted on the ground like nomads, cooking some kind of meal over the fire. Several meters from them, a painted sign on the door of a bar read "Cabaret! Huge fun! Allied troops only! The best German girls!"

"Dear God, where are we?" Olaf shook his head. He and the baron were driving past in an impressive Horch. Olaf, who was at the wheel, was now dressed in a stylish dark blue suit that fitted him perfectly. Washed, shaven, and rested, he now looked too much like the "blond superman" that Hitler's propagandists loved to depict on their posters to claim the superiority of the Aryan people.

"Where are we?" the baron sneered. "We're in Germany, that lost the war. Someone once said about us, 'Beware defeated Germany! If they don't manage to drown the world in blood, they'll flood it with their own tears!' But enough bitching and moaning, Olaf. Let's get down to business."

"I'm listening."

"Now you will be a legal expert working for the International Military Tribunal…"

"I hope that I won't really have to get bogged down in paperwork and quibbling about petty details."

"We'll see."

"Don't scare me, Baron."

"I think that after all you've been through, scaring you wouldn't be easy."

"These days only a Russian patrol could scare me. Thank God there aren't any of them here, just the Americans."

"You'll have to face the Russians very soon now."

"Where?"

"At the tribunal. The list of accused has already been drawn up, those who couldn't take their own lives or die a brave death. Even

Bormann is on the list, even though he's gone missing. They'll try him in absentia."

"They say he's in hiding."

"If he is, I hope it's in the hereafter. Although... The Americans might have recruited him."

Olaf looked at the baron in astonishment.

"I know, but what's wrong with that? They promised to save his life in exchange for all the secrets he was entrusted with. At any rate, I would have done the same in their place. Alright, then, let's forget about Bormann. Even if he's still alive, he'd never appear in public."

"And what am I to do during the trial?"

"You will act as a lawyer and carry out my instructions."

"A lawyer?"

"Yes, the Americans are currently looking for lawyers for the prosecution. It's not an easy task, so I'm helping them," the baron laughed. "The Americans do pay quite decent fees, so they will eventually find willing people. And with your help, I hope to learn of everything that happens at this tribunal. Both inside the courtroom and outside."

"Have they already announced where the trials are to be held?"

"Yes. At first the Allies argued about it. The Americans proposed Munich. The Russians wanted everything to be held in Berlin. In the very lair of the fascist beast, as their newspapers put it so vividly."

"Do you read Russian newspapers?"

"Of course. I must know my enemy. Anyway, they eventually settled on Nuremberg."

"Nuremberg... Good old Nuremberg."

"Where the German emperors convened their parliament, Hitler held his parades, and if you want to believe in rumors, its cathedral guards the Spear of Destiny itself."

"You surely don't believe in its power."

"I believe in the irony of history. In downtown Nuremberg, which was completely obliterated, the old Palace of Justice and the prison survived without a scratch, as if they were saved specially for this tribunal. It's awfully convenient. There's no need to transport the accused anywhere, there are no risks. Why did the bombs spare the Palace of Justice? After all, they bombed downtown Nuremberg ruthlessly. Maybe we should look for God's hand in this? Perhaps the Lord is sending us some message? We just have to figure out what it is."

At the crossroads their way was blocked by an American patrol. The baron flashed some identification and it impressed the American sergeant who initially had been rude. At the same time, a group of German prisoners surrounded by an American convoy were coming down the road.

"Where are they being taken to?" Olaf asked.

The sergeant narrowed his eyes at him and, without ceasing to chew gum, muttered, "To look at the ditches that have been excavated, where bodies from the concentration camps were buried. There are so many of them…" After a pause, the sergeant thought it necessary to add, "They'll turn away, hide their eyes, and claim they didn't know about any of it. We were thousands of miles away from Germany and we knew what was happening, and you Germans didn't even see what was happening right under your noses!"

Olaf gripped the steering wheel with all his might. The sergeant noticed this and laughed. He clearly liked to show who was boss now.

"By Gen. Eisenhower's order, Germans get ration cards only if they can show a used ticket to a documentary screening about what the Nazis did in the camps. Let them see themselves in it. Ugh, if I had my way!"

The column of prisoners finally moved past. Olaf put his foot on the gas pedal. The sergeant watched the car go and eagerly chewed his gum.

Nice little two- or three-story brick houses surrounded a small parking lot on which the American flag flew from a pole.

"What's this place here?" Olaf asked as they pulled in.

"A concentration camp," the Baron said in a detached way.

"A concentration camp?"

"Indeed," the Baron replied. "Just one for senior German officers. Wait for me here." He got out of the car.

He disappeared into one of the houses while Olaf, who rested his hands on the steering wheel and looked up at the American flag, remembered the camp where he had been held for a few days. It was an empty field, surrounded by barbed wire, into which prisoners were driven indiscriminately. Dysentery raged. They slept like animals, leaning against one another. Their guards amused themselves by throwing cigarette butts and watching the fights that would immediately break out. Olaf escaped after two days, not waiting to see what the camp would be like as it was further built up.

A jeep dashingly screeched to a halt next to him. A young man jumped out of it with a cigarette in his mouth and his hat pushed back on his head. A typical American, the type that Olaf had already seen enough of.

"Hi. Who's in charge here?" the American asked, his teeth shining dazzling white.

"I don't know, I'm German," Olaf said morosely.

"Me too," the American laughed. "Only my parents left Germany about a hundred years ago."

"I was born here."

"Unlucky you. I hope you're not Gestapo? Or SS?"

"No, I'm a lawyer."

"Wow, to be a lawyer under Hitler! It must have been a fascinating profession!" said the American, shaking his head. "Alright then, I'll go have a look around. I hear there are German generals here, a lot of them. You wouldn't happen to know what they're doing here?"

"Probably giving testimony."

"I'd love to be a fly on the wall, then. Probably that's not a bad good to peddle these days. I think it could be sold for quite some profit…"

Olaf shrugged as if to say, who needs it.

"I'm a trader," the American explained. "I buy and sell the best memories of the Thousand-Year Reich, which managed to last just a dozen or so years. By the way, you wouldn't be interested in sharing your reminiscences along the lines of 'I Served Justice under Hitler'?"

The American, satisfied with his own stupid joke, walked whistling towards the houses. Olaf watched him go with molten hatred.

Around an hour later the Baron came out of the house with a man in a German uniform without insignia. For a while they strolled down the asphalt and then said goodbye.

When they were driving away from the camp, Olaf asked, "I think that was Gen. Zeitzler from the General Staff."

"The very same."

"Can I ask what they were doing here?"

"They are drawing up reports about how the Wehrmacht's campaign went. Mainly on the Eastern Front."

"Who needs such reports?"

"The Americans, of course. You want to know why? I think they want to avoid the same mistakes that we made on the Eastern Front."

Olaf looked at the Baron in surprise. "Surely you're not saying that they are preparing to fight the Russians?"

"Is there something bothering you?" the baron asked. "Just imagine, everything could have turned out differently in April. Then Mr. Churchill announced that new times call for new situations. British forces got the order to store up Germany's trophy weapons, and the German soldiers and officers that surrendered were sent to Schleswig-Holstein and southern Denmark in whole divisions. That means they could have been turned into combat-ready units at any moment. At first we couldn't understand why the UK prime minister did this, but after President Roosevelt's death everything became clear. Churchill suggested to the new American president that they firmly stop Russian forces from advancing, by making threats of their own strength and the possibility of a new war. The operation had already been drawn up by the British brass and given the code name Unthinkable. It was to have involved the participation of those same German divisions I told you about, the ones that were never disbanded. A date was even set for the start of the new war: July 1."

"It sounds so unreal," Olaf couldn't believe it. "Truly 'Unthinkable.'"

"And yet, it was real politics. Churchill wanted to stop the Russians at any price. To not let them into Europe at any price."

"And what stopped him?"

"The Americans didn't go along. Their generals could imagine what fighting with the Russians would be like. Furthermore, they were counting on the Russians to help with the Japanese. Without the Russians their fight against the Japanese might have gone on for years and led to enormous casualties. But President Truman in turn was very hopeful that the atomic bomb he dropped on Japan would scare the Russians."

Olaf was quiet for a time, then smiled and said, "I even feel sorry for the Russians, that they got such a stab in the back from their own allies."

"What do you expect from an Englishman?"

"I wonder if the Russians knew about that? About Unthinkable?"

"I think they had some inkling of it, because they decided to take Berlin as fast as possible, whatever it cost them, so that they could show their fine allied friends what they are capable of. The Americans and British weren't up to such fighting. Only two nations in the world could fight like that: the Russians and the Germans. And if they fought side by side, no one could have held out against them. But for some reason they are constantly fighting each other…"

Their car was heading down a forest road when a tree suddenly fell right in front of it. Olaf barely managed to brake in time. Then a tree fell behind the car with a crash. All paths were cut off. For a while, complete silence reigned.

Olaf put his hand under the seat and drew a pistol out.

"Who could this be?" the baron asked.

"It's not the Americans, and hardly the Russians either," Olaf said calmly. "Maybe it's some kind of gang that was brought here to work, or starving Germans…"

"Dammit, this is ridiculous. Are we really going to die at the hands of starving people?"

"I'm getting out, baron. You stay here in the car and lie low. Don't close the door. If they start shooting at the car, try to get out." Olaf opened the car door and shouted, "Don't shoot, we're Germans! Let's talk about this."

The only answer was silence. He slid out of the car and looked tensely from side to side, trying to determine where the danger might be coming from.

Finally, there was a rustling in the branches in front of him and out came a man in body armor with a Schmeisser in his hand that he held with the barrel facing downward. He walked unhurriedly towards the car, jumped over the trunk that blocked the road and came up quite close to them.

"Goodness, Günther!" Olaf cried. "It's you!"

"Who else?" Günther smiled. "Wow, you've become so ritzy now. Maybe you can spare a smoke?"

"Sure thing." Olaf turned back towards the car and grabbed a pack of cigarettes laying on the back seat.

"Who is this?" The baron asked.

"My old comrade Günther Tilkowski. A month ago, we were hiding in the forests together. Just a minute, baron, just a minute."

After Olaf handed Günther the cigarettes, he asked, "Where have you been hiding?"

"Yeah, I don't want to sit in a POW camp eating American gruel, you know," Günther scowled as he lit his cigarette.

"Are there a lot of you here?"

"A few groups of people. But as you know, we don't need whole divisions. A dozen guys like you and me can do many things. By the way, this evening we're shifting to a new location, that's why we're in a bit of a hurry."

"Are you moving far?"

"Nuremberg."

"Nuremberg?"

"Yes. They say there's going to be serious business there."

"I won't keep you, then. I'm also going to Nuremberg, we'll see each other there."

"We'll be on the same side, I hope. I wouldn't want to have to fight you, buddy."

"I wouldn't like that either. It's just that I'll be working undercover."

"Well, I'll be sure not to confuse you with someone else."

They thumped each other on the back. Then, Günther signaled and several guys in camouflage came out and hauled the tree off the road.

When they had driven some distance Olaf, who had been lost in thought, said, "Günther says they're heading to Nuremberg."

The Baron nodded. "I heard."

"What does that mean?"

"That means there are people who want to organize an attack on the tribunal, free the prisoners, and spirit them away to Paraguay or wherever."

"Do you think that's possible?"

"First, it would be good to find out who will be guarding the tribunal and what forces might be required for that kind of operation… But you know where I stand. Even if I managed to save them, I wouldn't bring them to Paraguay. They are something already worn down by history and as long as they still live they can only get in the way. Unfortunately, it's not up to just me to decide things."

Notes

The US Embassy in Buenos Aires is investigating reports that Hitler and Eva Braun arrived in submarine U530 to Queen Maud Land in Antarctica, near the South Pole. Soon after this, U530 surrendered to the Argentinians.

Newspapers are reporting that a German settlement known as Berchtesgaden had been founded on the island during a German expedition there in 1938–39. Perhaps U530 was one of the submarines that left German ports at the very end of the war and headed for Antarctica.

CHAPTER XVI. THE NAZI GOLD

In his Berlin quarters Gen. Filin was writing up another report to Moscow when Rebrov came in.

"You called me, Sergei Ivanovich?"

"Yes. We're moving to Nuremberg, so get ready for departure. By the way, you will have accreditation at the trials as expert staff from our delegation."

"Expert in what?"

"Historical, legal, international… Whatever you like. Remember those lines of Mayakovsky?" Filin smiled.

"What am I going to do there? What will my duties be?"

"Well, as far as your duties go, I'll let you know. Mainly, you'll be a completely freelance individual in Nuremberg. Feel free, but don't go too far. There will be a special brigade of SMERSH counterintelligence there to solve any operational issues. Col. Kosachev will be in charge. He has the habit of solving issues in the harshest ways."

"Yes sir, comrade general, I won't go too far."

"And now for the most important thing. Our agent will be working in Nuremberg, the one codenamed Hector. We need to develop a reliable way of obtaining information from him. Considering how many American, English, and other countries' special services will be there, we need to come up with something out of the ordinary. You and I are not to expose this agent. That is completely out of the question. By the way, here is his last message, it came through Moscow."

In the camp where, under American orders, the German generals are examining the course of the war on the Eastern Front, an enormous number of documents have been brought in. It cannot be ruled out that as the Germans discover these documents, they might destroy some that could be used against them. This concerns especially documents proving that they spent a long time carefully preparing their attack on the Soviet Union. At the upcoming trials they intend to completely deny this.

"What, they're going to prove that we attacked them?"

"That they were forced to attack us, you see. They made a preventative strike, with the purest intentions. To protect the West from Bolshevik aggression, as Germany was and still is an outpost of the West…"

"But who would believe that!"

"Whoever needs to will believe it. Or pretend to believe it. By the way, you'll be able to ask Mr. Goering about all this personally."

"Ask who?!" Rebrov stared at Filin in amazement.

"Reichsmarschall Goering," Filin repeated. "I'm sure you've heard of him? The Americans have finally allowed us to interrogate him, but all of our investigators are still in Moscow. You won't even need an interrogator. So, let's not miss the opportunity, you'll do a little investigative work for now. It's simple enough, just ask him a few questions. Just get him warmed up before our investigators take over. You'll be going to Mondorf, it's in Luxembourg. Just have a heart-to-heart with Goering. By the way, ask him about the Nazi gold. Hector tells us that the Americans are very interested in it. I'll help you with the questions."

"What do we know about it? About the gold?"

"Let's see. Back before the war, Hitler dug eight secret mines in the Alps that were kept carefully concealed, and he stored gold and platinum bars in them. It was his stash for a rainy day. By the time the war was going on, there were thirteen such mines. All of the men who worked to dig them were killed by the SS. Then, the men who killed them were killed in turn. The Americans think that, besides Hitler, the location of the gold might be known to Himmler, Goebbels, Bormann, Goering, and Ley, the people closest to Hitler. Himmler and Goebbels are dead, and Bormann has disappeared, so that leaves Goering and Ley. Both of them are in the Americans' hands. The Americans won't let us interrogate Ley, by the way. He's supposedly in a bad state, either he's sick or he lost his mind from alcohol. So, ask Goering about this gold."

"Do you think he'll just spill everything right away?"

"No, but watch his reaction."

"Maybe we shouldn't ask about the gold."

"Why not?"

"Well, the Americans are going to be noting everything down. Why let them know that we know about the Nazi gold?"

"But you are to ask exactly this," Filin insisted. "Let them know that we know. And that they won't be getting their hands on the gold on the sly."

Notes

On April 6, 1945 the American 12th Army Group under Gen. Patton discovered in an underground salt mine near Merkers, Germany gold bars and coins, chests containing nearly three billion Reichmarks, and knapsacks full of goods that the Germans had confiscated from concentration camp victims. There were also works of art estimated to amount to a quarter of everything held in Berlin's Museum of Fine Arts. Patton was concerned about getting all this treasure out before Soviet forces arrived, so he brought trucks, tanks, air cover, and a Ranger battalion.

CHAPTER XVII. BLUE SUITCASES

Rebrov, accompanied by a young American officer, walked down a corridor of the Grand Hotel in the Luxembourg town of Mondorf-les-Bains.

"We bring them here from all over Germany," the American readily explained as they walked. "We're waiting for the prison in Nuremberg to be ready, and then we'll send them there. We bring them to their senses here. There's Robert Ley's cell. Do you want to see the man?" The American called the sentry who was patrolling the corridor and the sentry opened the door of the cell.

Ley met them standing at attention. He already looked like he had sobered up. It felt downright embarrassing to look upon this elderly man standing erect and staring intensely at his visitors.

When the door of the cell had been closed again, Rebrov asked, "Is that a prison rule, to stand at attention when someone enters?"

"No, they like to stand like that on their own, so straight you can hear their bones crack. Germans, what do you expect? They've got order and discipline in their blood. Prison does a lot of them well, by the way. Take Ley, when he was brought here, he was totally out of it. He smelled like a saloon. But now he's constantly asking for paper and ink to write something."

"Do you read what he writes?"

"No. There are special people here who do that. A whole team of them," the American laughed.

"I see."

"And Goering! You should have seen how many suitcases he brought here with him. And they were all blue leather. Can you imagine? Blue suitcases! I've never seen anything like that before. He had bags of crosses and gold rings! There were several marshal's batons encrusted with diamonds, and he was still complaining that his Reichsmarschall's baton had been stolen from him! You can't imagine what a pile of junk he had, we simply had nowhere to store it all. He had suitcases with all kinds of food in them, too. And then we found a whole bunch of pills, which turned out to be morphine substitutes. He took handfuls of them day and night. We wanted to take them away, but the doctors said that if he suddenly stopped taking them, he'd go totally crazy. So, now we're gradually reducing his dose. We're making a man out of a wasted drug addict. Thanks to that detoxification regime we can interrogate him now. Ah, here's the interrogation team. You get settled, they'll bring him out now."

Two tables were placed in a small room. At the one in the corner, an American officer with an incredibly neat mustache was seated along with two young ladies in military uniforms who were chewing gum.

"Here are our investigator, translator, and stenographer. They will be present during the interrogation and transcribe what is said," Rebrov's garrulous companion explained.

When he had left, Rebrov sat down at the empty table by the window. He placed in front of him a piece of paper and pencil that he had brought with him, and then ran his hand through his hair. The young ladies stared at him unabashedly and twittered among themselves, exchanging their impressions.

"Have you already managed to interrogate Goering?" Rebrov asked the mustached investigator. He was slightly nervous – it was Goering himself! It had been impossible to imagine just a couple of years before.

"Yes, and more than once," the investigator yawned. It had clearly become a wearying routine for him.

"What can you tell me about him?"

"He's a very strange and spiteful man. And besides that, he's a master of pretending and cracking jokes. He acts differently every time… In my opinion, he's a professional liar and an amazing son of a bitch."

At that moment two soldiers ordered Goering into the room. He was wearing a baggy tunic with the insignia removed, as well as trousers sized too big even for this fat man. Goering looked much thinner than on the newsreels that Rebrov had seen, haggard and somehow dilapidated. He sat down in the chair indicated, smiled, and looked affably at Rebrov. He seemed to show that he was completely ready to cooperate, and he was completely not any "amazing son of a bitch". The American in the corner watched him with a sardonic smile.

After introducing himself only as a Russian major, Rebrov asked a question that he had thought would be unexpected and knock Goering off balance. "Do you speak Russian?"

Goering was completely taken aback for a moment, but then he affably replied, "No, I only know only a single Russian word, *velikiye* 'great.'"

"Why does that word mean so much to you?"

"We faced great difficulty fighting near Velikiye Luki. I ordered then that someone tell me what *velikiye* means."

"Goering seemed open to sharing old memories but Rebrov, briefly noting down Goering's answer, abruptly cut him off. "How did you feel about the fact that Germany attacked the Soviet Union?"

"When I learned of Hitler's plans for war, I was simply horrified. I repeatedly tried to convince the Führer not to go to war with the Russians, but he was simply carried away with the idea and I couldn't talk him out of it. He said that it was an order from on high," Goering smiled and pointed to the ceiling. "He was a great mystic. He would go to Nuremberg to speak with the spirits of ancient Germanic warriors…"

"Why Nuremberg?"

"Because it's there, in St. Catherine's Church, that the so-called Spear of Destiny is kept. He was certain that the Spear would protect him from defeat. Hess told me that Hitler believed a campaign towards the East was sanctioned by some kind of center on Earth that received communications from the cosmos, and therefore it had to happen no matter what."

"But in your public speeches, hadn't you already spoken of your hate for the Soviet Union, that 'the Soviet Union will be crushed'?"

Goering looked at Rebrov in surprise. Then his surprise was replaced with gentle reproach. "I would be very surprised if you could show me just one speech along those lines", he said, carefully choosing his words. "Your question was not about love or hate for the Soviet Union but about the expediency of going to war with it. I believed that going to war with the USSR was not expedient, but at the same time I have always been opposed to your worldview. I have nothing to hide in this regard. The whole world knows what I think."

"How much had Hitler been trusting you with official secrets lately?"

"Since Martin Bormann, my nemesis, became secretary of the Nazi Party Chancellery, they tried to keep me from talking to Hitler. Never in my life did I have as much influence on Hitler as Bormann in these last years. You know what some of us called Bormann behind his back? 'A little secretary, a big plotter, and a dirty swine,'" Goering recounted with relish.

"How was your relationship with Hitler personally?"

"My relationship with the Führer was excellent until 1941," Goering proudly stated. "It got worse during the war and then completely broke down. Hitler relieved me of my duties, expelled me from the Nazi Party, and sentenced me to death. On April 22 he announced that he would remain in Berlin and die there. In the bunker, they gradually went mad. If you only knew what happened there!"

"Tell me about the state of Hitler's staff just before the surrender."

"No one among the staff was allowed to mention surrendering. Even as late as April 20 Hitler was talking about the possibility of bringing the war to a victorious end. About some wonderful weapon and secret forces that would save him… When I saw him for the last time, he was a ruined man. He hung his head, his hands shook, and he spoke quietly and indistinctly. However, he would still issue death sentences without a second thought, he didn't trust anyone. He seemed to truly hear voices and he only paid attention to them. That was generally the end of it."

"How did you feel about Hitler's racial theories that he made the basis of his politics?"

"In such a strict form as Hitler believed, I never shared his views. All this about us being godlike, I never believed that."

"Did Hitler?"

"For Hitler it went without saying. A godlike man with the Spear of Destiny at the ready," Goering chuckled and even seemed to wink at Rebrov.

"You do understand that you will have to appear before the International Tribunal, which will examine your actions and their consequences for various countries."

"I do understand. But I don't believe in the justice of any court convened by the victors over the defeated. This is a political undertaking, the verdict is forgone, I have already prepared myself for what will follow." Goering suddenly changed. He straightened to a haughty posture and his voice took on an authoritative tone. "I am prepared to accept responsibility for what is on my conscience, but not for what is on the conscience of other people."

Rebrov decided to cut him down a notch. "Not only the victors, the Germans too think that what is on your conscience will be quite enough,"

"You shouldn't listen too much to what the Germans are saying now. They have been defeated and are simply licking the winners' boots. As for what they might say about me, I don't give a damn. I remember well what they used to say just recently, and how they would weep from joy at the sight of the Führer. As long as everything went smoothly they adored and worshiped us. Don't worry, I know our people!"

"Yours is an interesting account," Rebrov remarked.

Goering smiled in a self-satisfied fashion.

"Are you convinced that Hitler killed himself? You don't think it was a cowardly thing to do?"

"Cowardly? No. Hitler had already told everyone beforehand that he and Eva Braun would depart this life, by themselves. He was the Führer of the great German Reich. I can't imagine him sitting in a cell and awaiting trial as a war criminal. A trial arranged by foreigners! He was too great a man for that!"

"Didn't he want to shoot you towards the end of the war, though?"

"That doesn't change anything. He was the symbol of Germany. No, I would never want to see Hitler subject to the justice of the victors. I'd enjoy seeing Himmler like that, though. Let him answer for himself and his cronies! I could never understand how he and his SS generals could do such terrible things! How could they live with themselves? I just don't get it."

Rebrov saw with some amazement that Goering was saying all this with almost pure, unaffected indignation. One might even think that he himself had had no idea of it all. Rebrov glanced at the American officer, who shrugged as if to say, I warned you. Rebrov then looked back at Goering; if he was so upset now, maybe it was time for sharper questioning.

"What can you tell me about the so-called Nazi gold? Do you know where they hid it?" The American officer's ears immediately pricked up. Rebrov noticed this out of the corner of his eye, but he continued to press Goering. "I'm talking about the gold that was plundered from the countries you invaded and hidden in mines under the mountains."

Goering closed his eyes. Now he resembled a balloon that had been poked with a needle.

"I'm tired. My heart hurts. They took my medicine away from me, you see."

His face had, in fact, really turned gray and was covered with sweat. It was obvious that interrogating him further would be senseless.

The guards led him out. "If Bormann was a dirty swine, then what are you?" the mustached investigator yelled after him. "Geez, you listen to him and you'd think he was the best friend the Jews ever had."

"In Hitler's inner circle he was referred to as the 'fat pig,'" Rebrov laughed. "They were all pigs there. And yet they considered themselves the kings of the world! With connections with on high. I'd rather they all hang."

"Is that all for today?" the American stretched. "Maybe we could go for a drink, wet our whistles?"

"I'd still like to talk to Keitel."

"Keitel it is, then," the American waved his hand. "They'll bring him out now."

"How does he come across, this… field marshal?"

"He's quiet and obsequious. He bows to everyone and tries to convince them of what an insignificant figure he was. He was only the supreme commander of the armed forces, that's all. He didn't have any power or authority. He just relayed Hitler's orders to the troops and monitored how they were carried out. Just a quiet functionary, though a field marshal."

Field Marshal Wilhelm Keitel presented himself outwardly as a typical Prussian officer: dry, direct, the sort of man that others would say had a stick up his rear. He had gray hair that was kept carefully parted and a small ashen mustache. Like all of the other prisoners, his uniform lacked rank or any other insignia.

Rebrov decided to speak with him in a direct, business-like fashion. "You are a general and field marshal, Chief of the Supreme Command of the German Armed Forces," he began harshly. "I ask that you clearly answer my question: when did Germany begin preparing for war against the Soviet Union and what was your role in this undertaking?"

Keitel cleared his throat and stated:

"The General Staff had information that in early spring of 1941, the USSR had begun massively concentrating its forces along the border, which attested to its readiness to, if not openly take military action, then at least influence Germany's foreign policy by military means. All the preparations we carried out prior to the spring of 1941 were of a defensive nature, should the Red Army attack. Naturally, in the course of these preparations we decided to choose the more effective option, that is, to prevent Soviet Russia's attack and smash its army in an unexpected strike. However, I must emphasize that our plan did not involve the total conquest of Russia."

It was clear that Keitel would answer any questions with formulations that had been well thought out and honed from long repetition. Obviously this had been the only thing that occupied him in prison.

"And what was your plan?" Rebrov asked dispassionately, though he was seething with rage inside. Sure, they only wanted to prevent an attack, that's all!

"Our aims with regard to Russia after defeating the Red Army were only to set up a military administration. As for what was to be done afterwards, I am not aware of anything. I know at least that when plans for a western campaign were drawn up, the German command and political leadership never specified the political forms that these states would take after they were occupied."

"Were you not aware of the plan to break up the USSR? To reduce the Slavs to slavery? To wipe out the Jews and communists?"

"Of course not," Keitel sat up in his chair. "I never heard of such plans. Never."

"Alright, how do you explain this, then?" Rebrov drew from a folder the documents that Filin had prepared. "On September 16, 1941 you issued an order to the German forces that stated, 'A human being's life in unsettled countries counts for nothing, and a deterrent effect can be attained only by unusual severity.'"

Keitel closed his eyes and muttered, "I don't remember any such order. I'm a soldier, not a member of some punitive expedition."

"Alright, then."

Rebrov did not go deeper in this theme, because it was now time to unveil his main question, which Filin had tasked him with asking Keitel specifically.

"What do you know about Vlasov's army? What role did German command set for Vlasov himself?"

"As far as I know, Gen. Vlasov was taken prisoner in the 18th Army region. The Army's propaganda division started distributing leaflets signed with his name. That's how the whole story with Vlasov's army started. I don't quite remember, but I think that initially Vlasov was noticed by the Ministry of Foreign Affairs… The General Staff began paying serious attention to Vlasov starting in the spring of 1943."

"After your forces were defeated at Stalingrad and Field Marshal Paulus was taken prisoner."

"Precisely. The General Staff proposed that Russian units be created and equipped under the command of Gen. Vlasov. However, Hitler strongly opposed the creation of any armed Russian units, and he ordered me to ensure that his directive was observed. I then put Vlasov under house arrest and kept him in one of the districts of Berlin. Himmler was also opposed to the creation of any Russian units under the aegis of the General Staff."

"How did they end up on the front if everyone was against them?"

"In October or November of 1944, Himmler's views about Vlasov changed. He specially visited me to find out where Vlasov was being kept and to talk with him. He suggested that I talk with the Führer about the need to form Russian units and use Gen. Vlasov. I strongly refused. However, after that Himmler managed to get the Führer's permission to create a Russian division which, as far as I know, was sent into battle in April 1945 south of Frankfurt-am-der-Oder. Vlasov's protection was assured only by Himmler and the SS… And in general, I must say that the German army was trained in the fine principles of Prussian warriors, and not the disgrace that the SS created."

When Keitel had been led out, the American shouted, "Don't believe a single word he says! Even when they show him the documents, he denies everything. How could these miserable little creatures do such great evil?"

Notes

A Danish young man found a sealed bottle near Roskilde with a German label. Inside was a letter from a German sailor. The letter was written in Fraktur. The bottle itself had been made for one of the Holstein breweries.

The letter read:

"This is the last message of one of the survivors of the submarine *Nautilus*, where the Führer of the German nation Adolf Hitler took refuge. The submarine was sailing from Finland to Spain when it ran into a sunken ship and began taking on water. We could hold out another 15 hours or so under the water and during that time I have written this letter…

"When the disaster happened, the Führer was in the [illegible word ending in *kammer*], which was locked, so he was separated from the rest of us.

"I am making this known in order to refute any claims that Hitler's body was burned in the Reich Chancellery…

"With a triple 'Heil!' for our beloved Führer I am leaving the ship. Soon we will again be free! We will restore Germany to its former strength and greatness!"

[Signature of Hans Rotenbürger]

CHAPTER XVIII.
DON'T FORGET TO DRAW THE CURTAINS!

Chekhova sat in her armchair while Frazer strolled about like he owned the place. He had swept into her house a few minutes before so unexpectedly that she hadn't even managed to draw the curtains as she had agreed with Rebrov. Now she was wracking her brains what to do. The summer evening was too bright, it would have drawn Frazier's suspicions if she drew the curtains now. Frazier, meanwhile, kept approaching the window and looking out at the front yard warily.

Frazier went to the telephone and, after asking her permission, dialed a number. "Excuse me, Maj. Bradley… Yes, I'm at her place… I hope that she'll be more reasonable today," he said, his eyes on Chekhova.

"What does all this mean, Mr. Frazier?" Chekhova calmly asked as he was yet again looking out the window. "You seem rather excited today. Are you suddenly competing against others for my memoirs about my intimate relationship with Hitler? Maybe you should draw the curtains so that no one can see us."

Frazier looked her for a moment, thinking, then firmly drew the curtains closed. Chekhova even sighed with relief: she had done it.

Frazier now took a chair sat directly opposite her. His gaze was cold and sinister. "Mrs. Chekhova, enough with the irony, let's be serious. All the offers I've made you with regard to contracts and your memoirs are and will remain available. These are real American business offers. But they will be valid only if you accept one more offer, a secret annex to them, so to speak," he grinned wryly.

"And what is this secret?"

"You work for the Russians… Yeah, yeah, don't deny it! And I don't mean during the war. I mean right now. You flew to Moscow and spent a pretty long time there. Too long for it to be by accident. You met your handlers from the Russian secret services there, and here you're living under Russian monitoring and regularly meeting with Russian officers.

Don't tell me you're just chatting with them about everyday life and how you feel."

Chekhova remained silent. What could she say? She did meet and talk with them.

"I'm not asking you to stop meeting them," Frazier assured her. "For God's sake, it's your business. We just want to be kept informed about your business with the Russians, first of all. And secondly, we want you to pass along some information that we give you to the Russians. There won't be any danger in this. Plus, you can expect a Hollywood contract…"

"Goodness, you've got a mistaken impression about me!"

"I don't think so. If you don't agree to this, then we'll simply knock you out of the game," Frazier answered harshly.

"How so?" Chekhova sat up. "Are you going to kill me?"

Frazier waved her question away. "Why get our hands dirty? We'll just drop the Russians some hints about your ties with the current Nazi underground, which is seeking at any cost to disrupt the trials of the Nazi leaders in Nuremberg. And since you speak regularly with the Russians about this, they'll think that you're handing their secrets to the Germans, and then they'll take you away. Not to Moscow this time, straight to Siberia."

Chekhova closed her eyes.

"You have no choice, Mrs. Chekhova," Frazier said insistently. "You should realize this and stop being so stubborn and silly!"

Suddenly a knock was heard at the door. Frazier froze. "Who's that?" he whispered.

Chekhova shook her head. She had no idea.

"Olga Konstantinovna, it's me, Rebrov!" said a voice from the other side of the door.

Frazier stood up, drew a pistol from the inside pocket of his jacket, and aimed it at Chekhova. "Open it, but don't you say anything. Otherwise, I'll shoot!" He silently approached the door and stood beside it. The pistol remained aimed at Chekhova. She straightened her hair, took a deep breath, and opened the door.

Rebrov, this time in civilian clothes, smiled at her. He held a cardboard box in his hands. "I've come to say goodbye, Olga Konstantinovna…"

Chekhova was unsure what to do. She only looked at him with desperation. Rebrov nodded slightly.

"What has happened?" Chekhova asked as calmly as she could. "Why goodbye?"

"I'm leaving. Here, I decided to bring you some food. Who knows when we'll see each other again. Can I come in?"

Chekhova, at a loss as to what was going on, stepped aside and Rebrov came into the room. Frazier, whom Rebrov hadn't noticed, came behind him and hit him upside the head with the pistol with professional technique. Rebrov collapsed to the floor. Chekhova gasped and rushed to his side.

"Is that your Russian handler?" Frazier asked.

"No, just a Russian officer. He's just a young guy."

"Just a fan, you mean?"

"If you've killed him," Chekhova was frantically probing at Rebrov's head, "the Russians will find you!"

"No, they won't," Frazier laughed. "Soon I'll already be in the American zone. And nothing's wrong with this young man of yours. I just knocked him out for a while. Don't worry, he'll come to soon. Just don't think about telling the Russians about our plans. For your own good. Otherwise we'll get even with you."

"Enough trying to scare me! If you're leaving now, what do I tell the Russians? How do I explain who attacked him?"

"Tell them that you were attacked by supporters of Hitler that hate you, especially as they make up half of Germany these days." He smiled.

Chekhova looked at Rebrov's deathly pale face and ignored Frazier, who now headed for the door.

At the same instant Soviet soldiers burst into the roof, rifles in hand…

Denis, occasionally rubbing the back of his head, was now interrogating Frazier. The latter had been ordered to sit in the same plush armchair where Chekhova had been sitting not long before.

"So, who are you? And don't give me that story about Paramount Studios."

Frazier shrugged. "That part about her memoirs is completely true. Mrs. Chekhova's intimate recollections could bring good money in America."

"You're no literary agent."

"That's just my hobby. You ought to know that every American is interested in doing business."

"Who are you really?"

"I'd like it if they could leave us two alone," Frazier nodded towards the soldiers. "Don't worry, I don't aim to hit you over the head again."

"Now it's my turn to administer the beatings, so keep that in mind. I've got every right to hit back, and I know how to do it if necessary. Plus, it's our occupation zone. Don't forget that."

"I understand."

When the soldiers had left the room, Rebrov asked again, "Well? Who are you and what do you want from Chekhova?"

"You and I are colleagues," Frazier smiled. "And, I should remind you, allies. So you really ought to let me go."

"So, you represent American intelligence?"

"You might say that."

"What, are the American spy services interested in publishing an actress's memoirs?"

"If that actress is associated with the senior leadership of Germany and the USSR, then… You understand. As for the information that Chekhova possesses, we wanted to determine what things might especially interest the Soviet prosecutors in the Nuremberg trials. After all, you asked her the same questions, didn't you, my colleague?"

When Rebrov and Chekhova were saying goodbye, they both suddenly felt that the events of the past days had, imperceptibly but quite firmly, brought them closer together. However, they both realized that this closeness was accidental, a product of the situation, and could not last. Nonetheless, at that moment it was extremely vital for them both. They would remember it for a long time, if not forever.

"Didn't you notice the curtains were drawn?" Chekhova asked.

"I did. I just decided that it wasn't worth storming your house," Rebrov awkwardly tried for humor. "I hoped I could do everything quietly and on my own."

"What's going to happen with this Mr. Frazier?"

"Nothing special, I think. They'll find out who he really is, how he got here, what he's up to. Then they'll contact the Americans and work something out. Where are you off to? Or is it a secret?"

"I'm heading for Nuremberg."

"Aha, you'll be judging these…"

"No, I'm no judge. Others will do the judging. I'm just going to watch."

"I wonder if we're going to see each other again."

"I hope so."

Notes

Top secret

Moscow, People's Commissariat of Internal Affairs of the USSR

To: Comrade Beria
The newspaper *Courier*, published in Berlin under the control of the French military authorities, printed on November 14 of this year a brief article entitled "Olga Chekhova honored". As the newspaper reports, the movie actress Olga Chekhova was personally honored by Stalin with a high Russian decoration for courage. Since the first days of the war, the newspaper reports, Olga Chekhova… had at her disposal a room at Hitler's headquarters and big receptions were held for her there… She played this dangerous game for many years without being exposed by the Gestapo. Only in the final days, when the Red Army was already fighting within Berlin, was her handler arrested, but she herself managed to avoid being shot.

Resolution: "…To: Comrade Abakumov, Comrade Merkulov. What do you suggest should be done about Olga Chekhova? — Lavrentiy Beria, November 22, 1945."

CHAPTER I.
YOU ARE CRIMINALS, THAT'S ALL!

Two US military transport planes emerged from the clouds one after another and landed heavily at Nuremberg's airport. They were immediately surrounded by armed American soldiers in jeeps and trucks.

A group of elderly, wizened men made their way with difficulty down the planes' exit ramps. They were dressed in a motley fashion: some in civilian clothing, others in military uniforms without insignia. They had threadbare shirts or jackets of unknown origin. The prisoners left through the crowd of soldiers in a bus with barred windows. Assorted suitcases and bags were thrown out from the plane and then the soldiers loaded them into one of the trucks.

The column slowly moved through the ruins of Nuremberg and the men in the bus silently and sullenly looked out upon the city. Only a few streets had been cleared of rubble. Among the ruins one could suddenly make out smoke from bonfires; people sat around them without paying them any attention and one would think they lived there. Holes and gaps in the walls of buildings had been carelessly covered with wooden boards. In the ground-floor lobby of one massive building stood the wreck of an anti-aircraft gun…

After going down the wide and straight Fürststrasse, the column suddenly entered a neighborhood with buildings that had remained practically untouched. In their midst was the four-story Palace of Justice behind an imposing double gate of wrought iron. The column rounded the Palace and drove along a long building perpendicular to it. This building looked quite severe: cold, ancient walls, rows of small barred windows.

"Prisoners, you are now in the prison," said Col. Andrus, the prisoner commandant, to the men before him. A stout figure with hair trimmed short, he might have resembled a stereotypical American sheriff, but he wore glasses and thus looked more like an impenetrable bureaucrat. The colonel was a professional soldier, who had done everything in life according to regulations or orders. He could not be swayed either by entreaties, flattery, or threats. A former cavalry officer, he always walked with a staff in his hand, occasionally tapping it against his boots.

"There are strict rules here which will be strictly observed. No exceptions. You all were in Mondorf and you ought to know that it's futile to try to beg me for lenience, threaten me, or scare me with complaints. You can complain only to the good Lord, but he'll extend no helping hand to criminals like yourselves."

After a pregnant pause, Col. Andrus went on. "Soon you'll see the inside of your cells. You are forbidden from keeping pencils, paper, photos of family, tobacco, or toiletries. Anything." He again gave the prisoners a moment to absorb what they had heard.

"You will be kept under nonstop guard. When a prisoner lies down on his cot, his head and hands must remain visible. A prison barber will shave you. Reading glasses will be issued to you during the day and given back to us at night. The cells are lit from the outside, so there is no electrical wiring inside them, no point trying to commit suicide by electrocution. Several times a week you will be searched without warning. God help you if we find anything you aren't authorized to have. You will wash once a week. Every morning you will clean your cells."

"Forgive me, but we are prisoners of war," Keitel couldn't keep silent. "There are the Geneva Conventions that deal with treatment of prisoners of war…"

Andrus cut him short, "I don't care about the Geneva Conventions. Here you are only prisoners awaiting trial, and you are subject to prison rules."

"Do not forget who you are dealing with, colonel!" Goering, who had lost more weight now, seethed. "You should be ashamed of the role you're playing now!"

"I won't forget even for a second who I've got in front of me here," the colonel grinned.

"I demand that my medicine be always kept in my room," Goering said. "I cannot live without it. Or do you mean to kill me?"

"You can only take medicine prescribed by the prison doctor. As for the drugs you've been hauling around in your dozens of suitcases, you'll go on taking them just like you did in Mondorf: in a quantity that ensures you stay alive until you're sentenced."

Goering got red in the face. Some of the other prisoners looked at him with open glee, others more detached. It was clear that these men were not united among themselves. Each of them was concerned only with his own fate.

"Don't forget, colonel, that you are dealing with historic figures, no matter what they accused us of," Goering continued to seethe. "You are no one!"

Andrus laughed defiantly in response. "Let me repeat, this is a prison for criminals. Remember that. Any protest against the conditions of your incarceration are not only groundless, but unlawful. Your idea of your status is mistaken."

Casting a disdainful gaze on the prisoners, the colonel explained again, "I'll repeat for those who didn't understand. You are not captured officers or simply prisoners of war. You are among the men who used international laws and treaties as toilet paper. You believed they could be used for your personal benefit, that you could violate them without fear of punishment when it comes to others, especially those of 'un-Aryan race'. You thought yourselves outside the law and you became outlaws. And now you'll be led to your cells. Every cell shows the prisoner's number and last name."

Goering, wanting to have the last word and show that he wasn't broken, loudly asked, "Since I am the most important person here, I trust I have been assigned cell number one?"

Andrus spat and tapped his staff against his boot. "You'll stay in the cell you've been assigned."

The former lords of the Thousand-Year Reich watched with satisfaction as the American put fat old Hermann in his place. They had no idea what a miserable sight they all were.

Notes

From the rules for prisoners in Nuremberg prison:
— Prisoners may not come within 4 feet of a window.
— Use of knives or any other sharp object is strictly prohibited.
— Any food should be mashed up to such a degree that it can be eaten with only a spoon.

— Prisoners shall be shaved by the prison barber using a safety razor and only under the supervision of a guard.
— Prisoners may use reading glasses, pens, and pencils when working with court documents only under the supervision of a guard.
— Prisoners and prison staff are prohibited from greeting one another other than with a nod of their heads…

CHAPTER II. THE EXPERIMENTERS

Robert Ley's cell was no different than the other cells in the prison: three meters by four meters in size, the height of a man, with a small window looking out at the prison's courtyard. The door had another window in it which remained always open and behind it stood a guard. In the corner there was a toilet. Next to a small table stood a hard chair without armrests, and across from it was a cot with a thin, coarse blanket.

Ley sat on the bed and squirmed miserably. In the chair sat a man with his legs crossed, dressed in civilian clothes and wearing a hat that he hadn't even bothered to take off. He looked like a typical representative of the American special services. Standing at the door, covering the little window in it, was forensic psychiatrist Maj. Douglas Kelly.

"Dr. Ley," Kelly said quietly, "this man is from the American military administration. He has considerable authority. You can call him Mr. Smith."

Ley readily nodded. His entire face beamed with an unfeigned joy. In his rumpled American military clothes and felt slippers he looked like a worthless bum.

"Mr. Smith has come at your request to hear your thoughts on the present state and future of Germany, and, if necessary, to relay them to the highest levels," Kelly said, then went on to clarify, "In the event that your thoughts are considered promising and beneficial for the United States and Germany." He showed enviably white teeth.

"You two talk, and in the meantime I will visit the other prisoners," Kelly said and went out.

As soon as he was gone Ley, a large-headed man with a bulging forehead and anxious eyes, started to speak hastily and stuttering, as if he had long been waiting for this moment. "We were experimenters, sir. But as we experimented on human material, we left behind the wrong words in the documents: 'destruction', 'elimination', 'amputation'. Even if it's a matter of cutting off rotten tissue, the documents should always use the right words: 'creating', 'building', 'solving problems'. Then no one would call you to account at some kind of tribunal, even if you cut off much more living tissue than we did. So, the right words and a strong army and… America stands above all, isn't that so?"

"And what 'right words' did you intend to use to explain Dachau, Auschwitz?"

"The Spaniards wiped out the Indians of South America and you Americans did the same in the North! Mankind just accepted it. It would have accepted every prisoner at Auschwitz if we had won this war! And words… Words can always be found when the army is strong."

"Let's start from the fact that you lost," Smith cut him short. "You got smashed. You surrendered unconditionally. You are now at the mercy of the victors, who can do with you whatever they well please. That's what you should be constantly keeping in mind."

"America should keep in mind that the Soviet Union's victory over Germany is a triumph of Marxism, which is a threat for the West. And not just Marxism! It's an Asiatic attack on Europe. Germany was always a dam against the Asiatic hordes, and then the Bolsheviks. Now that dam has been breached. The German people cannot rebuild it on their own. They need help in this matter of history."

"And who ought to help"

"America should rebuild that dam, if it wants to survive. For the German people and for America there is no other option!"

"And what will the new Germany be?"

"National Socialism has unfortunately tarnished itself by going to lengths that American society won't accept. I would not accept them either. Unfortunately, Hitler didn't have the right people around him. But the National Socialist idea, cleansed of antisemitism and joined with a reasonable democracy – that is what Germany can offer our common cause."

Mr. Smith fell silent, pondering something. Ley looked at him without speaking.

"There is theory," Mr. Smith finally said, "and then there is practice. In life everything comes down to people, specific people. Who are they, the ones who can build this new Germany?"

"They are the most respected and enterprising men in the country: *gauleiter, kreisleiter, ortsgruppenleiter…*"

"If I understand correctly, those are Nazi Party officials – local ones, regional ones, and so forth…"

"Yes. These are the most organized and capable men in Germany. The country ran on them."

"That was Hitler's Germany," Smith reminded him.

"Hitler is no more, but Germany remains!" Ley exclaimed with enthusiasm. "And America needs it. There are also the heads of the army, intelligence, industry, the whole backbone of the country . They need to be released from camps and prisons, released and encouraged towards a reborn German spirit. But one without any extremes, without extremes! The ones that got Hitler killed."

"But you must understand that after everything that happened, this would lead to public outrage all over the world, including America."

"I do understand," Ley said readily. "This operation should be carried out under complete secrecy. Without any publicity. The American hand shouldn't be too visible. Rather, these men should simply quietly come back and take up leadership positions, for there is no one else. Trust me, I know what I am saying! You won't find anyone else who can do it."

"What future do you see for yourself, Dr. Ley?" Smith asked.

"I think my experience in organization will also prove useful here. I wrote a letter to Mr. Henry Ford, where I offered my experience with building up the Volkswagen factories. With American help we will build absolutely the best automobile industry in the world."

Mr. Smith rose. "Well then, I've listened carefully to what you have to say, Mr. Ley. But in order to work with you, we need to be convinced of your sincerity."

"I'm ready to prove it! How can I?" Ley looked Mr. Smith up and down like a dog, his moist eyes bulging in excitement.

"For example, we are interested in the matter of the Nazi gold. Do you have anything to say about that?"

Ley, downcast, lowered his head and said nothing.

"There you go, Dr. Ley," Smith reproached him. "You immediately backed down. I guess you are not sincere after all, you're just playing games with us. You hope to trick us, lay it on with the cheapest goods of all: words, which you're all so fond of. I wouldn't do that if I were in your position. If the matter goes to court, or rather to the tribunal… You understand the difference, don't you, doctor? A court judges people, a tribunal condemns them. So, you've got to realize that no one can save your jolly bunch gathered here. Some might still save their necks from the hangman, though, but there would have to be good reasons."

"I don't know anything… about any gold…" Ley said through trembling lips.

"You don't know anything," Smith smiled. "You know how to re-make the world, but you don't know anything about any gold."

"I just don't know…"

"You see, you're still trying to wriggle and lead us astray. Incidentally, among your ideas there are some reasonable ones, but you've got to understand one simple thing: they can be implemented without you. No one needs you personally for that, Dr. Ley. Just like your accomplices in these neighboring cells. With your reputation for being butchers and sadists, you can't be used in any kind of open political intrigue."

Ley lowered his head and wept.

"And soon the Russian investigators will come for you. You constantly complain about the Bolshevik threat, about the need to stop it, but you yourself are helping the Bolsheviks."

"Me?"

"Martin Bormann, who's the subject of so many rumors right now, might well still be alive. They haven't found his body, you see. And since he disappeared in the Russians' territory, he might be in their hands. He wouldn't keep quiet for long. The Russians either beat all his secrets out of him, or he quietly started cooperating with them. Bormann, unlike you, is practically under no illusions. That means the gold will wind up in Russian hands, and then…"

Smith stuck his hands into the pockets of his trench coat. "All your talk about our common efforts is meaningless. Worse yet, your silence, your reluctance to cooperate with us, means that you're working for the Russians… Willingly or not, what difference does it make to us? While you're trying to lead us around in circles here, the Russians are finding out where the gold is being kept. Save your own skin, Dr. Ley. I told you how you can try to do this. If you manage to remember something, then let us know."

Smith left the cell. Ley watched him go with the eyes of a madman. Then he jumped up and paced around the tiny cell.

Notes

American intelligence shielded dozens of Nazi war criminals and their accomplices from trial, as attested in a 600-page report by the US Department of Justice that long remained classified. One of the war criminals that the CIA worked with was Otto von Bolschwing, who had a direct role in drawing up the plan to rid Germany of the Jews. Many figures from the Third Reich ended up under CIA protection. One was armament factory head Arthur Rudolph, who relied on forced labor from prisoners of war who were forcibly transferred to Germany. The CIA closed their eyes to this and sent him to America, as he knew a great deal about building rockets. Later he would be called the father of the American Saturn 5 rocket.

CHAPTER III.
MARBLE TOMBS AWAIT US!

"They are nobodies!" the baron said irritably. "Why the hell should we save them? Who needs them? They don't care about anything if they can just save their miserable lives. All their insistent claims of love for Germany are just a lie. Do you know what that crippled freak Goebbels said before he killed his children? That the German people have not proven worthy of its leaders, so let them perish along with them. How do you like that, adviser?"

The stately man standing at the window with his hands behind his back shrugged. "I don't like this at all, baron. But I do know that Goebbels was a master of propaganda, and his lessons are still relevant to us."

"Do you really expect that the Germans will again seize on Nazi ideology?"

"On an ideology that doesn't have the extremes that Hitler and Himmler allowed themselves. You and I know that Hitlerism contained a lot of things that were already in Germans' minds before him. And they will go on existing. That can't be denied."

The baron cut this line of conversation short. "This is all theories and philosophical talk, let's postpone it for a better time. Now we need to get down to practical matters. For example, the Nazi gold."

The man whom the baron called the adviser didn't argue against this.

"You want to find it and spirit it away from Germany?" the baron asked.

"I'm afraid that now we won't be able to do that. I'm not under any illusions. That's why our task is to ensure that it doesn't fall into the hands of the Russians or the Americans. Don't you agree?"

"What is the situation here? Among the ones who have survived, Bormann, Goering, or Ley might know of the gold… Bormann has disappeared and it would be best that he's dead, and not in the hands of the Russians or the Americans. As for Goering, if he knew about it, then he couldn't keep his mouth shut and he would have already made some deal with the Americans, but from what we know that hasn't happened. So, he simply doesn't know. That's understandable, considering that Hitler didn't trust him recently."

"He might have learned something before he fell out with the Führer."

"His information would be out of date. The gold was moved last time things went south between him and Hitler. So, that leaves Ley. They tell me that in prison he's tormenting himself with visions of the postwar order, as if anyone asked him to! But the Americans need something else from him entirely. Right now he's keeping quiet, but you can't trust in the mental state of a longtime alcoholic, especially once he's made to stop drinking."

"Of course. The best thing to do in this situation would be to neutralize him," the adviser said calmly and then asked, "How is the prison guarded?"

"Not bad, though the Americans are careless enough. After their victory, they're starting to slack. But why do you need any of this? Do you really want to try to free them?"

"Baron, I know what you think of the accused, but I won't hide from you the fact that in our secret council, we have decided to try to bust some of them out of prison. We have already found some people from Otto Skorzeny's group that are free men, they are the best experts in creating diversions. Plus, there are a lot of Germans working in the Palace of Justice, either prisoners or civilians. If we arrange something with them… Yes, there are several camps with prisoners from the SS quite near to Nuremberg."

"You know what I think about those men in prison," the baron said implacably. "I think it would be a big mistake to make any attempt to save them. Let them answer for their actions. They should serve as a sacrifice to redeem us."

"We know everything," the adviser shrugged. "Moreover, some members of the secret council share your position. But we have made our decision."

"Well, that's some fine German discipline, then! But tell me, why do we need them to be free? What would we do with them? They aren't Napoleons… Remember, adviser, that most of them were handed over to the Americans by the Germans themselves. Nobody wants them! Do you really think that there is anyone who wants to fight for them"

"As a matter of fact, there are."

"Sure, sure, a few desperate types could be found. But as soon as you slip out, the Allies will declare martial law and smash everything they haven't managed to smash yet."

"We cannot allow a trial that will break Germany's back. We will demonstrate the power of our spirit. That's the most important thing!"

"God, again this mysticism! Next you'll be telling me that we've got to get the Spear of Destiny back, wave it, and the world will be on its knees before us."

"It *was* on its knees, baron," the adviser reminded him. "People believed Hitler because he himself believed in his own destiny. And today, when the Germans are demoralized and going crazy, they need a new symbol to believe in. We need to show that we have strengths and capabilities, that we are not sheep that will simply be led to the slaughter or be castrated."

The baron took a deep breath. "*Okay*, as our American friends say. I won't try to convince you and your secret council otherwise. Onward, and may the Spear bring you luck."

"It would be nice to find it, for a start," the adviser laughed.

"Oh, so you don't have it yet, then! Where could it be?"

"Probably with the Americans. But we'll try to get a hold of it. We need symbols, baron, symbols! You are too materialist, and when you talk with the Americans you turn into an outright businessman. But Germans need spiritual symbols. That's how they're made. We don't need Hitler himself, he just became a wreck in the end, but we need the power that lifted him up to the top, and which abandoned him when he stopped heeding it."

"Ugh, I've had enough of these Germans!"

"What do you intend to do yourself, baron?"

"What I think is the most realistic option we have: discrediting the tribunal itself. The Germans, the entire world, should see that this is not a real, just court, but just a way for the victors to settle scores and get revenge."

"You're also a German dreamer, baron. Are you going to find lawyers who can prove that Kaltenbrunner and Goering are perfect angels? Can you imagine what documents are going to be presented? What witnesses? What an impression they'll make?"

"I can imagine. But the Allies have a multitude of sins on their conscience. If you can bring them up, hammer on them with good lawyers, and prove that the victors and the defeated were all the same… You might be able to drag out the trials and turn them into a mockery."

"They'll hardly allow us to do that, but we can try," the adviser agreed. "Let's work from two directions, then."

The adviser paced the room, smiling at some thoughts of his own. "By the way, Goering claims that in fifty years, the Germans will consider him and all the other defendants heroes. They'll rebury their half-rotten bones in marble tombs in a great temple and pray over them."

"Ha, fat, greedy Hermann thinks he's a saint! He should have ended up in prison a lot earlier, he'd have fewer sins on his conscience. And as far as bones go, he's mistaken: after they hang them, the Allies are going to make sure that no one ever finds their moldering remains anywhere. They'll simply be disposed of."

The adviser laughed. "They told Goering the same thing. And you know what he answered? That they'll just take any old bones, claim that they're Goering's, and place them in a marble tomb all the same. Then pilgrims will come by the millions to venerate the relics of this great martyr."

"Dear Lord, who does that fatso think he is?"

"Now he's as scrawny as a scarecrow. The skin's hanging off him like an elephant's. You could even make a hiding place in it."

"Ugh, how awful," the baron shuddered. "A fine symbol of the nation!"

After seeing his guest off, the Baron came back inside. Olaf came down the stairs to meet him.

"Well, did you hear?" the baron asked.

"Yes, and now I understand who ordered Günther Tilkowski to move with his people closer to Nuremberg, and why."

"Do you think they want to use him?"

"Sure, they are clearly preparing an assault on the Palace of Justice. They've been training specifically for this. And what are we to do, baron?"

"Us? We will observe."

"Just observe?"

"For the time being, yes. We'll see how things turn out for them, though I'm sure it will all come to nothing."

"I daresay, baron, you don't understand what Günther and his men are capable of."

The baron looked at Olaf quizzically. "What, do you still want to fight a war? And receive a bullet from the Americans?"

Olaf guiltily looked down.

"We need to soberly and responsibly keep an eye on things, my boy."

"But we've got to do something…"

"You've got something to do. Right now I'm busy with that old drunk Ley above all else, a man who loves to keep his head in the clouds and a master of delivering high-flown speeches that mean nothing. The Americans might extract information from him about the gold, if they promise they'll let him take part in some fanciful project. They'll just wind him around their finger. Or administer something that will help loosen his tongue."

"What should we do, then?"

"We need to take any illusions away from him. Regarding his own fate, first of all. Then he'll curl up into himself and retreat into his own dreams, and there… Can we do this?"

"I'll have to think about it."

"Start right now."

Notes

Aggressive leaders have been recurrently produced by the German people, who then follow them blindly. Detailed knowledge of the personalities of these leaders would add to our information concerning the character and habitual desires of the German people, and would be valuable as a guide to those concerned with the reorganization and re-education of Germany. The convicted be shot in the chest, not in the head, as it would be desirable to have a detailed autopsy, especially of an undamaged brain…

From an appeal by a committee
of American psychiatrists
and neurologists

CHAPTER IV. WHY RUDENKO?

Nuremberg's Johannisfriedhof cemetery was encircled in a wrought iron gate. Behind it stood ancient gravestones huddled close together, crosses, the occasional tree, and a brick wall. Nearby, half a meter above the ground, a tomb stood marked with two coats of arms in metal and adorned with an inscription, announcing it to be the resting place of the great German artist Albrecht Dürer.

When he had stood for a while at the most famous grave in Nuremberg and cautiously glanced around him, Rebrov went to a tree growing nearby and put his hand into its hollow. After finding something there, he quickly thrust a fist into his pocket. He spent a while more at Dürer's tomb and then quickly left the cemetery.

The old Palace of Justice, separated from the street by an iron fence, resembled some kind of gigantic office: endless corridors with cold, gray stone walls and innumerable office doors on either side. Crowds of people with papers, folders, and heavy briefcases walked the halls, but unlike an ordinary civilian building, here there were a lot of military wearing uniforms of different countries, as well as American military police. A distinct presence among this multitude were young men with stretchers, brooms, and brushes, dressed in greenish-brown camouflage overalls marked "POW" on the backs; the Americans were heavily using captive SS men to prepare the Palace for the trial of the Nazi leaders.

One had to admit, the Yanks had spared no expense: the US army had sent an entire regiment to manage the work of the tribunal, with drivers, encryption experts, telephone operators, copyists, guards, and more. The Palace now hosted its own post office, international switchboard, currency exchange, garment repair, barber, several bars, and even a nightclub. The Americans didn't want to skimp on comfort or give up any of the pleasures of life.

The Soviet delegation took up a separate section of the building. Over the entrance hung an impressive plaque with the words "Delegation of USSR."

In one of the offices Rebrov was pouring over the encrypted message delivered from the Johannisfriedhof cemetery.

"Well, have you finished?" asked Filin impatiently as he burst into the office.

"Yes, Sergei Ivanovich, I'm practically finished with it…"

"Go on and read it, then!"

"'The prisoners are observed and their words recorded around the clock, whether in their cells, the cafeteria, or during visits. The prison psychologist, Kelly, is also providing information to American intelligence and investigators. Lately the Americans have been actively working on Robert Ley. They think he might know where the Nazi Party's gold is hidden. In exchange for that gold, they drop hints that Ley might be able to live freely in South America.'" Rebrov looked up. "That's all, comrade general."

"So, they're trying to shake Ley for information…" Filin paced around the office, then headed for the door. "If anyone asks for me, I'll be at Alexandrov's."

Grigory Nikolayevich Alexandrov, head of the investigative branch of the Russian delegation, could easily pass as Filin's brother. This thin and bald man with the air of a classic Russian intellectual resembled a military type as little as Filin did. They clearly felt a sympathy for one another, and thus they quickly became friends.

"Well then, you still haven't perished under a mountain of documents?" Filin asked with a smile as he entered the office. "Your life is slowly slipping away while you pour over them, like Koschei."

"Rather like Pushkin's miserly knight, who realizes the power of the wealth in front of him," Alexandrov joked.

He looked tired, but undoubtedly upbeat. Filin noticed this right away.

"Well, don't be shy, I see that your face is shining with joy. What have you found? Have you been digging deep in the Nazi mines?"

"It's impossible to hide anything from you! We've found Operation Barbarossa, the plan for war against the USSR, right down to all the details!"

"Congratulations. Very nice. Considering that they're going to claim that we attacked them, then their entire defense will crumble. Did you already tell Moscow?"

"I'm preparing a report now. What have you been up to?"

"The Americans have started working on Ley."

"What about?"

"They think he might know about the secret Nazi gold. Ley looks like the best person to shake for that information."

"What about Goering?"

"Goering, they feel, is in an aggressive funk, it would be a lot of work to shake him. Who knows how long it would take, and what he'd demand in return. He's not easy to scare. But Ley's easy to break, to trick. He's an alcoholic with a shattered mind. He's also convinced that he has a chance to work together with the Americans."

"Well, you know, they're all convinced of that! Now they all imagine themselves the shining warriors of the West, defending it from the Communist threat. Any suggestions?"

"Can you demand to interrogate Ley and ask him about the gold?"

Filin's advice surprised Alexandrov. "With the Americans right there? Any interrogation would be carried out with their permission and with them present."

"Let it be with them present. Let them know that we've also got some information about this. Granted, I'm sure that they won't let us get to him right now. He's not even in his cell right now, he's in the prison hospital where they transferred him to. When it comes to the gold, all doors are closed..."

"Yes, they only open with some effort. They allowed us to interrogate some of that gang for the first time only at the end of June. They had already been interrogating them since early May, right after they were brought in..."

"The Allies are, to put it simply, a second front. Our agent obtained the text of a US State Department message to the British ambassador Halifax. It explicitly said, 'Until the information obtained from the prisoners proves valuable, interrogations should be carried out solely by British or American officers. In the interests of the USA, prisoners captured by the US army should not be interrogated at this time by either Polish or Russian officers.' There you go."

"Well, we won't display all of our secrets, either. Any other news?" Alexandrov looked at Filin with slight suspicion. "You weren't just feeling sorry for that drunkard Ley."

"I do have other news. The chief prosecutor for the Soviet Union will be Roman Rudenko, the Ukrainian prosecutor."

"So, not Vyshinsky, then."

"Vyshinsky will oversee the Soviet delegation's work from Moscow, as the chairman of the Politburo commission. Of course, he'll come here for a visit, too."

"So, it's Rudenko," Alexandrov said pensively. "Why do you think that is? He's 38 years old and they make him the chief prosecutor from the USSR? For a trial that is completely without precedent?"

"And so large in scale! That American prosecutor Jackson thinks that this is his ticket straight to the White House…"

"Rudenko wouldn't think anything like that. It wouldn't even come into his head, ever. Do you want to know what I think? This decision was politically very clever. If Vyshinsky came, it would immediately create undesirable associations with the trials before the war. I think Moscow took that into account. But as far as Rudenko goes… What did your Jackson see? I mean, with his own eyes? He might have read American newspapers or seen newsreels. But Rudenko spent the whole war at the front, he saw with his own eyes what the Nazis did. Plus, he has already participated in some trials against Nazis and their collaborators. He's already got experience, he has an idea of how they'll behave…"

Notes

We must ensure that the lives of the Germans in the colonized eastern lands is connected as little as possible to the local population … Considering how many children there are in each family there, we will only benefit if their girls and women use contraceptives to the greatest possible degree. We must not only allow unlimited trading in them, but also we must encourage them, for we are not in the slightest interested in the growth of the local population.

Adolf Hitler, Führer
of the German People

CHAPTER V. GRACE AND LADYSHIP

With a month remaining until the start of the trials, work in the Palace of Justice was proceeding at a feverish pace. This mostly consisted of processing countless documents and translating them into the languages of the victors.

Rebrov was walking with Arkady Gavrik, a young employee of the Soviet secretariat with dark hair, a perpetually anxious look in his eyes, and a fast manner of speaking. They were going down a narrow corridor to the Russian section of the translation department, where translators from America and France translated selected documents to and from Russian.

"I'll try to get them to translate our report faster," Gavrik said anxiously. "But I don't know if it will work."

Several steps from the door, Gavrik stopped and asked, nearly in a whisper, "Do you know who's in charge there?"

"No, I don't."

"Her Grace, Princess Tatyana Vladimirovna Trubetskaya," Gavrik reported with an air of great importance. "Can you imagine? Her Grace…"

"Are you sure she's Her Grace and not Her Ladyship?" Rebrov smiled.

"What's the difference?"

"I think that Her Ladyship is more important… But I'm no expert in aristocratic titles, and it's all the same to me, count or prince. That's all from a past life. You and me are Soviet people."

In the department, behind a table laden with papers, sat a young woman with her head wrapped in a warm kerchief. She had been reading something attentively, but now she lifted her radiant eyes towards them, and Rebrov suddenly realized that he had seen her pure and pretty girlish face somewhere before.

"Excuse me, we've got one text here, it's very important, and we'd ask you to translate it quickly," Gavrik blurted out, clearly embarrassed. "Can we do that? I realize that you've got a lot of work, but…"

An aged man in an American officer's uniform entered the room. After greeting them, he spoke with the young lady in English and she said something in reply. The man turned towards Gavrik and Rebrov with an unhappy mien and said several vehement words in English. Gavrik was confused.

"What is he saying?" Gavrik turned to Rebrov. "Do you understand?"

"He says it's completely impossible to do this translation quickly," Rebrov translated. "They are simply buried under other urgent tasks. He's saying this as the head of the office."

The young lady smiled and said something to the imposing officer. He looked at her with surprise.

"She's saying let us Russians agree on something among ourselves," Rebrov whispered in Gavrik's ear.

The man in the uniform shrugged his shoulders and went out, muttering something to himself.

"He said he can't pay her anything for doing it express," Denis translated.

"Give me your document," the young lady held out her hand. She had delicate, beautiful fingers.

"Excuse me, are you really the Princess Trubetskaya?" Rebrov asked.

"No, are you kidding! Tatyana Vladimirovna is at lunch." She looked at the clock and added, "We've still got five minutes until the lunch break is over. My name is Irina. Irina Yuryevna Kurakina."

"Kurakina…" Rebrov repeated.

"Are you also a princess?" Gavrik asked. "Your Grace? Or Your Ladyship?"

"No," Irina laughed. "I am a princess, but… It doesn't really mean anything."

Gavrik pulled at Rebrov's sleeve. "Well then, shall we go? We've got to…"

"Go, I'll catch up," Rebrov waved him off. Rebrov realized that he couldn't just up and leave so quickly.

Gavrik shrugged disapprovingly and left. Kurakina looked at Rebrov with her sweet smile.

"What were you reading so attentively?" Rebrov asked. "The Charter for the International Tribunal? Or the record of some gruppenführer's interrogation?"

Irina shook her head. "Bunin. The new story by Ivan Bunin that has been published here. It's called 'Pure Monday'. Levochka went to Paris and brought it back with him. There are already a few people lining up to read it." Irina pointed to the magazine.

"Who is this Levochka?"

"Levochka Tolstoy. Leo Tolstoy's great-nephew. He's working as a translator for the French delegation."

"I see. Will you let me read that Bunin?"

"On one condition."

"What's that?"

"If you tell me your name."

"Oh God, I didn't even introduce myself! Denis Rebrov. Just Denis will do. I'm not a prince, or even a count."

"So what? You know, it seems that every other Georgian is a prince. Ivan Bunin isn't a prince either, or even a baron. Are you from the Soviet delegation?"

"Yes. I'm… a specialist."

Rebrov suddenly felt the need to make sense of what had happened to him. And there was no doubt about what had happened. "So, I'll drop by later this evening? For the magazine."

Princess Kurakina nodded in response without speaking. Right then a young, fair-haired young man with a cheery face came into the room. When he saw Rebrov, his smile immediately vanished. He only nodded dryly, sat down at the table, and demonstratively sank into his reading.

That evening, after he had made his way through the scaffolding and over the cracked flooring to the sole renovated floor of the Grand Hotel, Rebrov lay for a long time on his bed, still dressed and oblivious to the ordinary hotel noises coming from the hallway.

Something had happened in his life. Something very important had taken place. He understood this very clearly, irrefutably. It was Irina Yuryevna Kurakina's eyes, her sweet Russian face, her chilled shoulders under her warm kerchief, her delicate fingers and voice… Goodness, look what things can just come along one day, and they remain with you always and forever…

He got up and went to the window. Even in the darkness of that night one could make out ugly piles of iron and stone, but he seemed not to notice them.

Notes

It is extremely important to ensure that we do
not awake any sense of dignity in the local
population. We must be especially careful here,
for after all, a complete lack of self-worth
among the conquered peoples is one of the major
prerequisites for our work.

                              Adolf Hitler, Führer
                              of the German People

CHAPTER VI.
NO DEFENSE AGAINST SUCH CHARGES

In the streets of Nuremberg, now and then he came across people carrying firewood and brushwood. They carried it on carts, on bicycle racks, on all kinds of makeshift trailers. Potatoes were unloaded from the covered bed of a truck, apparently brought from a nearby village. People were hurriedly packing the potatoes into sacks and backpacks and they handed the farmers not money but various goods. In the center of the city, twisted iron stuck out from the heaps of stones at him like skeleton hands, whether in supplication or deprecation…

Olaf, wearing dark glasses and a glued-on mustache, went down to the basement of the ruined house and knocked on the door. It was opened by a man who was no longer young and who showed fear on his face. From the dark room behind him a child's crying could be heard.

"Mr. Holzenbein?" Olaf asked, looking the man intensely in the eye.

"Yes, that's me," the man nodded in fear. "Excuse me, but who am I speaking to?"

"That's not important. Do you work in the hospital at the Palace of Justice?"

"Yes, in the prison hospital. But how do you know that?"

"That's not important, either. Just be quiet and listen. You clean the hospital ward. In one of the beds is Dr. Robert Ley…"

"But…"

"No buts!" Olaf angrily cut him short. "I'm going to give you a note which you will pass on to Ley today. Do it discreetly when you're cleaning his room…"

Holzenbein shook his head. "I can't do that!" Tears streamed from his eyes, he held his hands over his chest imploringly. "They'll send me away at once, and my children will die of starvation! This is the only job I have! My children, my wife, my elderly mother… Please, I beg you. The war is already over, why all this? Why? Everything's over already…"

Olaf grabbed the man by the throat with a gloved hand, like he had once grabbed the girl in the street. He looked the man in the face with cold eyes, and with a passionless expression on his face he lightly squeezed with his fingers. The man's eyes became dull.

"It's an order," Olaf said. "An order that won't be discussed, and you must carry it out. If you still want to moan and complain, I'll throw this grenade into that stinking hole of yours right before your eyes. And then you'll have to scrape the bloody remains of your children and your elderly mother from the walls."

Olaf's appearance was indeed terrible. The man, drenched in sweat, whimpered helplessly.

"Shut up. And don't try to trick me," Olaf said with disgust. "Otherwise I'll come back for you and your pathetic spawn."

At this time Ley was lying on his bed in the tiny hospital ward in the prison, staring at the ceiling. His face was like a frozen mask.

An American soldier opened the door to admit Holzenbein with his mop and bucket. The soldier remained outside in the hallway. He looked around from side to side, whistling and throwing a coin up in the air. Holzenbein began to clean demonstratively, and as soon as the soldier's back was turned, he slipped a tiny lump of paper into Ley's hand and immediately rushed to the door, barely avoiding spilling water from his bucket over the American.

Several days later Ley was led from the hospital back to his cell. There Col. Andrus, accompanied by two guards, announced in an unusually solemn tone, "Prisoner Robert Ley, I am US Army Colonel Burton C. Andrus. I have been authorized to serve you with the charges for the International Military Tribunal."

The colonel held out a rather impressive typewritten volume, which one of the guards had handed him.

With some horror, Ley took it into his hands.

"Here's a list of attorneys who have agreed to work at the trials. You are free to choose any of them as your defense."

Ley, spellbound, looked at the list.

When Andrus had left, Ley sank to the bed and covered his face with his hands. "You were right," he whispered in despair. "You were right, my dear. They had everything already decided, but I still hoped for something..."

He was still in this same state when he was found by Maj. Kelly and the recently appointed expert psychologist – and, simultaneously, US military officer – Gustave Gilbert.

"Good evening, Dr. Ley," Gilbert said affably and with a smile as he stood looking intently at Ley. "We would like to know how you feel after the charges have been announced?"

"How do I feel?" Ley roared theatrically. "How would I feel if I were accused of crimes I do not have the slightest awareness of?"

"Well, you've got more than the slightest idea," Kelly said softly.

"I do not have the slightest idea!" Ley said stubbornly. "But if, after everything that has happened, you're looking for new victims, then well, I'm ready!"

Ley got up from the bed, stepped over to the wall, stood with his back against it, and struck the pose of Christ crucified.

"You're looking for revenge! You want to feel like a big winner! Well then, just put me against the wall and shoot me. The victors can do anything they want!"

Ley leaned dully against the wall. Kelly and Gilbert exchanged understanding glances.

"Sit down, Dr. Ley, sit down. And calm down."

Ley obediently stepped away from the wall and sat on the cot.

"Better we discuss how you intend to defend yourself from the charges against you?" Gilbert asked gently, like a real lawyer.

"Defend myself? How can I defend myself from such charges? There is no defense against such charges! Why torment me and drag this trial out like… like…"

"You are being tried like a criminal. Did you expect that all would be forgiven you?" Kelly asked in surprise. "You are an intelligent man, you were a major state figure. You should have realized what everything was leading up to."

Ley put his hands over his ears. "Lies," he muttered, "Complete lies!"

"You just rest now, Dr. Ley. We'll visit later and discuss your situation. In the meantime, we'll visit the other defendants."

Notes

From the comments made by the defendants on the charges filed against them:

Hermann Goering, Reichsmarschall, Hitler's successor, member of the Hitler Council: "The victor will always be the judge, and the vanquished the accused."

Rudolf Hess, Deputy of the Führer and member of the Hitler Council: "I do not regret anything." Joachim von Ribbentrop, Reich Minister for Foreign Affairs, member of the Hitler Council: "The charges have been filed against the wrong people."

Wilhelm Keitel, Field Marshal, Chief of the High Command of the German Armed Forces, member of the Hitler Council: "For a soldier, an order is an order!"

Ernst Kaltenbrunner, Chief of the Reich Main Security Office: "I bear no responsibility for war crimes, I only did my duty as head of the intelligence agencies, and I refuse to serve as some ersatz Himmler."

Alfred Rosenberg, Nazi Party Reichsleiter for Ideology, Reich Minister for the Occupied Eastern Territories: "I reject the charge of 'conspiracy'. Antisemitism was only a necessary defense measure."

Hans Frank, Governor-General of the Occupied Polish Territories: "I see this trial as a supreme court pleasing to God, called to examine the terrible period of Hitler's rule and bring it to an end."
Wilhelm Frick, Reich Minister of the Interior: "These charges are entirely based on the assumption that I have participated in a conspiracy."

Julius Streicher, editor-in-chief of the Nazi newspaper *Der Stürmer*, Gauleiter of Franconia: "This trial is a triumph of world Jewry."

Hjalmar Schacht, Reich Minister of Economics, president of the Reichsbank: "I cannot understand why I have been charged."

Walther Funk, Reich Minister of Economics, member of Hitler's Council for defense: "Never in my life have I done anything consciously or unknowingly, which would have given rise to such accusations. If I have been ignorant or mistaken and committed the acts listed in the indictment, then my guilt should be seen in the perspective of a personal tragedy, but not as a crime."

Karl Dönitz, Grand Admiral, Commander-in-Chief of the German Navy, Hitler's successor: "None of the accusations has anything at all to do with me. They were invented by the Americans!"

Baldur von Shirach, head of the Hitler Youth: "All of these problems stem from racial politics."

Fritz Sauckel, General Plenipotentiary for Labor Deployment: "The chasm between the idea of a socialist society, which I nurtured and defended in the past as a sailor and worker, and these terrible events — concentration camps — deeply shook me."

Alfred Jodl, Colonel-General, Chief of the Operations Staff of the Armed Forces High Command: "This is a mix of unfair accusations and political propaganda."

Franz von Papen, Vice-Chancellor: "The charges horrified me, because I was now aware of the recklessness with which Germany plunged into war and created a global catastrophe, and secondly because of the crimes that my compatriots committed. Those crimes are psychologically inexplicable. I think that years of godlessness and totalitarianism are to blame for everything. It is them that turned Hitler into a pathological liar."

Arthur Seyss-Inquart, Chancellor of Austria, Reichskommissar for the Occupied Dutch Territories: "I hope that this execution is the last act of the tragedy of the Second World War."

Albert Speer, Minister of Armaments and War Production: "This trial is necessary. The process is necessary. Even an authoritarian state does not absolve each person from responsibility for the terrible crimes committed."

Konstantin von Neurath, president of the Privy Cabinet Council, Protector of Bohemia and Moravia: "I have always opposed accusations that cannot be defended against."

Hans Fritzsche, head of radio and press for the Reich Ministry of Public Enlightenment and Propaganda: "These are the most terrible accusations of all time. Only one thing could be more terrible: the looming charges that the German people will make against us for misusing their idealism…"

CHAPTER VII.
A CALL FROM THE HEREAFTER

Helmeted American guards paced the prison corridors, occasionally looking into the cells, which were lit through the window in their doors by a bulb affixed outside. When a guard glanced into Ley's cell, he saw that Ley wasn't sleeping but walking about the room in a frantic state and muttering something to himself.

"*Schlafen!*" the guard ordered in German, then added in English, "Sleep!"

Ley turned and stared with mad eyes at the guard through the little window in the door. "Sleep?! How could I sleep?"

The guard again ordered Ley to go to bed and then he moved on to the other cells. The remaining prisoners were already sleeping in accordance with the order that their hands remain visible on top of their blankets. Only Keitel was sleeping with his blanket pulled over his head. The guard beat on the door of his cell and shouted, "Hands!"

Keitel rolled over on his back, placed his hands over his blanket, and again closed his eyes.

When the guard had ensured that everything was in order, he walked on. When he met his partner who was walking down the other side of the corridor, he lazily asked him, "How's it going? One of my guys is bouncing off the walls."

"God, I'm so tired of seeing their faces!" his partner complained. "How the hell did we end up here? Everyone else is already home in the States, basking in glory, girls hanging on their necks, and we've got to watch these creeps!"

"But later we can tell everyone how we guarded the entire Nazi bunch," the first guard reassured him. "It's just a shame that Hitler ain't here! It would be a gas to guard that jackass. I'm sure I'd find a chance to spit right in his face, then I'd tell all Kentucky about it!"

"Yeah, that would have been great."

The guards laughed and then parted. When the guard came back to Ley's cell, he looked through the window and could not see the prisoner; the bed was empty. He shined his flashlight around the cell and found Ley sitting on the toilet. Disgusted, the American walked on.

The guard again returned to Ley's cell some time later and saw that Ley was still sitting on the toilet "Looks like he's got stomach problems," he chuckled to himself. "Maybe fear has gotten to him." He shouted through the window, "Hey, prisoner! Go to bed!"

No answer came. Ley sat with his head thrown back. Something was protruding from his mouth.

"Something's wrong! Call the captain! Now!"

Within a minute the officer on duty was running down the corridor, swearing frantically. He opened the door of Ley's cell: Ley was still sitting on the toilet, a rag in his mouth, and around his neck was a wet towel that, when it had dried, had contracted and strangled him. Col. Andus pushed the assembled soldiers aside and rushed into the cell.

Awoken by the noise and the stamping in the corridor, the prisoners lay in their cells listening intently to every sound.

The next morning Andrus, who had not slept a wink and who had been thoroughly chewed out by his superiors, was answering a crowd of journalists, ever more of whom were drawn to this sensational trial by the day. He held his beloved staff in his fists, which were bloodless from stress.

"From now on, each cell will be supervised around the clock by an individually assigned guard," Andrus explained the changes made to the prison rules after Ley's suicide. "We will keep the prisoners in our sight at all times. We will not allow what Ley did to happen again. Keeping a continuous watch on a cell is extremely tiring, so our guards will be rotated more frequently than before."

"People are saying that your rules here are too strict."

"You should tell that to the survivors of Auschwitz," the colonel angrily retorted. "And these men are regularly visited by military doctors, nurses, and dentists. They include not only Americans but also four Germans. With regard to their prison conditions, the brother of that scoundrel Goering is serving as a witness and was released from prison. He officially requested that he be sent back to prison, as the conditions here are better than the conditions Germans on the outside are living in.

"Did you allow him to come back?"

"It wasn't my call to make. But for my part, I recommended that his request be refused. Let him live the same as the people he stirred up and brought to their present state."

"Colonel, you never call your charges prisoners of war. Why is that?"

"The status of prisoners of war applies only to the Germans who work in the prison and do not number among the defendants. For us, the rest are only prisoners, accused of the most terrible crimes in the history of mankind."

"Do the other prisoners already know about Ley's suicide?"

"Of course, you can't cover up something like that."

"And what was their reaction?"

"What? Goering said, 'Thank God!'"

"Did he really say that?"

"Yes, that's exactly what he said. And he added, 'That moron would have only embarrassed us!' Mr. Gilbert is here and can tell you more about that."

Gilbert, who had been standing behind Andrus, stepped forward.

"Goering said, 'It's good that Ley is dead. I was very worried about how he would act in court. He was always so absent-minded and would go off on long-winded speeches. I have no doubt that he also came off as ridiculous during his interrogations. So, I'm not surprised he killed himself. Under normal circumstances, he would have drunk himself to death.' That's everything he said, in fact. Nothing especially heroic."

"When the trials begin, you will see how they get along with one another," Andrus said. "They all hate and suspect each other. They're ready to bite at each other's throats."

While Col. Andrews was fighting off the journalists who kept pressing him, Mr. Smith went through the papers that remained in Ley's cell. He was still occupied with this when Dr. Gilbert found him.

"Were you looking for me?"

"Yes. Come in, doctor. Maybe you can help me understand this crap that our heroic suicide left behind. You do speak German well."

"What happened?"

"Do you know about his wife, Inga Ley?"

"I don't know much about her. She was a very beautiful woman, and Ley drove her crazy with his rowdy living and shamelessness. She took her own life a few years ago, during the war."

"That's right. But how do you explain this then, doctor?"

"Explain what?"

"This letter I found in Ley's papers. Here, read it. Maybe I didn't understand something correctly with my poor German?"

Gilbert began reading and translating the letter into English: "My dearest Inga, when I received the news from you, I literally gulped it down. You were right when you warned me that I am trapped here. I couldn't even hope that you were waiting for me, that you forgive me. Now I know what I must do…"

Gilbert, astonished, looked up at Smith. "What is this?"

Smith gave a wry smile. "From what I gather, it's a response to a letter from his wife, who committed suicide three years ago. Or do you have some other explanation?"

"Just one: this is a letter from a mentally ill individual. Such people live in their own make-believe world. They often talk with people who aren't there, who might not even exist at all. Ley may have really imagined that he received a letter from his wife. Apparently, he always had a complex about her, feelings of guilt. Yesterday's events, when he was served with the charges and there was no hope of escaping justice, only sped up the process…"

Mr. Smith stuck the letter into a folder. "There's something about this that I don't like. I don't know exactly what, though. But what's important is that the bastard got away from us. He offed himself without saying anything."

At this same time, in the baron's house, a servant was pouring into a glass the best wine that had been found in the homeowner's cellar.

"To your health, my boy!" the baron said, raising his glass. "Great job! Sending Ley a letter from his dead wife that he drove to suicide, asking him to join her in the next world! A fantastic idea! I always knew that you could come up with things few other people can!"

"Thank you, baron. After all, you taught me yourself to carefully approach matters and look for unexpected solutions."

Notes

As the Soviet intelligence agent Hector reports, under pressure from the Americans the West has decided to abandon its earlier agreement to divide up the confiscated Nazi gold among the

four victor countries. It was decided that the
gold be sent to strengthen the International
Monetary Fund, the World Bank, which is led by
the Americans, and support the "international
dollar". While the USSR's position remains
unclear, the secret of the gold will be kept
from Moscow.

CHAPTER VIII.
THE SCOURGING OF HARLOTS

On the central stand in Nuremberg's stadium, where tens of thousands of people had once gathered during Nazi Party rallies, and where grandiose parades and torchlight processions had once taken place, American tourists parodied the Führer with scowls and laughter and took pictures of each other, taking turns at the place that had been reserved for Hitler. A dark-blue arrow dividing the stands pointed towards it.

"It must be nice to be an American," Irina said as she watched the tourists. "Unlike us Russians, they know how to have a good time."

"They just don't know much about life," Rebrov remarked. "Or in any event, less than we do."

Rebrov and Irina had come to this site of Nazi Party gatherings to get away from prying eyes. Rebrov realized that his acquaintance with Princess Kurakina was fraught with severe consequences for him should anyone find out, but he could not help himself. He was irresistibly drawn to Irina. Not just as a man is attracted to a woman. Through this delicate young lady, he, a completely Soviet man in his thoughts and views, sensed a vast and exotic world which he had hitherto thought long gone in the past, never to return. Yet, this world seemed to still exist, it lived on and was intriguing beyond words.

"Do you understand why the main character of 'Pure Monday', a woman who is so young, beautiful, rich, and loved, suffers so much?" he asked.

Irina looked up at him. "You don't?"

"To be honest, this life that Bunin describes is so distant… Like the reign of Ivan the Terrible, or even further back in time."

"Ivan the Terrible… Do you remember who those characters in Bunin's story meet during the Art Theatre revue? The actor Kachalov! By the way, he's still alive, and I think he has even been honored as a

People's Artist of the USSR. But you were talking about Ivan the Terrible..." She looked around the stadium. "What an odd conversation for such a creepy place... Typically Russian."

"Irina, what brought you to Nuremberg? All these destroyed buildings, dead bodies, Nazis, awful documents, why do you need any of this? You could be living in Paris. I've heard that it was hardly touched by the war at all."

"Well, to some degree this is a way to earn a living."

"Is that so important to you?"

"You think that if someone was once a princess, it's like walking on easy street?" she smiled sadly. "My father worked as a taxi driver until he died – he died at the wheel. My mother worked as a servant for many years, for different families. We simply didn't have anything to eat. But here they offered really good money, and then I suddenly felt that I had to get out of Paris, get out of France altogether."

"Why?"

"Do you know what *collaboration horizontale* is?"

Denis shook his head.

"I think that all France lost their minds. They are now hounding women who took up with German men... Prostitutes and those who were simply trying to survive. Their heads are shaved, they are stripped naked and driven through the streets, and people hit them and spit on them. Just imagine, guys are beating wives and mothers right in front of their husbands. It's terrible! The country is mocking helpless women. Some of them can't stand it, they go crazy or kill themselves."

"But why?"

"I think that this is how they are trying to wash away the sin of betrayal from themselves. After all, not so many French people became maquis, fighting for General de Gaulle's resistance. There were many who served the Germans, collaborated with them, and lived quiet lives. Now they want to feel like they are heroes and winners who fought against the enemy. I didn't want to see this any more, so when they offered me the job, I immediately agreed. There weren't too many people who speak Russian, French, English, and German. But I did not think the work would be so hard."

"Have you heard about Olga Chekhova?"

"The actress Hitler was in love with? There are so many rumors swirling around her these days."

"Yes, there are all kinds of rumors, but that's not what I mean. She was afraid that after the war, the Germans would all suddenly become opponents of the Nazis and they wouldn't forgive her for her past, her acquaintance with Hitler. As it turned out, the Germans can't forgive her for her present, either. They spit on her and call her a traitor."

A strong gust of wind blowing through the empty stadium made them turn away from it and nearly huddle together.

"By they way, who's that young man who's working together with you in the office?" Rebrov asked when the wind abated as suddenly as it had struck. "He looked at me like he didn't much like me, I'd say."

"That's Baron Pavel Rosen. He's also a translator."

"Rosen? Is he a German?"

"Come on! Dear Pavel is already a third-generation Russian Orthodox, a completely Russian person, though from the Baltics. But…"

"What?"

"He hates the Soviet Union, or that 'bunch of sovoks' as he calls it. He says that now, after the war against Hitler, nothing has changed. During the revolution, some drunken sailors shot his father in a train station lavatory. His mother and sister died of typhus, all their property was confiscated… All in all, a typical story for our circle. After the victory over Hitler, many of us changed our opinion about Russia, but he didn't."

"Have you known him for a long time?"

"Since we were children. We grew up together. My mother literally picked him up off a street in Crimea after his parents had died. Pavel lived in our home for quite some time, then some distant relatives were found and he went to live with them."

"So there must have been some childhood crush involved, am I right?"

"Well, maybe to some degree, but…" Irina hesitated, as if she was afraid of saying something important.

Rebrov waited impatiently.

"To be honest, it was only from one side," she finally said.

"I hope it was from his part."

Irina didn't have time to answer – suddenly their path was blocked by two men who had appeared out of nowhere. They wore dark coats with the collars turned up and hats pulled low over their eyes. They were clearly up to no good. Irina, frightened, grasped Rebrov's hand. He squeezed her tightly-clenched fingers, let go, and quietly said, "Get behind me."

When Irina had done so, he asked in German, "*Was ist los*?"

"You are, you bastard!" one of the men giggled and drew a knife. "You think I wouldn't recognize you, red scum? I could tell a commie from a mile off. What don't stay home in your precious USSR? Why do you got to come over to the American zone? Now we're going to cut your belly open, and then we'll take your dame with us. We'll have a good time together, she's so fine-looking…"

"It's just a shame I've only got you guys to fight," Rebrov laughed. A pistol in this situation wouldn't hurt, he thought to himself, but he would have to manage without one. He wasn't worried about himself: dealing with two thugs, even if they had knives, wasn't the most difficult thing in the world. Moreover, judging from everything, these two didn't have any special skills and they couldn't have imagined what training he had once undergone.

The man holding the knife grunted and waved his blade in front of Rebrov's face. Slightly stepping back, Denis quickly grabbed his opponent's hand and with a single motion twisted it back so that the man's knife went into his own stomach up to the hilt. The man gasped, bent double, and wheezed and he pressed his hands to his stomach. Rebrov kicked him away and turned to the second man, who he had been constantly keeping in his sight. When the second man saw how his friend was writhing in pain and kicking his legs, he yelped and ran away.

Rebrov turned to Irina, who was frozen with fear. He put his arm around her shoulder and led her away.

When they were already in the car, Irina asked, "Who were they?"

"Probably some *polizei* who fled, hidden among the other Germans," Rebrov shrugged.

"They are constantly trying to scare us with stories of SS men lurking about. In my worst nightmare I couldn't imagine that I might die for the Soviet regime," Irina smiled faintly.

Rebrov was absentmindedly strolling down a hallway in the Palace of Justice when Gavrik caught up with him.

"Let's have a walk."

"Where to?" Rebrov didn't understand.

"Let's just go for a walk while it's still light out," Gavrik said, pulling him by the arm.

They went out from the Palace just as the changing of the guard was taking place. Soviet men had been on duty, tall and strong boys with medals and ribbons, yellow and red stripes for being wounded in combat, holding bayonet-equipped rifles. Some of the omnipresent American tourists with cameras applauded when the Soviet soldiers marched off theatrically.

Further down, newly recruited German police in their dark blue uniforms were lounging about. When they saw Gavrik in his military uniform, they immediately stood at attention.

Rebrov and Gavrik walked in silence as far as the river Pegnitz. Here there was an ancient bridge that had miraculously survived intact, as well as the ruins of a cathedral over which two damaged towers awkwardly rose.

"Well then, what secret did you want to entrust me with?" Rebrov said, deciding to finally break the silence. He had long understood that it wasn't for a mere walk that Gavrik had forced him out of the Palace.

"I wanted to warn you, Rebrov," Gavrik replied in a serious tone. "Really warn you. As a friend."

"Alright, then, what about?" Rebrov smiled, but he already knew what Gavrik was going to say, and that he was not going to like to hear it.

"Watch out that you don't get into trouble because of this princess…"

"What does the princess have to do with anything?" Rebrov asked stupidly, and he realized how silly his question was.

"Come on!" Gavrik insisted. "What, you don't think I've noticed how you look at her?"

"Don't be silly."

"I'm warning you as a friend. You can't imagine what trouble this might bring you. A lieutenant from the guard platoon met a couple of times with the same French translator, and he was immediately sent away from Nuremberg. No one has ever seen or heard from him since. They are categorically forbidden from associating with members of other delegations or the local population."

"Well, that's the guard!" Rebrov shrugged. "Obviously they are closely watched. Sorry, but I work for another department."

"You've completely lost your mind, I see," Gavrik sighed. "I'm not from the guard either. An Englishwoman, a translator, came up to me during a reception. She asked where I was from, whether I miss home. We chatted for five minutes, that's all. The next day, I was called in and they started to ask me what our conversation was about. 'It was nothing,' I said, 'Just pleasantries!' An officer wearing colonel's stripes, Kosachev is his name, told me, 'Remember, comrade Gavrik, I only call someone in twice. The first time is to warn him, and the second time is already the last. If I see you here in front of me a second time, your mama is going to be spending a long time searching for you…'

"That's rough."

"Did you think it would be otherwise? It's becoming even stricter, they're trying to ensure we don't fall under the influence of the Americans. So, watch out with this princess. Maybe nothing will happen to her, but they won't forgive you or me for meeting with people like that."

"Listen, Gavrik, aren't you too scared of this Kosachev?" Rebrov angrily asked. "I'm not like that lieutenant from the guard, you know!"

"Listen, Rebrov," Gavrik imitated his words. "Maybe you haven't bumped into Kosachev yet, but he's…"

"I know who he is, he's the head of the investigative brigade at SMERSH."

"Exactly. And no one knows what powers he might have exactly, so they prefer not to be involved with him. He acts accordingly. That's one thing."

"Is there something else?"

"There sure is. Are you really certain that this princess isn't a secret agent? For the French or Americans? Do you think they hired her as a translator just like that? Just because she wanted the job, or because of her background? You want to bet your life on the fact that she's not gathering information? Well? Have you nothing to say?"

"It's not like that," Rebrov suddenly felt embarrassed. Such a thought, so reasonable and natural in his line of work, had not even come into his mind. Of course, it wasn't possible to link Irina with any intelligence services, but he knew what kind of things that seemed impossible at first glance played out among secret agents.

"It's not like that…," again Gavrik mimicked his words. "Honestly, you're like a child. Have you forgotten where we are? And if you want to know, I also don't want to be sent off somewhere like that old lieutenant from the guard. And you know why? Because I want to see these monsters sent to the gallows. I want to see that with my own eyes, see how they shit their pants in fear. I've got personal scores to settle. They simply burned all of my family: my mother, my sister, my grandmother… When we took Lublin, we saw the Majdanek camp. The Germans didn't even manage to burn all the bodies in the crematorium, they just stacked them on the ground and set fire to them. We arrived to find bonfires made from bodies that were still burning. My boots were white from human ashes." Gavrik gritted his teeth. "Next to the crematorium was a ditch, with thousands of bodies with bullet holes in the backs of their necks. On top of them a little boy was lying, still holding a teddy bear in his hand."

When they were close to the Palace, Rebrov couldn't resist asking, "Hey, Gavrik, was it really so obvious?"

"Was what so obvious?"

"Well, you know…"

"Your thing with the princess? You know, if I were Col. Kosachev, I wouldn't even call you in a second time."

"Why?"

"Once would have been enough, and it would be the last time. By the way, that's his car there." Gavrik nodded at a luxurious black-and-white limousine with red leather seats, which looked utterly fantastical among the ruined buildings. "They say it came from the garage of Hitler himself."

Notes

As our agent Hector reports, in Bavaria Ukrainian nationalists have appeared, who formerly served in the SS division named "Galicia". Several of them have been seen in the vicinity of Nuremberg. There is every reason to believe that they arrived in Germany from Rimini, Italy, where they had been held in a POW camp. The Vatican views them as "good Catholics and devoted anti-Communists."

CHAPTER IX. THE WHITE AND THE RED

Denis came down from his room to the restaurant that had newly opened in the Grand Hotel, where he suddenly caught sight of Irina at one of the tables. A young man was sitting opposite her, the same American that Olaf Todt had met in the camp for German POWs.

"Let me introduce you, gentlemen," Irina said. "This is Alexander Kraft, he's an American from New York."

"Just call me Alex," Kraft grinned widely.

"And this is Denis Rebrov from the Soviet delegation," Irina continued.

"Does it bother you that I am a little German?" Kraft jovially turned to Denis. "I must immediately warn you that my ancestors sailed for America long before Hitler…"

"Why should that bother me?"

"Well, not long ago your famous writer Ehrenburg called on everyone to 'Kill a German!'"

"That was during the war."

"Revenge is a powerful feeling," Kraft shook his head understandingly. "It's hard to make it subject to reason."

"What, are you also against this tribunal? Do you also think it will simply be a trial of the victors over the defeated? Revenge, not justice?"

"Honestly?" Kraft narrowed his eyes.

"Why lie?"

"Really, I don't deny that a person has a right to revenge. As an American, I am for an honest and unbiased court. In this case I am prepared to look past a lot of things, because I realize it couldn't be otherwise. These men did things that were too terrible. What about you, Irina? How do you feel about this tribunal?"

"I thank God that they didn't win the war, because if they had… Then, it would have simply been the end of the world."

"Did you wish victory for the Russians? Or rather, the Soviets? Even if they forced your parents to leave the country, and they called you aristocrats a class of parasites to be eradicated?"

"One of my uncles was an officer, a lancer. When Hitler attacked the Soviet Union, he said, 'They've attacked us.' You see, Alex, that's what he said, 'us'. In Paris we lived literally right next to the Gestapo. They would walk down our street on their way to work… To work. My uncle would listen to reports from the front on the radio, though the Germans forbade people from doing that. You could go to prison for it. One night he heard about the victory in Stalingrad. Do you know what he did? He dyed an old sheet red and hung it on the balcony, and then with his conscience clear he went to bed. Fortunately, my cousin came home at dawn and saw the red flag before the Gestapo did. He took it down and hid it somewhere, and my grandfather gave him a beating for it."

"You Russians are a mysterious people," Kraft sighed. "It's hard for us to understand you."

"What are you doing here in Nuremberg, Mr. Kraft?" Rebrov asked. For some reason, his question sounded a bit rude, as if he was suspecting Kraft of something. Irina caught this and looked at Rebrov with a slightly noticeable surprise in her face.

"Alex! I told you, just Alex would do," Kraft said as if he had not noticed anything amiss. "What would a real American be doing here? Business, of course. I'm signing contracts for memoirs with anyone who might interest our reading public. We think this will make good money."

"Have you also made any agreements with the defendants?"

"Of course! With them first of all. It's a good business today, there's no need to spend money on advertising. The advertisements are in every newspaper. Granted, you can only deal with them through their lawyers, and the lawyers want to get their piece of the pie, too. But it's not just money, the lawyers want to dedicate what they can write and what they can't. As you know, often it's what a person can't write that is most interesting."

"The American guards at the prison don't sympathize with you?"

"You don't know Col. Andrus! He's not a man, he's pure stone."

"What if they don't manage to write their memoirs for you? What if they are hung before then?"

"Well, first of all, I get the feeling that these trials are going to be stretched out, for a long time."

"And second?"

"Secondly, they won't all be hanged. Of course, there is some risk, but there is no business without risk. Without risk, it's a planned economy, a five-year plan. Or do you possess some information about this matter? With regard to the timing and the verdict?"

"No, of course I don't have any such information."

"I see. By the way, when will your chief prosecutor be arriving, Mr. Rudenko?"

Denis shook his head. "I don't know. As you can understand, that's not among my responsibilities."

"Damn, you can't find out anything about him!" Kraft said contritely. "Maybe you can tell me something? By the way, couldn't you arrange a meeting with him for me? His diary during the trials would be very interesting… We can pay a lot of money for that kind of material, good money!"

"Alex, calm down," Irina said with a smile and aiming to come to Rebrov's rescue, as Rebrov appeared to be getting tired of Kraft and his countless business ideas. "We're not in America. It's not appropriate for you to be pushing like that here, and more importantly, it's not going to bring you any success."

"What a pity," Kraft could not hide his disappointment. "But just think about it, Denis. All my offers remain valid. Maybe you'll come up with some of your own. In the meantime, I will bow out. By the way, everything is already paid for," Kraft cast his hand over the table.

When Rebrov and Irina were left alone, he asked her, "Have you known him for a long time?"

"Two days only. Why?" Irina looked at him with clear, attentive eyes.

"Alright, then. I thought it was a lot longer. He's a very slippery character. How did Bunin put it? 'A serpent clothed as a man…'"

"You remembered."

"More than that, too."

"What else?"

Rebrov was silent for a moment, and then he closed his eyes and recited, "How this was all to end, I did not know and tried not to think."

Irina didn't say anything, but she laid her delicate, light fingers on his hand.

As Rebrov was entering Filin's office, he almost ran into a man in a uniform with the stripes of a colonel. He had a jowly, habitually unhappy face.

Rebrov immediately slowed. "Good afternoon."

"Good afternoon," the man smiled maliciously, sizing up Rebrov from head to foot with a heavy gaze. He then turned to Filin and asked, with the same unpleasant grin, "Do I understand that this is our man? Alright, then. Well, I'm off, Sergei Ivanovich. I've already gone over everything."

Filin, drumming his fingers on his desk, looked at Rebrov. He looked weary and deep in thought.

"I gather that Comrade Kosachev has already told you everything?" Rebrov asked.

"Most of it, but everything? I don't know, you didn't tell me. But you seem to be keeping busy…"

"What do you mean?"

"I mean that you have new adventures daily. At the stadium they nearly killed you. At the restaurant, you were being recruited by some American gentleman almost openly. And both times, this Kurakina was with you… How am I to understand this?"

"A coincidence. A pure coincidence."

"Are you sure?"

"It was my suggestion that we go to the stadium. I am convinced that running into those former Nazis was just a coincidence. Maybe they were simply robbing tourists there. If they were watching us, I would have noticed them."

"Was it also you who invited her to the restaurant?"

"No, she said she would be there in the evening."

"And you went, like a lamb to the slaughter! And an American guy with mysterious intentions just happened to be expecting you there, and he just asked you to arrange a meeting with Rudenko. Was that all? Or have you got something else?"

"There was talk about Paulus."

"About who?" Filin suddenly stopped drumming his fingers on his desk.

"About Paulus."

"Was that so? And why did that come up?"

"The conversation happened to come around to Stalingrad…"

"It just happened to," Filin mocked him. "And who just happened to turn the conversation that way?"

"Him, Kraft."

"And what about her? Did she just remain silent?"

"No. Everything started from her remembering her uncle, who hung a red flag up in Paris when he heard about the German defeat in Stalingrad."

"How touching. He hung a Soviet flag in Paris? German-occupied Paris? Right under the Gestapo's nose? He might be quite a trooper."

"A lancer."

"What?"

"This uncle was a lancer."

"That's great," Filin smacked both palms on the table. "You know a lot about this uncle?"

"That's about it."

"I thought… So, what did he want to know about Paulus?

"Whether I knew where he is now and how he's doing. And whether he intends to return to Germany."

"Aha," Filin bit his lip. "And what did you tell him?"

"I told him that I have no idea."

Filin looked intently at Rebrov and sighed heavily. "I think you realize that your meetings with Irina Kurakina could not remain unnoticed."

"I do," Rebrov said with a sigh.

"And you realize that Col. Kosachev told me about you and Princess Kurakina, and that his men are watching you?"

"I do."

Filin sighed once more. "Denis, I have to warn you. Kosachev and his team are doing a very important job here. They are assigned to deal with all kinds of operational issues. He directly reports to Abakumov in Moscow, he's got that authority. He's a difficult and dangerous man. Dangerous, I say. I know him a little bit…"

"Have you worked together?"

"In a sense. He was the investigator in my case. Yes, don't look at me like that. It was back before the war. A whole team of our agents abroad immediately collapsed. It was clear that someone had betrayed them from Moscow. So, they started going after people left and right. Kosachev had only just started his career, so he was trying his best. Fortunately, they found the traitor before he… Well, before they had to take more serious measures. Anyhow, that's all in the past now." With a clear gesture, Filin put an end to the subject.

"Did you forgive him," Rebrov asked.

"What should I forgive him for? He was following orders. If it wasn't him, it would have been someone else. Granted, he was trying hard. I understood then that he doesn't have the slightest sense of mercy… Well, then, let's get back to our problem. I told Kosachev that in meeting with Kurakina, you were following my orders and trying to make her into an informant for us…"

"Informant," Denis grimaced. "You might have said 'agent.'"

"I might have," Filin raised his voice, "But I have no grounds to do that yet. That's unfortunate, as we could use such an informant. But watch out, Denis. Watch out that you don't switch roles."

"What do you mean?"

"Watch out that you don't suddenly become an informant for her."

"Come on! She's a completely different kind of person, from a different world."

"I know she's from a different world. But Denis, this is classic espionage, using a beautiful woman to get results."

"Sergei Ivanovich, haven't you thought that she's just a Russian young lady, who…"

"I don't intend to 'think', I should *know*. But we don't know anything yet! And remember, peace has come for others, but our war continues. You and I are still at war like before."

"So, I'm no longer allowed to meet with Kurakina?"

"Well, why shouldn't you? It would seem suspicious now if you didn't. Meet with her, but remember that you are carrying out a mission here, a very serious and extremely important one. Do your job now and think about girls later, even girls like Princess Irina Kurakina. You think I don't understand what kind of girl she is? But God forbid you lose your head in this, and end up making a closer acquaintance with Kosachev. He knows no mercy!"

Notes

When he found out about the German defeat at Stalingrad, my grandfather — an officer in the Russian army and member of Lev Alexandrovich Kazem-Bek's White Guards — hung a red flag on the balcony of our Paris apartment, just a stone's throw from a Gestapo branch. We only discovered this "banner of victory" the next morning and took it down. Pavel Tolstoy-Miloslavsky told us about it…

When my grandfather explained to his indignant fellow White soldiers why he had hung a red flag,

he said, "Since the Germans attacked Russia
this color symbolizes only the blood shed by
our people. And it will continue to do so until
the enemy is fully defeated! Then our people,
victorious, can decide what color to make their
national flag."

From the memoirs of
Prince Z. M. Chavchavadze

CHAPTER X. ESCAPE FROM HELL

Irina was walking with a friend to work past the ruined buildings surrounding the Palace of Justice. It was a warm and sunny autumn day. In the suburb where the French delegation was staying, everything was tinted gold and crimson by the fading foliage, and autumn roses, no longer scented but still beautiful, were blooming. Here, however, everything stood as a reminder of the horrors of the war. It was as if everything was wrapped in a smell of woe and despondency.

Among the ruins, works were going on at an unhurried pace. Young men in frayed military uniforms without insignia were dismantling the bricks and stacking pieces of iron that had been warped by bombing and fire. Their guards, a few American soldiers, were sitting on some boxes on the sidelines, basking in the sun. As the Americans were chatting and chewing gum without paying much attention to the prisoners, the latter were left to themselves and didn't feel compelled to great effort.

Irina and her friend got some overt male attention from the SS men. The girls involuntarily quickened their pace and lowered their gaze.

"How do you like this story about Ley!" Kraft asked Irina after he had sat down at her table in the Palace bar. "They're saying all kinds of things about what happened, even more than what's in the press."

Irina squeezed her coffee cup in her hand as if seeking warmth. "I don't know… Maybe his conscience was bothering him?"

"Conscience?" Kraft looked at her with genuine amazement. "Really, you Russians are obsessed with emotional suffering. Only you could have come up with writers like Tolstoy and Dostoyevsky. What conscience could Ley have? He oversaw foreign slaves brought by force to Germany. It was either fear or madness, nothing else."

Irina, wrapped up in her own thoughts, did not reply.

"What's wrong?" Kraft asked in a sympathetic tone. "What's happened?"

"You know, Alex, today I suddenly feel like I'm practically back in occupied Paris…"

"Why?"

"The car that brings us to the Palace broke down, so we had to come on foot. I walked with a friend past the ruined buildings, and there were German prisoners of war there. You know, in Paris it was horrifying every time you had to walk past them, because they could do whatever they wanted to you. And suddenly they're here again today, and there's no one who can protect you…"

"But they must have been under guard," Kraft consoled her.

"Yes, a few of your GIs were basking in the sun. But the way those German men were looking at us…"

"Yes, I see. By the way, the Russian delegation has repeatedly protested their presence here, asked that they be removed, but… From what I know, the 1st American Division that occupied Nuremberg answered saying that the war is over and the prisoners are only prisoners, plus there are the Geneva Conventions and people shouldn't exaggerate the danger."

"Do you think the same?"

"Me? Hell, I haven't even thought about it! They don't scare me for some reason. And they look pretty pitiful."

"You just never had to deal with them when they were in charge. In the French delegation there are always rumors that there's a conspiracy to free the men on trial, and it'll happen with the help of these same German prisoners…"

"Hell, I ought to introduce you to Col. Andrus some time. He'd put your mind at ease. In any event, he told me once, 'No men under my watch will escape.' Well, look here, let's ask our Russian friend," Kraft said and waved to Rebrov as he walked into the bar.

Rebrov seemed to be deliberating whether he should go to Kraft and Irina, but ultimately moved in their direction.

"Hello, Denis! Have a seat at our table! By the way, you should comfort Irina, she got scared today because of some German prisoners who were cleaning out a ruined building. I've reassured her as best I could, I told her they pose no danger. They won't start any new war! But she talks about some conspiracy to free the men on trial. What's with this conspiracy that everyone keeps talking about? Have you heard about it, too? You want a coffee?"

Rebrov brusquely refused, "Thanks, but I'm in a hurry." He tried not to look at Irina.

"What about this conspiracy?" Kraft would not let up. "What are they looking to do? What could they achieve?"

"They could try to disrupt the trials," Rebrov explained, rather reluctantly.

"How so?"

"For example, by spiriting some prisoners away. It would be such a mess that the trials would have to be postponed indefinitely, and ultimately they might never happen."

Irina looked confused. She clearly did not understand what was happening.

"That's an interesting theory," Kraft mused. "But Col. Andrus is sure that this would be impossible. He has already considered every trick. As you may know, you can only get from the prison to the courtroom through a special tunnel. Both ends of the tunnel are under heavy guard, and they can shoot the whole length of it. At the slightest sign of trouble, all exits are immediately blocked."

"That may be true, but among the German veterans there might be some real experts in their field. Saboteurs from Skorzeny's team, for example. They managed high-risk operations like getting Mussolini out. So, if I were your colonel, I wouldn't think that everything is accounted for. He missed Ley."

Kraft answered this by pursing his lips, bulging his eyes, and throwing up his hands.

Rebrov stood up. "Sorry, but I've got to go."

When he had left the bar, Kraft couldn't contain himself. "I'll be damned, Irina, he's jealous. Jealous of seeing me with you. It's as clear as day. Yes, yes, Irina, he's obviously in love with you. What a story, a Russian princess and a Soviet hard worker!"

Irina leaped to her feet and left the bar without a word.

Kraft finished drinking his coffee, smoked a cigarette, and muttered thoughtfully, "Poor Russians, everything is so complicated for them."

After retrieving the agent's report from the drop point, Rebrov returned to the Palace where he set to work on decoding it. Then, when he finished, he went to report to Filin. Among the details in the encrypted message was that American intelligence officials who were working with the prisoners, thought it likely that Ley had somehow been driven to suicide from the outside. They believed that this could have been done by someone from the German underground or Russian agents who didn't want Ley to reveal the secret of the Nazi gold to the Americans.

"Well, taking into account that you and me didn't poison Ley," Filin said mockingly, "the only remaining possibility is some Nazi underground, which undoubtedly exists. It is clear that they're aiming to disrupt the trials. The question is, what lengths are they willing to go to in order to do this? What opportunities do they have?"

"Here, the Palace is full of people who were working around him and ready to do a lot of things…"

"These captive Germans trouble you?"

"They don't trouble you?"

"They do, but what can we do? We are on someone else's territory here. We talked to the Americans about it, but they are convinced that there's nothing to worry about. What can you do? Guard the prisoners yourself? It's impossible. The only realistic option is to find out who these men are and warn our allies about them. But how can we find out who they are? Let's try to think here… What task could this underground assign to the German prisoners working here? Not some completely fantastical task, but something that's realistic and can be carried out? Everyone's thinking that they might try to free all of the men on trial, but that would be really hard, perhaps impossible. But what if the goal is just to kill them? That, you must agree, is a lot more achievable. Especially if the task is not to kill everyone, but just a few specific men. Or even just one particular person…"

"But who?"

"If it's about the gold, then whoever knows about it like Ley did."

"Then that person would be Goering."

"It would seem so. Let's imagine that Bormann is still alive; his body still hasn't been found. Bormann, who probably wants to take hold of the gold personally. Plus, he hates Goering. So, the operation to free the men, like everyone thinks, might really be an operation to kill them… Granted, there's also Rudolf Hess, who might have some information on this matter. They promise that he'll be delivered from England in just a few days now."

"Well, where there's one body, there might be a second one."

"That's right," Filin didn't argue. "By the way, all kinds of rumors are swirling around Hess. They say that he simply lost his mind."

"Or he's just pretending to be a madman."

"We'll try to find out. Prepare a message for Hector. But Denis, the main task for you and me is to ensure at all costs that the trials are not disrupted… The gold would be nice, of course, but the main thing is the tribunal. We need to think about how we can twist the Americans' arm to get all this German prisoner labor out of here. Official requests aren't working, so we'll have to scare them somehow. Think about how we can do that. I'm off for a few days, first to Berlin, then Moscow. When I get back, I expect a plan from you. Think, Denis, think!"

Notes

In the summer of 1945 Gen. MacDonald sent to US Army Air Forces headquarters in Europe a list of six underground factories that they had managed to locate. Each of them produced, up to the very last day of the war, aircraft engines and other special equipment for the Luftwaffe.

A few months later, in a preliminary report on underground factories and laboratories in Germany and Austria sent to US Army Air Forces headquarters, it was stated that "a larger number of German underground factories have been found than previously suspected." Underground structures were discovered not only in Germany and Austria, but also in France, Italy, Hungary, and Czechoslovakia. The report further noted, "Although the Germans did not engage in large-scale creation of underground factories until March 1944, by the end of the war they had managed to get around 143 such factories running." To this one can add another 600 caverns and mines, many of which were turned into stockpiles and laboratories for weapons production.

CHAPTER XI.
PUTTING THE CAT AMONG THE PIGEONS

Olaf and the baron were dining. Everything was like in former days: a white tablecloth, rare Meissen porcelain made and painted by hand nearly two centuries before, with its world-famous logo of two crossed swords; heavy silverware; and an old, well-trained servant who personally served the dishes and poured wine into their glasses.

"So, the first day of the trials is getting closer," the baron turned the conversation to serious matters as they finished with the first course. "But as far as I know, the parties cannot find agreement on many issues. I hear that the American chief prosecutor is complaining that the thinking of the Russians is so different from Westerners that they are hard to understand even with a good interpreter."

"Yes, there are disagreements. The Russians are very stubborn and insisting on their own views. However, I think that things shouldn't be exaggerated. They'll manage to overcome these cultural clashes."

"What if we shatter their idyll of cooperation?" the baron smiled.

"How?"

"There are documents that could blow the whole tribunal apart. And I've been promised copies."

"Who? Someone from Hitler's privy council?"

"No. They will be provided by our American friends."

Olaf looked at the baron as if he could not believe his own ears. "American?"

"Yes, indeed. Of course, not the ones who are working against us with these trials, but those who are against the tribunal…"

"And they can confirm the authenticity of these documents?"

"No, of course not. You're asking too much of them. They will generally remain on the sidelines. It's up to us to put the cat among the pigeons, as the old German proverb has it."

"A dead cat?"

"A living one. That's the whole point, that it's a living one, my boy."

Olaf waited in silence for the baron to explain.

"Sorry, my boy, but for the time being I cannot yet tell you what it is all about. Everything has its time."

"Forgive me, baron, but what are these American friends of yours trying to achieve? Why have they decided to expose the Russians?"

"Well, let's just say that they don't believe that a long-term alliance with the Russians is possible. And they don't want the Russians to get too strong."

"I see. So what do you need from me?"

"We need to think about how we can throw our 'cat' into the tribunal. You see, the document shouldn't just be thrown out there. We need to ensure that it is officially entered into the record of the trials, and then it will have a much greater destructive force. From what I gather, the Americans and British aim to put on a real trial, so one of the lawyers can ask for this document to be read in court. And then… Do I have to explain what kind of lawyer would agree to do this?"

"Would he have to be especially determined?"

"I think so. Because the Russians will be furious. You understand, resisting the Russians under the present circumstances is not easy to do. A person has to be either desperately brave or grotesquely conceited."

"Or just be paid well for it."

"He'll get his reward."

"Will he have to hide his sources?"

"No, why would he?" the baron smiled. "I think that he can just say that a copy was given to him by an American officer who had been studying Third Reich archives… It was received anonymously. Under the cover of darkness. Let the Russians never forget what kind of world they live in."

"I know a lawyer like that."

"Good. But let's not be hasty. We'll need to examine him closely."

After drinking his wine, the baron finally settled into a good mood. "How is the situation at the Palace of Justice?"

"The Americans call it 'the office'. It's full of onlookers, journalists, dealmakers. They say that even Marlene Dietrich herself will come to the first day of the trials."

"Yes, the Americans love to turn everything into a big show. Nonetheless, we shouldn't have gone to war with them, or the Russians either for that matter. The Europeans would have been enough."

Olaf nodded absentmindedly.

"It seems like you want to say something."

"Right next to the Palace of Justice I saw Günther…"

The baron raised his eyebrows questioningly.

"Günther Tilkowski, my friend from the special operations unit. Remember, they stopped us in the forest?"

"Of course I remember. What's the matter?"

"He ended up in a camp where they are detaining the Edelweiss division. They're being brought over to work on the ruined buildings next to the Palace. Some of them are even working inside the Palace."

"So?"

"Günther is not the sort of man who would just stay in a camp and break bricks apart."

"What, is he some fanatic whose greatest joy in life is to shout 'Heil Hitler'?"

"He's a professional. As I understood, they are getting ready to carry out some kind of action in the Palace…"

"I know. There are people who want to use these men to carry out some operation. Freeing a few prisoners, obviously. You saw one of these people at my home, the adviser. So what, is there a specific date to make the attempt?"

"As far as I understand, not yet, but it is said to be a matter of days."

"Well, let them try, then… Ultimately, they can always be used, whether they are successful or whether they prove unlucky."

"How's that?"

"All kinds of ways, my boy, all kinds. Let the Americans finally understand that not all of Germany is in their hands and under their control. And let them feel in great danger. But remember, you're not a part of all this business. We just need to think how we can draw some advantage of our own from it."

Early in the morning of the next day, before the prisoners were brought to work near the Palace, Olaf hid himself in the ruins. He patiently awaited the sound of engines and the lazy cries of the American soldiers to announce that the prisoners had arrived. Olaf was not afraid of being detected by the Americans, as they didn't poke their noses into the ruins from fear of breaking a leg or their neck among the craters, broken floors and collapsed staircases.

Olaf made his way to a window and began to look for Günther. When he saw him, he signaled by him by whistling the special way they used to whisper in their unit.

In a few minutes Günther Tilkowski was standing in front of him. They thumped each other on the back.

"You've been visiting pretty often recently. Don't tell me that you simply miss your old friend," Günther laughed. "I just won't believe you, Olaf Todt. You're playing some kind of game."

"Is that a question?"

"No, I'm certain of it. I won't even ask what kind of game, because it's clear that it isn't your game."

"Let's say that it's not just my game."

"What, then? Can I help you? How?"

"I just want to know what exactly you're up to and when you'll finally act."

"It's just…" Günther looked out the window at the destroyed streets of Nuremberg, reflecting on something.

"Listen, Günther, I'm not asking you to give anyone up," Olaf said in a serious tone. "I'm not asking, because I know more or less what you intend to do. I even know who assigned you this task…"

"You always knew more than other people."

"Do you have weapons?"

"A few. Are you going to ask where they are hidden? Here… We just need a few more days to bring another batch here, and then…"

"They can't find them here?"

"Who? The Americans? They don't walk around here."

"Are you sure this is something worth doing?" Olaf asked. "Is it worth it for you? If you want to know my opinion…"

"I don't want to think about anything, my friend," Günther interrupted him. "Germany is no more. Everything I see around me is horrifying, it makes me ashamed. I don't know what is going to exist here, but it won't be my Germany any more. You might want to live in it, but not me. I've got a task in front of me. They promised me that after I carried it out, they would send me somewhere in South America. That's all. I don't want to know any more than that. I despise the men who I've got to break out, I know the people who proposed I do this, and I know they are capable of anything. including giving me over to the Americans if I'm not successful or just tricking me. But I don't have any other choice. Either I play this game, or I go crazy. Or I blow my brains out."

"I wouldn't want that to happen, Günther. Come on, I'll help you break out and lie low for a while."

"There is only one thing you can do for me: don't get in my way. I'm not asking you for help. Just don't get in my way. And then we'll see what happens."

Notes

Together with Hitler's will they found a photograph of a 12-year-old boy, which led the American authorities to suspect that Hitler had a son. In the boy's photo one could make out a strong likeness between his features and Hitler's… US intelligence began going through all materials relating to Hitler's private life in the hope of finding pointers to this mysterious boy.

An officer of the Third United States Army claimed that "the resemblance between the boy and Hitler is striking."

CHAPTER XII. PEGGY APPEARS

Rebrov walked out the gate at the Palace of Justice, not knowing where to go. Gen. Filin had left for Berlin and he had been practically left to himself. He didn't feel like going to the hotel. It was already dark outside and snow was falling, so light it was almost unnoticeable. This snow, early for these parts, seemed a harbinger of new times, changes at hand.

"It will be New Year's soon. A new year without the war…"

Rebrov turned sharply – Irina was standing in front of him. They hadn't seen each other for several days now. After that meeting in the bar, when he had pretended not to notice her, he thought that there could no longer be anything between them.

"It doesn't bother you if we are seen together?" Irina asked. "It won't get you in trouble?"

He hadn't managed to answer before a jeep suddenly braked to a halt alongside them. Kraft was sitting in it, while a beautiful red-haired woman in a US army uniform was at the wheel. She had a thick army jacket with a white belt, pants tucked into white stockings, and shoes with thick soles. Her military cap somehow held fast to her magnificent hair.

"Hi there," Kraft waved and smiled. "Let me introduce you, this is Peggy. Peggy Butcher. She's a correspondent for some New York magazines. You can't keep a secret from her. Our Peggy can get through any doors."

Peggy laughed merrily. "We're going to a press camp to celebrate the start of the trials tomorrow. We're tired of waiting! Come along with us!"

Irina and Denis stood there silently, unsure of what to say.

"Come on, come on," Kraft urged them. "If you need any Nuremberg secrets, no one knows more than Peggy."

Irina resolutely climbed into the back seat. Rebrov, after hesitating for a moment, got in next to her.

Peggy daringly bit her lip and then tore away so quickly that the car nearly skidded. It was hard to understand how she could find her way among the ruins that arose on all sides like black hills.

In one of the cleared spaces she stopped the car in front of a peculiar monument: on a brown pedestal a jeep had been placed. The vehicle had been in some kind of terrible accident and resembled a crushed can. There was an inscription in four languages: "I drove too fast!"

"A warning for drivers who can't take it easy," Kraft explained.

"Nah, for bad drivers," Peggy snorted.

"I hear the military police have been ordered to catch and severely punish anyone who drives over 50 miles an hour," Rebrov teased her.

Kraft laughed. "Did you hear that, Peggy?"

"I did," she waved the matter away. "If they want to punish me, they'd have to catch me first."

"And here they are," Kraft nodded.

A military jeep was rushing towards them and frantically signaling.

When she saw it, Peggy immediately put her foot on the gas. "Hold on tight. If they catch up with us, I'll pay for dinner."

"If they don't, then I'll pay," Kraft laughed. "Just do your best, darling!"

"Put the money up, baby."

Peggy pushed the jeep to its limits. Her hair was fluttering wildly on her shoulders, her face was lit up, and her eyes shone madly. Nonetheless, she drove with cold calculation. Eventually she managed to get away from their pursuers, who had gotten confused among the ruins.

"Well, that's all, baby," she turned to Kraft. "And you guys should order the most expensive thing on the menu today. Our friend Alex is paying for everything. Let it be his punishment for thinking so badly of little Peggy!"

"No rush, darling," Kraft warned her. "You seem to have forgotten they have walkie-talkies, and now they'll really get you."

The jeep was already heading down the road, which had remained unscathed in the bomb, that led to the press camp when another patrol car appeared behind them and sounded its siren.

"Ha, you got caught, baby!" Kraft rejoiced. "You won't get away this time."

Peggy however made a sharp turn, braked, and rolled the car into the darkness behind a ruined building. The two MP jeeps drove by none the wiser. After Peggy had waited for some time, she got back on the road to the press camp. There was no longer anyone after them.

After they had burst into the protected zone of the press camp, Peggy stopped the car at the main entrance. "I'll meet you in the restaurant. I need to change clothes. I've had enough of being a soldier today."

After Kraft had ordered, he asked with a smile, "Well, how do you like dear Peggy?"

"Is she really a reporter?" said Rebrov.

"Yes, and a very good one. When it comes to obtaining information, at any rate. Especially since she's not shy here. For example, it's no problem for her to say that she's ready to sleep with anyone who will give her the details she needs."

"Does she actually keep her promise?" Irina was amazed.

"I don't know," Kraft shrugged. "I'm not one of her sources."

"What an incredible feeling of freedom," Irina said. "I envy her. Such independence from other people's opinions and prejudices."

"I think you're a very free person, too," Kraft said in a serious tone. "Only you don't show off your freedom like Peggy does, but it's still there inside of you. What do you say, Denis?"

Rebrov nodded in agreement.

"But you Soviet people, it's like you're constantly guarding some military secret," Kraft squinted. "Even your journalists are such a tight-knit bunch – they all go into a bar together, and then all leave together. I heard that when one of your guys meets a foreigner, he gives a different name every time. Apparently, he considers his own real name to be a huge state secret!"

"Well, you'll find strange people from any country," Rebrov said defensively.

At that moment Peggy reappeared. She was wearing a short, girlish dress with a modest bow at the neck. Her hair was smoothly combed into a bun. Now she looked like a nice girl that would never do anything naughty.

"Have you already done your homework, little girl?" Kraft asked sternly. "But don't think you can have some champagne, I don't want to go to jail for corrupting a minor."

Peggy only smiled enigmatically. Now she was completely withdrawn into herself, in her own little world.

"Have you driven for a long time?" Denis asked.

"I have always driven. I feel like I was born in a car," Peggy answered. "Has it been a long time since you left Moscow? That's somewhere I should really go. Do you have good roads?"

"We've got all kinds. Some are country roads, I think it you'd find it interesting to drive on them. Especially in winter."

"It's agreed, then! Tell me, is Field Marshal Paulus, who surrendered at Stalingrad, still alive?"

"As far as I know, he is. But why did you bring him up?"

"I know his wife, Elena von Paulus. As you might know, she was born as the Romanian countess Rosseti-Solescu. When Paulus spoke out against Hitler, she was ordered to publicly condemn him, renounce her marriage, and change her name. She refused and was sent to a camp, and her son and daughter were arrested..."

"She's just like those Russian wives who would follow their husbands to Siberia," Kraft remarked.

"The Decembrists," Irina quietly said.

"Yes, yes, very similar."

"Well, I don't think so," Irina said just as quietly, but stubbornly. "The Decembrists led an uprising in their own country against the tsar, but Paulus was captured thousands of miles from his homeland. In the Volga steppes, where he had been sent to kill Russians. Can you imagine what it would have been like if they won?"

"But he's not among the war criminals that are going on trial. The Russians didn't list him among the accused," Kraft said.

"The Americans aren't trying everyone they caught either," Rebrov broke in.

"Well, what can you do? In America, unlike in the Soviet Union, there are different points of view about what is going on here in Nuremberg. Just a few days ago the New York Times published statements by prominent American generals. They were fundamentally against blaming soldiers for following orders that were handed down by politicians. As for the charges against the German high command, they consider it an attempt to discredit the military profession as such. Could such statements ever be possible in Russia?" Kraft defiantly asked.

"If the Germans had gone to America and did what they did in Russia, you'd hardly find anyone in America who would think that," Rebrov said glumly.

"Perhaps," Kraft conceded. "By the way, almost seventy percent of Americans think that Goering should be shot without any trial. Well, or hung…"

"Alex, come on, let's not talk about that fat pig now," Peggy interrupted. "By the way, soon all the journalists in Nuremberg will be lined up in my room."

"Is that so?!" Kraft grunted. "What for?"

"I found this guy who is going to work as a guard over the Nazis in the courtroom. He used to work in the circus. He's got a phenomenal memory. During his circus performances, spectators could read him any text, in any European language, and he could recite the whole thing back word for word, even if he didn't know the language. In exchange for payment he's going to tell me what Goering and Hess talk about, even if he doesn't know German."

"Peggy, you're an angel. Or a devil. I don't know which exactly," Kraft smiled. "But let's drink to the health of our Russian friends. I think that some misunderstanding has occurred between them. Sorry, guys, it might not be any of my business, but damn it, you're a good match for one another. Honestly. It's even downright symbolic. Looking at you, I think that there are two Russias that you represent, and you can bring them together…"

All evening Rebrov thought about how to explain his behavior to Irina, but he couldn't reach any decision. And then she left with her friends from the French delegation.

Notes

The Czechoslovak police have arrested in Bohemia a 12-year-old boy who may be Hitler's son. The boy was found with forged papers under the name of Friedrich Schulz. He had come to Bohemia from Berlin two months before. He bears a striking resemblance to Hitler.

CHAPTER XIII.
JUST A FEW MINUTES OF FEAR

After the dinner in the press camp's restaurant, Rebrov and Irina didn't see each other. It wasn't that they tried to avoid one another, but rather they simply didn't try to meet. It was clear to both of them that their relationship had reached some serious line that they could not cross, and they sensed this clearly. They understood that the consequences of taking a further step could be grave. They had to step back from this line and return to their former lives. Yet they listened to their own hearts trying to guess whether to go on or not. They had neither the strength nor the will to fight what was happening. They also had to see after their own duties, which were becoming increasingly more burdensome and difficult as the start of the trials approached.

As Rebrov was reflecting on Filin's order to think of a way that the Americans could be convinced to remove the German prisoners working in the Palace, he suddenly remembered fearless redheaded Peggy, whom Kraft had introduced as a correspondent for many American news sources. After he made some inquiries, he determined that Peggy really was a famous and respected reporter. Her scandalous coverage had brought serious consequences on a number of occasions.

He found Peggy in the press room, an enormous space where dozens of journalists from many countries were working round the clock on their reports. The hammering of typewriters made an unbelievable din, but the journalists themselves, so wrapped up in their work, hardly noticed it.

Rebrov walked up to Peggy and said something in her ear. Peggy nodded to show agreement. Rebrov heard for the bar, where he ordered two cups of coffee.

Soon Peggy floated in, her face still red from the zeal with which she had been typing up her dispatch. She sat opposite Rebrov and shook her head in surprise. "Honestly, I didn't expect such an invitation! I'm just dying to hear what it is!"

"Peggy, are you looking for a sensation?"

"How much?"

"What?"

"How much is it going to cost?"

"Just a few minutes of fear."

"Well, then it's practically free, then."

"We'll make things even. I'm offering you a little excursion…"

"Where?"

"One of the circles of hell. How do that sound?"

"Interesting. Is it far?"

"These days hell and Nuremberg are practically one and the same."

"That's right. When are we leaving?"

"Tomorrow morning. Just bring all your accreditation with you, it is very well respected in hell."

"It's been so long since something interesting came along!" Peggy licked her thickly painted lips.

The next morning, they drove Peggy's jeep out of Nuremberg and headed down the magnificent autobahn, built by Hitler's Reich just before the war. The autobahn was strangely empty, with only rarely a thick-wheeled cart drawn by a horse seen on the shoulder of the road, or people on bicycles who avoided looking at the jeep. The entire region seemed to be nearly lifeless.

Suddenly, several yards from the road, they saw a tavern with several cars parked around it. A large handmade sign hung at the entrance, depicting an enormous hand that pointed at the door, and a text in English and German: "Frederick the Great, Bismarck, Hitler, Roosevelt, Churchill, or Stalin never stopped here. But there's always great beer and great people. Come in and see!"

"Maybe we should go in?" Peggy nodded towards the sign. "Maybe there are still great people in Germany after all."

"Let's do it on the way back, Peggy."

"Alright, then. Is it still a long way?"

"No. From what I remember, we've practically there already."

They soon reached the autobahn exit, only to find their way blocked by a square bunker made from sandbags with several machine guns sticking out of the narrow opening. The pillbox was surrounded by coils of concertina wire.

"You'll have to open negotiations, Peggy," Rebrov shrugged. "Remember our story?"

"By heart," Peggy assured him. "You can't imagine how much I loved playing cowboys and Indians as a kid."

A freckled American officer emerged from the pillbox, stretching and obviously still quite sleepy, but the closer he got to the car, the more gallant and respectable his bearing became. The sight of Peggy, as Rebrov had already seen on a few occasions, had a magical effect on Americans.

"Well, goodness gracious, it's Peggy Butcher herself!" a smile appeared on the officer's face. "I read all your articles, they're great! Who is this here with you?"

"This man is staff at the International Military Tribunal. He's Russian, but he speaks good German. Gen. Donovan allowed me to take him along as an interpreter and representative of the Allies. You don't have any secrets here that he might sniff out?"

"Besides crowds of prisoners, there ain't no one else here."

"They're exactly what I would like to have a look at. Are they scary?"

"Now they're peaceable, ma'am, though who knows what they're really thinking. Just a second, ma'am, I'll call the camp commandant and let him know you're here."

The officer went into the pillbox. Rebrov looked at Peggy with an emphatic reverence. "All doors really are open with you along."

"Americans love celebrities and they greatly respect the press," Peggy explained. "I've got a famous name, but I can assure you, I had to work to earn it."

The officer came back out and, looking from under the visor of his cap at Peggy with enamored eyes, he said, "You can go on, ma'am. The commandant is waiting for you."

The way to the camp led through a heavy gate made from thick metal sheets. As the guards checked their papers, they happily joked with Peggy. After the pair had left the car at the gate, they entered the camp territory. A stout officer rushed up to meet them. His jolly face was red with delight. "Miss Butcher, my God! I'm Major Steve McBride, the camp commandant. It's a huge honor for me to welcome you here today."

"Just call me Peggy, major," she said with the generous and condescending air of a queen. "You know, I've never seen a POW camp…"

"I'll show you around, ma'am. There are some things to see here. These damn krauts knew how to organize things."

"This was a German concentration camp during the war, you see," Rebrov explained. "For Soviet prisoners…"

"Not just Soviet ones. They threw all kinds of people in here. Actually, not much has changed since. The house I'm living in, it belonged to the German commandant before me. He was a real bad guy."

They entered a huge officer decorated with heavy furniture.

"I've hardly touched anything here," the commandant gestured around the office. "It was all the same under Hitler. I just threw that madman's portrait in the trash and hung up one of our president Truman, and our flag too, of course." The stars and stripes hung in the corner of the room from a specially placed stand.

"Tea, coffee, whiskey, gin?" He looked at Rebrov and added, "Vodka?"

"Whiskey," Rebrov smiled. "With soda and on the rocks."

"And for me a coffee," Peggy asked, lounging on the leather couch. "And who are the prisoners in your camp now, major?"

"Now mostly former SS, ma'am, from the Edelweiss division. They were hiding around here. People would catch them in the forest or cellars and bring them here. We're keeping watch over them."

"Are there a lot of them here?"

"Unfortunately, I couldn't give you an exact number. We just haven't made a good count yet, but it's a lot. I honestly wonder where they found so many of them."

"You're not afraid that they might run away?"

"Run away? Where? How? To starve in the forest like a pack of hyenas? Here we give them decent food, military rations according to the Geneva Conventions. There are doctors here who treat the wounded and sick…"

"Even the Germans?"

"Of course. There aren't any Americans here for them to treat. The camp administration provides for the prisoners' leisure time," the major cheerfully reported. "On Saturdays and Sundays there are concerts that they put on themselves. Movies three times a week…"

"What kind of movies?"

"American ones. And before them, we show newsreels about Nazi crimes. They're hard to watch, I can't watch them myself."

"What effect does it have on them?"

"Frankly, not much," the commandant answered dejectedly. "A lot of them just look to the side or at the floor. It's hard to tell what they are thinking at that moment. But they aren't thinking about escaping. You can talk to any of them, and he'll tell you he's happy here and has no complaints. I can assure you."

"But these are SS men, major!" Peggy reminded him. "Professional killers! Could they change their stripes so fast?"

"I know, ma'am, but… They were soldiers and just following orders. The US is a democratic and humane country, it takes care of all prisoners. We can't be like the Germans who killed people here."

"And what if they decided to escape anyway?"

"I can assure you, none of them has shown any desire to. At least for the time being."

Rebrov decided to enter the conversation. "Tell me, is it prisoners from your camp that are taken to work in Nuremberg?"

"Yes," the commandant turned towards him. "They work at the Palace of Justice and oversee the repairs. Now they're tearing down ruined buildings. We haven't heard of any incidents or complaints."

"It's like a scout camp here, so quiet and comfy," Peggy smiled. "Has there really been nothing unusual going on, nothing out of the ordinary? You see, major, for my dispatches I need something that will hook American readers."

"I understand, ma'am. Let's have a walk through the camp, and I'll show you some things," the commandant gallantly suggested.

German order and cleanliness reigned in the camp. As the commandant approached, the prisoners stood at attention. Many were still wearing their black uniforms, only without insignia and with boots that were now clearly worn out. The commandant mechanically acknowledged their greeting by bringing his hand to his cap. It might have seemed as if a senior was meeting his subordinates over some business, Rebrov thought. While Peggy was talking with the commandant, he had kept silent, for Peggy worked professionally and asked precisely those questions that he was concerned with.

Naturally, the prisoners couldn't take their eyes off Peggy's seductive figure, which was dressed in a carefully maintained military uniform that perfectly emphasized her curves. Peggy herself was not at all embarrassed to be an object of desire for a large number of young men who hadn't seen a woman in some time. On the contrary, she seemed even inspired by it.

"There's one guy here…" said the commandant. "I'll order them to bring him out." He said something to the soldier accompanying him. The soldier went to a low building standing at a small distance from the barracks and brought out a 15-year-old teenager. He was an awkward young man in a loose-fitting suit with an expressionless, even anemic face and flowing blond hair.

"This is the former camp commandant's son," Maj. McBride explained. "His name is Max. His father hardened him and brought him up as a true Aryan. On his birthday, he was allowed to shoot as many prisoners as there were candles on his birthday cake: eleven, twelve, thirteen…"

Max listened to this completely indifferently. It seemed as if nothing disturbed him any more.

"What?! How could you do such a thing?" Rebrov asked him in German.

"Against that wall over there," Max gestured. He was clearly used to answering this question. "They would be put up against the wall, and the machine gun would be over there, right on the ground. They laid out a carpet, and I'd get down on it and shoot…"

"Did you see their faces?"

"No, I don't have very good eyesight. I can't see far away without my glasses. But they were all the same: thin, in striped clothes and caps. It was already hot outside – my birthday is in May. Then they were finished off by the guards, because I couldn't shoot straight. The machine gun had a very strong recoil and I couldn't aim it right. And then they were hauled off and buried in a ditch, over there… The last time was last year, when I turned fourteen. This year it was supposed to be fifteen."

"He never got to shoot fifteen men," the major explained. "Our forces entered the camp first."

"When did this all start?" Peggy asked calmly. "When did you shoot a man for the first time?"

"The first time? When I was ten. Papa said that it would make me strong. I was a weakling, and they made fun of me at school. Papa said that I had to learn to be tougher."

"Enough!" Peggy sighed. "Get him out of here, I can't take any more."

The American shoulder slightly shoved Max forward. Max said "Goodbye" in the same indifferent tone and awkwardly stumbled back towards the same low building, almost tripping over his own feet and swinging his long, slender arms.

"His father is gone, and I'm still here," the major explained. "We're keeping him separate from the other prisoners. We just don't know what to do with him. Put him on trial? He's underage. But we can't release him. Too many people know about his 'birthday presents'. I don't think he would survive long out there."

They stood and watched as Max walked up the porch steps, glanced back, and then disappeared into the building.

Peggy drove the jeep down the autobahn without speaking. When she saw the same jolly tavern again, she braked sharply. "After everything they showed me, I really need a drink," she said forthrightly. "If I get drunk, you'll have to drive."

The tavern, neatly maintained, was empty. They settled in a corner and the waiter brought two large mugs of beer without asking anything first.

Peggy eagerly drank from one of them, but then categorically stated, "This beer is horrible."

"Well, they'll get back on their feet soon," Rebrov said. "The Germans can't live without beer, and soon they'll have real German beer again. But how will they live with themselves?"

Peggy lit a cigarette. "Well then, did you take poor Peggy all that way just to meet that little monster?"

"I must admit, I didn't even know about him."

"What was your real aim, then? Come on, come on, I can see that you're up to something. Only I don't like being used or tricked. You've got to deal honestly with Peggy."

"I could guess that right from the start. Anyway, I wanted you to see with your own eyes what conditions those SS thugs are being held under now, and how they are kept convinced that there's no reason to escape from that so-called camp."

"Alright, let's assume I saw all that. What then?"

"Peggy, yesterday weapons were found in a ruined building next to the Palace, completely by accident. They said that they had been there since the war, but who knows? How many more weapons might be hidden in secret stashes near the Palace?"

"Wait, you're saying that..."

"I'm saying that if these SS guys are thinking about attacking the Palace and freeing the men on trial, they could easily do so. Only a few days are left before the tribunal begins. If something is going to happen, it'll be in these next few days, to stop the trials from even starting."

Peggy listened, her eyes on the tip of her cigarette.

"The Soviet delegation tried to alert Col. Andrus to this danger, but he can't even admit that such a thing is possible. By the way, before Ley committed suicide, he didn't think that was possible either."

"And what do you need me to do? Go to Andrus myself and share my impressions of visiting the camp?"

"No, I just want you to do your job as a reporter. If you write about what you saw with your own eyes, and it gets published in a newspaper, then Col. Andrus and his staff will be forced to respond. In America the press is greatly respected, and so is Peggy Butcher's reporting in particular!"

"It might prove a sensation," Peggy said pensively. "Those weapons in the ruins. Did they really find something like that?"

"As far as I know, they did."

They fell silent for some time and looked each other in the eye.

"Peggy, I'm being honest. I want those criminals to be tried."

Peggy sipped her beer, not longer paying any attention to how it tasted. She seemed to already be putting together her sensational reportage.

Notes

Heinrich Hoffmann, Hitler's photographer, was interrogated by Allied intelligence and he declared that in his opinion, the 12-year-old boy arrested in Czechoslovakia with forged papers in the name of Friedrich Schulz was not Hitler's son. He felt sure that Eva Braun, whom Hitler married on April 29, 1945 before his suicide, never had children. Rather, the boy was the son of Martin Bormann, one of Hitler's closest companions, who had disappeared without a trace. He greatly resembled the boy in the photograph found with documents belonging to Hitler.

CHAPTER XIV.
FROM THE WORLD OF HALLUCINATIONS

After their "outing" to the POW camp, Peggy disappeared and Rebrov didn't see her again for several days. When Rebrov ran into Kraft in the corridor in the Palace of Justice, the latter said with a smile that Peggy had devoted herself madly to her work – she was writing something sensational and wouldn't yet reveal exactly how she was going to shock the world.

In one of the Palace's other rooms, another crowd of journalists, tired of waiting for the trials to begin, were tormenting David Amen, the head of investigation. He was a short, heavy-set and mustached man, resembling a retired middleweight boxer. Rebrov decided to listen before he went on to the investigation department of the Soviet delegation.

"Where are the interrogations of the prisoners held?"

"On the second floor there is a special section with eight rooms specially equipped for interrogations. To ensure complete security, they are connected to the guardroom with a special alarm system."

"How are the accused brought there?"

"By an underground passage leading straight from the prison."

"How do the investigators work?"

"They work according to a special schedule, so that the prisoners meet different investigators. Each interrogation shouldn't last any more than six hours. So, they are usually done at a fast, very intense pace."

"How do the accused feel about the interrogations?"

"They like going to them," Amen laughed. "They all like to talk, though it's not always in response to what they've been asked. By the way, after they go back to their cells, many of them start writing notes to the investigators."

"To complain?"

"No, to fill in what they forgot to say during the interrogation."

"Will all this testimony be used in the trials?"

"The testimony that the prosecutors will use in trial consists of written statements made under oath. They are signed by the person giving the testimony and the person overseeing the swearing of the oath."

"Will the interrogations continue after the accused have been formally indicted?"

"Only with their agreement."

"Are the Soviet investigators leading any of the questioning themselves?"

"No, only the Americans. The Soviet investigators receive answers to their questions in the form of written reports."

"But that's not fair!"

"An agreement was made that it would be done like that," Amen shrugged. "The same holds for the prosecutors from Britain and France."

Alexandrov, who Filin had allowed Rebrov to consult in case of acute necessity, looked worn out and frustrated. Rebrov knew what the reason might be: Gavrik had told him that Col. Kosachev had sent Alexandrov a report from Moscow. What the exact contents of this report might be, Gavrik hadn't said, but it was clear that they weren't good. There was no time for a more delicate approach, however. He wanted to ask that Goering be interrogated about some matters that he had agreed on with Filin before the latter flew to Moscow. Granted, now after hearing what Amen had to say, he understood that this might be difficult to arrange, at least for the time being.

"We've insisted many times that they let us interrogate the prisoners ourselves, but…" Alexander shrugged his soldiers irritably when Rebrov asked if he might be present at the questioning. "The Americans only make promises… We've got a list of questions that the highest levels in Moscow approved, but the way the Americans are leading the interrogations, we haven't got any answers to them yet. They've got their own way of dealing with things. The accused are divided up among the investigators without any logic to it, and the investigators change frequently. For them, the only thing that matters is respecting the schedule they drew up. They throw out question after question without really delving into the answers they get. They practically never ask follow-up questions. And they're constantly looking at the clock. As soon as lunchtime comes or it's the end of the working day, everything is immediately wrapped up. They don't like working overtime."

Rebrov had the impression that Alexandrov was explaining the situation not so much to him as to some other person, most likely the high-ranking brass that Kosachev's report had been directed to.

Alexandrov shook his head. "Honestly, I sometimes wonder if they even understand what is going on. These aren't real interrogations, it's more like a formal request for getting information of some kind."

"You think they don't care?"

"The way they run things, it seems that way. Unlike in the USSR, they hardly do any preliminary investigations. Everything is decided during the trial when the prosecutor and defense attorneys have it out. And some people don't want to understand this!"

"I wanted to ask that Goering be questioned. By the way, I already talked to him, in Mondorf."

"Maybe that can be arranged later. Now the Americans are trying to get what they need out of him. Once they get it, only then they'll say 'You all can come in now!'"

"Georgy Nikolayevich, the matter of the gold hasn't come up during the interrogations?"

"Not in our presence."

"And we didn't ask about it ourselves?"

"Gen. Filin didn't think this was practical yet."

The ringing telephone didn't allow him to finish. Alexandrov picked it up. "Yes, that's me. What happened? I see. Thanks for the invitation. We'll be there. I'll be with Mr. Rebrov, the interpreter."

Rebrov looked at Alexandrov quizzically.

"Col. Amen has invited us to his office," Alexandrov explained. "He says something extraordinary will happen there."

In the special department for interrogations on the second floor of the Palace, where the accused were brought straight from the prison by a tunnel, Alexandrov and Rebrov showed their passes to the American guards and then entered Col. Amen's office.

The owner of the officer sat at his desk by the window directly across from the door. To his right was a stenographer in an American army uniform who transcribed the interrogations on his special typewriter. To Amen's left was his interpreter and assistant.

A row of chairs was set along the wall all the way to the door. At the end sat a soldier in a white helmet, with white gloves and a white holster. Alexandrov and Rebrov settled onto their own chairs, and after some time had passed, several more people in military or civilian clothing took their seats alongside them, as if at a theatre performance.

"There are always a lot of people coming in to watch when the Americans are doing their interrogations, as if they just walk from one office to another and see what's on," Alexandrov whispered in Rebrov's ear. "It's like a zoo."

Col. Amen looked around the room and said in a solemn tone, "Gentlemen, yesterday Rudolf Hess was brought to Nuremberg from England. I have invited you here to witness his first interrogation, which will be held right now."

In recent weeks Rebrov had seen prisoners from vastly different positions in Nazi Germany, but the appearance of Rudolf Hess, Hitler's right-hand man in the Nazi Party, Reich Minister, Reichsleiter, Obergruppenführer in the SS and SA, and considered the third most powerful person in the state, greatly impressed him.

Two American soldiers led in a strange creature in handcuffs that were connected with a chain to one of the escorts. He was inhumanly tall, with dangling arms, an untidy skull shrunken into his shoulders, and unbending knees. His eyes were unusually deep-set, almost invisible between his thick brows and his pathologically prominent cheekbones. With lips so thin he seemed to have none at all, his mouth was merely a hole.

After Hess sat down on the chair set right across from the investigator, he looked gloomily down at his own shoes in huge, threadbare boots.

"Name?" Amen began the interrogation.

Hess frowned and remained silent.

"Prisoner, did you hear my question?" Amen raised his voice.

Hess finally let out a response, "I don't remember."

"What were your duties in the German leadership?"

Hess furrowed his brow. He was breathing heavily and irregularly. "I don't know."

"Are you married?"

With his thin lips twisted Hess grunted, "I don't know."

"Do you have children?"

Hess shook his head.

"Who was Hitler?"

"I don't know anyone by that name."

"You were his deputy in the Nazi Party!"

"I just don't know."

"What is *Mein Kampf*? Answer, please!"

"I don't understand."

"It was a book by Hitler that you wrote for him! Hitler trusted you with everything!"

Hess suddenly struck his knee with his fist.

The soldier at the door and Amen's assistants jumped up, intending to set upon Hess, but he again fell into total passivity.

"Enough for today," said Amen, then ordered, "Get him out of here!"

Hess went out, dragging his legs as if he were wearing a prosthesis. His eyes were indistinct beneath his frowning eyebrows.

"So, what do you say, Mr. Alexandrov?" Amen asked when the public, impressed by the performance, had also left the room. "Is he really crazy, or just pretending to be?"

"He really does resemble a psychopath," Alexandrov answered cautiously. "I have met a few such men among criminals. But he might be faking it."

"A psychopath or a real madman?" Amen sought to establish. "Is he ill?"

"In such a case we should resort to a forensic psychiatric examination. Experts can quickly make a diagnosis that we can trust in."

"Maybe you're right," Amen agreed. After thinking for a bit, he slapped his palm on the desk. "Alright, then, before we go ask the doctors, I want to do an experiment. Come here again tomorrow at two o'clock. You'll find it very interesting, I promise you."

Over tea in Alexandrov's office, they naturally looked back on the incredible story of how Hess was originally captured.

In May 1941, the "deputy führer" of the Nazi Party, Rudolf Hess, who had served as a pilot in World War I in the Richthofen squadron led by Hermann Goering, took off from the airfield in Augsburg. He was flying a Messerschmitt Bf 110 with only enough fuel for a one-way journey. Hess was dressed in the uniform of a Luftwaffe lieutenant and he carried a map of his planned route. He intended on landing his plane not far from the estate of Lord Hamilton, a member of the British royal family, whom he had met at the Berlin Olympics in 1936. However, he could not find a suitable place to land, and when he ran out of fuel he parachuted out and gave himself up to local farmers. He initially presented himself under a fictitious name, but soon admitted who he really was.

Hess behaved in quite a strange way. He was long disappointed that British officials could not understand what he was trying to achieve, and that they were refusing to meet with him. Finally, one of the officials from the foreign affairs ministry agreed to hear what Hess had to say. Hess presented a document with the terms under which Hitler might sign a peace treaty with Great Britain, end the fighting, and combine forces for a joint battle against Bolshevik Russia. Furthermore, Hess stated that since Hitler was not willing to sign an agreement with Churchill as prime minister, the latter should resign. Hess considered the Germans and English to be "Aryan brothers in blood", and it was a great tragedy and error for them to be fighting each other. He hoped to get these ideas into Parliament with Lord Hamilton's help. However, by Churchill's personal order Hess was sent to the Tower of London, where he remained as a high-ranking detainee until the end of the war and his transfer to Nuremberg.

After the English had announced Hess's arrest in a radio broadcast, Hitler ordered his propaganda minister Goebbels to tell the whole world that Hess was crazy. Goebbels stated, "Clearly, Nazi Party member Hess lived in a world of delusions, and as a result he believed that he could find a mutual understanding between England and Germany... The Nazi Party believes that he has fallen victim to insanity. And so, his actions have no effect on the continuation of the war, a war that Germany was forced into."

However, it was hard to swallow all this. Gen. Filin, with whom Rebrov had occasionally discussed the matter, was convinced that behind Hess's proposals were Hitler's real wishes. Hitler was preparing to wage war on the USSR and did not want to fight on two fronts. If the British had only accepted these terms, Hess would have been called a hero, not a madman. Furthermore, he had real grounds to assume that the British were prepared to ally with Hitler. Who knows what would have happened if Hess had reached Lord Hamilton safely and unnoticed. Did he perhaps fly over on an invitation from the British secret services? The British had avoided discussing this mysterious story and they had classified all documents relating to it.

"Indeed, Mr. Churchill is capable of playing the most complex game," Alexandrov concluded. "First he set Hitler on us, and then he started helping us..."

"What can we expect from him now?" Rebrov asked.

"I think that we will soon see."

The next day at two o'clock, Alexandrov and Rebrov again entered Amen's office. Hess was already sitting in his chair. His apelike hands, bound in handcuffs, were dangling over the floor. Then, the guards brought Goering himself into the room. Goering carefully looked around at the men present and after his gaze lingered briefly on Rebrov, he calmly sat down on the chair indicated by the guards.

Amen began the questioning. "Rudolf Hess, do you know Reichsmarschall Hermann Goering?"

"No!" Hess shouted, unexpectedly sharply.

"Let me repeat: Reichsmarschall Goering," Amen slowly repeated.

"I don't know anyone by that name!" Hess croaked.

Goering, who had been silently watching these events and clearly did not intend to give Amen any help, eventually could not take it any longer. Who would dare not recognize him, Hermann Goering himself!

"Hess, it's me, Goering! Look at me, open your eyes. Or did you go blind over there in England?"

Hess, without looking at him, only grumbled something unintelligible.

"Enough fooling around!" Goering was more than upset; Hess's behavior seemed to enrage him. "If you want to act like a madman, don't think that anyone here will believe it!"

Hess turned his beady little eyes on Goering but said nothing.

"And who was Hitler, do you know?" Amen interrupted the old Nazi Party comrades.

Hess shook his head.

"You worshiped Hitler! You crawled down on your knees before him!" Goering said. "You thought he had talents sent down from heaven that would make him ruler of the world! You told me this yourself a million times."

"I don't know anything," Hess muttered stupidly.

"He doesn't know!" Goering, quite offended, threw up his hands. "You really don't remember the Führer?"

"I had someone's portrait on the wall of my room…"

"Someone's portrait! That was Hitler! Do you remember what he said about the destiny of the Reich and the German people?"

"The portrait didn't talk to me," Hess smiled. And at that moment, he did not look crazy.

"You have got to be kidding me!" Goering, furious, jumped up. A soldier laid a hand on his shoulder and he collapsed back onto his chair.

"Instead of pretending to be insane, you ought to think about how we should all be acting here! How we can avoid embarrassing ourselves! You just decided to hide in your little burrow, but it won't help you, you fool!"

Goering waved his hand and demonstratively turned away from Hess, muttering curses under his breath.

"Alright, that's enough," Amen ended the interrogation. "Get the prisoners out of here."

When Goering and Hess had been led out, he sighed wearily. "You know, when you're in the presence of a psycho like that, you always feel in danger. And when he's got a face like that! It's awfully tiring."

"I think that we can't do without real psychiatric expertise," Alexandrov calmly restated his original proposal..

"That may be," Amen agreed. "And still, I just can't understand. How did slimeballs like this have all Europe on its knees?"

Alexandrov didn't agree. "They look like that now. But in Germany there were many other people, much more capable and tougher standing behind these men."

Notes

After the fall of France in 1940, Britain was forced to confront Germany alone. Churchill knew that if Germany concentrated its forces on the fight against Britain, the latter would be defeated. The only option left was to draw things out, to search for allies and create a second front. He wanted two countries to be Britain's allies: the USA and the USSR. For the Soviets however, who were then collaborating with Germany, it would have been too dangerous to risk war with Germany. Churchill thus needed to get Hitler to declare war on the USSR himself.

British intelligence in Berlin established contact with Rudolf Hess and through him had a channel to Hitler himself. Hess was told that if Germany declared war on the USSR, Britain would cease military actions. Hess convinced Hitler that he could trust in this. British intelligence fabricated an invitation with Churchill's signature on it and gave it to Hess. Hess ended up in Scotland after his secret flight over and he got an opportunity to meet with British officials. He announced that Hitler would attack Russia. He was told in return that Britain would also fulfill its part of the arrangement. A record was made of this meeting and sent to Moscow. "The cat was out of the bag". The war had broken out.

CHAPTER XV. A REAL SOVIET MAN

The USSR's chief prosecutor Roman Andreyevich Rudenko spoke Russian with a slight Ukrainian accent. If judge Robert H. Jackson was called the most typical American out of all typical Americans, then with the same stroke Rudenko could have been labeled a real Soviet man.

He was born one of the many children of a Ukrainian farm laborer, but the Soviet regime gave him extraordinary opportunities to shape a new destiny for himself. This simple peasant son, then an active member of the Komsomol, was hired by the Soviet prosecutor's office, which had just been founded then, and he soon began moving up the career ladder. Before the outbreak of the war, there was a moment when his life was literally hanging by a thread. He had been reprimanded by the Party, dismissed from the nomenklatura, and fired from his very prestigious position as prosecutor of the Donetsk region. This should have been followed, according to the laws of that time, by his arrest and then either a long sentence in a labor camp or execution. For more than a year he waited with his fate in the balance, but he was saved by the war, when men with professional education were sorely needed. They remembered Rudenko, and he asked to be sent to the front, so they assigned him to work in the Ukrainian SSR prosecutor's office. By June 1943 he had already become chief prosecutor for Ukraine. Thus he made a blazing trail in the war years.

Just as Jackson believed that the USA was the greatest country on earth, and to be an American the greatest fortune, Rudenko was utterly sure that the Soviet Union was the most just of societies and the hope of all mankind. The outcome of the war only strengthened his conviction. Being a true Ukrainian peasant by nature, he was not normally inclined to take things on faith. Rudenko had of course seen many things which could not be reconciled with his belief in Communism, but he sincerely believed that these were only exceptional excesses on the great path to a brighter future. He accepted his appointment as chief prosecutor at

Nuremberg without fear, as if it were just another order from the Party that had to be carried out. Moreover, he had been sent to do the job by comrade Stalin himself.

In Nuremberg he felt himself to be a prominent figure. After all, he had behind him the power of a country that had defeated fascism. He was accustomed to working meticulously and precisely, without expecting anything to happen on its own. In addition, several trials of Nazi men in 1945, where he had served as prosecutor, had taught him a lot. He already understood clearly that no triumphal march awaited him and his country, but rather a battle with a cornered enemy that hoped to get out of its situation by any means possible. An enemy that would seek to drive a wedge between the prosecutors of the victor countries and even set them against one another.

Rudenko was reflecting on this as he sat in his office in the Palace of Justice and listened to a report from Alexandrov's investigative branch.

"We want to determine before the start of the trials what line the accused are going to stick to," Alexandrov was saying. "Otherwise we might make fools of ourselves at the trial."

"We can't allow that," Rudenko interrupted him. "We cannot allow being made fools of. Moscow would have it in for you like you can't imagine."

"That's what I mean. Now these men, the defendants, seem pitiful, they wriggle, look you in the eye, but... I feel that Goering's got a sting in him and Mr. Jackson will have a hard time with him."

"You think he's a real animal?"

"He sure is! You can already occasionally glimpse a real predator waking up inside of him, one with absolutely no mercy."

"I warned Jackson about this," Rudenko shrugged, "But he strongly believes in his mission and his own eloquence. Too much so. He can't imagine that the men will be able to object. And I've already seen these gentlemen in court. They'll dispute what he says at any opportunity."

"Yes, Roman Andreyevich, a person needs more than fine speaking to deal with Goering. At the slightest opportunity, Goering will make a laughingstock out of him."

"Jackson is a very stubborn fellow. He's convinced that all these villains will come crawling to him with their hands up," Rudenko stated bluntly. "Some of them might, but certainly not all of them. He doesn't know anything, he hasn't had to deal with men like this, but I have. They need to be confronted with facts, evidence, logic..."

"But what about the interrogations, Roman Andreyevich? Please don't forget to ask Jackson about that."

"Alright, fine, today I'll demand once again that your men be allowed to question these villains directly, and ask them our questions. By the way, how are these former lords of the earth behaving under questioning?"

"Most of them are very calm and polite."

"Get out of here!"

"Yes, sometimes they are unbearably courteous… When they come into the room, they bow and scrape. They don't sit down before they've been given permission to. Granted, Frank once got angry when an American investigator suddenly attacked him, and he called the American a pig."

"He really said that? And did the American just take it like that?"

"No, Frank was just immediately dragged out of the room and back to his cell to cool down. The cells don't have any windows for security reasons, so it's not so hot in there now."

"So, he hasn't really found peace with himself…"

"No way! Sometimes such a fury appears in his eyes! Incidentally, when they see us, with our Soviet uniforms, they look at us with great apprehension, I'd say."

"Well, how else could they look at a Soviet officer?" Rudenko laughed. "Huh? How else!"

Rudenko's words with Jackson clearly had an effect, as the next day Alexandrov and Rebrov were able to lead their own questioning of Goering. The American investigator and his assistants were only spectators.

When the guards brought Goering in, he looked at the Soviet investigators with curiosity and sat down with ease on the chair indicated. To Rebrov it even seemed like Goering winked at him, remembering the interrogation in Mondorf.

Goering had, judging by everything, not fallen into depression but, on the contrary, he was in an upbeat and combative mood. The treatment of his drug addiction and the strict prison rules had had a positive effect on him, and he looked quite self-assured. Compared to the other prisoners, his manner was very jaunty. Though he was wearing a light gray tunic with a turndown collar and riding breeches, and his boots hung off his feet as though on a hanger, he didn't at all come across as pitiful.

Alexandrov explained to Goering that he would now be questioned by the head of the investigative department of the Soviet delegation. Goering nodded in a friendly fashion.

"List the positions and duties you held in the German Reich," Alexandrov began.

Goering began to list his countless positions and titles at length and with great pleasure, but at a certain moment he simply smiled and waved his hand. "I think that's it. Or maybe not…" He glanced at Rebrov and affably asked, "Forgive me, but haven't we already talked?"

"Yes," Rebrov nodded. "In Mondorf."

"Yes, we did, I remember. We talked about the Spear of Destiny and Hitler's belief in its miraculous power… But you Russians are materialists and don't believe in miracles and supernatural forces."

"Well, you're not a great mystic either, it seems to me," Rebrov smiled.

"Yes, I keep my feet on the ground. But as for that Spear of Destiny, the Americans have probably already stolen it, and sent it overseas," Goering gestured somewhere aside and squinted at the American investigators, who immediately began whispering among themselves.

"You know anything about that?" Alexandrov asked sternly.

"No, I just know the Americans. They are clever people. By the way, if they find out where Bormann and Himmler hid the gold, they're hardly going to tell you about it. They'll just spirit it away over the ocean," Goering laughed.

Rebrov involuntarily tensed. He had been constantly thinking about when he would be able to ask Goering about the hidden gold, but Goering had suddenly brought it up himself. What could one conclude? Clearly he was already used to talking about this, and he could have only done it with the Americans, not just under official questioning but also during secret meetings in the prison. So, the reports from agent Hector were confirmed.

"Tell me, might Hess know where they hid the gold looted from occupied countries?" Alexandrov asked, a question that they had agreed on beforehand.

Goering smiled condescendingly. "I didn't know the Russians were so keen on valuables…"

"These 'valuables' belong to countries that Germany plundered, and they must be returned to those countries," Alexandrov said dryly. "We now speak on their behalf. By the way, in the investigation's files is a message you sent to Rosenberg, where you wrote, 'I now possess what is probably the most valuable collection of Old Master paintings in Europe.'"

Goering shuddered, his face became gray and angry. He quickly got a hold of himself, however, and decided to abandon this subject that posed such risks to himself personally.

"You ask about Hess?" Goering said. "Maybe Hess once knew something, but now he hardly remembers anything at all. Only Bormann could know – he oversaw the Nazi Party's finances and even Hitler's. But Hess… He complained that the English were poisoning him with some chemical to brainwash him, so he ended up a vegetable."

"Let's get down to the matters that will be discussed at the trial," Alexandrov cut him short. It was clear that Goering would not say anything further about the gold. "You are familiar with Adolf Hitler's book *Mein Kampf*. How do you relate to the ideas in it?"

"Hitler wrote it with Hess's help in prison, but I must admit that I never found time to read it. It's quite a thick book," Goering grinned. "So, I don't want to give an opinion on something I know nothing about."

"But are you familiar with the racial theories presented therein?"

"I've heard about them. I think they are wrong."

"And do you know Alfred Rosenberg's *The Myth of the Twentieth Century*?"

"I've heard about that book, too, but it never felt necessary to read it. Why do I need to know about every crazy theory? Ultimately, these were works by private individuals."

"Let me remind you that in 1934, Hitler appointed Rosenberg as his 'Commissar for Supervision of Intellectual and Ideological Education of the Nazi Party'. In that way, The Myth of the Twentieth Century went from being the 'work of a private individual' to practically the official expression of Nazi ideology. In his view, the German race is eternally opposed to the corrupting influence of the Jewish race…"

"Perhaps you know more about Rosenberg than I do," Goering shrugged. "But you aren't right to make his ideas out to be the view of the entire Nazi Party. Many people didn't agree with them. I personally had other ideas."

"Did you take part in developing the plans to attack Britain and the Soviet Union?"

"I was against going to war with Britain, and I had nothing to do with the war against Russia. In fact, I asked Hitler not to go to war with Russia. I pointed out that we had other countries against us, especially America, and we would be fighting the whole world alone. But Hitler didn't want to listen. He told me, 'Goering, this is my war. I act as a higher power directs me to!' He had probably gone to Nuremberg the day before and again met with the Spear of Destiny, so when he met with me, he had already made his decision. 'Now, no one can convince me otherwise,' he said."

Goering looked at all those present and shrugged his shoulders sadly, as if to say "What do you want from me?"

"Did you know of the large-scale looting of the occupied Soviet territories?"

"It was war. To the victors go the spoils, it has been like that since the world was first created. Whatever resources we capture in war are ours. What has changed? I can imagine what is going to happen to poor Germany now: I think that they'll haul off everything they can from it."

"You even carried off agricultural soil from the USSR," Alexandrov reminded him.

"Well, agricultural soil had nothing to do with me," Goering said.

"Nothing to do with you. The most valuable soil in Europe…"

"Well, that was an exaggeration. You know how fishermen and hunters boast in an innocent way, pretending to be simple folk," Goering decided to explain. "And also, you must keep in mind that when I collected all those paintings, I saved them from destruction. Thanks to me, they have remained the heritage of all mankind… I think that our descendants will appreciate this."

Goering looked around triumphantly at everyone present and suddenly winked at Rebrov again.

"You could have not remained unaware of the crimes committed by German forces on the occupied territories," Alexandrov decided to raise his voice. "Of the experiments on the people in concentration camps, gas chambers, reducing people to slavery…"

"Why should I have known about all that?" Goering asked, offended. "I was doing other things."

"After you spent half an hour listing all your duties and positions, a person can't imagine that you didn't know about what was happening in Germany."

"Yes, I was a prominent figure. But nonetheless, a lot of things were done without my knowledge and without my participation. If things had gone differently, I would have been the first person to…"

Immediately after the questioning, Alexandrov and Rebrov went to Rudenko's office, where the latter was expecting them…

"Well, what are your impressions of the 'number-two Nazi' as they're calling him?" Rudenko asked. "What kind of creature is he?"

"It's hard to say," Alexandrov ventured. "He's a serious type, but an actor can pass himself off as an idiot or simpleton, and he might even imagine himself leader of all Germany. Everything depends on his mood and what he thinks would give him the advantage. We must keep in mind that he's from a well-known family that has produced generals and important officials in the past. So, he can only pretend to be a simpleton. By the way, he had a special department to eavesdrop on the telephone conversations of all the Third Reich leaders. He worked just as hard as the Gestapo did, tracking everyone… He will defend himself to his last breath, turn things around, lie, try to redirect accusations against other people…"

Rudenko turned his pencil in his fingers.

"Alright. And how should we deal with him at his trial?"

"Without getting too philosophical or lyrical. He is capable of talking at length about anything. We need to get him with facts, nail documents to the wall, hit him mercilessly. There can't be any repentance in him. If he suddenly starts to regret something, it means that he's lying. The only thing he really regrets is that everything's over and they lost."

"Ha, he thinks he's the cock of the walk," Rudenko said, scratching his head that was already noticeably balding in spite of his young age.

"Will you allow me, comrade general?" Rebrov stepped forward. "Goering, as I've noticed, is very vain. We can work with that. If we allow him to puff himself up and act heroic, he might start admitting things."

"Well, that would be something," Rudenko nodded. "Alright, Georgy Nikolayevich, you hold on here. I'm off to Moscow for a meeting of the committee overseeing the trials."

"Were you urgently called back?" Alexandrov asked.

"It's more than that," Rudenko raised a finger. "I can feel that they aren't happy with us there, but why? God knows."

"Good luck, Roman Andreyevich."

"Thanks," Rudenko took out a briefcase and began stuffing it with papers.

When they were already at the door, Alexandrov suddenly remembered, "Roman Andreyevich, there are some problems here that are really getting in our way with the work…"

"What else do you need?" Rudenko, shutting his briefcase, rushed him.

"Our Russian typewriters are terrible. We need ones that work decently, and a couple of experienced typists."

"There's always something. Alright, send me a request when I'm in Moscow, I'll talk to them there about typists."

In the hallway, Rebrov said pensively, "Gen. Filin is also flying to Moscow from Berlin."

"I know," Alexandrov nodded. "Something is going on…" After a pause, he glanced sharply at Rebrov. "Why did Goering wink at you, huh?"

"Hell if I know! He probably remembered our talk in Mondorf."

"Watch out. If Col. Kosachev finds out, you'll end up in your own Mondorf!"

In the half-empty plane flying from Berlin to Moscow, Rudenko encountered Filin.

"So you're also going to Moscow," Rudenko said ominously. "And, as I understand, you're also going to a meeting of the Politburo."

Filin only sighed.

"Vyshinsky will be leading the meeting," Rudenko noted, settling more comfortably into his seat.

"Vyshinsky?"

"Yes, Andrey Yanuarevich Vyshinsky," Rudenko said, still with ominous undertones and looking Filin right in the eye.

Each of them had their own relationship with the man nicknamed "the Great Leader's right-hand man" or "the Jaguar". For Rudenko, Vyshinsky had recently been the big boss, a formidable prosecutor at the very top, and a man very close to Stalin. Thus, with Rudenko's country wisdom, he treated all aspects of Vyshinsky's character as a given, like a natural phenomenon that had to be watched out for and avoided whenever possible. At the same time, Vyshinsky even seemed sympathetic to Rudenko and it was said that he had proposed him for some high-ranking position in Moscow back before the war and before Rudenko had been dismissed from his post. Rudenko wasn't at all flattered by this, however, as he knew that the Jaguar loved to beat on his own so that others would fear him. Plus, Rudenko knew well that Vyshinsky had very much wanted to be the USSR chief prosecutor at the Nuremberg trials and dazzle the whole world. Rudenko's appointment to this position awoke in the Jaguar, no, not envy, but rather annoyance, which he with his distinct character would inevitably act on. The only question was how. Would he do it openly, in the form of an address to the Politburo meeting, or when he reported to Stalin?

Filin's relationship with the punishing right hand of the Great Leader was much more acute. He believed that Vyshinsky, a brilliant orator and lawyer, was by nature an unscrupulous adventurer capable of serving or betraying anyone as needed to stay afloat himself. Filin was convinced also that Vyshinsky reveled in his power over people, he liked to humiliate others, destroy them, reduce them to madness. Stalin needed him because of his abilities and readiness to crush any obstacle in his path, but also because he himself could easily be destroyed at any moment: one need only point out that Vyshinsky had signed an arrest warrant for Lenin in 1917 when Vyshinsky was working for the Provisional Government… After the war broke out, Vyshinsky was somewhat pushed aside and he dreamed of a grand spectacle he could put on before the whole world during the trials of the Nazi leaders. However, Stalin knew a Vyshinsky serving at the international tribunal in Nuremberg would always be compared to the Vyshinsky serving at the prewar trials in Moscow. Any memory of these show trials, where many things were fabricated and set up beforehand, would be very inappropriate and dangerous for this important business. For this reason, Stalin kept Vyshinsky behind the scenes in Moscow. Knowing the Jaguar, Filin could easily imagine him complaining to the great leader about the mistakes that the Soviet delegation in Nuremberg was making without his critical eye and harangues.

Filin also knew that he might end up being discussed in the committee's proceedings. So, when the plane had taken off and was on its way, he drew from his briefcase a document he had received from Nuremberg the day before, and he handed it to Rudenko. "Here, have a look at this, Roman Andreyevich, so you're prepared…"

Rudenko carefully read through the document and gave it back to Filin without saying anything. Then, he quietly asked, "What, you think that it's only because of this?"

"Not only because of it, but rather this just acted as the trigger. And in Moscow…"

They were silent for some time, trying to imagine what would happen at the meeting and how all this might end.

"Well, whatever happens, happens," Filin said as if trying to brush off the thoughts that had been troubling him. "There are more important things at hand." He leaned towards Rudenko and said in a low voice, "We just got a report from our agent… Someone has provided the Americans with photocopies of our secret non-aggression pact with Germany, and now they are deciding what to do with them… And this, you know…"

Rudenko froze. He understood how things might turn out. "You think they might make this public at the trials?"

"We still don't know. We don't even know who found them. The American leadership directing the trials involves all kinds of people. There are even a fair few who are ready to lay any accusations at us and even disrupt the proceedings of the trial."

"But we have clear agreements with them about this! That we will not use in the trials any material that would call into question the right of the victors to judge those who committed crimes."

"We do have agreements with them, but we cannot be sure they will be strictly observed."

"So, the trials might be over before they've even begun. Moscow will not allow the non-aggression pact to be disclosed, and we would even be willing to withdraw from the trials to ensure this. And who needs that?"

"The Americans understand. But some of the American hawks really want to do this."

"What, they are willing to disrupt the trials?"

"They might do everything through a third party."

"Like who, for example?"

"The German lawyers, for example."

"How so?"

"The lawyers will present these documents in the defense of their clients. Or they will try, in any case."

"Good Lord!"

Notes

The occupation authorities "purged" the spiritual life of Germany of all traces of Nazism. The Germans themselves were actively attracted to this cause and they showed great zeal, sometimes bordering on the absurd. In Berlin, a special committee was founded to remove "Nazi literature" from libraries. Through its decisions, nearly 700 authors of literature and 1500 authors of political and scientific works from different eras somehow ended up being categorized as "Nazis", even as they had nothing to do with Nazism, and their books were removed from library shelves.

A list was drawn up of 15,000 book titles and 150 magazines with "fascist and militaristic content" that might propagate racial theories or be directed against the policies of the Allies. They were subject to confiscation and destroyed.

CHAPTER XVI. TRUTH SERUM

Vyshinsky was visibly nervous. His thin lips twitched under his gray mustache.

"So, we must conclude that during the preparations for the trials in Nuremberg, various issues that are unpleasant for the Soviet side are constantly leaking," he said in a harsh, unpleasant voice. "In particular, people are doubting the 'suddenness' of Germany's attack on the USSR, which the Soviet side must deal with on the orders of comrade Stalin."

The men present at this meeting of the Politburo committee sat with tense faces. All of them, the USSR Prosecutor Gorshenin and the People's Commissar for Justice Rychkov, the Supreme Court chief justice Golyakov, the heads of the state security organizations, knew that through Vyshinsky they were hearing from Stalin himself. Vyshinsky had been meeting with Stalin especially often in recent days. Rudenko and Filin were aware of this, too, and now they had to represent the Nuremberg delegation and answer for all its achievements and shortcomings.

"And if we don't manage to do that," Vyshinsky's eyes flashed ominously, "then it is mainly because the Soviet Union's chief prosecutor Rudenko has no clear-cut plan for how to manage the trials…"

The men present looked at Rudenko. His face had turned pale.

"One gets the impression that he is simply not prepared for the trials, he does not understand their importance. He does not understand how comrade Stalin feels about them."

"I do understand," Rudenko said, without looking at Vyshinsky.

"However, I don't understand, comrade Rudenko, what your report means about the Allies questioning the treacherous attack of Nazi Germany on the Soviet Union! Who won the war? Who broke the back of the Nazi beast? How could they not heed our demands? Perhaps you simply haven't talked with them? You don't know how to explain matters and make demands?"

Rudenko, his teeth clenched, remained silent.

"Why has our categorical demand not been carried out, that we obtain an agreement from US chief prosecutor Jackson that the Soviet side be given all documents relating to the USSR? What is this, sabotage? Or have all you there in Nuremberg ceased to obey the Kremlin? Have you become bourgeois?"

"That's impossible, comrade Vyshinsky," Rudenko started to explain. "It's impossible to get a hold of every document…"

"What are you saying, impossible?" Vyshinsky interrupted him rudely. "In wartime we didn't know the meaning of 'impossible'!"

"They cannot hand all documents over to us, because it was decided that the American delegation would deal with the matter of conspiracy at the trials. It would be impossible for them to do that without these documents."

Vyshinsky hissed, "Again 'impossible'. We hear from you too often this explanation that things are 'impossible'! In the meantime, the situation is heating up and threatens to get out of control. Gen. Filin, what information would you like to bring to the committee's attention?"

Filin stood up. He understood that he needed to direct the threat away from Rudenko. "According to reports from our agent Hector, representatives of certain American circles close to the State Department intend to publicly present at the Nuremberg Trials a copy of our non-aggression pact with Germany…"

The faces of everyone present were aghast.

"How?" Vyshinsky cried. "Who exactly would do this? Why? We've made an agreement with the Allies about this!"

"We aim to determine this now," Filin said calmly and businesslike. "But judging from everything, these people want to reveal the non-aggression pact not simply in the press, but in the course of the trials, so that these facts are entered into the official record."

"We categorically cannot allow that! Categorically!" Vyshinsky beat his fist on the table. "Even if we have to delay the trials, or cancel them outright!"

"But what legal value do these documents have?" USSR prosecutor Gorshenin turned to Filin. "What do they really say about themselves?"

"As our agent informs us, it is a matter of photographic reproductions that are not certified with any seals or signatures. So, their authenticity is subject to debate."

"So, they'll have to prove they are authentic," Gorshenin shrugged. "Maybe we're panicking for no reason?"

"Just imagine how explosive the appearance of these documents during the trial would be. Plus, there are living witnesses that a non-aggression pact was signed, and they might also appear at the trial. And there's one more thing. The Americans and British have photocopies of all existing original documents of the Germany Ministry of Foreign Affairs. They can go there and see the original certification. So, they need only begin."

Vyshinsky struck the table with his palms and said, "Everything is clear, then! Since the chief prosecutor's opening remarks, which I sent to the Kremlin with revisions, hasn't come back yet, and in light of these circumstances, we need to delay the opening of the trials by two or three weeks, and then we'll see."

Rudenko shook his head. "The Americans won't agree."

"What do you mean, they won't agree? Comrade Rudenko, if you don't understand how serious the situation is and if you are not able to do something about it, we can find another chief prosecutor!"

Rudenko could only shrug.

"In the meantime, we need to study these materials and take stock of the situation. We need to buy time and prepare ourselves. Most of all, we need to draw up and approve a list of matters that are off-limits for the trials. We need to win the agreement of the other chief prosecutors that they shouldn't touch on any of these issues in the courtroom under any circumstances. Not because we are afraid, but because it is completely impermissible for the USSR, the USA, Britain, France and other nations to be subject to criticism from the accused, from these war criminals and their defense attorneys! The world cannot forget that we are dealing with major war criminals for which there can be no forgiveness. They have already admitted their guilt, this was announced by representatives of the victor countries. Comrade Rudenko, how realistic would it be, delaying the start of the trials?"

"We'll do everything we can," Rudenko said cautiously.

Fury began to rise again within Vyshinsky.

"We'll try," Filin intervened. He knew that there was no point arguing with Vyshinsky now. "We will see there what can and cannot be done. By the way, the chief justice, Lord Lawrence, recently said, and I quote, 'We are not here to find out whether other countries have committed violations of international law or whether they have committed war crimes …We are here to sort out these points with the defendants already present here!' Those were literally his words."

"Well then, good job, comrade lord!" a smile suddenly appeared on Vyshinsky's face. "He's our kind of guy. So, hold firm to this line, comrade Rudenko! Bargain with them, convince them, prove the need for it, but the trials should run according to our script. And what if we can slip the lawyers some documents? Do we not have anything we can present to the Allies?"

"The Americans really don't want there to be any discussion of their role in arming Hitler's Germany," Filin continued to lead the conversation away from Rudenko. "That's why, incidentally, they didn't want to see any German industrialists or financiers among the defendants who might have stories to tell. The British don't want their bombing of Germany cities, which made no sense militarily, to be brought up, or their 'unlimited warfare' on the seas when they sank passenger ships under the Red Cross flag. On the SS Cap Arcona, which incidentally was laying at anchor, more than seven thousand refugees and former concentration camp prisoners were killed. Their bodies were being cast ashore from the sea all summer. Something can also be said about atrocities committed by the French."

"Well, naturally they don't want the world to know just how they were fighting against the fascists," Vyshinsky grimaced. "So, don't shy away from a fight, comrade Rudenko. The Soviet Union is behind you. Don't you forget that for a second."

"I'm only afraid, comrade Vyshinsky, that the American prosecutor Jackson will not want to postpone the start of the trials," Rudenko cautiously stood his ground. "He's eager for a fight."

"He would have been eager for a fight when there was talk about opening up a second front. How long did they wait? Years! It doesn't matter, let him be patient. And you, comrade Rudenko, you will stay in Moscow for the time being. We will announce that you are ill. Your subordinate in Nuremberg will take care of ensuring the beginning of the trials is delayed. Let them try to start without us! Is that all for today?"

The portly General Kobulov, Deputy People's Commissar for Internal Affairs, raised his head. "Here's how things are. Our people who are now in Nuremberg should report any defiant behavior by the defendants when they are interrogated. Goering, Jodl, Keitel, and the others act aggressively under questioning. Their responses often include anti-Soviet views, and our investigator Alexandrov is weak at parrying their thrusts."

"Let them just try if it were me doing the interrogation!" Vyshinsky's face twitched. "Comrade Rudenko, inform our investigators that they must, wherever necessary, cut the accused off. We must decisively fend off any anti-Soviet attacks in the strictest, most decisive way. If this investigator, Alexandrov, can't carry out the interrogations properly, then let's recall him. Let him interrogate small-time crooks or pickpockets, if he's afraid of Goering!"

Filin cleared his throat. "If you'll allow me…"

"What else is it?" Vyshinsky scowled. "Everything is clear now."

"I wanted to offer some clarification," Filin said softly but insistently. "This information was sent from Nuremberg by Col. Kosachev from the special counterintelligence team SMERSH…"

"How do you know of it?!" Kobulov rudely interrupted him. "Are you tracking our men?"

"No, we are not tracking your men. It's just that Col. Kosachev, when he was drunk, said himself that he had denounced Alexandrov in a report to Moscow, and that after this, Alexandrov was certain to be sent to the gulag."

"And why was he unhappy with Alexandrov?" Vyshinsky asked.

"The fact of the matter is that Kosachev was sleeping with a young lady interpreter. The entire Soviet delegation knew of it. Alexandrov tried to reason with the colonel…"

"Does this committee really need to follow who is sleeping with whom?" Kobulov interrupted.

"That's not the problem," Filin was unperturbed. "The problem is that investigator Alexandrov wrote a memo for the committee after Col. Kosachev threatened him. He asked me to bring it to the committee's attention."

"Is that so?" Vyshinsky asked. "And what did he write?"

"Will you allow me to read it aloud?" Filin again cleared his throat and read in an even tone:

> In connection with the allegations that have come to my knowledge about what supposedly occurred in Nuremberg, where during the interrogations of the defendants in the case of the top-level war criminals, they made attacks on the USSR and me personally, I wish to report the following.
>
> Firstly, during the interrogations were present, besides me, Col. Rozenblit and, as a rule, Col. Povkrovsky, and our translator and expert staff Rebrov.
>
> Secondly, no attacks were made against the USSR or against me personally, either by the defendants under interrogation or any questioned witnesses.

Thirdly, the event that supposedly occurred involving me, in fact happened in my presence at an interrogation on October 18 of this year with the American Lt. Col. Hinkel of the defendant Hans Frank. At the end of the interrogation, Frank did indeed call Hinkel 'a pig'. During this interrogation, I was present as an observer. I personally began leading interrogations later.

I believe that in this case, government authorities were misinformed about the actual way in which interrogations of the defendants were carried out. I ask that any sort of rumors about the interrogations of the defendants be put down, as it creates an unhealthy atmosphere and gets in the way of further efforts...

Filin closed the folder open in front of him, looked around at the men present, but made no further comment.

"I know about this matter," Rudenko broke the silence. "Frank really did insult the American prosecutor during questioning, as a result of which he was immediately sent back to his cell. It should be noted that the Americans do not forgive such behavior. They are generally quite harsh and resolute with the defendants. And this slander of Alexandrov is groundless, he is a decent man and a professional."

"Frank should have been punched in the face so that he'd never forget," Vyshinsky grunted. "Enough for today, comrades. As for this Kosachev, you deal with him, comrade Kobulov. If he can't tell a Soviet investigator from an American one... then he probably confuses our intelligence men with American spies."

Filin and Rudenko were walking slowly past St. Basil's Cathedral, occasionally turning their backs to the icy wind that swept across Red Square.

"Do you think that we'll manage to delay the start of the trials," Filin asked, holding his cap on with his hand against the wind.

"It will be hard, very hard," Rudenko sighed. "The Americans are extremely insistent about sticking to the schedule that was agreed upon."

"That's easy to understand. The more the trial gets delayed, the more interest in it declines. Plus, Jackson has already had his brilliant opening remarks prepared for quite some time. He worked so hard on them. They say that he considers the speech to be a masterpiece and it will bring him glory in front of the whole world. He's rather a provincial American idealist."

Rudenko smiled sadly. "I fear that I am one, too. What else are they saying now over there in Nuremberg?"

"They say that the French representative will insist that they not start without you present. But Jackson is very determined."

"I have been summoned this evening to a meeting with comrade Stalin," Rudenko involuntarily lowered his voice, as if someone might hear them. "I think after it, things will finally become clear."

That evening, when Rudenko left for the meeting with Stalin, Gres and Filin, who were both wearing civilian clothes and looking quite peaceful and quiet, though tired after a long day at work, sat drinking tea in Gres's spacious office.

"So, their line of defense is clear for us now," Gres concluded, wiping sweat from his brow. "By the way, what kind of people are going to be defending these Nazi gentlemen? I mean, who are their lawyers?"

"All sorts of people. There were, incidentally, some American and British lawyers who wished to serve as defense, but the tribunal wouldn't allow it. So, the lawyers are only German. There are quite some colorful figures among them. And there are some who are only in it for the money."

Gres was surprised. "Are they going to be paid well for it?"

"For Germany as it is these days, it's quite decent money. Some of them are aiming to make their fortune, and some of them are ideological supporters of Nazism. Some of them are afraid that the tribunal is going to accuse all Germans of crimes and they seek to defend not so much the defendants as Germany. These men, we have to admit, are all experienced in legal chicanery."

"And how are they going to act at the trials?"

"I think they'll take a serious approach. The first fears after Germany's defeat have already passed, and if they feel that many things are going to be allowed them, then it won't be easy to deal with them."

"And is it really the case that many things are going to be allowed them?"

"Certainly. For the chief justice, Lawrence, the most important thing is that there be no doubt about the legal validity of the trials. The thing he fears most is that the newspapers will criticize him for being biased, and that's why he'll give the defense attorneys a lot of leeway. It won't be easy for our prosecutors."

"But we've got so many incriminating documents! The facts are irrefutable!"

"Anglo-Saxon law is based on precedence. But there is no historical precedence for all this."

"How is our agent Hector doing? Are reports coming in?"

"Regularly. And very valuable reports. According to the most recent one, American intelligence is seriously considering the idea of questioning Hess with truth serum."

"Really?"

"Injecting the defendant with truth serum will supposedly loosen his tongue, and he'll unwillingly answer any of the questions he is asked. General Donovan of the OSS thinks that every prisoner should be administered truth serum so that they can get the information they need. So far Col. Andrus, the Nuremberg prison warden, is categorically opposed to that. He's afraid that the drug could prove lethal. Such incidents have occurred before, when it was administered to certain patients. Chief prosecutor Jackson also knows about the idea, but he's unsure of it. He asked Washington and is waiting for their answer."

The phone rang. Gres picked it up and listened to the voice on the other side without saying anything. He looked troubled. Finally, he hung up. Filin looked at him without speaking.

"Sergei Ivanovich, there's something else…" Gres sighed. "An agent has been identified here in Moscow, too. They've intercepted some of his encoded messages and managed to decipher them. His code name is Spitz, and his mission is related to Nuremberg. He has access to the most important information. They haven't managed to determine what yet."

"Where does he come from?"

"I think he's a German agent. Apparently the Germans gave him over to the Americans. Or sold him. His radio operator made a broadcast immediately after the meeting of the committee yesterday."

"And what about the radio operator? Have they caught him?"

"They did, but he took poison while he was being held."

"Well, that's already something. It's unlikely he has many radio operators to rely on. He'll have to find a new one."

"What if he is capable of broadcasting himself?"

"He'll hold off himself. Do we know what was reported?"

"That the Russians are trying to delay the start of the trials. That we know about the photographic reproductions of documents concerning the secret pact and the plan to make them public at the trials…"

"He's good," Filin was surprised. "The meeting was in the morning, and by the evening he had already managed to pass details of it on. So, the Americans will be already prepared when it comes to our proposal to delay the trials. It won't come as any surprise for them."

Notes

The trial effort being mounted by the victors is colossal. The evidence that has been amassed by the prosecution is a crippling burden for us, because we have no documents of comparable quality on the German side to put in against them. All we can do is to try to piece together opposing evidence by an intricate process of mosaic work.

Dr. Otto Nelte, defense attorney
for Field Marshal Keitel
at the Nuremberg trials

CHAPTER XVII.
THE PRINCESS HAS LEFT FOR PARIS

As Filin flew in from Moscow, he was met in the airport by Rebrov. When they were going down the autobahn, Rebrov asked, "How were things in Moscow?"

"Moscow," Filin sighed, "is like always. A lot of rushing about and having orders barked at you. How have things been for you here? Have you managed to accomplish any great feats? Or has nothing come up so far?"

"We'll find out today," Rebrov promised in a jolly voice.

Filin looked at him suspiciously. "Don't scare me."

"Yes, never mind, it's nothing," Rebrov shook his head foolishly.

When the Palace of Justice loomed in front of them, Filin asked in amazement, "What's going on over there?"

"Where?"

The road was suddenly blocked by an American patrol jeep. Soldiers were holding submachine guns at the ready and seemed quite determined to use them.

A sergeant came up to the car and gruffly saluted. "Papers, please." He was looking at Filin and Rebrov cautiously.

After carefully examining their papers, the sergeant explained, "You can't drive any further. You'll have to go on foot from here."

"What is the matter?"

"There is a special operation going on. You'll have to leave the car here, they'll keep an eye on it."

Among the ruins next to the Palace, where the prisoners of war had been working, a series of military trucks were lined up one after the other. Americans with assault rifles in hand were marching the SS men out of the ruins with their hands up and forcing them into the trucks.

"It seems something has happened here," Filin said anxiously.

"It sure does," Rebrov agreed.

At that moment two SS men appeared from the ruins, bent under the weight of a large wooden box. One of them was Günther Tilkowski. After quickly looking around, Günther whistled and he and his partner threw the box down. The two rushed back into the ruins, screaming "Bomb! Bomb!" and disappeared. The Americans could only look on in confusion, but then they rushed after the two men. A moment later, bursts of rifle fire could be heard.

Filin and Rebrov, after exchanging glances, quickened their step.

At the gates of the Palace of Justice stood heavy armored personnel carriers with the white star of the US Army painted on their sides. In the courtyard, several tanks loomed at the corners of the building, with their guns pointed at the nearby street intersection. The courtyard was full of American soldiers, they were to a man all chewing gum and carefully inspecting each civilian who entered or exited the building.

An excited crowd had gathered in the enormous vestibule, chattering in many languages. Rebrov and Filin encountered Gavrik, who was craning his neck in every direction.

"Gavrik, what has been happening here?" Rebrov grabbed him by the arm.

"Rebrov, it's you! Nobody knows what the hell is going on! The Americans suddenly got spooked this morning, they brought in all these soldiers and equipment. They say it has something to do with those prisoners of war from the SS who are put to work here…"

At that moment Peggy suddenly flew into Rebrov, triumphantly holding up two fingers in a V shape. "Victory!", she shouted excitedly into his ear and then ran off again.

Filin, who had been coolly watching this tumultuous crowd, turned towards Rebrov resolutely. "Maybe you can finally tell me what is going on here, comrade major? Who was that woman? What did she tell you? And why has your face lit up like a bride on her wedding day?"

Rebrov, who was indeed finding it difficult to hold back a smile, reported merrily, "That's Peggy Butcher, comrade general. She's a famous American reporter. She sent in an article about how captured SS men were put to work in the Palace of Justice and around it, and if they wanted they could easily try to free the defendants. They could hide the weapons they needed in the ruins nearby, where the American soldiers never look. Plus, in the POW camp where they're being held, she saw with her own eyes that they aren't being watched over carefully, and it wouldn't be difficult to escape from there. Yesterday this report hit the

papers in America and got picked up pretty widely, and today the brass of
the American occupying forces got on Col. Andrus' case, and he decided
to carry out an operation to prevent any attack. And to put an end to the
presence of these captured SS men in the Palace and the area around it."

"You seem to know an awful lot about this Peggy," Filin grumbled,
then scrutinized Rebrov carefully. "Part of your job?"

"I just explained some things to her and helped her obtain some information," Rebrov answered modestly. "You know, comrade general,
that our dashing Col. Andrus can wave away any complaints that our
delegation makes to him, but he can't get away from the American press."

"And you didn't think it necessary to consult your superiors? At least
let them know about things?"

"This is just how things developed, comrade general. We had to act
quickly, but you were in Moscow."

"Just how things developed. Fine, then. Good job. I'm going to the
investigative department, but you stay here and keep an eye on what's
happening."

Filin walked away from the crowd, and then Col. Andrus appeared in
the vestibule, accompanied by several soldiers. As always, he held a staff
in his hand. The reporters present rushed towards him.

"Colonel, is it true that the POWs were readying an attack on the
prison to free their former leaders?"

"Yes. Yesterday it became known to us that several men had escaped
from the POW camp where some of the prisoners had been put to work
on clearing rubble," the colonel answered dryly.

"With weapons?"

"No. But we had already received word that among them are some
who want to break in and free the defendants. That is why I took preventative measures."

"Is that the real reason? Or was it because of Peggy Butcher's article?"

The colonel breathed heavily for a moment, as if to stay calm. When
he had regained control of himself, he said, "Miss Butcher was correct to
raise the issue of security over the defendants and the need to supervise
the prisoners of war more carefully. And although I am convinced that
any attempted assault on the prison would end in failure, we felt it necessary to respond to the statements in the press…"

"But is there any chance that the defendants could still escape or be
freed by others?"

"Put it in your dispatches like this: 'Any possibility that the men
under my watch might escape is strictly ruled out. The measures we

have applied have a strong psychological impact.' If you knew how we're guarding them now, you would undoubtedly agree."

"What happened to those two SS men who ran and hid in the ruins? Did you manage to catch them?"

"One of them was killed during the pursuit. The other one might have been killed, too, but we haven't found his body yet. Searching for him in the ruins would be very dangerous for my men – everything has been shaken by bombing there and the ground might give out under them." He concluded heatedly, "I don't want my men to wind up cripples or die after the war is already over! Now if you'll excuse me, ladies and gentlemen, I've got work to do. But I can assure you, you won't see any more of those SS men around here!"

Notes

A budding SS officer had to immediately realize that he was joining the holy inner sanctum of the state, an elite organization. He had to believe that the Germans are an elite nation, and the SS was the cream of the German people.

SS men were generally selected according racial principles. Their bloodline had to be one-hundred-percent "pure". The requirement of racial purity also applied to the wives of SS men. Lower-ranking men had to prove that their ancestors were all Aryan at least back to the year 1800, but higher-ranking officers or candidates for promotion were required to show that their direct ancestors did not have a drop of non-Aryan blood at least back to 1750.

The SS were convinced that they were a racial elite. The result of this is that they considered it their right and duty to decide whether others had any right to exist.

Membership in the SS involved a large number of
rituals. The rules existing in Nazi Germany put
the SS in a completely unique position. Even
their direct privileges (they did not undergo
compulsory service in the Wehrmacht, they were
paid more than all other professional soldiers)
were endowed with a sort of ideological
asceticism: a person who receives more, is asked
more of.

SS officers were not subject to
the jurisdiction of ordinary courts.
They had their own special courts.

CHAPTER XVIII.
I WON'T FORGIVE AND FORGET

That evening in the press camp's restaurant, Peggy's fellow reporters congratulated her on her success. All of them, professionals with long experience, knew how important it was to make a splash like that. Kraft, cheerful as always, was naturally present, and next to him sat Irina, who was wrapped up in a warm handkerchief in the Russian fashion. Among the diverse, multilingual crowd that filled the restaurant, Irina's was for Rebrov the most welcome and dearest face. Rebrov had been dragged here by the ever-rambunctious Peggy.

Denis felt that the painful break in the relationship between Irina and him in recent days was about to come to an end, and it would have to end with some definitive explanation or step after which there would be no turning back.

Irina suddenly stood up and walked away from the table. He watched her go, enchanted, but then she turned and he caught her glance. He got up and followed her.

The dimly lit park surrounding the press camp was deserted. The black branches of the old trees, woven into a single web, mysteriously swayed and rustled under the unexpectedly warm and humid air. The light of the moon, piercing through the crowns of the trees, shimmered and reflected from puddles. Indistinct sounds came from all around that were mysterious and full of vague premonitions and anxieties…

"Do you remember the short story I gave you?" Irina suddenly asked. "By Bunin? 'Pure Monday'?"

"I do."

"Near the end, when the man and the woman are coming back from the revue at the theatre, and she tells him to let the driver off. And she also says that she had been thinking a great deal about him. I've also been thinking…"

Driven by a sudden impulse, Rebrov embraced her. She did not pull away. She only tilted her head back a little and looked into his eyes. It was clear that something had happened that was more important than anything in his life had ever been before or would be after. It left its mark forever.

Irina suddenly opened her hand and Rebrov saw that she held a key in her palm.

"The princess, Tatyana Vladimirovna, has left for Paris. She left me the key to her apartment…"

The next day, Rebrov was walking down the endless corridors of the Palace of Justice, oblivious to everything around him. He had never been so happy in his life. He was thinking about the previous night, about Irina, and he couldn't quite believe that it had happened to him. He had wanted it to last forever. But for some reason, his memory was continually drawn back to the last minutes that they were together, which had been particularly moving. Denis could still hear Irina's voice as they said goodbye in which, it seemed to him, there was an alarming note of disquiet. This sense of disquiet passed into him as well, and it lay heavily and restlessly on his soul. It still seemed to him that their meeting had gone by with a certain tinge of separation. Suddenly he literally ran into someone and looked up to see who it was. Baron Pavel Rosen was standing before him with wild eyes. His face was deathly pale.

"Forgive me, I was lost in thought," Rebrov apologized and stepped aside to let Rosen past. This was precisely the man who Rebrov did not want to see right now, as he had been hopelessly in love with Irina since they were children.

Rosen continued to stand in his way.

«Sir, I need to discuss something with you,» he said, somewhat grandiloquently.

Rebrov was surprised at this. "Discuss something? What has happened?"

"Let's step aside here. Our conversation should not involve any passersby."

Rebrov considered this and then agreed. He understood that Rosen was presently in a state where he might make a big scene, and that was completely to be avoided.

"Very well. There's a little room at the end of this corridor where no one will trouble us."

When they were away from the eyes of others, Rebrov asked calmly and as graciously as he could, "What did you want to talk to me about? I'm listening, baron."

"It is about Irina Yuryevna Kurakina… I must ask you to end your relationship with the princess. Just let the princess be. Do you hear me? Let Irina be!"

"Excuse me, but did she ask you to talk to me like this?"

"Of course not, and you know that perfectly well!"

"Then let us stop our discussion of the matter. Anything that Irina Yuryevna feels necessarily, she'll tell me about it herself. I have no interest in discussing with you my acquaintance with her. It's a matter only for the two of us. Now, if you'll allow me…"

Rosen nervously grabbed Rebrov by the arm. He was shaking all over. "No, you listen to me. I'm going to ensure this happens!"

"Take your hands off me. Otherwise, this is going to end badly for you…"

Rosen jerked his hand away. "Well, I knew it would be pointless to try to talk to you. To try to get you to understand what a terrible situation Irina is in…"

Rebrov, who was already headed out of the room, stopped. "What do you mean?"

"Irina…" Rosen hesitated, but then went on, "is attracted to you, as a representative of the 'victorious Russian army'! There are many among us émigrés who think that it's the Russian army! The fools! They think that now everything in Russia is going to change, that now it's time to forget the past. Forget everything that happened during the revolution and after it…"

"But you aren't one of those people, I take it?"

"I am not, and I will never be. I don't intend to forgive and forget. I will not betray the memory of those close to me who were wiped off the face of the earth by the boots of drunken proletarians!"

"Fine, I understand. I only ask you to realize that I was born after the revolution, and so it's odd to blame me for what happened then."

"You are nonetheless one of them. You are their successor. But Irina is from our world, and our world has nothing in common with yours. Already people are whispering behind her back, spreading monstrous rumors that she has been recruited by Soviet intelligence, that she's working for you. You cannot imagine what this will do to Maria Alexeyevna."

"And who is Maria Alexeyevna?" Denis asked in a dull voice.

"Irina's mother, who will never forget what your revolting sailors did to her husband and sisters… You don't understand how important Irina is to her family. You don't realize what will happen if your relationship with Irina becomes known! Irina can't go against the wishes of her mother, but if, God forbid, she did, then one of them would certainly take care of her…"

Denis was silent. What could he say in response to this? Then, trying to keep calm, he asked, "What do you want from me?"

"Damn it all," Rosen exclaimed. "I knew it wasn't worth trying to do this! That our tears mean nothing to you. What could you understand, huh? During the revolution it was considered fashionable for your commissars there to make use of aristocratic girls. You're all the same! I hate you!"

Rosen turned on his heels and walked away, clasping his hands behind his back…

Notes

The letter I received from her two weeks later was a short one — an affectionate but firm appeal not to expect to see her any more, not to try to search for her: "I shan't return to Moscow, for the time being I shall do penance, then perhaps I shall finally take my vows in a convent… May God give you the strength not to answer me — it is useless to prolong and add to our misery…"

Ivan Bunin, "Pure Monday"

AND IT WILL BE GIVEN TO YOU

CHAPTER I. DO THIS!

The colossal motor of the international tribunal, something completely unprecedented in history, was gathering momentum and spinning ever faster.

The tribunal rolled like a squeaky wheel, because it was extremely cumbersome and hastily designed. Besides, it faced many opponents who said that a legally impeccable and unbiased trial would be impossible in these circumstances. Yet it practically could not be stopped, for the whole world was crying out for justice. Even the apparent clashes between the legal approaches of the two main actors, the Russians and the Americans, could not stop events from proceeding.

The Soviet investigators had finally won the agreement of the Americans to lead the questioning of the defendants themselves. So far, only American investigators had been able to do so, and the other delegations faced the same limitations as the Russians. The USSR's chief prosecutor Roman Rudenko personally approved the list of questions that would be put to the accused.

In addition, it was vital to determine how the Nazi leaders would behave during the trials, what to expect from them. Would they act in concert, or would each fight to only save himself and heap blame on the others? This was the task of Rebrov who, acting on the orders of Gen. Filin, was present at nearly every interrogation as an assistant to the investigators.

The tension and anxiety in the investigative team, as well as among the entire chief prosecutor's staff, had abated after the meeting in Moscow, where thanks to Gen. Filin the denunciation made by Col. Kosachev had been neutralized. Now they could continue their work at ease. However, wise Gen. Filin warned Rebrov that Kosachev would not forgive his defeat, and that probably Filin and Rebrov would serve as the target for his hatred.

"Now he'll be after us, so don't leave yourself open to attack," Filin warned him. Did he get the hint? It wasn't difficult to tell that Filin was talking about Irina.

After what had happened between them at the home of Princess Trubetskaya, Denis and Irina met seldom, in fits and starts. This was not only because it was hard to meet away from others' eyes, or that both of them were weighed down by responsibilities at work. Rather, it was because both of them understood that what had happened at Princess Trubetskaya's home was a boundary that would either mark the end of their relationship, or turn it into something completely different. Each of them had to decide for themselves about this important matter that their entire future lives depended on. Due to this indecision, any meeting, even any mere glance, seemed to be the last, a farewell pang, or a promise of a future that was as yet unknown but could not be denied.

It was all this uncertainty, which he didn't know how to deal with, that Rebrov was pondering in the interrogation room, where he and Alexandrov were waiting for Joachim von Ribbentrop to be brought in. Ribbentrop had been Minister of Foreign Affairs for the Third Reich. Next to Alexandrov sat a new interpreter, who had arrived from Moscow only days before. She was a very beautiful, elegant, and fashionably dressed woman of around thirty.

When Ribbentrop was brought in, he struck everyone with his appearance. This figure who had once wore smartly fitting tuxedos or the tight uniform of an SS general, now wore a colorless and threadbare shirt with a worn-out collar, over which hung a shapeless brown jacket. On his feet were rough shoes without laces, as the American guards forbade them. Ribbentrop's thin face with sunken cheeks was covered in stubble. After he sat down on the chair placed in the middle of the room this man, who had not long ago been dictating the will of Germany and Hitler to entire countries, leaned forward in a supplicant pose, indicating a complete willingness to answer any questions.

As was the custom of the Americans, the room also filled with onlookers who behaved as if they were witnessing a theatrical production. After Ribbentrop, there unexpectedly appeared none other than Kraft. He perched on a chair in the corner and merrily winked at Rebrov, as if to say, it's been a long time…

"Oh, I have always been a faithful friend of the Soviet Union," Ribbentrop said, looking Alexandrov right in the eye. "In order to get our non-aggression pact with Russia, I had to overcome the great prejudice

against your country in Germany's highest circles. A very great prejudice!" Ribbentrop raised his index finger in emphasis.

Alexandrov nodded and reached for a pack of cigarettes lying on the
table. After taking out a cigarette, he absently slammed his palm on the
table in search of a box of matches that were lying a bit to his side. Ribbentrop suddenly leaned forward quickly and reached out to take the box. He
hurriedly lit a match and held it up to Alexandrov's cigarette. Alexandrov
looked at him in surprise, began smoking, and even nodded in thanks.
Ribbentrop smiled proudly.

"By the way, Herr Alexandrov, haven't we already met in Moscow," he
asked casually. "I remember that among the Russian diplomats, there was
a man with such a name."

"No," Alexandrov answered dryly. "I have never worked for the Ministry of Foreign Affairs."

"Oh, what a pity!" Ribbentrop seemed disappointed. "I still have such
great memories of my visit to Moscow. Everything could have turned out
completely differently if…"

Alexandrov hit the table with his palm. "Mr. Ribbentrop, we're not
here this evening to reminisce but to interrogate you. What relationship
did you personally and your ministry have on drawing up plans to attack
the Soviet Union?"

Ribbentrop placed his hand over his eyes and slightly bent forward, as
if he was racking his brains to remember something. This happened each
time that he had to think over his answer. To buy time, Rebrov noted. But
it wasn't only for that. Ribbentrop's morale had been shattered, he was tormented by fears and his memory often did fail him, though he was able to
endlessly recount insignificant details. And generally he was a weak man,
easily dependent on the will of others.

"I didn't know anything about any plans for war with Russia," Ribbentrop finally came back out of himself. "Nothing. Hitler decided everything
himself or with a narrow circle of associates that I wasn't a member of."

"But there was some diplomatic preparation for the war, to ensure
that Germany's allies would participate in it."

"I wasn't part of that."

"How could that be?" Alexandrov laughed. "You were Minister of
Foreign Affairs and you weren't part of it?"

Ribbentrop threw up his hands in a feminine gesture. "I can assure
you, you won't find any official agreements about that with my signature
on them. None! Germany got support through an oral agreement between Hitler and the leadership of our allied nations."

"But in the plans for Operation Barbarossa, it clearly states that the German military command together with the Ministry of Internal Affairs – which you led – would ensure the participation of Germany's allies in the war."

"I didn't know anything about Barbarossa!" Ribbentrop said, looking Alexandrov right in the eye. "It was not among my responsibilities."

Alexandrov only shook his head in disappointment. "When did you find out that a decision had been made to attack the Soviet Union?"

Ribbentrop again put a hand over his eyes. "I learned of that only on June 22, 1941. Literally hours before German forces entered your territory at Hitler's command. Yes, yes, I realize that that might sound strange to you, but the way things worked in Germany, matters were assigned in such a way that the Ministry of Foreign Affairs didn't know about a lot of things. Often it was the last to find out."

"It seems to have missed out on a lot!" Alexandrov grinned. "Apparently everything."

"You're right," Ribbentrop agreed without batting an eyelid. "That's how things worked."

"But before the attack, you, as minister, convened a meeting of various Third Reich departments and directed the propaganda efforts: a war with the USSR should be depicted for the international public as a purely defensive one, and the Soviet Union should be blamed for everything."

Ribbentrop suddenly sniffed. "I don't remember such a meeting."

"But we've got documentary evidence of it…"

"Maybe there are documents where something to that effect is written, but that doesn't mean it really happened. I was against war with the Soviet Union, and that's why they hid the war preparations from me."

"Tell me, do you know anyone by the name of Bagration-Mukhraneli?

"Who's that?"

"In 1942, a congress of Georgian émigrés in Rome recognized Irakli Bagration-Mukhraneli as the lawful pretender to the throne of an independent Georgia. I'll ask you to note the year and the place: 1942, Rome, the capital of a country ruled by Germany's closest ally and sympathizer Mussolini. The German forces are aiming for Stalingrad and the Caucasus, and it's time to draw up plans to dismember the Soviet Union, including setting our friend the king on the Georgian throne."

"I don't remember anything like that. I didn't deal with these issues."

"But there was a special task force for separating the Caucasus from the USSR after victory. What, the German Ministry of Foreign Affairs didn't know anything about it?"

"Rosenberg dealt with those issues!"

"But Rosenberg claims that you were actively assisting him. Which, you must agree, makes sense considering your position."

Ribbentrop gave Alexandrov a look of entreaty and reproach. "Why are you tormenting me like this? You can't imagine what position I was in. You can't! It was so painful…"

Rebrov, exchanging a glance with Alexandrov, suddenly asked, "Tell me, what if now, after everything that has happened, Hitler appeared here and said, 'Do this!'…"

Ribbentrop looked at Rebrov with astonishment. "Good Lord, how did you guess? I often think about that…"

"What would you do?"

"Oh, I'd obey him. Yes, even after all that has happened. He had such an incredible, diabolical power. Without any doubt, he had been trained by the devil himself. We, ordinary people, easily yielded to him. We worship strength like an idol. Hitler was such an idol for the Germans."

"Are you saying that Hitler forced the German people?"

"Oh, no, he didn't force our people. He seduced and corrupted them. Just like a man seduces a woman. You can't imagine what madness came over us Germans then."

"Over you personally?"

"Me, and every German. It was madness, insanity! You didn't experience this fever! When we were all carried away by that power! First Hitler enchanted us, then he stirred up the whole world, and after that he simply disappeared and left us here to answer for everything that happened. Us, ordinary people, the 'bacilli of the planet'…"

"What are you talking about?" Alexandrov didn't understand and looked at the lovely interpreter in bewilderment. "The 'bacilli of the planet'?"

"That's exactly what Hitler called the human race. We were only its shadow, and now they are going to try us," Ribbentrop's voice was now barely audible. "For what? Why do we need these trials? Is it really not possible to find a more peaceful solution? The victors are going to heap up hatred upon hatred. These mountains of hatred will destroy us all, they'll cover the whole world. I am ready to accept any sentence, but without this awful trial." Ribbentrop looked completely pitiful, his eyes were filled with tears.

Kraft, who had been sitting in the corner, got up and headed for the door. At the threshold, he looked back and made a sign to Rebrov that they should talk.

When Ribbentrop, weeping and barely able to move his legs, had been taken from the room, Alexandrov, Rebrov, and the interpreter were left alone for some time in the empty room.

"Am I free to go?" the interpreter asked, gathering her papers.

Alexandrov nodded.

When the door had closed behind her, Alexandrov said thoughtfully, "She's new here, just arrived. Her name's Beletskaya. She knows German like a native, but…" He raised a finger in warning. "She's got a husband. And not just any husband, a general."

"Well, so what?" Rebrov asked, surprised. He was still impressed by Ribbentrop's interrogation and how the man had behaved.

"Never mind," Alexandrov smiled, thinking his own thoughts. "It's just that she's a very beautiful woman, major. Everyone here started looking at her, and you can see why."

Rebrov shrugged and asked impatiently, "Georgy Nikolayevich, do you think that he'll act the same way at the trial?"

"Who?"

"Ribbentrop."

"Oh, him. Who the hell knows. That remains a mystery, and it is precisely what you and I need to figure out."

Notes

In the early hours of June 22, 1941, I waited with Ribbentrop in his Wilhelmstrasse office for the Soviet Ambassador Dekanosov… I had never seen Ribbentrop so excited as he was in the five minutes before Dekanosov's arrival. He walked up and down his room like a caged animal.

"The Führer is absolutely right to attack Russia now," he said to himself rather than to me… "The

Russians will certainly attack us themselves if
we do not do so now."

From the memoirs of Hitler's
personal interpreter Paul Schmidt

CHAPTER II. COUNTER-ACCUSATIONS

Naturally, Rebrov found Kraft in the press bar. He had a few bottles of beer in front of him, was smoking a cigarette and constantly nodding in greeting to acquaintances, and he seemed, like always, extremely pleased with life.

"I didn't know you visit the interrogations," Rebrov said. "Why?"

"Well, first of all, it's interesting to see close-up those monsters who almost conquered the world," Kraft laughed. "And secondly, business. I'm looking for materials for my publishing company, things that would make a lot of money. Mr. Ribbentrop, they inform me, is constantly writing something. Why not obtain the rights to it, if it's interesting?"

"Well, I don't know who would be interested in that. A minister who hurries to light someone's cigarette! He's a lackey, and he doesn't even hide that's he a lackey. Plus, he's constantly lying and half-crazy from fear…

Kraft smiled at Rebrov's vehemence. "You still haven't mentioned that before he became minister, he went around hawking champagne."

"Exactly! He's a pathetic salesman!"

"Well, you see, it's not so simple. Hitler in his time was a crazy homeless man that no one was interested in. Unemployed, too. And then what happened? By the way, when World War I broke out, Ribbentrop was living quietly in Canada and doing business. But he came back to Germany completely voluntarily to fight, and he hid the fact that he had had a kidney removed. He was awarded the Iron Cross and promoted to 1st Lieutenant. So, he's not the worm he might have seemed to you today. Or he wasn't always a worm, at any rate. By the way, from what I hear, the other defendants don't like him and even look down on him."

"Why?"

"Well, you see, he's an outsider for them. He only joined the Nazi Party quite late, in 1932, shortly before they seized power. For the old Nazis, he was this opportunist that wormed his way in. They had been fighting Communists back in the early Twenties in the Munich beer halls, beating each other over the head with benches and mugs. But now this salesman comes along, and a guy who added the aristocratic tag 'von' to his name. But Hitler really liked him after being invited once to his home. It was a nice little middle-class home, where Hitler seemed very touched by how Frau Ribbentrop kept house with motherly tenderness. It was her who taught the Führer how to use a knife and fork. Ribbentrop told Hitler a lot about his life in Canada and America, where Hitler had never been.

"But he did become a Nazi!"

"I don't think he became a real, genuine Nazi. He might have sympathized with some of their views, but Ribbentrop was never an anti-Semite. There were a lot of Jews among his business partners and friends. He could have hardly subscribed to the Nazi's racial theories, so he certainly wasn't a fanatic. He wasn't a Goebbels, Rosenberg, or Himmler. But he was simply fascinated by Hitler personally and he subordinated himself to Hitler. On the other hand, he was very afraid of Hitler. Once Hitler yelled at him, and the horror marked him for life. So, he would do anything the Führer asked of him without questioning it. He might not have agreed with what was being done, but he was simply in no state to resist. He was physically incapable, you see. Just like many other people."

"You know, sometimes I wonder if that Spear of Destiny really did help Hitler. Otherwise, how could you explain how this nobody, who now everyone claims didn't know anything, became such a superman for the Germans? How can you believe that looking at him? It's a real mystery."

"Well, maybe you prefer mystery! But you know, our American psychologists are very fond of doing tests now. They measure intelligence with all kinds of questions. They've even tested these 'nobodies', as they seem to you. It turns out that these pitiful little men have quite a high IQ."

"That's hard to believe."

"Testing showed that the average IQ across the defendants was 120. They only found a lower IQ in three of them."

"Do you remember who they were?"

"Well, it was Streicher, Sauckel, and Kaltenbrunner. The others had higher IQs. Goering, Schacht, Seyss-Inquart, and Dönitz showed very high scores. *Very* high!"

"What about Ribbentrop?"

"Pretty high. So, you shouldn't think these are all idiots and psychopaths. These people managed to take advantage of their historical situation, to ride the wave as they say. But now each of them has been shot down and only cares about saving himself. Each of them is only thinking about how to survive, at any price, and is ready to do anything for it, though they don't know how or if it's possible at all. Plus, a person can't bear such a crushing fall from the height of power down to nothing. Prison breaks people who aren't used to it. But the hell with them! What about our lovely, beautiful Irina. You don't know?"

"No," Rebrov managed to get out with an effort. "What happened?"

"She looks like she's tired and has a lot on her mind. Well, that's how you Russians usually look. But I thought she was worried about something specifically.

Rebrov shrugged and stood up. He tried to avoid looking Kraft in the eye. "I've got to go. I've got a lot of work…"

"Yeah, I understand. The closer the start of the trials, the more things to worry about."

Kraft looked at him with understanding and even sympathy, but Rebrov found both unbearable.

Gen. Filin was hearing Rebrov's report on Ribbentrop's interrogation. He listened attentively, but not for a second could he stop thinking about some things of his own.

Rebrov, who had remained unpersuaded by his talk with Kraft, didn't hold back in describing how pitiful Ribbentrop was, how he wasn't ashamed of his horror in front of the court, how he ingratiated himself to his interrogator and guards. How he tried to show in everything that he was deeply struck by the pain that all humanity had suffered due to the Nazis' actions, which he now understood were criminal. But when he came to his own fault in it, he immediately struck the pose of an innocent person who had been slandered.

Filin, however, as he was listening to Rebrov's heated comments, was thinking about how the entire tribunal seemed to largely depend on the shattered and defeated Ribbentrop, who was now openly despised by his fellow defendants. Moscow had made a categorical demand that if the non-aggression pact signed between Germany and the USSR had to come up at the trial, then it was only to be according to a version offered by the Soviets – for example, just as it was stated in Molotov's telegram: "On June 22, 1941 a Hitlerian conspiracy, perfidiously violating the non-aggression pact, attacked Soviet territory without any declaration of war, and therefore initiated an aggressive war against the USSR." Not a word more was to be said, under any circumstances, and they must ensure that at any cost. Any mention of a "secret protocol" to the pact, which might be the subject of much speculation, was not to be permitted. The same went for any political interpretation of the events leading to the signing of the agreement which the British sought.

As far as the political interpretation went, matters were clear. It could be wielded in any direction. Before the war broke out, everyone was searching for a way to avoid a confrontation with Germany, which was aware of its might, but they wanted to do that at someone else's expense. All attempts by the USSR to forge an alliance with the West against Hitler had been fruitless. The West hemmed and hawed, intending to ultimately leave the Soviet Union one on one with Germany. Even Churchill referred to that policy as the greatest foolishness, admitting that the Kremlin had lost faith in the ability to establish joint security with the Western powers, and so Russia had to go it alone. But much time had passed since then, Hitler had been defeated, and now many sought to prove things. Yet, in the Russians' actions a person could, if he wished, find many things that didn't fit with his ideas of good and evil. But where were such people with their ideas when the Russians were drowning in their own blood at Moscow and Stalingrad!

"Comrade general, are you listening to me?" Rebrov was looking at Filin with surprise.

"Sorry, I got lost in thought. OK, when it comes to Ribbentrop, on one hand everything is clear."

"And on the other hand?"

"On the other hand, it's completely unclear how he's going to behave during his trial. What can we expect from him? Send a message to Hector that we are interested in precisely this."

"To me, everything is clear: he's going to act like a sycophant and weasel out of questions. He'll lie. He'll try to pretend that he doesn't remember anything. That's all. You couldn't expect anything else from him."

"Fine, then. But what if he's capable of suddenly making counter-accusations? Or if others can push him to do so?"

Rebrov didn't understand. "What counter-accusations could he make?"

"Alright, we'll talk about it some other time," Filin sighed. "Now I really need to look in at Pokrovsky's, and you prepare an encrypted message for Hector."

Notes

Altogether, the information which their intelligence work was able to collect through clandestine operations in World War II useful to the defense of the Soviets was about as good as any nation could hope to get.

Allen Dulles, CIA director

CHAPTER III. SECRET AGREEMENTS

The desk of the Soviet deputy chief prosecutor, Col. Yuri Vladimirovich Pokrovsky, was so piled high with papers that there no longer seemed any possibility of finding any one of them. Thin and gray-haired with round spectacles and the square mustache favored by many Soviet high-ranking officers of the time, Pokrovsky was clearly shaken as he read through the telegrams that Moscow had been sending him in Rudenko's absence.

Pokrovsky stood up as several men entered the room one after another: Alexandrov, Filin, and the assistant to the USSR chief prosecutor Maj. Gen. Nikolai Dmitriyevich Zorya, a handsome, dark-haired man of around forty. During the war Zorya had been a military prosecutor in the army, then an assistant to a senior prosecutor at the front, and before he was assigned to Nuremberg he had worked as the head of the legal department for the Soviet office of the Allied Control Council in Austria, though he remained a mere colonel. Everyone who came in the door was a general and so he felt somewhat awkward. Filin sensed this awkwardness and hurried to get down to business. "How did the meeting of the prosecution go?"

"They went ape," Pokrovsky showed a gesture of distress. "When I said that we ask that the trials be slightly delayed because Rudenko has fallen ill, Jackson practically hit the ceiling, he was so angry. And then he said that the United States would start the trials at the designated time, even if they had to do it alone."

"And the British?" Zorya asked.

"Well, like always they side with the Americans. They said that the Soviet Union should officially announce that it takes responsibility for any further delays. The French are on our side, though. They even threatened to pull out if the trials went on without the Soviet prosecutor. There was a big fuss, basically."

"How did it all end?" Alexandrov asked anxiously.

"We agreed to meet again in the evening."

"Have you already reported this to Moscow?" Filin asked.

"I did. Here's the latest telegram from them: 'If, at the meeting of the prosecution, the majority are against our proposal to delay the trials, then you should announce that you are not authorized to take part in the trials should they begin without the USSR chief prosecutor, and that you will have to inform the Soviet government about the rejection of their proposal and the situation that results from this.' Those are my instructions. What should I do now?"

"Well, that's a tough equation to solve," Filin shook his head mockingly.

"I also sent them an explanation: 'Our proposal contains a threat to withdraw from the trials should they start, but is not yet a complete refusal. Thus, our proposal is a way of putting pressure on the other prosecutors in order to achieve our goal.'"

The pause that followed was quite long.

"You're in trouble, Yuri Vladimirovich," Alexandrov raised his eyebrows. "That's not just an equation, that's a whole proof!"

Pokrovsky looked around at everyone, clearly seeking support. "There's another thing. It's easy to understand Jackson. The order of opening remarks is supposed to be the following. Jackson will address the court first and his remarks will be built upon the documents, on examination of the evidence, and so will take two or three days. After Jackson speaks, his assistants will read to the court all of the documents that Jackson referred to in his remarks. That will take another few days. The second person to speak will be the UK prosecutor, and that will take at least one full court session. Then, the documents will be read to the court. The third to speak is the French prosecutor, and then we have Christmas and New Year. Rudenko will be the last to address the court, with concluding remarks. The British are saying, why delay the trials if Rudenko is going to appear in a month at least?"

"Of course," Alexandrov threw up his hands, "but just try to explain that to Moscow. And it's easy to understand Moscow, too. How could the trials start without us? What did we shed so much blood for?"

"I think that Moscow is more concerned about undesirable questions," Filin said thoughtfully. "And the pressure on the committee is connected with this. Moscow wants to rule out any possibility of provocations."

"Well, a lot of efforts have been made, even while comrade Rudenko was still here," Pokrovsky seemed relieved to report. "A general resolution of the prosecution committee was adopted: the prosecutors intend to energetically avoid any slippery issues and not let the accused take over or get the court bogged down in discussion. In that light, they saw it would be good to draw up a list of matters that shouldn't be discussed at the trials, so that they can be immediately steered away from in the courtroom."

"Does Moscow already know about this?"

"I told them about it today."

An officer knocked on the door and then entered the office with yet another telegram in hand. He handed it over to Pokrovsky, who read it and then looked around at the other men present. "Moscow does not object to the trials starting in Rudenko's absence. He himself will be in Nuremberg at the earliest opportunity."

"Moscow, Moscow…" Filin said in conclusion to no one in particular. Each of the men could understand his crowning remark in his own way.

Filin and Alexandrov left Pokrovsky and Zorya to resolve some matters of their own. In the corridor, Filin asked, "Do you also think, like Rebrov, that Ribbentrop isn't capable of any surprises?"

Alexandrov was slow to answer. "The way he looks now, no, I don't. What could happen? But if someone knew him well and knew how to put pressure on him… The question is, who?"

"Yes, there are two possibilities. Either the Americans, or his own fellow Germans. Among his fellow Germans, the only person who could do it is Goering, who is now making himself out to be the leader of all the accused, like a prison Führer. He'll place his bet on trying to spark a fight between us and the Allies. Ribbentrop has an obedient nature, he'll listen to Goering, but not to the point of putting himself in the line of fire."

"Perhaps," Alexandrov agreed. "At least for the time being…"

"The other possibility is the Americans. We don't know what they have been up to in the prison. We know they've been up to something, but not what exactly. They've been noting down everything that the prisoners say among themselves when they think that no one is listening. And then they've got these so-called prison psychiatrists and psychoanalysts. In fact, they are probably hired and trained to talk with the prisoners confidentially, prick them, assess their morale, and find their weak spots. For the prisoners, they are like a light through the window. The reports of their conversations in the prison cells will immediately get to the American prosecutors and US intelligence. And of course, one can not only listen, but give advice, direct them, and advise them to, for example, bring up the matter of secret agreements.

Notes

Leon Goldensohn, a young American doctor and psychiatrist, observed the mental state of the prisoners and main witnesses. All of them, he claims, were yesterday the devil's henchmen. Now, frightened, each of them tried to make a good impression on the Americans, obtain some small advantage, and thus possibly save his own life.

As a rule, they didn't hold back in giving information, especially if it added to the guilt of others. They all thought themselves completely unimportant and innocent.

Goldensohn, a good listener and observer, with even an understanding of the language of gestures, talked with them in German. These were conversations with figures from a world frozen over, as he would later write…

CHAPTER IV. ARE YOU WITH US?

In this half-underground beer hall in a part of Nuremberg that had survived, it seemed that every speculator, prostitute, and other dark figures of the city gathered. In spite of the terrible beer, the place was thick with smoke. Olaf slipped the owner several dollars and the latter immediately brought out a separate table and three chairs and set them in the corner. After wiping the table with his towel, he asked what they would be having.

"Do you have real beer?" Olaf asked, sitting with his back to the wall so that he could see the entire space and the entrance.

"We do, for especially distinguished guests, but…"

"Don't worry about money," Olaf said, setting a pack of real American cigarettes in front of him. A couple of brightly made-up girls with greedy eyes immediately drew closer to his table. "And tell your whores not to bother me," Olaf said firmly, looking into the owner's eyes with an unblinking glance.

The owner nodded understandingly and waved the girls away with his towel like flies. The girls sighed heavily and turned, disappointed, to look at the other customers.

Olaf looked over this filthy crowd and thought that under Hitler – and here one had to give him credit – none of these people had been around. They either didn't exist back then, or they didn't stick out. The might of the Reich hung over their heads and threatened to crush anyone without mercy. Now this might had been destroyed by the weapons and bombs of the Allies, and the Germans had been turned into a herd of loose and greedy wimps. Or perhaps into hungry, frightened sheep. To everyone his due.

The owner set a mug of beer in front of him, but he didn't hurry to leave – he waited for Olaf to judge its quality. Olaf took a sip. It was real beer, German.

"Good," Olaf nodded. "That's how it should be. When they arrive, bring me the same."

The owner nodded in a soldierly fashion and withdrew. This man remembers what order is, Olaf thought.

Recently, thanks to the baron, he had started looking much more calmly at what was happening around him. Germany's defeat had lifted up a filthy foam, the baron felt, but soon everything would settle down. The Germans would remember their eternal virtues as a people and get to work. There would not again be a complete catastrophe and national humiliation like after the First World War, when Germany was trampled upon, on its knees. The Americans didn't at all seek to turn Germany into a "potato field", and they concluded that its complete collapse would only benefit Russia. Moreover, the West could soon use Germany's might to counterbalance the Soviet Union's incredible power. So, Germany would not be destroyed, they would let her rise up, and then they would see. Today no one could tell how the new postwar world would turn out; it was clear only that there would be a confrontation between the West and the Soviets. That confrontation was already on the way and gathering strength by the day. Only the upcoming trials over the Nazi leaders still held them together…

"Are you Olaf Todt?" A young, dark-haired woman with resolutely pursed lips and wearing a tightly buttoned coat was standing by his table. She might have been called pretty, if not for the overly severe, even fierce expression on her sickly pale face.

"Maybe."

"Günther sent me."

"But where is Günther?"

"He'll be here soon."

"He sent you here to scout," Olaf laughed, "while he's lying in ambush…"

The girl didn't appreciate his joke, she only looked at him with cold eyes, occasionally throwing a cautious glance to the side.

"Sit down," Olaf nodded at the chain. "Or people will think you're a prostitute trying to get a higher price."

The girl sat down.

"What, you think I look like a prostitute?" she asked, without any particular interest.

"Not really. Although these days there are a lot of German girls who behave that way."

"I'm not one of them."

"I see that. What is your name?"

"Giselle."

The owner appeared at their table with two full mugs in his hands. "The same stuff," he said emphatically, placed the mugs on the table, and then respectfully withdrew.

"Try the beer," Olaf said. "You won't regret it."

The girl answered nothing, but she took a sip of the beer. She was damn taciturn, and probably occupied by some thoughts of her own. Like any extremist should be. Olaf wondered what relationship she had with Günther and what linked them.

At a neighboring table, an elderly gentleman threw his empty mug down on the table and loudly cried, "Is this really beer? This is water! Look at what those Nazi scoundrels have reduced Germany to! When will the Russians and Americans finally take care of them? Let them all hang!"

Giselle cast a fleeting glance at the man, one that Olaf noticed was full of contempt and hatred. Clearly, the girl had been through the Hitler Youth and they had done a pretty good job with her.

"Hi, Olaf! I'm happy to see you again, buddy." Günther Tilkowski was standing in front of them. He was wearing a coat with the collar turned up and a hat pulled low over his eyes.

"God, you look like an American spy!" Olaf laughed.

"I'd be one, but I don't know if they'd take me," Günther chuckled as he sat down across from him. He picked the full mug up and took a long draft from it. "Ha, now this is beer! Usually they serve complete crap here. The same crap as all of Germany now! But all the beer you get in the Palace of Justice is real, I take it?"

Olaf nodded. "We need to talk one on one."

"I don't think that Giselle would bother us, but if that's what you want…" Günther turned to the girl. "Go have a walk, I'll be back soon."

Giselle stood up with the same mask-like face and left the beer hall.

"Where are you staying now?" Olaf asked.

"What difference does it make!" Günther waved the question away as he again drank from the mug. "Well, at Giselle's. But so what? Better you tell me what you need."

"I want to know what you're planning to do. I've received information that a plot is being hatched…"

"What do I have to do with it?"

"Knock it off, Günther, I'm being serious. You want to free that fatso Hermann and the rest."

Günther leaned forward and said defiantly, "No, Olaf, I want to show those American warriors that they're in Germany, not Alabama. I want to show them that Germany still lives, that there are people in it to be reckoned with. That's what I have in mind."

"And how do you intend to do that?"

"How?" Günther was silent for a moment. "You know you don't blab to outsiders about things like that. But I can tell Olaf Todt. If Olaf Todt betrayed me, then there's nothing left for me in this world. Now, the plan is very simple. We'll infiltrate the Palace of Justice, take hostages from among the Americans and British, and demand that they release the prisoners in exchange for them."

"Are you sure you can do it?"

Günther drank down the rest of his beer with relish. "Everything's already decided. Do you really think that Günther Tilkowski is just going to submissively haul bricks around and sing for his prison soup? Plus, we've been given good money for this operation. If everything goes well, we will immediately be moved to South America."

Olaf was silent for a moment. "What about Giselle?"

"She's with me. She's part of our plan. A very important part. I've known her for a long time."

"What is she, some kind of fanatic? She worshiped the Führer?"

"She's a German and she loves Germany."

"I see. Hitler Youth school."

"All her family died in the bombing of Dresden, when the British tried to wipe the city from the face of the earth along with everyone living there."

"Incidentally, Goering, who you're trying to save, swore that no bombs would fall on German soil."

Günther shrugged. "You and I made promises, too. Times change."

"Yes, times are changing and a person has to see that."

Günther looked at Olaf with a serious mien. "You don't need to tell me what kind of world we live in now. I know that no less well than you do. But I've already made my decision, and Giselle has already obtained a pass for the Palace, through one of the American officers guarding it. Now she's studying the whole building, all the entrances, passages, emergency exits. She has already established that the best time for an attack would be lunch or dinnertime, when the prisoners are brought to the cafeteria down a narrow staircase next to an emergency exit. The personnel guarding them during that time are negligible. Plus, our POWs are working in the kitchen. We need to establish contact with them, and some of them are sure to help us. You're working in the Palace now, what do you think about our plan?"

"It's very risky. It's got a lot of gaps and assumptions. Plus, since you escaped, the prison guard has been on the alert. If you want to act, then do it a bit later, when the Americans have calmed down."

"So, are you with us?"

Olaf was silent for a moment. "Well, I'm not against you, at any rate, Günther."

Notes

It is difficult to describe the hypnotic effect that Hitler had on the people who encountered him. Even those who were utterly opposed to the Führer recognized the power that he radiated and felt an irresistible attraction to him, though later they felt confusion and guilt. This quality is usually inherent in strong personalities, and it was charisma, not an emanation of evil, that was Hitler's most prominent trait.

Traudl Junge, the youngest
of the Führer's three secretaries

CHAPTER V.
PROFESSIONAL MISCONDUCT

Rebrov was lying on his bed in his hotel room, absentmindedly staring at the ceiling. His thoughts were confused, one moment he was thinking about Irina, the next trying to make sense of the latest message from Hector where the agent had given his own report about the games being played with Ribbentrop.

It seemed that Goering, who had become increasingly emboldened in recent weeks, was trying to convince Ribbentrop to pay special attention to the secret protocol of the Germany-Russia non-aggression pact and announce its existence at the very first opportunity. He was being supported by Frank, who claimed that Ribbentrop should say that there was a pact between Hitler and the Russians, and so Stalin and Molotov should be sitting in the dock next to them. Ribbentrop was ignoring this or saying that these agreements were being given too much importance, that they had meant nothing. Goering was threatening Ribbentrop that if he himself "wasn't up to it", then Goering would himself announce the facts to the whole world. But Ribbentrop realized that disclosing the secret protocol meant taking all of the responsibility for it on himself, as Hitler was no longer around! And why should he, Ribbentrop, anger the Russians? Especially when there was no original copy of this pact.

Rebrov got up and went to the window. Stone and twisted iron lay piled in front of him in the red glow of the setting sun. Although he had long since grown used to this landscape, this time it seemed especially terrible and foreboding. On the windowsill lay the notepad with the hotel's letterhead that he had found in a drawer the day before. In blackletter script it proudly declared that Nuremberg was the *Parteitag* city, the site of Nazi Party congresses…

As usual, he had to force his thoughts to focus on the situation with Ribbentrop and the prewar agreements, for the war – everything he had seen and lived through during it – had pushed the prewar era so far away into the past that it was hard to believe in its reality, or in the importance of what had happened then. God, what difference did it make when everyone knew that war was on the horizon and they could only hope that it wouldn't break out the next day but just a little later.

Rebrov graduated high school with top marks (receiving a "golden diploma", not yet the red diploma of the later Soviet years). He had found it easy to study, because he had remarkable powers of memory. When he got new textbooks at the beginning of the school year, he looked through them and remembered much of their contents from the first reading. He was not yet 17 years old at the time, so he was not called up for military service but rather went straight to university. Over all his student years he could only think about one thing: would he manage to complete his studies, or would war break out first? Nearly everyone was sure that the war would be with Germany specifically and so Rebrov dived into studies of German. When the USSR signed the non-aggression pact with Germany, everyone thought it was only an attempt to ward off a war and that was all. Rebrov often spoke about this with his father and was under no illusions on this account. Now, when the USSR had won the war at the cost of countless victims and enormous suffering, there was a need to make sense of what had happened then, who had signed treaties with whom. As Rebrov's father had said to him a few years before, everyone had been trying to conclude pacts among themselves or with Hitler, but they all clearly understood that this wouldn't save them. They only hoped to draw out the days of peace a little bit longer.

He was drawn out of his thoughts of the past by a knock at the door. Rebrov opened it to find Gavrik standing there.

"Come in."

Gavrik entered the room and nervously glanced around.

"Why do you look like that, Gavrik?" Rebrov asked, surprised. "What happened?"

"Something happened," Gavrik giggled.

He paced around the room and suddenly let out, "I have committed professional misconduct."

"You?"

"That's right." Gavrik drew an envelope from his trouser pocket and handed it to Rebrov.

"What's this?"

"It's a letter to the leadership of the Soviet delegation."

"Well, I'm not one of them. Why did you bring it to me?"

"I wanted you to read it. Don't worry, the envelope is already open. Come on, read it already!"

"Alright then," Rebrov said in a reassuring tone. "Why don't you have a glass of water or something in the meantime."

While Gavrik was pouring himself some water, Rebrov quickly scanned the message. "I would like to bring to the Soviet command's attention that its staff member Denis Rebrov has entered into an intimate relationship with an interpreter from the French delegation. The nature of their relationship is such that information, even of the most serious kind, could easily leak." There was no signature.

Rebrov folded up the sheet of paper and stuck it back in the envelope. "Where did you get this from?"

"That letter was brought by American courier along with a set of interrogation transcripts," Gavrik explained. "He threw it down on the table like he usually does and didn't ask for a signature. Since the letter looked unusual and I was the officer on duty, I opened it. No one else has seen it. Right after I got off duty, I brought it here to you."

"Thanks, Gavrik," Rebrov sighed. "But you could get in real trouble if they found out. Especially if our friend Kosachev gets wind of it."

"I'm telling you, no one else saw it. No one knows anything. The courier, as you know, couldn't care less. So, we can just dispose of the letter. But you've got to understand that everyone is already talking about your relationship with Kurakina. You're lucky that Kosachev doesn't know yet."

"He knows."

"He does? Then it's strange that you're still here!"

"That's just how things are. Filin told him that I've been meeting Kurakina for work-related reasons."

"You think he believes that?"

"I do, but not entirely. In any event, I get the feeling his men are watching me."

"I'd imagine so!"

"But it's not about me. I'm not worried about myself."

"I understand. If a letter like that reached the French delegation, the poor princess is going to be in trouble."

"Yes, that's the thing! I've got a cover, but she has nothing."

"What jerk would scribble a message like this, huh?" Gavrik, normally mild-mannered, was fired up. "You know, judging from everything, it wasn't one of our guys who wrote this."

"Well, it's not a very big secret," Rebrov grinned. "But indeed, it's not from one of our guys. I didn't expect something like this from him!"

"You think you know who it is?"

"I'm ninety-nine percent certain, but I've still got to make sure."

"What are you going to do?"

"You have any advice?"

"You wouldn't listen to it anyway," Gavrik waved his question away. "But you need to plug this leak. If you need my help… I think she's a very nice person."

"Who?" Rebrov, who was now thinking deeply, asked distractedly.

"Her Grace, Princess Kurakina, that's who!"

Rebrov looked at Gavrik in surprise. "Listen, Gavrik, you haven't fallen in love with her, have you?"

Gavrik's face suddenly turned red and he shook his head desperately. "You're crazy, Rebrov! You're talking nonsense!"

Notes

SMERSH operatives working in Nuremberg have asked Moscow to issue them passports, as due to the large influx of foreigners, the Americans have tightened the rules for residency and carried out a number of police measures. At the same time, they have intensified their intelligence and counter-intelligence work among the Soviet delegation. The lack of passports has impeded their ability to move around the city and carry out operations.

From the SMERSH archives

CHAPTER VI.
IT'S A MATTER OF YOUR HONOR

He waited for Baron Rosen in the hallway leading to the French delegation. Rosen walked with his head down, as if he didn't see anything around him. Rebrov caught up with him and gripped him by the arm strongly. Rosen, startled, turned and stared wordlessly at Rebrov with his wild eyes open wide in surprise.

"Mr. Baron, we need to talk," Rebrov said, in a voice that would not take no for an answer.

"Let me go!" The baron tried to jerk his arm away. "What the hell is this? I have nothing to say to you, Mr. Chekist!"

"It's in your own best interest, Mr. Baron. Otherwise…"

"Don't try to scare me!" With a frenzied effort, Rosen finally pulled his arm free. "Don't even bother! We're not in the basement of Lubyanka where you can do whatever you want!"

"I'll be expecting you in 15 minutes at the fountain in the square," Rebrov calmly said. "It's a matter of your honor. Exactly fifteen minutes."

A light rain turned into snow and then suddenly stopped. Rebrov was standing by the fountain with his hands stuffed into his pockets. He was looking at the sculpture of a nude woman that adorned the fountain. She had miraculously survived the war unscathed and her nude figure was particularly absurd among the rubble.

He didn't even hear Rosen approach. The baron halted a step away and looked at Rebrov with his chin pointed forward. He looked like he was ready for anything.

"Why did you do something so mean to me?" Rebrov asked coldly.

"First of all, I don't understand what you're talking about," the baron said arrogantly, though his voice faltered. "Secondly, when it comes to people like you, there can be no talk of meanness."

"Of course, I'm a bloodthirsty Chekist."

"That's right. Your predecessors called my parents terrible vermin that had to be eradicated at *any* cost."

"Look, baron, we've already gone over that. I'll remind you again that during the revolution I hadn't even been born yet."

"That changes nothing," Rosen gritted his teeth.

"Fine," Rebrov nodded. "So as far as I go, things are clear. When it comes to me, you can allow yourself any action or any thought. But Irina… You do love her, after all. And yet you do something so mean, something that could destroy her."

"Don't you dare talk about my feelings for Princess Kurakina! Do you hear me? Don't you dare!"

Rebrov suddenly felt pity for Rosen. He really did love Irina, with a long and desperate love, and he could not help himself. But he could not blame Rebrov for the fact that Irina did not share his feelings, that was just how life had turned out.

"I'm trying to save her," Rosen suddenly burst out. "But now it's already hopeless, you have already ruined her. The only thing that could save her is if you went away. That's why I need you to disappear. Whether you're sent off to Siberia or Magadan, it's all the same to me. I don't owe you anything, you don't deserve any pity from me. You have ruined her life, and the only thing left for me is to destroy you, at any cost. No, I won't just calm down. You hear me? I won't!"

Rebrov looked at his face distorted by rage and thought of how this man was leaving him no choice. One might feel some understanding and sympathy for him, but he had to be stopped.

"Calm down, baron. Just calm down and knock it off. Stop doing mean things, things that are going to embarrass you later. Otherwise, I will destroy you."

"How? With a bullet in the back of my neck? A noose around my neck? Those are the methods your kind uses!"

Rebrov shook his head. "There's a more terrible punishment for you, baron. You are a member of the aristocracy, and you should understand the concept of honor. If you continue to write such ridiculous denunciations, then your spiteful actions will become known not only to everyone here, but in Paris as well. You'll look in front of your friends and loved ones like the person who gave Princess Kurakina up to the Soviet authorities." Rebrov turned and walked away without saying goodbye.

"I hate you!" Rosen whispered as he watched him go. "I hate you!" Tears came into his eyes.

They stood naked at the window in Princess Trubetskaya's apartment and watched the mysteriously gleaming branches of the trees outside, which remained encrusted in a transparent shell after the icy rain the night before. This garden of ice seemed unreal, an invention or fantasy, just like everything that had happened between them.

Irina ran her fingers lightly along the scar on his shoulder.

"What's the matter with you today?" Rebrov turned to her. "What's wrong?"

"They told me that something bad might happen to you because of me. You could be sent to Moscow or even to Siberia."

"Who told you that?"

"It doesn't matter."

"Was it Rosen?"

"What difference does it make?"

"Don't listen to him, he's just jealous. I even feel sorry for him."

"Do you really?"

"Can you believe it? But what about you, too? Nothing bad could happen to you? Do you realize who you've gotten involved with?"

"I don't know, I haven't really thought about it. Well, they could send me back to Paris. But that wouldn't be the end of the world. Just think, I might lose my job! We Russian princesses aren't used to poverty…"

Notes

In late 1944 de Gaulle made a visit to the Soviet Union. He wanted most of all to establish contact with Stalin. His main goal was to sign a pact between the USSR and France. De Gaulle said that it was necessary to "somehow restore French-Russian solidarity — which was the natural order of things — both in the face of the German threat and the attempt to establish an Anglo-American hegemony.

Konstantin Melnik,
a Russian emigrant's son and,
under de Gaulle, the de facto
head of the French secret services

CHAPTER VII.
A DREAM GIRL FOR MEN
WHO AWAITED DEATH

The courtroom on the third floor of the Palace of Justice looked not just severe but gloomy, even foreboding. The dark-green marbled walls covered with panels of dark wood made any person who looked at them shudder with a sense of piercing cold. All of the windows were tightly curtained so that daylight could not enter the room.

A long table for the tribunal's judges was set on a raised platform. Behind their chairs hung large flags of each of the victor nations: the USSR, USA, Great Britain, and France.

The defendants' dock with two rows of seats was located at the other end of the courtroom opposite, so that the judges and the defendants were always facing one another. A whole line of American soldiers with white helmets, white shirts, and truncheons in their hands stood behind the accused. In front of the accused, as if to protect them from the judges, were three rows of seats where the defense attorneys fluttered, resembling in their black and purple robes a flock of crows.

Rebrov, who had been occupied with yet another message from Hector, arrived late to the beginning of the first court session. He made his way to the onlookers' balcony when the US chief prosecutor Jackson was already speaking:

"May it please Your Honors: the privilege of opening the first trial in history for crimes against the peace of the world imposes a grave responsibility. The wrongs which we seek to condemn and punish have been so calculated, so malignant, and so devastating, that civilization cannot tolerate their being ignored, because it cannot survive their being repeated…"

As Rebrov stood up on his toes to better see Jackson, he suddenly noticed Peggy's impressive head of hair in the first row. She was dressed today in an American military uniform and leaning on her arms on the railing, attentively looking over the courtroom. Remarkably, there was an empty chair next to her.

Denis thought for a brief moment and then made his way forward and sat down next to her. Leaning over and saying in a low voice, "Hello, Peggy," he was immediately hit by a wave of expensive perfume. "We haven't seen each other for some time…" The words had continued to tumble out, but he now realized that it wasn't Peggy next to him: it was Marlene Dietrich herself, whose arrival at the tribunal had been the talk of all the newspapers. She looked at him with a mixture of surprise and amusement.

Rebrov coughed with embarrassment. "Forgive me, Miss Dietrich. I mistook you for someone else."

Marlene even clapped her hands in surprise. "It's been a long time since anyone confused me with someone else. That's quite extraordinary!"

"Again, forgive me."

Without taking her eyes off Rebrov, Dietrich suddenly drew from her breast pocket a pack of lozenges, placed one in her mouth, and then offered another to Rebrov. He nodded in thanks and began in an obedient fashion to chew. The candy was mint.

Amazing, Rebrov thought, I didn't recognize Marlene Dietrich, a world-famous movie star. A native German, she had been begged to return to Germany by even Ribbentrop himself when he was Minister of Foreign Affairs, but she spurned his entreaties and demonstratively renounced her German citizenship. When the war broke out, she headed to the frontlines to sing for American soldiers, who adored her. She was a dream girl for men who awaited death.

"What makes this inquest significant is that these prisoners represent sinister influences that will lurk in the world long after their bodies have returned to dust," Jackson was saying. "They have so identified themselves with the philosophies they conceived and with the forces they directed that any tenderness to them is a victory and an encouragement to all the evils which are attached to their names…"

"Hey now, who are you? Dietrich asked gaily when a court recess had been declared.

"My name is Denis Rebrov. I am from the Soviet delegation."

"Oh, you're a Russian! But why aren't you in uniform? Those other Russians in their uniforms with those gold epaulets look the way victors should. What, you didn't fight?"

"I did fight, but now…"

But Marlene was not listening to him. She was lost in her own thoughts. "You know, I've never felt so happy as in the army! My German spirit was stirred at the front. The Germans are a nation of warriors. I saw the war in a grimly sentimental way: struggle, death, duty, I know all that. It's something every German can feel."

"But you were in the American army," Rebrov gently noted. "You performed for American soldiers who were fighting against the Germans."

"Of course. After all, who was I supposed to be performing for? Not for these guys…" she gestured disgustedly towards the side of the courtroom where the accused had been led out to lunch by their American guards.

"Olga Chekhova sang for German soldiers," Rebrov said for some reason.

"Well, everyone has their audience," Marlene shrugged indifferently. "Everyone chooses what suits them."

"You know, not long ago a German girl spat right in her face."

"Well, considering that Hitler called her his favorite actress…"

"It wasn't for that."

"What was it, then?"

"She attacked Chekhova because of rumors that are going around that she was a Russian agent."

"Was she really one?" Marlene asked, clearly interested.

"I don't know, I didn't work with her."

"Why did you tell me that?"

"Aren't you afraid that the Germans are going to treat you the same way as Chekhova now? As a traitor, and not as someone heroic?"

"That's their problem. The Germans themselves went in for Hitler, and they stayed with him until the end. They have nothing to complain about. I can assure you, though, they wouldn't dare spit at me. The Germans know how to behave with the winners."

Right then Peggy came flying towards them. This time she was dressed in a severe business dress.

"Hi, Marlene! God, I'm so happy! We haven't seen each other for ages!"

Marlene hugged her. "Last time it was in Paris, my dear, right after the liberation…"

"Are you going to be in Nuremberg a long time? Are you maybe making a film about the trials?"

"No, so far none of this looks like a good movie. I hope that when the Russian prosecutor comes out… By the way, what rank is he, Denis?"

"He's a general."

"I hope your general will be wearing a full uniform and boots. And that at some point he'll pull out a pistol and shoot Goering! Now that would be a good movie!"

"Yes," Peggy agreed. "That would be a sensation."

"Well, that will hardly happen," Rebrov smiled. "It's completely impossible, I can assure you. Gen. Rudenko knows how to stay cool."

Marlene was now starting to sign autographs and smile at the public that had thronged around her.

"Let's go to the bar and have a drink," Peggy said, taking Rebrov by the arm. "It's good that I didn't wear my military uniform today, I would have looked like a miserable Marlene Dietrich imitator. And then I would have had to shoot myself."

In the bar Peggy looked at Rebrov through squinting eyes. "Where's our princess? I haven't seen her for a long time."

"She is feeling unwell."

"Oh, I hope it's nothing serious! She's such a very nice girl! The aristocracy really has something… I love aristocrats," Peggy provoked him. "Though someone from a proletarian state like yourself probably doesn't care for them."

"Well, you can't call American society aristocratic either," Rebrov parried. "But what about you, Peggy, you don't have any blue blood?"

"Me? Goodness, no. My father was a simple Irish drunk and he beat my poor mother mercilessly. And me and my brothers, too. I spent my whole childhood hungry, ice cream was something we could only dream of. But later I figured out how the world works."

"And how does it work, the world?"

"Oh, it's very complicated. But there is one rule that you've got to follow," said Peggy, who had now turned completely serious.

"And what's that?"

"Don't let anyone hurt you," Peggy said stiffly. "Never. People can tell right away who is capable of fighting back and who isn't. Who you should mess with and who you shouldn't. I am the sort that you shouldn't mess with. But I can go to very great lengths for my friends…" She then looked pointedly at Rebrov. "Would you give me a present? A front-page sensation from the Russian delegation, hmm? I'd know how make it up to you…"

Rebrov laughed. "Peggy, you already owe me. Who gave you that sensation about those prisoners from the SS?"

"I remember, and soon I will give you something in return. But couldn't the Russians prepare some sort of surprise?" Peggy pressed on. "It seems to me like your man Stalin likes all kinds of surprises."

"Peggy, I'm sure you know a lot more secrets than I do. I only deal with boring legal discussions here, going through papers and translating documents…"

"You think I believe that? You are very secretive, Mr. Rebrov, and mysterious. You're a real spy of some sort!" Peggy winked.

"Come on, what kind of spy would I be!" Rebrov waved her claim away.

"Fine, fine. But you can be sure that Peggy is only talkative when she needs to be."

"I'll keep that in mind."

"Incidentally, how do you like Marlene Dietrich in the flesh? That was probably the first time you ever saw her up close."

"She's a real star."

"Yeah, yeah, Marlene knows her trade. I've known her for many years now. It just so happened that my first ever interview for a newspaper was with her. Being the girlfriend to every American soldier is the best role Marlene ever played, and definitely the most loved. It's what brought her her greatest success. But if you believe everything she says, you'd think she spent years on the frontlines under fire, and she was constantly at risk of getting killed. Or, what's worse, falling into the clutches of the Nazis who would immediately start raping her. First, she convinced the public of that, and then she started to believe it herself. In fact, with all her comings and goings our little star was in Europe for hardly more than a year, and between those concerts for soldiers she was flying off to New York or Hollywood."

Rebrov raised his eyebrows in surprise. "You sound awfully jealous of her, Peggy."

"Me? No. But I'm a journalist and I ought to recognize the truth. I might make up some big sensational news, but for myself I ought to recognize the truth. The truth is a strange thing. It isn't capable of much on its own, but it pulls you. You want to know more and more, even if the truth makes you worry or brings you trouble. But once you know the taste of the truth, you wouldn't confuse it with anything else."

She fell silent for some time, then said, "As far as Marlene goes, she did what she could for American soldiers, but there were a lot of other women who did everything that they could, and they got nothing for it. But she's become a symbol of victory. Do you understand what I'm saying? I'm saying that Marlene was one of those people who knew how to get something in return for their efforts, and they never accepted a bad deal."

At that moment Kraft appeared next to them. Like always, he was in a jolly mood and had a smile on his face. "And here I am! What are you guys talking about? But wait, let me guess: Peggy is trying to get some secrets out of you, Denis, about the Russian delegation?"

"You didn't guess right, Alex," Peggy stopped him. "I've just been telling our friend about Marlene. Sitting next to her, he was just blinded by her beauty and greatness."

"Is that so? I thought you liked a whole different type of woman," Kraft looked at Rebrov playfully. "I mean, a different sort."

"I like different types," Rebrov growled.

"Ha, and right you are!" Noticing that Rebrov didn't like the way the conversation was going, Kraft immediately changed the subject. "By the way, about Marlene: she has a sister named Elisabeth. The British found her in one of the worst concentration camps, Bergen-Belsen. Of the sixty thousand prisoners in the barracks, ten thousand of them were already dead, and several thousand more died in the first days after the camp was liberated. It turned out that Marlene's sister and her husband had just been running a cafe near the camp where those butchers would hang out. Elisabeth and her husband were very mild-mannered, respectable citizens of the Third Reich, who just did their jobs. Elisabeth was a beautiful, healthy, well-fed lady, but right next-door thousands of people were dying from torture and starvation. But this isn't a story about Marlene at all, really, it's a story about the German people. And about those men who are now being tried."

"Are you finished?" asked Peggy, who liked to make speeches herself.

"Basically, yes. But there's one other thing that will greatly interest our Russian friend. Just a few days ago the American delegation lost one of its staff under scandal. You know what it was? He said that the American delegation had too many Jews who had only recently become US citizens, either just before the war or even during it. This guy says these émigrés from Germany that fled the Nazis weren't thinking about justice but revenge. So, he didn't want to participate in a farce of a trial where there was no place for law and justice."

After a short pause, Peggy said, "It feels to me like something's missing in this story."

"Yes," Kraft agreed. "It's missing our man's name. It's a good German name, you see. He himself is one of those German émigrés."

"Just like you," Peggy stuck her tongue out at Kraft.

"Alas," he lowered his head. "Not everyone has the good fortune to be born Irish."

Notes

I propose that a film about the Nazi crimes be shown to the witnesses in the wings, to rid them of any swagger they might have before going to the witness box.

I am talking about people like Hess' secretary, Fraulein Speer — she is a fanatic who insists that the Nazis did not do anything wrong, and any reports of atrocities are just propaganda.

I am also talking about the other militarists who believe that the Wehrmacht's honor remained unstained even as they obeyed Hitler without question.

Gustave Gilbert, an American
psychologist who observed
the defendants during the trials

CHAPTER VIII.
SHE WILL SACRIFICE HERSELF

The reception that the Americans had put on in the Grand Hotel restaurant, meant to celebrate the start of the trials, was now in full swing. Drinks were flowing like a river and the excited guests had already started to dance. The stunning Marlene Dietrich was naturally at the center of everyone's attention. A group of Soviet interpreters suddenly broke out in an old song by Dmitry Sadovnikov. The Americans and British loudly applauded them. Rebrov, absentmindedly watching the proceedings from behind a marble column, suddenly noticed Princess Trubetskaya heading for the exit and he rushed after her.

"Good evening, Tatyana Vladimirovna," he greeted her quietly in the empty foyer.

The princess turned. "Ah, it's you, young man. I've decided to head off from this celebration. I'm tired, you know. I'm no longer used to such things. And then all the French left, and I felt I had to stay, because I'm here to represent France after all."

"What happened?"

"What happened is that your boss, Mr. Vyshinsky, offended France. He said that he was raising a glass for the best and most noble allies that the USSR could have: the British and the Americans. He either forgot about the French or intentionally did not mention them. They got upset and left. But I stayed for a while and chatted with old friends."

Rebrov helped the princess into her very modest coat. "Tatyana Vladimirovna, I wanted to ask you, how is Irina Yuryevna?"

"She has come down with a high fever. The poor girl is just burning. But the Americans helped with some medicine, so everything will be fine. With time, of course."

"I could see you home, I've got a car."

"My God, what luxury! Your own car! Well, if you're serious. The weather in the city is awful now, a person wouldn't let his dog out into the street."

The half-lit streets and alleyways of Nuremberg were deserted.

"Tatyana Vladimirovna, I wanted to…" Rebrov hesitated.

"Oh, Denis – that is your name, isn't it? You don't need to say anything. I understand everything, but…"

"But why can't two people, young and free, just love each other?" he stubbornly exclaimed. "I just don't get it! Why does this bother everyone? Why does everyone want to get in the way? Interfere with a person's intimate feelings?"

"I understand, my dear," the princess sighed. "But the thing is, neither of you is free. You are bound hand and foot with heavy chains, because you both come from different worlds. Not just different worlds but hostile ones, and there can be no peace between them."

"God, we are both Russian people!"

"Russians, but not the same…"

"What can we do?"

"I don't know. I just feel very sorry for Irina, because she will do what a Russian woman ought."

"Which is?"

"She will sacrifice herself."

"What should sacrifice herself for? Why?"

"Because she could not do otherwise. That is our lot, the lot of Russian women."

"And what is she going to do with herself?"

"I don't know. Do you remember that story of Ivan Bunin? The main character gets a letter. It's an affectionate but firm request for him to not wait for her any more, to not to try to look for her. It's pointless to draw out and increase the torment. It's about her, about Irina. She will do just that."

"But how?"

"She will sacrifice herself."

Notes

Former men from the Vichy militia, who had done the Gestapo's work during the occupation of France, now masqueraded as former French Resistance fighters. Helping to punish women who had been in relationships with the Germans

seemed the most obvious way to show their loyalty
to the new regime. Punishing defenseless women
meant entering the circle of victors. Shaving
a silly girl bald and exposing her to public
mockery meant joining the rounds of Resistance
veterans. The crowd watched this humiliation
with pleasure.

From the memoirs of
a French Resistance fighter

CHAPTER IX. IT WAS AN AMERICAN!

After saying goodbye to Trubetskaya, Rebrov thought for a while and ultimately decided to return to the Grand Hotel. After all, in spite of everything else he still had to monitor the proceedings and make conclusions. As he was parking the car, he clearly heard two gunshots ring out.

A man holding a pistol was running from a sizable black car, parked right next to the hotel entrance, towards the ruins. He stopped for a brief instant, then turned and immediately disappeared among the fallen walls.

When Rebrov had run up to the car, he saw that the right door was open and the driver, a Soviet sergeant, was lying with his head on the steering wheel.

"Are you still there?" Rebrov asked, carefully shifting his body back onto the seat.

The sergeant moaned.

"Who shot you? Who was that?"

"An American," the sergeant whispered in a barely audible voice. "American uniform…"

Already several American military police were running from the hotel towards the car, but when they arrived, the sergeant was already dead.

"The Americans called to apologize," Rudenko said as he hung up the phone. He looked around at everyone present. For this morning meeting in Rudenko's office he had called Pokrovsky, Zorya, Alexandrov, Filin, and Rebrov as the immediate witnesses of what had happened.

"They don't believe that an American could have done it," Rudenko shrugged. "They say that our employee is mistaken or he didn't hear the man correctly. Comrade Rebrov, did you hear what the sergeant said correctly?"

"I did. I couldn't have misheard it," Rebrov stood up so that his answer would come across as more official and convincing.

"Come on, sit down now," Rudenko waved with his hand.

Filin, with whom Rebrov had discussed the situation late the previous night, intervened. "Now, comrade general, that doesn't mean that it was really an American soldier. What good would this do the Americans?"

"What are you saying?"

"It could have been a German dressed in an American uniform. He did run towards those very same ruins where those German prisoners of war used to work. He might have been one of them."

"He might have, but how could we determine that now? But first of all, why was this necessary?"

"Everyone's saying that this was supposed to be an attempt on you, Roman Andreyevich. The reporters have already given this version to the newspapers," Pokrovsky spoke up. "And an attempt on the chief prosecutor for the USSR would be a very serious thing. And it would serve many people's interest."

"'Many people' is too general," Rudenko snapped. "Who precisely did it? What am I to report to Moscow? And most importantly, how could this affect the trials? That is what worries me."

"Well, let's try to think again about what happened, from the very beginning," Filin said calmly. "Who would want to shoot Sgt. Bubnov? What sense does it make? Let's assume that they wanted to simply shoot a member of the Soviet delegation, it didn't matter who. Simply out of blind hatred for the Russians. But why do it right at the Grand Hotel during a reception marking the start of the trials? The most likely thing is that they thought there would be someone else in the car besides the driver, but in the dark and in his rush, the attacker just didn't notice there was no one else inside… Do you often take this car, Roman Andreyevich?"

"I've been in it a few times."

"So, the idea that it was an attempt on your life is a realistic one."

"Everything's clear," Pokrovsky swatted the air with his palm. "They were aiming for Roman Andreyevich himself, and the motive is very clear: they wanted the trials to be delayed or completely called off."

"They might have tried to spark a fight between the Allied delegations," Alexandrov entered the discussion. "The Soviet chief prosecutor is killed in the American occupation zone and immediately people start asking a million questions: did the attacker just slip through the net, or did the Americans know of it and intentionally allow it? And it happened in front of hundreds of journalists from all over the world. There would be a scandal like you can't imagine!"

"Yes," Rudenko sighed. "it would be a complete disaster."

"There's already a big buzz, but we haven't said anything yet," Zorya spoke up. "Maybe we ought to make some kind of statement? Or protest?"

Filin didn't agree. "What good would that do us? The Americans are tearing up the place now. Rebrov himself almost got arrested for it and we barely convinced them to let him go. If we protest, it will only look like we're escalating the situation. We don't need to escalate anything when the trials are going on."

"I agree, Sergei Ivanovich," Rudenko concluded. "I think there's no need to hurry. For us, the most important thing is the tribunal. It should proceed smoothly. So much effort has been invested in it, the whole world is counting on us. Let the Americans carry out the investigations and we'll just see what comes up, who they arrest…"

"I don't think they'll arrest anyone," Filin leaned back in his chair. "It wouldn't be advantageous for them. If the killer is German, then that means a failure on their part. If it's an American, it would be even worse."

"Well, let them feel guilty to us," Rudenko laughed. "It won't do any harm. If something ever comes up, we can remind them that they owe us one."

"Idiots! They are complete idiots, total idiots! Killing that Russian driver, why would they do that? What are they trying to achieve?" The baron was literally shaking with fury. "They only angered the Americans. And now the Russians can demand a tougher attitude towards the Germans. That friend of yours who you praise so much, does he have anything to do with this mess?"

Olaf shook his head. He was sitting in an armchair while the baron, who was usually a calm man, was pacing his office like a tiger.

"It's very stupid, baron, but…"

"What? What 'buts' could there be here?"

"Many Germans have simply sunk into despair. When I see them in the streets with bundles in their hands or carrying something on carts and bicycles, they look like ghosts that have no place of their own on German soil. Ghosts with empty eyes. People are simply going crazy from humiliation, humiliation that seems like it will never end!"

"But why then kill a Russian driver with the rank of sergeant?"

"I think the real target must have been that Russian general. If they had succeeded in that, then…"

"*If*," the baron laughed sardonically. "If Germany had won the war, then now she would be dictating terms! I can't imagine anything would have happened if they killed the Russian chief prosecutor. What would have changed? The Russians would appoint a new prosecutor, become ten times more harsh, and no one would object. But killing a simple driver, that is unforgivable stupidity! I assured the Americans that we've got all German forces here under control, that there would not be any surprises. Now I look to them like a man who just likes to boast and can't really do anything, which means a man who cannot demand anything!"

"Maybe just tell them that it was an individual extremist. A lone gun. There are people like that."

The baron looked at Olaf with reproach. "That is exactly what I told them. Because I could not have said anything else. But it's not enough, nowhere near enough! We need to prove that the Americans could not cope without us. After what has happened, we need to show them now how important and indispensable we are. I have already taken some steps."

Olaf looked at the baron quizzically.

"The Americans have sent in a special group of experts. They will search for anything related to the SS and Gestapo doctors' experiments with mescaline."

"Mescaline?"

"Yes. It is a drug extracted from some kind of rare cactus. The SS doctors were looking for a way to suppress a man's free will, paralyze him mentally, and alter his behavior in the direction they needed."

"I had heard that they carried out experiments on camp prisoners, especially Russian POWs. The Russian prosecutors are talking about that at the trials. It's one of the most serious charges."

"I know. But also, the Americans have created their Division 19, which is supposed to use the SS's findings to create drugs that highly secret American agents can use. We're talking about special-purpose weapons of a chemical, biological, or psychological nature. I had to give the Americans some of the documents that I had in my possession."

Olaf could not hide his astonishment.

"Yes, indeed, they were stored in my home and I wasn't intending to give them to anyone else, but... After that stupid assassination attempt, I had to sacrifice something to make it up to the Americans. Even that wasn't enough, though. We've got to give them something else, too..."

"If we knew where the Nazi gold was hidden, we could use that to make them happy. Well, not all of it, of course. Just a small part of it."

"No, let's not rush with the gold," the baron said thoughtfully. "We will save the gold for the time being. You told me about your friend

Günther Tilkowski and his team. Well, about their plan to kidnap members of the tribunal and free the prisoners…"

"I don't think that they will manage to do anything."

"They won't manage to do anything," the baron snapped. "Anything at all. Because they'll be arrested by the Americans."

"Are the Americans on to them?"

"Not yet, thank God. But they will be soon." The baron smiled enigmatically.

When Olaf saw his smile, he turned visibly pale. "But baron…"

"Yes, my boy! The Americans will be on to them, because you and I are going to betray them to the Americans," the baron spoke harshly and threw in a few expletives. "We'll give them up instead of the gold. We need the gold for ourselves, if we find it. A future Germany needs it. No one needs these idiots with their stupid plots." The baron waved his hand brusquely. "They would only get in the way. It's time to get rid of them. But we can't just dispose of them without getting something for ourselves out of it. Let them serve the great cause of Germany's rebirth. After all, they are Germans."

Olaf stood up. His voice shook. "You're asking me to betray a friend. I can't do that, baron. Günther and I risked our lives together. We've been friends since we were kids!"

"I understand how you feel, my boy." The baron walked up to Olaf and gave his shoulder a squeeze. "I'm not asking you to betray him, I've asking you to save him! Understand? Save him. If they tried something, they would just be swatted like flies. If the Americans arrested them in time before they could try anything, before they committed this stupid violence, then they'll stay alive. They'll even go free after some time. In fact, it won't take long at all, since their crime will look like a childish prank next to those men on trial. You must understand, Olaf, I don't want you to feel like a traitor for the rest of your life. You would simply be saving them from death, a death which would be senseless and wouldn't help Germany. At the same time, you would be helping our business. Find me Günther and his team. Find them, that's an order."

Notes

The "Butcher of Lyon" (Klaus Barbie, Gestapo chief in the French city of Lyon) was infamous among for the French for his extremely cruel methods of carrying out interrogations… Barbie was handed over to US Army intelligence and immediately taken on as a paid informant… Thus began a double game where, on one hand, the USA continued to look for war criminals for the Nuremberg tribunal, but on the other hand they zealously labored behind the scenes to ensure that "valuable men should not face their accusers".

Guido Knopp, a prominent
German writer and historian

CHAPTER X. REAL GERMANS

The Soviet prosecutor Lev Smirnov was presenting to the judges in the courtroom a large book bound in leather that resembled in its bulk a medieval tome.

"I present you a report from Maj. Gen. Stroop to his superiors on the successful liquidation of the Warsaw ghetto. It contains only the names of those murdered. Your Honor," he appealed to the chief justice, "I ask you to enter this book among the physical evidence."

He then went on. "And now I would like to quote from the diary of Governor-General of Poland Hans Frank, who is among the defendants. He writes, 'That we sentence 1.2 million Jews to die of hunger should be noted only marginally… Poland shall be treated as a colony; the Poles shall be the slaves of the Greater German World Empire…'"

Frank, who was sitting in the dock, hunched and tensed.

"It was Frank who gave the order to 'liquidate the Warsaw ghetto with total ruthlessness'", Smirnov continued. "In describing to his superiors how he carried out this order, Gen. Stroop writes, 'I therefore decided to destroy the entire Jewish residential area by setting every block on fire.' The SS men, assisted by military police, hammered the doors and windows shut and set fire to each building. Those who tried to escape the flames were killed. His report states, 'The soldiers carried out their duties unwaveringly and shot those people, thus ending their agony and sparing them unnecessary pain.' Those who managed to somehow get away and hide among the ruins were searched out with dogs. Those who sought refuge in the sewers were smoked out with gas bombs.

"'Thus, one day', Stroop tells us, 'we opened 183 sewer entrance holes, and at a fixed time lowered smoke candles into them, with the result that the bandits fled from what they believed to be gas in the center of the former ghetto. It must be stated that the Wehrmacht engineers, too, executed the blowing up of dugouts, sewers and concrete buildings with indefatigability and great devotion to duty…'

"I would like to draw the court's attention to the following remarks: 'The longer the resistance lasted the tougher the men of the Waffen SS, police, and Wehrmacht became. They fulfilled their duty indefatigable in faithful comradeship and stood together as models and examples of soldiers. Their duty hours often lasted from early morning until late at night. Officers and men of the police, a large part of whom had already been at the front, again excelled by their dashing spirit.' There you have it, ideal citizens of the Nazi state. This is an example of how those who stand accused brought up 'real Germans.'"

Smirnov set the book aside, cleared his throat, and went on, "In presenting evidence to the court on crimes against civilian populations, I would like to point to the following..." He turned to the table next to the podium. The table was covered with a white sheet, and when the prosecutor threw back the sheet, there was a deathly silence in the courtroom.

On the table, under a glass bell and on top of a marble stand was a human head with long, dark, and neatly combed hair. However, it was only the size of a large fist.

"The Nazi monsters made 'souvenirs' like this in the concentration camps, using technology that they developed there through unspeakable experiments. The camp commandant gave out these 'pieces of work' as souvenirs to high-ranking visitors."

A woman among the public seated on the balcony screamed. A young American soldier wearing spectacles that was standing behind the accused fainted and collapsed. His fellow soldiers quickly carried him out of the courtroom.

All of the defendants remained motionless like stone. Suddenly one of them hysterically either coughed or chuckled.

Notes

When you look at the defendants in the dock, you cannot help but think of an open enclosure at the zoo where wild animals are brought from their dark cages into the daylight. They are no longer dangerous, you can study their behavior, but you get goosebumps thinking about encountering one of these fearsome predators

when they were roaming freely and, with their
teeth bared, they went in for the kill.

Roman Karmen in the newspaper
Izvestiya, November 28, 1945

CHAPTER XI.
I LIVED IN ANOTHER WORLD

The seemingly endless light rain that had been falling since morning and resembled a fog finally ceased, and the sun appeared over the deserted suburbs of Nuremberg with a blinding light.

Rebrov stopped his car in front of a modest home which, in the fresh sunshine, looked like a theatrical stage set. "We're here," he turned to Irina who was sitting next to him. "This should be the place."

They got out of the car and just stood there for a while, stunned by the sense of peace and quiet and the lack of any terrible black heaps of rubble, which they had grown so used to in the center of Nuremberg.

"It's so quiet and pretty here," Irina sighed. "As if there weren't any tribunal, no Nazis, camps, nothing."

Rebrov went to the gate and called out. After several wearying minutes, a tall and thin man came out of the house. He wore a large knitted sweater and had long gray hair. After he had reached the gate with a few belabored steps, it became clear that he was quite old, but his hawk-nosed face with wrinkled cheeks was quite handsome in its own way, like a painting of Dürer.

"To what do I owe this visit?" he asked in a ceremonial tone. His eyes showed the familiar concern with which most Germans looked at those who had vanquished them.

"Mr. Glanz?" Rebrov asked with emphasized politeness.

"The very same."

"We're reporters accredited for the trials."

"Americans?" Glanz asked, examining Rebrov carefully and then fixing his gaze on Irina.

"No, we're from France."

"I see. France… How can I help you, sir and madame?"

"Mr. Glanz, many people consider Adolf Hitler to have been a student and follower of yours…"

Glanz moved his head, but it was unclear whether he was agreeing with Rebrov or protesting.

"We would like to know your opinion about what has happened with the German people and Germany."

"It's been a long time now since anyone was interested in my opinion about the Germans or Germany," Glanz muttered, as if talking to himself. "Why do you want to know?"

"We think it is very important to understand everything that happened with Germany and the Germans, and whether it could happen again."

"Well, if you really want. However, you know that this is not a pleasant subject for me. But you won the war…" The old man opened the gate and ushered Rebrov and Irina into the house.

He led them into the typical study of a bookish person: a massive writing desk near the window covered with a heavy curtain, the walls hung with old paintings and weapons. Glanz lowered himself into an armchair with a high, straight back, while Irina and Denis sat down on the bulky, rather uncomfortable sofa.

"Forgive me that I have nothing to serve you while you are here," the old man threw up his hands. "So, where shall we start?"

"Perhaps with your acquaintance with Adolf Hitler," Rebrov suggested as he took out his notebook.

"Well, of course… But he was not the same Hitler that today the whole world knows. He was quite young, living in real poverty, but he was very interested in history, or rather the world of the Germans of old, their beliefs and laws…"

"Excuse me, but why did he come to you?" Irina asked.

Glanz looked at her with a reproachful smile. "Because that was my world. I was one of those who saw it in my dreams, and then I talked about it to other Germans."

"And how did your interest in the Germany of old begin?" Rebrov inquired.

"When I rejected the vulgar and filthy world that surrounded me. Already in the 1910s I was passionately interested in Europe's medieval past and the religious orders of knights. It was a wonderful world of fairy-tale heroes who were completely and irresistibly great. I dived headlong into their history, legends, myths… I was so obsessed with them that I even decided to take vows in an abbey near Vienna, though my family was completely opposed. I became Brother George. The white-stone halls of the church with Gothic vaulting, the white slabs of the tombstones, the strict Romanesque style, the white robes of the monks, the secluded monastery garden, the stained-glass windows and the 12th-century tombs of the dukes of Badenburg... It was as if I went back to those times, I felt that I touched the sacred heights of ancient Germany. I started to write about what I felt and experienced. The first book that I published consisted of reflections on a gravestone image found under the slabs of stone at the monastery. The stone depicted a warrior striking at some terrible beast...

"That was quite a common legend of those times," Rebrov shrugged. "A knight defeating a serpent or dragon."

"Yes, but I immediately glimpsed the truth in this scene: an allegory of the eternal battle between the forces of good and evil, which is endless. By that time I was already ready to glimpse it. I was especially drawn by the bestial depiction of evil on this ancient tombstone."

"So you started to see evil as a terrible beast that threatened the whole world?" Irina asked quietly.

"Exactly. There is a terrible beast that lives inside many people and is the root of all kinds of evil in the world."

Glanz leaned back in his chair. His back was straight and his eyes half-closed. He was clearly carried away by his reminiscences, which had not interested anyone for a long time. From time to time he opened his eyes and looked at Irina. It was clear that he was speaking only to her. Rebrov thought that in the end, any man dreams only of being understood by a beautiful woman.

"I was carried away with my thoughts. I started to take up zoology. I studied the Scriptures, the Apocrypha, modern archaeology and anthropology... At some point, it suddenly became clear to me that the all that is good and blessed in the world is incarnated in the Aryan race, while dark deviations, evil, is incarnated in the Negroid and Mongoloid races and the Semitic inhabitants of the Mediterranean..."

"All these revelations are hardly in accordance with Christian dogma," Irina objected.

Glanz was unfazed. "Yes, these beliefs were, to put it mildly, unorthodox, and they caused some serious friction between Brother George and his superior in the abbey. Furthermore, by that time I had fallen in love with a woman, with a passionate carnal love. I was called to 'reject the temptations of the world and the love of the flesh', but my inclination to free thought was strong and I left the abbey. The world to which I now returned seemed horrible and impoverished, in spite of the achievements made in technology. Millions of people died in a murderous war unleashed for someone's personal benefit. People killed each other, were blown to pieces or choked on poisonous gas, and no one knew what it was all for. The savagery of these bestial men meant an end to culture and refined humanity…

"My thoughts again turned towards the orders of knights which had stood against the barbarians. They found themselves encircled ruthlessly by the Islamic forces of North Africa, the Near East, and the Balkans, and the amorphous Mongol hordes. Their world could survive only if they preserved their Aryan purity. After all, the Christianity of the time was a militant and aristocrat monastery-fortress, from which knight-monks went forth to destroy their encirclement by dark and aggressive powers."

"So the Middle Ages seemed for you the Golden Age of the Aryans?" Irina asked.

"Yes, it was a fascinating world. A world of brave knights, pious monks, magnificent castles, wealthy monasteries, and beautiful, chaste, and faithful women… It was supported by the racial and knightly cult of the religious and military orders. The royal dynasties of Germany cultivated the arts and talents in their castles and palaces, for them these were the only historical tool for progress. And, opposing them, there was always the dead weight of the lower castes, who posed a danger to the nation through their vulgar demands for power sharing. These castes of lower, subhuman creatures were unaware of their natural, racial incapability to govern. They were only able to spread corruption and vulgarity.

"Nonetheless, they were people, too," Rebrov noted.

"No, they were merely human-like creatures capable only of destruction. Thus, the Aryan Germans were absolutely right to spread their rule over the whole world. Germany could no longer allow itself to lose the 'golden fleece of the world', as the entire planet was a natural colony for it."

"So," Rebrov summed up Glanz's thought, "in our time, in accordance with the principle of racial purity, this meant a farm for every brave German soldier and an estate for every officer in the Crimea? And the slaves from the lower races were to labor for the Aryan Germans?"

Glanz closed his eyes, which had shone with a youthful gleam. "The specific way this would turn out did not concern me."

"Well, sure, it was left to Hitler and the SS!"

"But where is Christianity in any of this, Christian virtues?" Irina passionately interjected. "You are a Christian!"

"You're referring to the modern understanding of such things, but the religion of that time was not so tastelessly humane and effete," Glanz rubbed his temple with his fingers. "It was an extremely aristocratic cult of true Aryans who were aware of their power and their duty. A strict, militaristic, economic and political organization designed for heroic people. The religion of that time mercilessly wiped out subhuman species that bore bestial, animal traits… Or humanely kept them in Jewish ghettos so that they could not infect our beautiful world! It was a majestic and beautiful flowering of heroic religion, art, and culture, the bearers of which were true Aryans."

"That's what you think," Rebrov couldn't control himself. "But your mythical world lost its fight."

"Alas, the destruction of the Templars in 1308 marked the end of this era and the beginning of the triumph of inferior racial forces. From that time on, the racial, culture, and political achievements of Europe began to slowly fade. What replaced it was horror. The growth of the cities, which gathered in them all the impure things of the world, the spread of soulless capitalism, the emergence of the working class that was incapable of anything, all this led to compromised aristocratic values and ideas of racial purity."

"They simply proved to be incompatible with either the new order of things or Christian doctrines."

"Christianity," Glanz glowered, "has turned from a strict, selfless faith into a sentimental, altruistic fable that claims that all human beings are equal, that we have to love our neighbor regardless of his race and whatever his traits are. Europe fell victim to a long process of decay, and it ultimately ended in the triumph of the dark vulgar masses and demagogues, who patted themselves on the back with talk about equality and brotherhood. But the brave warrior that strikes at the terrible beast cannot be equal to it! He cannot be its brother."

"So, for you," Rebrov asked, "the world is divided into a light side of blue-eyed and light-haired Aryans and a dark side of non-Aryan demons? Behind one side is good, salvation, order, and the others are capable of only evil, chaos, and destruction? Did I get your ideas right?"

Glanz sighed, "Nearly, young man, nearly so. They were not so crude, they had a great deal of feeling in them, even beauty, unspeakable beauty…"

"Nonetheless, for you the Aryans were the source and instrument of all good, of aristocracy and creative achievements, while non-Aryans were automatically linked to corruption, weakness, and destructive tendencies. How exactly was this conflict to be expressed? In what actions?"

"At the time I was driven by the thought that a modern crusade was necessary to counter the political emancipation of the masses, parliamentary democracy, socialist revolutions based on the idea of universal equality."

"So, the world of superhuman, pure-blooded Aryans, so unlike what you saw around you, had to oppose non-Aryans in every possible way? Hence the need to found an Aryan German empire that would have no moral obligations to the rest of the world…"

"The way you put them, these ideas look so crude and harsh," the old man said thoughtfully. "For me this was more of a dream, if you like. A dream of a long-lost past. I had no ideas or hopes about putting them into practice. A person who is offended in his purest notions by a filthy and ugly reality will retreat into dreams, where everything is clearly defined. It was a dream of a perfect human being that everyone should strive for."

"And therefore you had to ensure the racial superiority of the Aryans," Rebrov insistently continued. "For that, you needed laws against interracial marriages, you needed to multiply pure-blooded Germans through polygamy, and you had to create Lebensborn homes where unmarried German women of good blood could conceive children of pure-blooded heroes…"

"Again I tell you that all this was merely the dreams of a common scientist and dreamer, as I was then. I was and I still am."

"But didn't the idea of Lebensborn homes for commendable SS men not come from there?"

"Probably," Glanz didn't argue. "Probably, when Hitler and Himmler thought of them, they were basing themselves on some thoughts of mine, but I never conceived of any SS, Gestapo, or concentration camps! By the way, if you are so well informed of my views, you should know that when Hitler came to power, they banned the publication of my works! The scientific teams that I led were broken up at the order of the Gestapo, our scientific journals were shut down."

"Apparently Hitler, who already thought himself to be a superman, didn't want anyone to know that his ideas weren't due to God's will but the dreams of an ordinary scientist that was ridiculed by many."

"Probably," Glanz shrugged. "But don't you dare insult me. You don't understand what moved me then, what tormented my soul, what fears

for this country afflicted me! Germany had been humiliated and insulted by defeat, chaos, poverty, the arrogant mockery of the West… Hitler
was, of course, influenced by my description of an ancient Golden Age,
these ideas were widespread back then, but he himself turned abstract
impressions and melancholy nostalgia into a racial movement that led
to a revolution and coup. I had never thought about such a thing! I
dreamed of hearing a fantastic chorus of heroes and perfect human beings, but instead there was the monstrous war of insane butchers."

"Tell us, did Hitler really believe that there is some power in that
Spear of Destiny that has been talked about so much?"

"At some point he might have believed in its power. He could have
convinced himself of that belief, because he had nothing else left. In each
person there is a desire to believe, though this desire might be stronger
or weaker depending on circumstances."

"Maybe he simply understood that with the Spear and your visions
of a Golden Age, he would appear before the people not as an ordinary
politician, but as a 'great and anointed one' endowed with great strength
and supported by demonic powers?"

"That's quite possible. He knew how to handle crowds and what to
say to them."

"But look, did you really not understand what was really happening
in Germany? Himmler and Goebbels seemed to be your ideals brought
to life."

"I'll say it again, don't you dare try to insult me. You asked me to talk
about the past and I did. It has nothing to do with the life I have now.
My life now consists only of thinking how to stay warm and fed. That's
all. Everyone I was close to died in the bombing. Or do you want to drag
me off to your court? Be my guest, I am not afraid of that. Send in your
soldiers."

They were already walking out when Glanz suddenly said, looking
at Irina, "I sense the aristocracy in you. You cannot fool me. Men have
done great feats for such women."

"But I don't have a drop of German blood," Irina objected.

Glanz said nothing in answer.

"There's another person who wasn't guilty of anything, didn't know
anything, didn't suspect anything," Rebrov said to Irina when the two
had walked out, and the he added, "All great ideas are merciless…"

The sun had already gone away and light rain had started to fall
again.

"You can't stop people from thinking and dreaming," Irina said softly. "But why did you look him up?"

"I keep trying to understand how a small group of dreary extremists managed to seize control of a huge European country, to subjugate all Europe, and openly proclaim the need to annihilate whole peoples. This is a story that mankind will never forget. People will continue to be attracted to this ideology with its rage and ritual savagery for a long time. How will they see it?"

"Well, I think that after all that has happen, they'll seen it quite clearly as pure cannibalism."

"I don't know. That old man might seem even kind and touching with his reminiscences, but he did declare the lower classes of society to be the descendants of the lowest races, and he blamed them for Germany's fall from greatness. He was bold enough to say that they should be simply eradicated. He called the Christian tradition of compassion for the weak and oppressed to be a lie."

Irina was quite for a time, then suddenly said, "Still, he has a certain charm, doesn't he?"

"True. That evil has a charm to it is a perennial problem for human beings. He looked at you with eyes full of rapture, but he did see women as a problem, inasmuch as he thought they are much more inclined towards animal tendencies than men. So, only strict submission to their Aryan husbands could, as he put it, guarantee the success of racial purification and the apotheosis of the Aryan race. And to speed up the process of eradicating the lower races, there were also humane methods: sterilization and castration."

"It's horrible," Irina shivered.

"So, this old man doesn't seem to have denied Hitler and Himmler. They were his disciples. They wouldn't have had the imagination and smarts to think all that up themselves."

They got into the car and Rebrov started the engine. After hesitating for a moment, he turned to Irina. "What are you thinking about? Something's bothering you, I can see it."

"Tomorrow they're going to call a witness, a French woman. She'll testify about what they did in Auschwitz, where they had sent her. I've heard some scraps of information, it was unbearable."

"I can imagine."

"But I heard her tell a friend of hers that she'll bring a pistol into the courtroom. And once the witness examination begins, she'll shoot at the accused until she is out of bullets."

"I think she was just suffering from a slight nervous breakdown," Rebrov reassured her. "And besides, it's impossible to bring a gun into the courtroom. The witnesses are searched."

Rebrov and Irina were standing by the entrance to the courtroom. Several steps away was Col. Andrus with two officers from the guard. They were discussing something and periodically looking to the side.

From the witnesses' room, a very thin and dark-haired woman of around thirty came out, accompanied by a bailiff. She was walking directly towards Rebrov with her head bowed and her arms around her shoulders. Irina nudged Rebrov, who nodded to Andrus, and the colonel resolutely blocked the dark-haired woman's path.

"I am Col. Andrus of the US Army," he solemnly introduced himself. "Witness, if you have any weapon, hand it over. It is strictly forbidden to carry any weapons into the courtroom."

"I don't have any weapon," the woman, bewildered, muttered. "And what do you want from me, anyway? I am a French citizen! You have no right to detain me!"

"Madame, I'm going to ask you once more to hand over any weapons. We have reason to suspect that you do have one. You will not enter the courtroom with it. We will have to search you."

"You wouldn't dare! You hear me? You wouldn't dare! Those fascists tortured me in the camps, don't you dare do such a thing here."

The woman suddenly drew forth a pistol that she had been hiding under her clothes and aimed it at Andrus' chest. "Let me through! I am only doing what I have to! I have to do it myself! Let me through or I'll shoot."

Andrus and the officers froze in astonishment. Rebrov, who had been standing just behind the woman, quietly rushed up to her, grabbed her hand holding the gun, and pressed her to himself so that she couldn't move.

The woman broke down in sobs and Rebrov yelled, "Doctor! We need a doctor!"

Notes

Many Russian women and girls are working at the Astra factories. They are compelled to work fourteen and more hours a day. Of course, they receive no pay whatever. They go to and from the factory under escort. The Russians literally

drop from exhaustion. The guards often whip
them. They have no right to complain about
the bad food or ill treatment. The other day
my neighbor obtained a servant. She paid some
money at an office and was given the opportunity
to choose any woman she pleased from a number
here from Russia.

From a letter that German
soldier Wilhelm Bock,
221st Infantry Division,
sent his motherfrom
the Eastern Front

CHAPTER XII.
TO WAIT AND KEEP THE FAITH

"It's time," Irina said. "Otherwise, I'll be late for the plane and I won't make it to Paris for Christmas. It's Catholic, of course, but Paris at Christmastime is still worth seeing."

That surprised Rebrov. "Wait, are you a believer? Do you believe in God?"

"Of course. Why do you look so scared?"

"It's just that I'm remembering that story by Bunin again. It just won't give me any peace. Do you remember it?"

"Of course."

"At the end, the woman enters a nunnery…"

"Yes, so that she doesn't draw out their torment any further…"

"I hope you aren't thinking the same?"

"No. So far, no. Though after everything I've seen here… It's a pity you can't come with me. Christmas in Paris! God, just a few days when I don't have to see these ruins, the Germans with their eyes full of fear and hate. I don't have to hear their testimony and stories, or translate reports of atrocities…"

Rebrov hugged her. "Did you warn the guards?" he suddenly asked.

"That the witness had a gun?"

"Yes."

"Pavel Rosen said that I shouldn't tell anyone about it."

"Why not?"

"He said that after all that this woman had been through, she had the right to do whatever she felt necessary. And that no one should dare judge her. He was sure that she would have been let off."

"I see. And you probably agreed with him?"

"I don't know. I feel like my mind has gone dull by everything that's going on here. I don't know how to live with all this. What are you going to be doing here?"

"Waiting for you to come back. Waiting and keeping the faith. However long I have to."

Notes

But as soon as I entered the grounds, figures
appeared from the church carrying icons and
banners. Behind them, dressed all in white, the
great princess walked with lowered eyes and a
large candle in her hands. Behind her came a
line of nuns, dressed the same in white, singing
with their faces lit by their candles… Now one
of the women in the procession suddenly lifted
her head, which was covered with a white scarf,
and shielding her candle with her hand, she
stared into the darkness with her dark eyes, as
if directly at me… What could she see in the
darkness? How did she sense my presence?

Ivan Bunin, "Pure Monday"

CHAPTER XIII.
MY ARM IS NOT SHAKING

Defeated Germany celebrated Christmas 1945 and ushered in the new year 1946. Barrel organs could be heard wheezing plaintively in the bombed-out streets, and somewhere there were even carousels spinning and Santa Claus making his rounds. Hungry children looked with greedy eyes on this semblance of a holiday, they stretched out their hands for meager little gifts, and their parents did not want to think back to how things had been quite recently. They thought only of how to survive and how to save their children from dying of starvation. If they were asked about Hitler or Nazism, they only turned and walked away.

Dr. Gilbert walked down the wide corridor of the prison, past the guards that were now standing outside of each cell. A two-week recess had been declared at the tribunal, and now anyone who wanted had already left that Nuremberg they were so fed up with. Dr. Gilbert could have left, too, but he did not. He understood perfectly well that fate had given him this chance, and he had to make the most of it. There would be more Christmases in his life, but there would never be another Nuremberg. The unique material that he was able to collect here would him fame, fortune, and prosperity. For the same reason, he was waging a secret war with the military psychiatrist Kelly, whom he felt to be a direct competitor when it came to eventually publishing sensational books about the secrets of Nuremberg. Kelly could be dismissed from his job by Andrus, and Gilbert insistently suggested to Andrus that the source of all those sensational details leaking out about prison life were coming from Kelly. Andrus had already had some stern chats with Kelly, and judging from everything, Gilbert would not have to wait long for his efforts to pay off.

In addition, Gilbert was supplying intelligence with much more information about the defendants' thoughts. His reports were highly appreciated by Jackson himself, who occasionally gave Gilbert direct instructions to find out this or that bit of information. True, in order to do this he often had to strain his imagination and think up something to ascribe to the Reich leaders, but he didn't mind.

Because this work was his life, he did not care about time off. During the court sessions he hovered constantly near the defendants' bench, striving not to miss a single minute lest something important slip by. He not only noted down the comments they made to each other, he also studied their body language: their reactions, gestures, and facial expressions. After each session he would enter the prison, visit the cells and again listen, seek information, ask the questions that concerned him. There was one more thing that Gilbert would not admit even to himself: he liked that all of these field marshals, admirals, Reichsmarschalls, and ministers not only spoke to him on equal terms, they even relished the opportunity to chat and at times try to ingratiate themselves.

Therefore, Dr. Gilbert spent the Christmas holiday in the prison. Moreover, he thought that the prisoners, sentimental Germans, would be feeling particularly lonely and melancholy during this time, so they might reveal more than they normally did.

He stopped outside one cell, over the door of which hung a spartan sign "Hermann Goering". The guard on duty saluted him, turned the lock, and opened the cell door.

Goering was sitting on the cot that served as his bed. He appeared to be in a gloomy mood, but not a depressed one. Gilbert set down on the single chair.

"How are you feeling, Reichsmarschall?"

"I haven't been getting letters from my wife and daughter, doctor." Goering pointed at a framed photograph on the wall.

"You see, before I *willingly*," Goering made an intentional pause, "gave myself up to the Americans, I personally appealed to the American commander Gen. Eisenhower and requested that my family be taken care of. This was promised to me. But now your prosecutors and judges are depriving me of communication with my family and clearly trying to break me. You'll find that to be in vain."

"I'll try to find out what is going on," Gilbert promised him.

Goering was unaware that the letters had been held back on the recommendation of Gilbert himself. Jackson believed that the upcoming examination of Goering, the main defendant, would be the most important moment of the trials, and he expected constant reports from Gilbert on Goering's morale. As Gilbert looked at the scowling Reichsmarschall, he thought it wouldn't be easy to turn this damn fatso into a repentant, sniveling little man. Goering's hubris was growing no smaller, in spite of all Gilbert's efforts.

"You have to understand that the American army has quite a few men who think that when it comes to you and the other prisoners, after all that you have done, they should be allowed to do anything to you. Do you know what suggestion the US president received from England? Use German war criminals instead of laboratory animals during atomic bomb tests in the Pacific."

Goering stared at Gilbert, then he grinned. "All people are the same. They just have different imaginations."

"Nonetheless, you should be aware of how the world sees you. But I promise that I'll look into the situation with letters from your family," Gilbert said, thinking whether it would be more profitable for him if the Reichsmarschall did not get his wife and daughter's letters and got angry, or if he did receive them and trusted him, Dr. Gilbert, more and opened up to him more…

"Thank you," Goering nodded. "I will be very obliged."

Gilbert now turned the conversation in a more serious direction. "Tell me, Reichsmarschall, don't you regret that for the sake of satisfying its imperial ambitions, Germany unleashed such an aggressive war?"

"Don't make me laugh. America, Britain, France, and Russia have always done the same to satisfy *their* imperial ambitions. Strong countries always behave that way. But since we lost, Germany's actions will always be called crimes. That's all there is to it. Let's see how America acts now, when so much is allowed it…"

"When you were making plans for war, did you really not give any thought to the fact that millions of people would die? Including Germans, so young, strong, and full of life?"

"War is war. Of course people don't want war. Why would some poor slob on a farm or in a factory want to risk his life in a war when the best that he can get out of it is to come back to his farm or factory in one piece? Naturally, the common people don't want war; neither in Russia, nor in England, nor in America, nor Germany. But after all, it's the leaders of the country who determine the policy, and it's always a simple matter to drag the people along whether it's a democracy, a dictatorship, or a parliament. In a democracy the people have some say in the matter through their elected representatives, and in the United States only Congress can declare wars. Voice or no voice, the people can always be brought to the bidding of the leaders. That is easy. All you have to do is tell them they are being attacked, and denounce the pacifists for lack of patriotism, and exposing the country to greater danger."

"You don't have a very high opinion of people. Or Germans."

"They're all the same," Goering retorted haughtily.

"But Hitler declared the Germans to be a superior race."

Goering shrugged and his face showed a contemptuous grimace. "People believe someone who tells them nice things."

"You didn't stand up against Hitler."

"Who stood up against him? The West? When we carved up Czechoslovakia, the French and British just approved whatever Hitler said. There were no objections. I was simply amazed how easy it was to decide the fate of an entire country. Hitler made demands, and there wasn't a peep against him in response. We got everything we wanted, we did!" Goering snapped his fingers. He looked as if he had gone back to that era and felt like a winner again, with the whole world at his feet.

"They didn't even ask the Czechs anything. They just told them, as they stood outside the door, that now they belonged to Germany. Hell, I even wondered then if that Spear of Destiny that Hitler was obsessed with really works. Everything had gone just like in a fairy tale, you see. It was some kind of miracle."

"How do you see things now? When you have lost everything?"

"The same way. The British and French then were the most afraid of war. They really did not want to fight. They wanted to live their ordinary bourgeois lives. They were moral defeatists. They wanted to live well and drink wine, and not fight! All the time, they waited for us to finally move on to the Russians and then we would drown each other in blood. That was their humanism: let someone else shed blood."

"Did you always have those plans, to attack the Russians?"

Goering uncomfortably fidgeted on his cot. "It was obvious that a confrontation with Russia was inevitable. But we did not intend to act according to the orders of the West. We had our own designs and our own plans. We were guided by the interests of Germany and not the too-clever plots of those miserable and cowardly impotents. We were alive then, full of energy, and they were exhausted and weak sybarites…"

On his prison cot that seemed close to collapse, Goering again looked like the same self-satisfied, arrogant man that the whole world had grown used to before the Reich's defeat.

"So," Gilbert asked, "when Britain and France signed the treaty in Munich, you took it as their direct agreement with Germany expanding its borders east at Russia's expense?"

"Of course! How else should I have taken it?" Goering smiled at Gilbert. "The British wanted wholeheartedly for us to start a war with Russia, and as soon as possible. They were like an open book!"

Gilbert stood up. "I've got to go. I will talk with my superiors about the letters from your family. I wish you a merry Christmas and a happy new year, Reichsmarschall!"

"I think you want to say a happy last new year," Goering said with a cruel gleam in his eyes.

"That doesn't depend on me."

Gilbert had already reached the door when Goering called out, "Doctor!"

"Yes?"

"Look." Goering was holding his arm out almost in fascist greeting, but his hand was in a fist. "You see, my arm is not shaking. It is still that strong. Let your prosecutors hear that. I am ready for a fight. A real fight."

As he walked down the corridor, Gilbert was thinking that he had to somehow increase the pressure on Goering's morale. For example, he might be isolated during meals, seated at a separate table, so that he could not speak with the other prisoners and he would not be able to communicate any instructions to them.

Notes

Once an American chief photographer came up to us and said that if we had camera flashes on us, we could go with him. He took us to a space around forty square meters in size. There were tables at the wall, but no lighting. Four people were seated at each table. At one table sat Goering, Rosenberg, Admiral Dönitz, and von Schirach. At the table closest to me was Keitel along with Jodl. I shot them with a flash. Keitel covered his face with his hand. Then I went over to the table where Goering was seated.

While other photographers — American and French —
had been taking pictures, Goering said nothing,
but as soon as he saw my Russian uniform, he
started shouting, "What is this? Can't I eat in
peace?"

Then an American lieutenant came up and ask,
"What's going on? Why is Goering shouting?"
I had no idea, I said that I just wanted to
photograph them. The lieutenant went over to
Goering and told him to stop shouting, but
Goering would not stop. Then the lieutenant
lightly hit Goering in the back of the head with
his truncheon. After that, it got quiet.

    Yevgeny Khaldei, Soviet photojournalist

CHAPTER XIV.
NO NEED TO DRAW OUT THE TORMENT

The court resumed on January 2, 1946. By the next day, examination of the defendants and witnesses had begun. Otto Ohlendorf, an Obergruppenführer of the SS, was called before the tribunal as a "witness".

The man seemed to have come straight out of a propaganda poster of "true German beauty". He gave the impression of a thinking, intelligent person, one who possessed extraordinary abilities. He had an impressive academic record, having graduated with two degrees in law and economics respectively. He had then made a blazing career: at the age of thirty-four he became head of the Amt III (SD-domestic branch) of the Reich Main Security Office and was promoted to the rank of SS general. Ohlendorf had seen the end of the war somewhere else, though, as he did not see eye to eye with Himmler's deputy Ernst Kaltenbrunner. He moved to the Ministry of the Economy as an expert in foreign trade issues. Women adored him, he would receive letters and postcards from them in his prison cell. Yet this was a man who, by his own calm admission, had personally directed the murder of tens of thousands of people in the occupied territories and on the Eastern Front. The "inferior population", as Ohlendorf put it, had to be "liquidated": people were shot by Einsatzgruppen, gassed in special vans, and whole villages were set aflame…

This tall, elegant man, who might have served as a paragon of "Nordic beauty" was sitting with his legs crossed in an armchair in front of a microphone. He was in a state of total calm and gave clear and exhaustive answers to the questions asked by the American and Soviet prosecutors. The courtroom, still half-empty after the Christmas holiday, was plunged into total silence. Otto Ohlendorf, commander of Einsatzgruppe D, recounted in cold blood how his team carried out the tasks assigned to them in early June 1941. Among their instructions, the liquidation of "persons of Jewish race and Soviet commissars" was the highest priority. All "inferior persons" were simply labeled "sources of resistance". Also included among them were random passersby or the inhabitants of communities that the SS did not like. The commandos spared neither women, nor children, nor the elderly. The deleterious effect on the civilian population was simply astonishing, especially considering the large number of children under the age of five killed and even infants.

SS Obergruppenführer Otto Ohlendorf calmly adjusted the parting of his hair, which was already impeccable.

Goering snorted in fury and muttered hoarsely to Hess, who was seated next to him and apparently oblivious to the proceedings, "Here's another man who sold his soul to the enemy! This pig expects to be pardoned, but they will hang him all the same."

Denis was sitting at a table in the bar, absentmindedly stirring sugar into his coffee. The events in the courtroom were being broadcast over the radio. Ohlendorf was now being questioned by the defense attorneys of the accused. They had only one goal: to prove that their clients had nothing to do with these "liquidations". The defense for Albert Speer, former Reich Minister of Armaments, asked whether Ohlendorf, a friend of Speer, knew that in 1945 he was preparing a plot to assassinate the Führer and save Germany and the German people, and to hand over Himmler to the Allies for all his crimes. Rebrov did not hear Ohlendorf's answer, but he did not really care whatever the Nazis planned then, when it was already clear that the end was near. Everyone was simply trying to save their own skin instead of getting a bullet in their Nazi brains.

Someone sat down at his table. Rebrov looked up to see Peggy.

"Hi," he nodded in greeting. "Welcome back."

"Thanks. Though coming back to hear all this… What do you think, why is this handsome general so open today?"

"I don't know."

"You think he has come to his senses?"

"Any normal people who came to their senses after all that would shoot or hang themselves."

"Maybe… Did you see what an uproar came from the Nazis when Speer said he was plotting to kill Hitler? Goering was just furious. He started to accuse Speer of being a traitor, of going over to the enemy, and Speer told him to go to hell! I think Dr. Gilbert is very pleased."

"Pleased at what?"

"That he managed to split the defendants, make them fight among each other."

"What difference does it make!"

"Jackson, who Gilbert works for, thinks that it's not just important to hang them, but also make them repent, show how pathetic they are."

"Well, then."

Peggy looked at Rebrov searchingly. "I need to talk to you about something…"

"Again with the Russians' secrets?" Rebrov smiled.

"No. I can see that you're not in the mood, but…" Peggy set a small book in front of Rebrov. "This is for you."

"What is it?"

"Just look at it."

Denis shrugged and picked up the book. It was a collection of short stories by Ivan Bunin. He looked up at Peggy with astonishment.

"I flew here straight from Paris. I saw our friend the princess there. She asked me to give you this. She said you would understand."

"Has something happened to her, to Irina?" Rebrov asked with difficulty.

"It's just that she won't be coming back to Nuremberg."

"She won't? Why?"

"Irina was fired. She said that the French delegation no longer needs her services. She will be replaced by other translators who will not enter into questionable affairs with Soviet agents. You know what's going on now in France with women… *Collaboration horizontale*! It's so appalling."

Stunned by this news, Rebrov fell silent and looked at the book. Peggy leaned over and whispered fiercely, "From what I understand, someone reported her, reported your relationship, saying that a Soviet agent was recruiting her and getting secret information from her. What nonsense! Thank God that it didn't wind up in the papers. It would have been quite an uproar. If it was about me, I'd just tell everyone where they can go, but Irina… She's different. She is terribly worried, and she feels guilty, though she has nothing to feel guilty about. And the Russian émigrés, they are a special world, they have their own laws and their own ideas of honor."

"Do you know who did it?"

"Did what?"

"Reported her?"

"From what I understand, it was one of the people here, who work here, in Nuremberg." Peggy took a drag on her cigarette. "I told her she should move elsewhere, to America, for example, or somewhere like Casablanca. I even offered her help with money, because she is quite badly off, your princess. Poor, even."

Rebrov remained silent.

"Denis," Peggy suddenly addressed him by his first name. "Alex taught me a Russian saying."

"What's that?"

Peggy pronounced with difficulty, "*Slezami goryu ne pomozhesh*, your tears won't be any help for your grief."

In the office where the French translators worked, only Princess Trubetskaya was left. She was wrapped up in a warm handkerchief and appeared to have come down with quite a cold.

"Tatyana Vladimirovna, can I see Mr. Rosen?" Rebrov asked sharply.

Trubetskaya loudly blew her nose in a fashion that was far from aristocratically elegant, then shook her head.

"Why not?"

"Why do you want to see him? He doesn't work here any more, my friend. He stayed in Paris. Or rather, I told him he should, so that he wouldn't run into you. You don't need to see him. Pavel behaved repulsively, of course, but he thought that it was the only way to get you away from Irina."

"So, he was the one who reported her?"

"Let God judge him for it."

"But why only God? What about other people?"

Trubetskaya looked up at him with eyes red from her cold. "Do you remember our talk about Irina?" she asked. "I told you that you and her were bound in chains of such incredible strength that they cannot be undone. So, it's not just Pavel's fault with his awful letter. Irina would not have come back anyway."

"But why?" Rebrov was not willing to understand.

"Because Maria asked her not to."

"Who is Maria?"

"Maria Alexeyevna, her mother, and an old friend of mine. She has suffered too much during the revolution and civil war. You simply cannot imagine what she had to go through. She cannot forgive and forget any of that, even if you have nothing to do with it. God… May everyone get their reward for what they've done…"

The princess adjusted her handkerchief, sighed, and continued resolutely, "So, I admit that even I told Irina not to come back to Nuremberg."

"Even you?" Rebrov was stunned.

"Even me. So that she would not draw out the torment. Nothing good would have resulted for Irina from this."

"What, is she cursed?!"

"It's fate, young man. Not only hers, but yours as well. Do you want to abandon your Russia? She can't abandon hers."

"And there's no way to bring them together," Rebrov muttered, his strength gone.

"Who knows. Maybe someday, but not now."

Notes

Soon after our rendezvous, she told me when I brought up marriage, "No, I am not fit to be a wife! I am not fit!" That was little encouragement for me. "We'll see!" I said in the hope that she would change her mind. What was I left with, besides hope?

Ivan Bunin, "Pure Monday"

CHAPTER XV. NOTHING CAN BE DONE

Gen. Filin was looking at Rebrov's glum face with the same pity he would be showing his own son were he still alive. Filin thought that the war had been largely won by young men like Rebrov, who only yesterday had been in high school or university. Without them, there would have been no pilots, tank drivers, artillerymen, or staff officers. With incredible speed they had filled the army's needs for junior and mid-level commanders, and this was one of the key factors in securing victory. And, Filin felt sure, it was they – or rather those who hadn't perished in the carnage of war – who would move the country forward. He had lost his son, but if anything happened to Rebrov, too, he would never forgive himself for it.

They reached Nuremberg's famous Fountain of Virtues and stopped.

"No one will hear us here or keep any recordings," Filin said in a raspy voice. "I know about everything that happened with Kurakina. Nothing can be done. Not now, at least."

Rebrov said nothing in answer.

"But you ought to keep one thing in mind," Filin, now growing angry, went on. "You met with Irina Kurakina at my order. You used her as an agent and got valuable information from her. That's exactly how it happened, word for word. Remember?"

Rebrov reluctantly nodded.

"And there were no feelings between you. At least from your side. I already had a talk today with Kosachev. About you. I think he wants to tell Moscow that he has found a spy in our delegation. You want to take a guess who that spy might be?"

"Well, me," Rebrov smiled wryly.

"Yes, you. There's nothing funny about this. I'm sure Kosachev has already thought about this and come up with an amazing story: you were seduced by a representative of White Guard émigré circles, and she turned you into her agent. When I told him that Kurakina had been arrested as one of our agents…"

"Arrested?!" Rebrov let out. "Was she really arrested?"

"Well, I exaggerated things a bit. No one was arrested, but I had to head Kosachev off. In any event, try to think what information we could have got from her. You can ascribe some of the reports we've received from Hector to her. It won't cost him anything, and it will make her look good. Why aren't you saying anything?"

"I can't stand any of this. What do I have to justify myself for, Sergei Ivanovich? And to who? I just can't."

Filin looked at him harshly. "He just can't! Well, now, do you want Kosachev to paint you as a traitor to your country? Then be my guest, or just give yourself up. Only keep in mind that if you do, then they'll take me, too, as your direct superior and someone who personally vouched for you. And not just me. Other people will go down for it, too, like Gavrik. You just think about that when you want to play the fool."

"I'm sorry, Sergei Ivanovich."

"Fine, what can I do," Filin waved the subject away. "I realize that you don't meet girls like that very often. Maybe once in your whole life. Well, you're still quite young, you've got your whole life ahead of you. Anything could happen."

"Well, then, Georgy Nikolayevich," Rudenko said as he turned to Filin. "Tell us, what's the big emergency here? What kind of a pickle are you in?" Rudenko said with a Ukrainian rusticness, which he loved to slip into his speech to give the conversation an informal, friendly quality.

Filin appreciated the gesture, but he decided to keep a serious tone. "It's not a pickle, Roman Andreyevich. It's just a very unpleasant situation. We need to think of something, or the entire Soviet delegation will be a laughingstock in front of the Allies."

"Is that so?" Rudenko scratched his large and already balding head.

"As you know, Col. Kosachev has long been forcing our young interpreter Lidia Korzun to carry out an affair with him. The whole delegation is whispering about it. Foreigners have caught wind of it, and soon they'll start printing stories about it: 'Look at what the Russians are up to during the trial of the century.'"

Rudenko, who could not stand dealing with matters like that, shrugged. "Maybe she herself fell in love with him? We just don't know."

"First of all, there's no love there, he's forcing her," Filin put it harshly. "Secondly, things have gone too far."

"How so?"

"Lidia Korzun is pregnant."

"What a dirty dog!" Rudenko exploded. "So, we need to send her to Moscow immediately. This is something we really don't need!"

"It's too late."

"What do you mean, too late? Let her fly home and give birth there."

"The problem is that Kosachev forced her to get an abortion, which, as you know, is against Soviet law."

"I know the law! Has he lost his mind?"

"I don't think so. I think he feels that now he can do whatever he wants and get away with it."

"Well, he's wrong. SMERSH is SMERSH, of course, but everyone has their limits! As for this abortion, did he carry it out himself? I don't think any of our doctors would have agreed to it."

"He didn't go to our doctors. His staff found a German doctor and brought Lidia Korzun there. The operation went badly. It appears that Korzun has come down with an infection. She's in a very bad state now, getting worse by the day. Kosachev won't let her see a doctor, he's afraid that things will become public. He has even set a guard at the door to her room. If Korzun dies, I can't imagine what lies in store for us…"

"That's the last thing we need!" Rudenko jumped to his feet. "He must have completely lost his marbles!"

"The situation is quite bad," Filin summed up. "According to the Soviet law banning abortion, Korzun has to be brought to trial. We're not in the USSR right now, but…"

"You tell me what to do, Sergei Ivanovich! Come on!" Rudenko sighed heavily. "And let me worry about the law."

"I think we need to get both of them out of Nuremberg. Korzun should be sent to a hospital in the Soviet zone to recover, but with Kosachev it's more complicated… SMERSH won't listen to you or me, but we can't have him around here any more. He's behaving in a completely unacceptable way. It's casting a shadow over the entire Soviet delegation. Can you imagine what the Western newspapers would make of this?"

"I can't imagine it very well. But you and I can't send him back to Moscow! Only SMERSH can recall him, or rather Abakumov."

"But we can't put up with this situation any more," Filin insisted. "Korzun is in a very bad state, she needs medication and a new operation. We need to save the girl."

"Indeed, we can't put up with it any more," Rudenko agreed. "I'll send my car and my bodyguards for the girl, they wouldn't dare stand in their way. Let them take her straight to the airport and off to the Soviet zone.

God help us that she doesn't die! Sergei Ivanovich, you send your man with my guards. They should do everything very carefully, so that no one knows or suspects a thing. We don't need any shooting among ourselves. Can you imagine what would happen?"

"I certainly do," Filin nodded. "What are we to do with Kosachev? He'll want revenge, it'll be the last straw for him."

"Well, we'll see about him. That dog has gone completely rabid! In just a few days, the Soviet prosecutor Gorshenin will be flying in. I'll explain to him this situation that has come up. He can speak directly to Abakumov. We might be abroad right now, but no one can violate Soviet law. That will be our argument, it will be a very weighty one."

Rudenko was walking around the office, muttering something to himself. Filin took a paper out of the folder lying in front of him. "Roman Andreyevich…"

"What, is someone else pregnant?" Rudenko grimaced.

"Not quite yet," Filin smiled reassuringly. "We have received through our channels word that the American prosecutor is preparing to question Goering. I wanted to show it to you."

"Well, that is interesting! What have our overseas colleagues come up with?"

"They've been working on Goering a lot. Partly their Dr. Gilbert has been occupied with this."

"I've heard of him."

"Until recently Goering, it seemed, was thinking about only one thing: dragging things out, trying to shirk responsibility, and paint himself as an innocent lamb. Apparently in the last few weeks he has undergone some changes. The prison barber says that Goering is increasingly using words and expressions that cannot be printed when he talks about the Americans. He is convinced that he'll be able to put 'that whiskey-sodden American provincial lawyer' in his place."

"Did he say that about Jackson?" Rudenko was astonished. "What a son of a bitch!"

"This is from a man who could not live without his drugs, and now he is clearly emboldened. Strict prison life has done him good, it seems. He is once more able to analyze the situation, reflect, and make some unexpected and daring moves. Do you know what one of the lawyers is calling him now? *Mordskerl*, back to his full strength!"

Rudenko looked at Filin, puzzled.

"*Mordskerl* in German means that he's a hell of a guy, a hotshot. In general, I think Jackson is in for a hard time, and he will need our help."

"Well, then, let's open a second front," Rudenko laughed. "How many times did we come to their rescue during the war, when the Germans had them by the tail?"

"Dr. Gilbert has provided Jackson with an in-depth analysis of Goering's personality. He describes his strong sides, self-defense strategies, and his most vulnerable spots. The American psychologist generally characterizes Goering as an aggressive extrovert, as a person without any spiritual interests and caring only about his own personal benefit. Goering is a heartless, cynical, and pragmatic man. At the trial he will attempt to prove that he was against war with Britain and he had tried to open negotiations behind Hitler's back. Operation Barbarossa, the plan to attack Russia, he will describe as premature. He will try to play a hero, an honest patriot and exemplary officer who was faithful to his duties as a soldier."

"Well then, let him just try."

"There are two chinks in Goering's defense: the atrocities of the Nazis, which he supported, and his own irrepressible greed and desire for his own personal enrichment. He will continually try to deflect attention towards other accusations that are less dangerous for him personally. For example, he'll draw parallels between the Nazis' actions and those of other countries. We need to constantly hit Goering with harsh and specific questions so that he cannot go off into endless abstract reasoning."

"Well, that is very sage advice," Rudenko said. "Let's see what Jackson can make of it. For my part, I think that we need to come up with a few surprises for Goering and the others. Surprises that they won't be at all prepared for, either in terms of their thinking or their morale. We do have a few surprises like that." He rubbed his hands.

Notes

As early as December 15–18, 1943, the first court trial of Nazi German criminals opened in Kharkiv. These ordinary butchers of the Third Reich were not high-ranking, and the atrocities they committed were only a small part of the monstrous chain of crimes that humanity eventually became aware of. However, this was the first trial over fascism and it made a historical precedent: for

the first time, the world convened a trial for
crimes against humanity.

The trial was covered by the Soviet and
international media, including the London *Times*
and *New York Times*, the *Sunday Express* and *Daily
Express*, and the Columbia Broadcasting Company.
The Soviet press was represented at the trial
by Alexei Tolstoy, Konstantin Simonov, Ilya
Ehrenburg, Elena Kononenko, and Leonid Leonov.

Victory was still far off, a long 705 days would
pass before the Nuremberg trials began when
in Kharkiv, which had survived 22 months of
occupation, stern words were spoken about the
inevitably of a day of reckoning for these
monstrous crimes. Words that kept the entire
world in hopeful suspense: "Arise, the court is
in session!"

From the materials of
the Kharkiv Holocaust Museum

CHAPTER XVI.
LET'S NOT DO ANYTHING
STUPID, COLONEL!

The black-haired and swarthy sergeant Grosman, one of Rudenko's bodyguards, was quite young, smart, and, judging from his actions, a clever guy. He was sitting next to Rudenko's driver and constantly turning his head, wrinkling his nose, snorting, and he clearly wanted to speak with Rebrov, seated boss-like in the back seat, but he couldn't convince himself to.

"How old are you, sergeant?" Rebrov asked.

"Twenty-two, comrade. Forgive me, I don't know your rank…"

"Just call me Denis Grigoryevich. Where are you from?"

"From near Odessa."

"Near Odessa," Rebrov smiled. "Have you been serving for a long time now?"

"Since '42."

"Wow, so you're quite a veteran."

"Since 1943 I've been serving in division intelligence, I was a platoon commander. I got to Berlin and even left my mark on the Reichstag."

"How did you wind up here in Nuremberg?"

"It was quite simple. Somehow the head of our division's political department calls me and says, 'Comrade Grosman, they've decided to transfer you to Nuremberg to guard the Soviet delegation at the trials over the major German prisoners.' I was baffled, I said, 'Why me?' The colonel answers, 'If I were you, I'd be raring to go. And anyway, it's an order. So, go to the tailor, they'll make you a new uniform so that you look appropriate.'"

"You must have been a dashing scout, sergeant, if they chose you out of the whole division."

"My commanders never complained."

"How good of a shot are you?"

"Pretty good. If it's a target, then 9, or rarely 8…"

"Do you always have a pistol with you?"

"Of course. I'm the bodyguard for our comrade general."

"Well, everyone knows that. But don't draw your pistol, sergeant, because under no circumstances are we to shoot. Everyone there will be our own guys. Well, it looks like we're here."

They entered a large, four-story building, went up to the second floor, and stopped in front of the door to the apartment they were looking for.

"So, sergeant, I'll explain our mission," Rebrov said as Grosman was fidgeting impatiently. "We need to get a sick woman out of here and bring her immediately to the airport so we can send her to Berlin. It's a simple matter, but one of our officers is standing next to her and he has been instructed to admit no one. I'll repeat: one of *our* comrades. So, we need to act calmly and delicately."

"What if he does something?"

"We'll try to convince him."

"And if that doesn't work?"

"Then we need to carefully neutralize him. Just do it gently, like he's family. I'll see to that myself. You just back me up, understand? The main thing is to not let him foolishly shoot."

Rebrov rang the doorbell. After a while, a stern voice came from the other side of the door. "Who's there?"

"Soviets, commander," Rebrov calmly answered. "We have come on the orders of Gen. Rudenko. Do you know him?"

"Can you prove it?"

"I've got his bodyguard with me, Sgt. Grosman."

The door opened slightly. A lieutenant stood behind it with a round, boyish face with a big frown. His hand was on his unbuttoned holster, which Rebrov did not like at all. The guy looked tired, clearly nervous, and he could do something really stupid since he was so tense."

"What's going on?"

"Do you recognize us, lieutenant? This is Sgt. Grosman, one of Gen. Rudenko's bodyguards." Rebrov tilted his head towards Grosman, who had sagely taken up a position not behind Rebrov's back but rather a step away to the side, which would allow him to quickly act if things came to a confrontation. "You know him?"

"I do," the unhappy lieutenant, clearly caught off guard, nodded.

"We come with orders from Gen. Rudenko to immediately take Lidia Korzun to the hospital. How is she?"

"She's delirious. I feel sorry for the girl. But I have been ordered by Col. Kosachev to let no one see her. No one."

"Even Gen. Rudenko?"

"He didn't tell me anything about comrade general," the lieutenant frowned.

"So, what are we going to do, commander?"

"Without an order from comrade colonel personally, I don't have the right to let anyone in."

"But we do have an order from the general," Rebrov threw up his hands.

The lieutenant shook his head vehemently. "Go look for comrade colonel. I can't do anything without him. I have my orders to open fire if anyone…"

Rebrov suddenly jabbed a finger into the lieutenant's back. "She's got out of bed!"

The officer turned to look. Rebrov promptly covered his mouth with one hand and with his thumb he pressed down on the officer's neck slightly below his ear. The lieutenant was still trying to grab at the holstered pistol, but Grosman, with a single cat-like movement, rushed forward and grabbed his hand. Together they carried the officer into the hallway and carefully sat him down in a chair.

"Wow, good work," Grosman said with burning eyes. "Will he be out for long?"

"He'll come to in ten minutes or so and raise the alarm. We're got time to spare."

They went into the small bedroom where a thin girl with parched lips was lying in bed. Her eyes were closed. Rebrov easily lifted her up and quickly headed for the door. Grosman grabbed her coat from its hook and rushed after him.

The plane had already soared into the sky when two cars sped right onto the runway. Col. Kosachev and three SMERSH officers ran out from them. Kosachev cast a glance on the plane that was already disappearing in the clouds, and then turned in fury to Filin and Rebrov who were standing a distance off. For a while they stood facing each other in silence, and then Kosachev's hand reached for his holster."

"Get a hold of yourself, colonel," Filin said calmly. "Don't do anything stupid. What example are you making for your officers?"

At that moment the doors of Rudenko's car, which had parked nearby, opened and Grosman and the driver jumped out and rushed to stand alongside Filin and Rebrov.

Kosachev, without saying a word, turned and got back into his car. His officers followed behind him. As he looked over the departing men, Filin quietly said, "Well, it's over." Then he smiled at Grosman, who was all fired up, and said approvingly, "And you, sergeant, good job! You came right when we needed it."

"We're frontline soldiers, comrade general, you can't stop us," Grosman sniffed. "We know our job."

"I see. Tell Gen. Rudenko that he's got a fine bodyguard." Filin turned to Rebrov. "You and I are flying to Berlin tomorrow, and then to Moscow."

Notes

The head of the SMERSH second department, S. P. Kartashov, returned from Moscow to Nuremberg and stated that he had established contact with the American occupation administration and familiarized himself with the way that war criminals were being held in the city's prisons. He noted that the defendants were poorly monitored while in their cells. The Americans assured him that procedures would be tightened. However, subsequent events showed that these promises were not fully implemented.

From the SMERSH archives

CHAPTER XVII.
YOU HAVE REALLY CHANGED...

In Olga Chekhova's home, nothing had changed since Rebrov's last visit. She remained the same, however: elegant, unperturbed, and well aware of her worth.

"I feel like we haven't seen each other in ages," Rebrov suddenly let out. "Though it hasn't been so long since we last met."

"That is because you have really changed in that time," Chekhova said as she carefully examined him. "I can sense that. You have experienced a very serious shock. I don't know whether it was personal or business, but it got to you. Am I right?"

"Perhaps," Rebrov didn't reveal anything more. "And how have you been doing here?"

"Thank you for asking. As far as my life in Berlin these days goes... The Russians are very kind to me. Soldiers ask me for autographed photos and repay me with vodka, sugar, grain... Many people could only dream of such things."

"What about the Germans?"

"Oh, the Germans! As always, they send me letters filled with curses, and in huge quantities."

"But they don't go too far?"

"You mean like that girl who spat at me and called me a traitor? No, nothing else like that has happened. By the way, I just read in the paper that the majority of Germans, who Hitler made suffer so much, still don't approve of Colonel von Stauffenberg who tried to assassinate him. They think that von Stauffenberg violated his oath. For the Germans, an oath is a sacred thing, it doesn't matter who you swear it to."

"Many Germans also consider Marlene Dietrich a traitor, but she doesn't care. I met her in Nuremberg at the trials, by the way. She considers herself an enemy of Hitler and fascism and is proud of it.

"Well, no one in Germany considers Marlene a German these days. For the Germans, she's an American."

"I see."

"You didn't happen to fall in love with her, did you?" Chekhova asked mockingly.

"No. But she inspires respect."

"I see. Not like me."

"I didn't say that."

"Marlene and I are just different sorts of people. From different stables, as she puts it. Besides, I do not like dressing up like a man. But God bless her! But it wasn't Marlene that brought you here, you are after something else. Or someone else. Who?"

"I need to ask you about Goering. How will he behave during the trial? What would the best way to deal with him be? Pressure him, humiliate him, insult him?"

"It depends to a large part on what state he is in now," Chekhova said thoughtfully.

"You know, prison has done him good. He has lost weight, he has been gradually weaned off drugs… He has generally recovered, and occasionally he even looks extremely lively and vigorous. But from time to time he becomes gloomy and depressed."

"I already told you, Goering is a great actor. He can play whatever role suits him: a simpleton, a merry fellow, a modest man. But his favorite role is the hero, leader, or knight. Goering was a pilot, and in Germany pilots were a special class. Everyone loved and worshiped them."

"Especially women."

"Are you alluding to Ernst Udet?" Chekhova calmly asked. "Yes, I loved him. You know, when he was a child they said he had a 'sunny temperament'. And then he became a famous ace, Goering's number-two man in the Luftwaffe…"

"But Olga Konstantinovna," Rebrov rudely interrupted, "I've heard that Udet was really an alcoholic and drug addict."

"It's very cruel to remind me of this. He shot himself, after all."

"Even though they announced that he died while he was testing a new plane?"

"In actual fact, he shot himself under the stress of everything that was happening to him. He was a famous pilot and a lousy commander. But the German people were given a heroic tale. Goering shed tears at his funeral, but later he said that Udet had destroyed the Luftwaffe, though he, Goering, had nothing to do with it. That's how he is, Goering. Once he descends into pathos, you can't stop him. But in informal conversations with him, it is best to be a little sociable and even seem like you are being open. In reasonable doses, of course. He might think that he really has won you over with his irresistible charm, and then he will give in even more."

"I see." Rebrov remained quiet for a while, aware that Chekhova had to cope with the reawakening memories of her long and passionate affair with Udet. Then he said, "I also wanted to talk to you about Field Marshal Paulus."

"He is not someone I have ever cared for! He is a typical Prussian. It would have never occurred to him, like it did to poor von Stauffenberg, to eliminate Hitler so that Germany would not be dragged down into hell with him."

"Does he have weak points?"

"His wife. Elena von Paulus, who was born the Romanian countess Rosetti-Solescu. She was quite a different kind of woman. She had what you might call a Mediterranean temperament."

"When he was captured, she refused to change her last name and renounce her husband."

"Yes, she preferred prison. I don't know if Paulus deserved such a heroic stance. But for her, he would go to great lengths."

"I see. Do you remember when you were blackmailed by a certain Mr. Frazier? Yes, the same man who hit me over the head. He hasn't been coming round here or troubling you?"

"No, thank goodness."

"Alright, then, it's time for me to go." Rebrov stood up.

Chekhova extended her hand and squeezed his fingers tightly. "You really are shaken by something."

"Is it really so obvious?"

"Yes."

"It's nothing. Everything is in the past. It's all over now."

Chekhova shook her head, not quite believing him.

Notes

The front page of the Stuttgart newspaper *Wochenpost* printed a photograph of an old film starring Olga Chekhova. Instead of a statuette, she held in her hand a Soviet medal. The caption read, "Olga Chekhova with the Order of Lenin, for loyal service as a spy". The newspaper also promised to reveal "juicy details about the famous actress". In the same report one could read the following:

Hitler never managed to identify the lovely Olga as a spy and he invited her, as a prominent representative of German culture, to every ball and diplomatic reception during the war, showing her off to foreigners. Only Goebbels, with his keen eye, always expressed reservations, but Hitler believed that the little doctor had experienced some fiasco with her and wanted revenge. Frau Chekhova denies that she received the Order of Lenin. Well, she knows best!

Unfortunately, we were not able to examine the award certificate in the Kremlin offices! Frau Chekhova also denies that she was engaged in espionage of Hitler's entourage. We cannot disprove it either, as we were not members of Hitler's circle, unlike so many prominent cultural figures of the Thousand-Year Reich…

CHAPTER XVIII.
HOW COULD HE HAVE SURRENDERED?

Outside of Moscow, a car was heading down a road blanketed after a massive authentic Russian snowfall. The January frosts had taken their toll, it was as if the still air was still cracking. Everything around seemed to be frozen and insensate, like in a painting. Rebrov, who was sitting in the front seat next to the driver, looked out at the white silence, so different from the warm and wet Nuremberg winter. He did not think about anything, he only repeated to himself Pushkin's lines "Frost and sun…"

Generals Gres and Filin, sitting in the back seat, were also quiet.

After they passed a road sign reading "Lunevo", the driver turned at a familiar intersection and several minutes later they reached the gates of a community of summer cottages surrounded by a fence.

Guards hovered at the gate, dressed in white sheepskin coats and felt boots and carrying assault rifles over their shoulders. They drove further through the yard along a little path kept carefully clean of snow. Suddenly they encountered a group of German officers in greatcoats without insignia, who were walking here and there on some business completely unguarded.

Near the staff building they were met by the commander of this unusual military base, a colonel, who had been alerted to their arrival by the guards. He waited as the generals stretched their legs after the long journey, and then he asked, "Shall we bring him right out, comrade general?"

"A little later," Gres told him. "In the meantime, have them make us some tea."

In the base commander's office, the generals settled onto a large leather couch while Rebrov discreetly walked up to the window and began to examine the courtyard covered in a blinding layer of snow. Among the heaps of snow as tall as a man, two German officers were walking down the path. One had pince-nez spectacles. They were carrying on a lively conversation about something.

"Well, I reckon you've already figured out where you are?" Gres laughed behind him. "It is a sort of camp with amenities for higher-ranking prisoners of war who have agreed to collaborate with us. With their help, incidentally, we have managed to prepare quite a few documents for our prosecutors in Nuremberg."

"And Paulus is being held here, I gather?" Filin asked.

"That's right." Gres got up and strolled through the spacious room, swinging his arms with evident pleasure. "So, what do we have? The field marshal, after our long efforts with him, has written his testimony, which will be read aloud at the trials in Nuremberg."

"What is in that testimony?" Filin asked.

"Everything we need. It is the testimony of a man who personally took part in drawing up plans to attack the Soviet Union, as the deputy chief of the German General Staff. This is already, as you know yourselves, something serious. After this testimony, all that talk from the accused and their lawyers about a 'preemptive strike', some threat from us, will be seen as pure blather." It was clear that Gres was very satisfied with Paulus' testimony and believed it of the greatest importance. "Upstairs," Gres jabbed his thumb towards the ceiling, "they also think so."

Filin leaned back on the sofa, paused, and then showed a crooked grin. "But the German lawyers will claim that the testimony was drawn up in the basements of the NKVD under torture, or deep in some Siberian mine under terrible cold where the poor field marshal was kept without military-issue long johns. They will demand that he be brought personally to Nuremberg so that he can tell everyone himself what was written. That's already something else entirely."

"Quite right," Gres did not argue against this. "But you aren't the only clever one. We here were thinking things over, too. And we have an idea…"

Filin looked at Gres quizzically.

"The idea is this: at the time it is necessary, we go to meet those lawyers and deliver Paulus to Nuremberg, so that he can repeat his testimony live. How does that sound?"

Filin considered the plan. "It's a bold idea. Only some issues might arise with it, very complex ones."

"I know," Gres waved his hand emphatically. "The first question would be whether Paulus himself agrees to speak in Nuremberg and unmask the men who were his colleagues just yesterday."

"Exactly."

"We are already working with him in this regard. We have been for a long time already."

"And?"

"Our field marshal is hesitating. That's why I have brought you here. I want you to talk to him as a person who has seen firsthand what's going on in Nuremberg. As a person who represents what is happening there. By the way, try to get an idea of his psychological state. We need to understand how risky it might be to take him to Nuremberg. You've seen him under different situations…"

At seven o'clock in the morning, a German officer emerged from the basement of the destroyed department store where Paulus's staff were headquartered. He held a white flag and reported to the commander of a nearby Soviet tank that the Germans were prepared to surrender. The tank commander relayed this to his superiors. A group of Soviet officers, including Filin in an overcoat with the insignia of an infantry captain, headed for the headquarters of the German 6th Army. In the cold room, lit by a dimly burning bulb and a candle stump, the German chief of staff Gen. Schmidt signed an order for his men to end further resistance and hand over their weapons. Paulus, who Hitler had promoted to field marshal the day before, wore a uniform with a colonel-general's stripes, but when they arrested him and referred to him as general, he sternly declared that he held the rank of field marshal and demanded he be addressed accordingly. Filin could not help but smile.

Thousands upon thousands of lice-infested, frostbitten soldiers, who no longer bore much resemblance to human beings, were taken prisoner. They trudged along, shivering with cold, in torn and dirty coats, with women's rags tied over their caps and straw overshoes dangling from their boots. They were hardly escorted at all; only a few Soviet soldiers were present, easy to distinguish by their hats with flaps over the ears, their short fur coats, and their felt boots. Later it became known that some columns of prisoners had marched without any guard at all. Each column was typically led by the senior-ranking German non-commissioned officer, holding in his hands a white sheet of paper with "Beketovka" written in Russian. This referred to the place where all prisoners were to gather. When the Soviet regulars saw this paper, they showed the Germans the way, and the Germans trudged onward in lockstep.

A German reconnaissance plane that flew over Stalingrad on February 2 at 2:46 a.m. radioed command, "No signs of fighting are visible in Stalingrad."

Hitler then screamed at a meeting at his headquarters, "How could he have surrendered to the Bolsheviks, huh? It's completely impossible!"

"It's totally unthinkable!" muttered Zeitzler, the Germany army's chief of staff, in bewilderment and looking away.

"He ought to have shot himself, like a real German soldier! It would have been so easy to do!" Hitler railed at his staff. "A pistol isn't hard to operate. What kind of coward do you have to be to be afraid of one? Really! Is it honestly better to let yourself be buried alive? And especially when he knew perfectly well that his death would help support the other places where our forces are entrapped. And now when he has made an example like this, we can't expect our soldiers to go on fighting!" Hitler looked around, upset, at everyone gathered.

"There is no justification for this, my Führer," said Zeitzler in a servile tone. "Paulus should have shot himself."

"They surrendered! But everything could have turned out differently: they could have come together, formed a circular defense, and kept one last bullet aside for themselves…"

Hitler walked up to Zeitzler and, as if delirious, started rambling, "You know, one very beautiful lady – oh, she was beautiful in the full sense of the word – was insulted once. Someone insulted her with a single remark. Something completely trivial! But she said, 'If that's what they think of me, I can take my leave of them!' No one tried to hold her back. She walked away, wrote a farewell letter at her home, and shot herself!"

Zeitzler, struck by this grotesque anecdote, remained silent.

"You see," Hitler explained heatedly, "the woman had enough pride that once she had heard only a few words directed at her in insult, she went away, locked herself in her room, and immediately shot herself. A woman did that! Can anyone respect a soldier who fears an honorable death and lets himself be taken captive?"

Hitler walked up to the table, laid his hand on it, and solemnly lifted his head. "I won't be awarding anyone else the rank of field marshal in this war! Anyone, under any circumstances! We'll have field marshals only after we have proved victorious! And I believe we will be victorious, in spite of Paulus's shameful cowardice."

After Hitler learned that Paulus had surrendered, Hitler tried to revoke his decree awarding him the rank of field marshal, but it was already too late: the decree had been read out over the radio and published in the newspapers. Two days before Paulus surrendered, Germany had celebrated a national holiday, marking ten years since the Nazis had come to power. The Germans in those days were told of the heroic 6th Army's willingness to lay down their lives for the Führer's sake. Paulus himself had sent Hitler a telegram on the eve of the festivities that spoke of "the flag with the swastika majestically flying over Stalingrad". Propaganda from Berlin immediately hoisted this banner on "the highest ruin of Stalingrad" and made appropriate statements about how German soldiers were unbeatable… But the soldiers who remained alive in the cellars of destroyed Stalingrad, around one hundred thousand of them, who had practically lost any resemblance to human beings and received each day a meager ration of lousy bread, were thinking only about how to survive, at any cost. Being taken prisoner seemed the best way out of the icy and fiery hell that they were living in.

On January 30 Paulus sent the Führer a telegram: "The end is no more than twenty-four hours away." On the night of January 31 Hitler's decree promoting Paulus to field marshal was broadcast over the radio. Another 117 generals and officers of his army also received promotions. They were showered in Iron Cross medals, which Berlin hoped would give them the strength to either maintain their defense or lay down their lives. "There is no historical precedent for a German field marshal giving himself up to captivity," Hitler pointed out as he explained his decision.

But in the mud, ashes, and reek of Stalingrad, Paulus's staff were living out their last hours. His chief of staff Gen. Schmidt sent away any officer who tried to come and congratulate Paulus. "Let him sleep, he can find out about his promotion tomorrow morning." Paulus, who woke up the next morning as a field marshal, asked everyone now standing around him a familiar question: "Should I shoot myself?" The members of his staff, filthy and battered, answered in unison their already well-worn answer, "No need to do that, sir. Our field marshal should share in his men's fate to the very end." Thus it was decided.

On February 3, German radio broadcast a muffled drum roll, then the announcer gravely read out a message from the High Command of the Wehrmacht, full of sentimental statements about the perishing of the 6th Army. This report also mentioned the "exemplary command" of Field Marshal Paulus…

After the announcer had fallen silent, the radio played Beethoven's Fifth. For the first and last time during the war, a "period of national mourning" was declared across the Reich to commemorate the defeated and captured 6th Army. Flags were lowered in the cities and towns, on ships, and even outside the offices of concentration camp commandants. As the *Völkischer Beobachter* wrote that day, "They died so that Germany may live." "Until their last breath, the faithful 6th Army under the exemplary command of Field Marshal Friedrich Paulus perished in the face of superior enemy forces and unpropitious circumstances. The final battle ended under a flag with the swastika set on the highest ruin of Stalingrad. The generals, officers, and enlisted men fought shoulder to shoulder to their last bullet."

The Führer personally took part in a symbolic funeral for Field Marshal Paulus, "who fell in the line of duty along with the heroic soldiers of the 6th Army." He even laid a diamond-encrusted staff on the field marshal's empty coffin. Hitler, it seemed, was very afraid that the example of this commander, so popular among the army, would become contagious.

The head of the Abwehr, Admiral Canaris, was crafting a plan over these days to rescue Paulus from captivity and spirit him away back to Germany. But while these dashing plans were being hatched in the Abwehr headquarters on Berlin's Tirpitzufer street, the captive Paulus and his generals were being delivered first to Beketovka, a district in the south of Stalingrad, and then to the small estate of Zavarygino on the steppes. A special battalion of NKVD forces was brought in to guard the prisoners.

Nearly as soon as he arrived at Zavarygino, Paulus demanded to meet with representatives of the Soviet command. Alexander Voronin, head of the Stalingrad branch of the NKVD, was sent to the wooden house that Paulus was being held in and was made personally responsible for the prisoner's confinement. Filin, who had already begun working with the prisoners, arrived here along with Voronin. As soon as Paulus, sitting at a table, caught sight of Voronin he began, without uttering a word in greeting, to rattle off his complaints and demands. They consisted of the following: the prisoners were served only one breakfast, but they were accustomed to two; secondly, they were not given any dry wine; and thirdly, they were not being provided with information on the situation along the front…

This all sounded appallingly impudent and comical at the same time. However, since it was clear that Paulus would be needed for serious political intrigues, they calmly heard him out. After Voronin had waited a while, he answered coolly, "I will deal with all your complaints, field marshal, but I must remind you that you are not at a seaside resort now, but rather a prisoner. Let me repeat, a prisoner! Wine, in this case dry, is produced in Crimea and it has been captured by your forces. Instead of wine, you are being provided with vodka daily, as I understand. Your adjutant and the other generals are receiving one hundred grams a day. You are being fed quite well. So, I think that one breakfast will be enough. As far as information on the war goes, newspapers will be delivered. Soviet ones, as we don't get German newspapers here."

"And coffee? I can't get through mornings without coffee."

"Coffee?" Voronin laughed. "We'll look for some. If we find any…"

Filin, who had been studying Paulus all this time, was thinking about how difficult it would be to work with such a man. It was obvious he was an arrogant Prussian officer, who considered himself the summit of creation, did not have a very broad outlook on life, and could think only in fixed routines and dogmas. But he could not, of course, be called a stupid man.

During these days the Germans had nevertheless begun to make attempts to rescue the field marshal. Several small landing groups of up to forty men were killed as they tried to approach Zavarygino. Reconnaissance planes were spotted above the estate. Another battalion was brought in to Zavarygino in order to increase security.

But after a day, the prisoners had been sent further away in Russia. First, they were brought to Saratov, and then the generals and senior officers led by Paulus were taken to Suzdal, where a camp for high-ranking prisoners had been set up in a former monastery. Not only Germans were held here but also Germany's allies: Italian, Hungarian, Romanian, and Spanish soldiers. They lived in the former cells of monks, but they were in no hurry to repent of their sins.

Filin was not to work on Paulus after all, however. He was immediately summoned to Moscow and assigned to a new mission. He remained aware that, all that time, serious efforts were being taken with regard to Paulus. As early as September 1943, a "League of German Officers" was formed, consisting of captured German officers and generals. It was led by Walther von Seydlitz, a general in the artillery. The League called on German officers to rise up against Hitler or lay down their weapons for the sake of Germany's future. Paulus's jailers were constantly trying to persuade him to join the League and he was even offered the chance to lead a German military unit that would be drawn up from prisoners of war. However, this plan did not come to fruition for many reasons, and Paulus, in spite of his jailers' long attempts, showed no interest in political involvement and continually avoided taking any specific action.

Around one year after Paulus had been moved to Suzdal, he was summoned to the office of the camp's commandant, Col. Novikov. The commandant handed his prisoner a letter from his wife. How this letter had managed to make it across borders from Berlin to Suzdal during the fighting, is another story. A Soviet intelligence agent, risking his life, had managed to inform Paulus's wife of his true fate, which until this time had remained totally unknown to his family. Nazi propaganda had disseminated to the world three versions of Paulus's fate: in one, the field marshal ingested the poison curare, which he had always kept with him; in another, he was gravely wounded when he was captured, and the Russians tortured him during interrogation; and in the third version, Paulus died like a soldier at his post. Even a pilot was found who supposedly flew over downtown Stalingrad on February 2, and who saw with his own eyes how the department store building that had sheltered Paulus's staff in its basement had been blown up. The Soviet agent managed to convince the field marshal's wife that he was telling the truth, and she even decided to entrust him with a letter to her husband.

This letter may have been the last straw that led Paulus to a decision he had long been shying away from. On August 3, 1944 he told the commanders of the camp that he was seriously willing to consider public action against Hitlerism, but he was "looking for an appropriate way of doing so that would not seem to Germany like stabbing the German army in the back." Already on August 8, 1944 Paulus appeared in a radio broadcast directed at Germany, in which he called on the German people to denounce the Führer and save the country. And to do this, the war, already lost, should be immediately brought to an end. Then the Nazi regime demanded that Paulus's family publicly condemn him as a traitor, break all ties with him, and immediately change their last name. When his family refused to fulfill these demands, the field marshal's wife Elena was sent to Dachau, while his son, Wehrmacht captain Ernst-Alexander Paulus, was imprisoned in the Küstrin fortress. They had survived to see the end of the war, and now Paulus could even be promised a meeting with them…

Paulus was brought into the office. He was wearing a fine civilian suit and was lean and taut, but also very tense. Filin was struck by the thought that since Stalingrad the field marshal had not seemed to grow any older at all. Rather, he was in even better shape, and clearly he had had enough wine and coffee. One had to admit that he still had his old bearing.

"Sit down, field marshal," Gres nodded at the chair and turned to Rebrov, "Alright, major, start interpreting for me."

Rebrov stepped away from the window, stood at Filin's side, and got to work.

"I'd like to introduce you to some of our staff who have just arrived from Nuremberg," Gres said as he sat down on the sofa. "I think that you'll appreciate getting the latest information from them."

Paulus nodded curtly and then dully asked, "How is Nuremberg looking today? I remember it well. It was a beautiful old city. A lot of flowers."

"Nuremberg looks like a city would after massive bombardment by the Allies," Filin said coolly. "Though there are neighborhoods that are practically unscathed, generally on the outskirts."

"And how is the weather there now?"

"There has been wet snow for a few days now, fog. It was hard to fly out."

"I see."

"As far as the trials themselves go… Goering and the other defendants are sticking to the same line, that they were all against war with the USSR and had no part in drawing up plans for it. Everything was thought up by Hitler. Well, or otherwise by Himmler and Goebbels. Of course they blamed them, they are already dead. As for your colleagues in the military…"

Paulus visibly tensed.

"They claim that Germany was always at risk of attack from the neighboring countries and that is why they prepared for war. Gen. Manstein, who will appear as a witness, claimed that Germany's war doctrine was based on its neighbors having claims on German territory. When the accused talk about the attack on Poland, they declare that it was Poland who had started the war, and so Germany was forced to attack, but only for defensive purposes. The attack on Norway? The German navy in northern Europe was only trying to ward off an attack on Norway by British forces…"

Filin paused, waiting for Paulus's reaction, but the latter remained silent. Filin then went on. "The invasion of Belgium and the Netherlands? Your colleagues have an answer for that, too. It is well known that Britain and France had long had a plan to use those countries as a springboard to attack Germany. If Germany had not seized them, they would have been taken by its enemies. And so on and so forth. The Soviet Union was preparing to attack Germany, and therefore Germany only preempted an enemy attack."

Paulus remained utterly silent just as before. Rebrov even asked if he had understood everything. Paulus only nodded.

"I want to draw your attention to one very important point," Filin stood a step away from him. "The accused are constantly working with the notions of 'Germany', 'the German people', 'the German army', i.e. it turns out that this wasn't about the Nazis who had seized power in Germany, dreamed of world domination, and wanted to have the whole world at its feet. No, rather this was all the will and desire of all Germans, this was the natural essence of Germany as a country. Do you understand what the consequences would be if this view on matters prevails?" Filin asked intimidatingly.

Paulus's silence was beginning to annoy him. The man was ultimately a prisoner and had to be aware of what that meant. Filin quickly suppressed his growing irritation, however. This was too serious a game for him to give in to his emotions.

"Let me tell you what all this means. Among the victor countries, there are two opposing points of view. The first seeks to distinguish Hitlerism from the Germans. The second aims to show the whole world that Germany is an eternally aggressive country that threatens the whole world, and therefore everything must be done to deprive it of the opportunity to pose any such threat in the future, to turn it into an agrarian country…"

Paulus involuntarily clenched his fists.

"'Germany has always posed a threat to others', that is their credo. The accused in Nuremberg are doing everything to prove that this position is correct. By trying to save themselves at any cost, they are ready to sacrifice all Germany. The tribunal in Nuremberg is intended to try Nazi criminals that committed atrocities and forced Germany and the German people to do its will. But they, to save their lives, are claiming that they and Germany are one and the same."

"I understand," Paulus let out heavily. "But collaborating – me personally collaborating – is not so simple."

"The way I see it, it is quite simple. Either the Nazis will be condemned as a criminal organization, or they will bring condemnation over all Germany. You have an opportunity to prevent this. If your duty to Germany and the Germany people is more than just noble words for you."

"I'll have to think about it, at least," Paulus gritted his teeth.

"Think about it. But don't forget that you don't have much time."

As their car drove into Moscow, Gres asked, "Well, what are your impressions?"

"He is hesitating," Filin sighed. "He's not any sort of politician at all. He's a fine example of a military man who always acts within his competence and authority. But we're suggesting that he step beyond those boundaries."

"Maybe we should put more pressure on him? We could, incidentally, make it known that we could put him on trial, too. We have gathered material on him…"

"You want to scare him? Break him?"

"So what?" Gres snapped. "What, is he made of some special stuff?"

"Well, first of all, as far as I know, there are plans to recommend him for a high-ranking position in postwar Germany, maybe even minister of defense. The Americans don't like that at all, by the way. They have already come up with their own list of ministers."

"Well, plans, so what. We've always got a lot of plans, but what matters is if they are workable."

Filin however did not let up. "And secondly, if you try to scare him, what guarantee do you have that he will act the way you want at the trial? Will he be able to withstand meeting with his former peers? Will he be able to oppose them? Will he withstand examination from the defense attorneys and all that they've got in store for him? After all, they will try to completely annihilate him up there on the stand. They will declare him a traitor and a coward, a man who betrayed his oath, gave himself up, and led the soldiers that his country entrusted him with to their deaths. If he stumbles there in Nuremberg, if he collapses into hysterics or remorse, then everything will be ruined beyond any repair. It would be better not to bring him there at all."

"You think he shouldn't be convinced to appear at Nuremberg?"

"Oh, no. Why? But you have just got to show him that a lot is riding on him, you must make him understand his task."

Rebrov, who was sitting in the front seat, coughed. The generals looked at him.

"Olga Chekhova thinks that he would go to great lengths if it meant a chance to see his wife," Rebrov said dispassionately. "You might promise him that she will be brought to Nuremberg. And then she might be allowed to visit him in the Soviet Union…"

Gres thought for a moment and then said, "Well, we can take that idea into account. We'll keep working on Paulus, and on the matter of his wife, too. But if he agrees and we feel that he's ready, there's another problem: how can we bring him to Nuremberg safely? After all, it is in the American zone, we cannot guarantee anything there."

"Yes," Filin agreed. "The Americans would start asking questions if we addressed them directly. Who knows what they would come up, and who they might tell about Paulus's arrival. I wonder if they already know about our work with him?"

Gres didn't follow. "What do you mean?"

"Information leaks," Filin sighed. "How is agent Spitz doing? Hasn't he managed to get anything out again?"

Gres ground his teeth. "He's been busy, the bastard!"

"If he somehow catches wind of our plans and tells them about Paulus, then we simply shouldn't bring him to Nuremberg…"

Gres cut him short. "So, think of a way to bring him there without anyone getting in the way. You know how things are there."

The plane back to Nuremberg would leave early in the morning. Filin, like always, had little desire to go to his empty apartment, where only a heavy and overwhelming anguish awaited him, so he decided to spend the night at work, in the small break room next to his office. He was already preparing to lie down when a gloomy Rebrov looked in. After a moment of hesitation, Rebrov said that he wanted to ask permission not to go back to Nuremberg. He was prepared to work in any other assignment than Nuremberg. He was ready to make a report if needed.

Filin was not surprised to hear this. In fact, he had been waiting for Rebrov to say something like this. "What do you intend to do?" he asked sharply. "I hope you won't just give in to drink, spending your time in bars and letting yourself go."

Rebrov looked up in astonishment.

"What are you looking at me like that for? You aren't the only one who has read Bunin." Filin looked at the weary and offended Rebrov and regretted starting the conversation in such a rude and tactless fashion. The man was clearly suffering, he was in pain. Filin paused and then went on in a different tone of voice, "You shouldn't want such a thing, Denis. For many reasons. First of all, I have no one there who can replace you, but things are serious now. You might say we are at a turning point. Secondly, I can't leave you here, because things might turn out badly for you here."

"I don't intend to become a drunk," Rebrov muttered.

"I don't mean that."

"Then what do you mean?"

"I mean that Col. Kosachev has managed to get off with a simple reprimand and he is already back at work. He has been assigned here in Moscow to carry out investigations. I know what kind of man he is. He would do anything to get revenge on you. And on me, too. Well, don't you worry about me, but I don't want something to happen to you here! And I won't allow it to. Do you understand me?"

"Yes, I do."

"Great. Let's make some tea."

Notes

In fact, in every Reich ministry, among the responsible authorities, there were Russian secret agents who would use secret radio transmitters to relay their reports.

Walter Schellenberg,
head of foreign intelligence
for the Third Reich

CHAPTER XIX. WATCH WHAT YOU SAY!

The morning was warm and foggy. When the fog had dispersed and the sun came out, it felt in the garden on Eichendorff-Strasse that spring was already on the way. Rudenko sat drinking tea in the kitchen and looking out the window. His wife Maria Fyodorovna sat across from him. She was looking at her husband with pity, frowning like an overly attentive grandmother. From time to time she shook her head slightly, troubled by some thoughts of her own.

Their impressive gray cat silently came into the kitchen. Maria Fyodorovna squinted at it and then said with pride, "Our little Murzik can't ever sleep without you here. He sits waiting for you. Yesterday he spent all night sitting on your armchair until you came home."

"He's a loyal guy," Rudenko laughed and scratched the purring cat behind its ears. "I'm going to have a walk now in the garden, I suppose. You can't imagine sitting in that courtroom all the time like a sinner in hell. Everyone's faces are blue, like drowned men."

Maria Fyodorovna nodded in understanding.

"Did you call our daughters in Kiev?" Rudenko asked as he was putting his coat on.

"I did. They said that they miss us, and that everything is fine. They are getting good grades at school."

"That's good." As he reached the door, Rudenko asked, "Now, where is my bodyguard?"

Sergeant Iosif Grosman, chewing something, jumped out from the room at the entrance to the cottage where the chief prosecutor's bodyguards were based.

"Will you keep me company while I go for a walk, comrade sergeant?" Rudenko asked politely.

"Yes, sir, comrade general!" Grosman answered right away.

"You are doing good, comrade sergeant," Rudenko complimented him and showed a slight grin. "For an order from one's superior, as everyone knows, must be carried out, even if it is asking the impossible."

To Grosman it even seemed that Rudenko winked just then and broke out into a smile.

In the garden Grosman sat slightly behind Rudenko and carefully scanned the surroundings. The wet garden was empty.

Rudenko suddenly turned to Grosman. "Comrade sergeant, do you have a personal score to settle with the men we're trying?"

"I do, comrade general, like every Soviet person. My father died at the front, and my uncle Iosif Nakhmanovich escaped from captivity and spent two years as a resistance fighter in Odessa before he too died. My grandfather Pinya and grandmother Manya, the Germans burned them alive during some punitive operation. When I visited the courtroom for the first time and saw those fascists up close, my stomach turned and my head was spinning. I wanted to take a machine gun and…"

"No need to do that," Rudenko said softly. "Now they will get what is coming to them."

He was about to continue his walk when Grosman decided to ask him something. "Comrade general, may I?"

"Go ahead, comrade sergeant."

"Is it true what they're saying, that Hitler is alive and hiding somewhere in Tibet?"

"In Tibet?" Rudenko shook his head. "No, he's not hiding in Tibet. We have proof now that Hitler took poison. His body has already been identified. Any talk that he is still alive is just rumors or… political intrigue for someone's sake."

"But comrade general, they're saying that there are some secret powers that helped him," Grosman decided to take advantage of this opportunity to ask the question that had long been troubling him. "How could he do all those terrible things without such powers?"

"Mystical powers, you mean?" Rudenko took off his cap and scratched his bald pate in his habitual fashion, then resolutely put his cap back on his head. "If those mystical powers really existed, comrade sergeant, then you and I wouldn't be having a stroll right now. But he might have tricked the Germans about having those powers in order to gain their complete obedience. Or perhaps he really believed in them himself, because he was a psychopath…"

At that moment, the honk of an approaching car was heard. "Well then," Rudenko sighed, "I guess our walk is over."

At the cottage, Filin and Alexandrov were standing outside the car. Rebrov was still seated at the wheel. They breathed in the air and turned their faces to the warm sun.

"Howdy!" Rudenko greeted them in his rustic Ukrainian way as he walked up. "Shall we go into the house or have a walk?"

"Let's have a walk, of course," Filin said in a cheery tone.

"Let's go then," Rudenko waved towards the depths of the garden. "And you, comrade sergeant," he turned to Grosman, "wait for us here. Don't worry, we won't wander off far. You'll have us in view the whole time."

"Comrade sergeant," Grosman frowned, "My orders are to strictly accompany you at all times…"

"Do you understand what you have to do when you get an order from a superior?" Rudenko's voice showed a slight strain.

"I do," Grosman answered, having caught the displeasure in the general's voice.

"So do it."

"Yesterday a message came from Moscow," Rudenko announced when he had been left alone with Filin and Alexandrov. "The decision has been made to deliver the witness to Nuremberg. He is ready to testify to the tribunal."

"When are they bringing him?" Filin asked.

"When and how is something that you and I will have to decide," Rudenko chuckled. "So, the success of this operation is completely up to us. There is just one condition: we've only got a couple of days for everything: to bring him here, have him appear in court, and then get him out of here. That is the schedule we have to work with."

"Of course. He has a huge number of enemies among the Germans," Filin said anxiously. "They consider him a traitor and responsible for the deaths of thousands of soldiers. So, every day that he's here means a higher chance of some provocation. They promised him in Moscow that they would find time for him to meet with his wife and son. He hasn't seen them in a long time."

"Well, that is up to you," Rudenko shrugged. "I personally don't mind, but you'll have to decide yourselves when. My job is to examine him without any complications or hitches."

They fell silent for some time, each thinking that using Paulus like this was a bold and effective move, but if it failed in any way,

Moscow wouldn't listen to any explanations. They would be held responsible and suffer the consequences.

"Let's go over the steps of the plan now," Rudenko broke the silence. "Step one: bringing the witness to Nuremberg."

"Doing that in an open and legal way with the Americans' permission is risky," Filin said resolutely. "It's still full of unrepentant Nazis, criminals, and all kinds of shady individuals that are capable of anything. Acting without the Americans' permission is also risky. You remember how not long ago they detained one of our planes and arrested the crew because it had landed without their permission? Right after the victory they were still willing to look the other way, but things have changed. The Americans might demand to interrogate Paulus before he appears in court if they learn that he's here, and then it will be hard to refuse them that. Just imagine what might happen when they are interrogating him or afterward…"

"Sure, all kinds of things," Alexandrov snorted. "In their interrogation room, they let all kinds of people in. People are constantly coming and going, it's like a zoo!"

"So, how are we going to do this?" Rudenko, troubled by these heavy thoughts, glared at Filin and Alexandrov. "Or you haven't thought of anything yet?"

"Well, we do have some idea," Filin sought to avoid troubling his superior any further. "I think that we need to bring him to Nuremberg secretly, observing every measure of caution, but with the Americans' official permission, to maintain decorum."

"I agree. But how can we do it?"

"The best thing to do is bring him by plane to Berlin, to our occupation zone, and then to our base at Plauen. From there, we can bring him by car to Nuremberg. It would only take a few hours. A lot of cars come from Plauen, the Americans are used to it, and if they inspect them it's a mere formality. If we just give them a few tins of caviar or some bottles of vodka…"

Rudenko was amazed. "Does that really work?"

"It sure does!" Filin laughed.

"Those sons of bitches! Alright, Sergei Ivanovich, you work things out with comrade Alexandrov and then act. Now for the second step of the plan: how and when should we have the witness appear in court? It's our big trump card, we need to play it right."

"I think that here, as our American friends say, we need to put on a big show," Filin suggested.

Rudenko at him quizzically. "What kind of show?"

"I mean that his appearance must be made in a very effective way, so that the entire courtroom is stunned by the surprise, and the reporters will rush to tell the whole world about this sensation."

"Oh, Sergei Ivanovich, you've let yourself get carried away with these American tricks," Alexandrov laughed. "The harmful influence of the West."

"No, he's right," Rudenko spoke up. "We need to choose the very best moment. And what harmful influence are you talking about? At Okulitsky's trial back in June of 1934, we always took into account that the trial was being covered by both our newspapers and Western ones, and some hearings were broadcast by radio to the entire country. We prepared some good surprises for the defendants. What you need there is some good drama! Anyway, I am going to take care of this part, I've got an idea..."

"There's another complication here," Filin said pensively.

"Yet another!" Rudenko was amused.

"We need to be one hundred percent sure that Paulus will make his appearance in the right way. It's one thing to assure Moscow of it, but another to act here. When he sees the ruins of Nuremberg and his former bosses, when he hears the accusations from the defense attorneys who will try to provoke him... I hope he won't cry too much. I don't want to sit in a puddle of his tears."

"The higher-ups, Sergei Ivanovich, have already thought of that," Rudenko smiled mysteriously.

"And?"

"They feel that the final decision as to whether he appears or not is something we should make here on our own, depending on the state he is in. Ultimately, if he gets cold feet, we can do without him. We'll just send him back if he isn't in a state to appear. Moscow is letting us have the final say, though that also means that we bear complete responsibility."

"Moscow, Moscow..." Filin sighed in his usual way.

Alexandrov turned his gaze to him sharply and his lips twisted into a smile. "Watch what you say!"

Filin shrugged. "Just some lines of verse, by Mikhail Lermontov."

Notes

As admitted by General von Schweppenburg, members of a group of high-ranking German officers created by the Americans to compile reports on the Wehrmacht's campaigns, had the opportunity to "withdraw from circulation any revealing documents that might be used at the Nuremberg trials."

Field Marshal Küchler, as the highest-ranking member of the group, claimed that it was impermissible that there be "any criticism of the German command" and he set about "erecting a monument to the German forces".

CHAPTER XX. THE TEUTONIC KNIGHT

At the entrance to the bar in the Palace of Justice, Rebrov caught sight of Peggy, who was pleasantly chatting with an assistant to the German defense. This young "Aryan" with an obvious military bearing had long drawn Rebrov's attention, as he bore little resemblance to the rest of the brotherhood of lawyers.

"Hello, Denis," Peggy waved to him gaily. "I'll talk to you in five minutes. I've got news!"

The "Aryan", somewhat demonstratively, did not turn to look at Rebrov.

"Well, what did that Teutonic knight have to tell you?" Rebrov asked when Peggy was already seated opposite him.

Peggy raised an eyebrow. "Ha, do I hear jealously in your voice? Finally! But why did you think that young German lawyer is a Teutonic knight?"

"Well, judging by the way he holds himself, before becoming a lawyer this fine man must have undergone some rigid schooling, and probably military training, too."

"You're observant. But he's a good guy," Peggy stretched like a tiger. "But just so you know, I met with him as a journalist. I asked what he thought of the French prosecutor's remarks that the German people need to be rehabilitated. No, not just rehabilitated, but made into something else."

"And what did he answer?"

"He said that re-educating the German people is something that Mr. Hitler already tried. And that now that the Germans have learned the whole truth about Hitler, they are capable of deciding themselves what they will be. He said that such talk sounds like an attempt to declare the Germans an aggressive people, as if some people want to weigh them down with a guilt complex for many years to come and use that for their own benefit."

"That's a good way of looking at things."

"Yes, not bad. But I needed to talk to you about something else than deciding the fate of the German people."

Rebrov's expression showed that he didn't understand. "And what's that?"

"A sensation, Denis. I need a real sensation! I can't go on reporting all the time about how Col. Andrus is toughening the conditions of the defendants' confinement! Otherwise, my readers are going to start feeling sorry for the poor old men who are kept huddled in the courtroom and held in the harshest conditions! Hasn't your great leader Joe come up with any good bombshells?"

The damned girl has caught wind of something, Rebrov thought. Her American informants have pointed her in the right direction.

"And remember," Peggy stuck out her chin, "if you refuse to help, then I'll have to come up with a sensation on my own!"

"I can imagine!" Rebrov laughed. "But don't try to rush things, Peggy. I can assure you that when our prosecutors start laying down the real facts, any made-up ones will pale next to them."

"I knew I wouldn't get anything out of you," Peggy sighed in disappointment. "You're not a man, you're a statue. But I'm not like that! Remember, you're just pushing me towards that Teutonic knight, and he won't refuse me."

After Peggy had dashed off, Rebrov sat deep in thought. The Americans knew of something. The question was, what exactly? How much did they know? That damned agent in Moscow!

"May I?"

Rebrov looked up. The beautiful Beletskaya was standing at his table and holding a tray with a cup of coffee on it.

"Yes, of course."

"Thank you." Beletskaya sat down. "That American journalist is funny," she said as she stirred sugar into her cup. "But most importantly, she's a good person. She's got a good heart."

"Maybe. You are good at recognizing people."

"You know, I am rather a psychologist," Beletskaya smiled. "I have a lot of experience in dealing with people in a troubled psychological state…"

"Have you worked with mental patients?"

"With people who are sick at heart," Beletskaya gently corrected him. "But even here it is very difficult for me, and again, I am a person who is used to this. Sometimes I simply don't have the strength to deal with all the negative energy that pervades this place."

"You mean the accused?"

"Not only them. I get the feeling that the entire city is marked by evil and grief."

"Very poetic. Excuse me, I've got to be going." Rebrov stood up.

"Of course," Beletskaya smiled. "Go on, then. Just don't give in to…"

"To what?"

"Despair? It won't be like this forever. Spring is already on the way."

From Hector's last message, it followed that the American secret services knew that Paulus might come to Nuremberg. Moreover, they roughly knew the route that he was to take, through Plauen.

When Rebrov reported this to Filin, the latter only threw up his hands in exasperation. Nothing could be done now, however. The plan had been approved by Stalin himself, and asking to change it would only alert the great leader that there was a secret agent in Moscow that they could not manage to ferret out. For Filin's friend Gen. Gres, this turn of events did not bode well; the consequences could be grave. Therefore, Filin decided – at his own risk and peril – not to tell Moscow about Hector's message, but instead to improvise a way to safely deliver Paulus to Nuremberg.

Hector also reported that, by all accounts, the Americans themselves did not plan to do anything. Bringing in their witnesses was the right of each of the Allies, and so no use of force from the Americans would be expected. However, the American side included people with a very wide range of views, and there was a real chance that one of the secret services, playing its games, might tell some gang of Nazis hiding in a basement about Paulus's arrival, and those people might take the most extreme measures… There was already little time. The plan, which Filin had thought up just after their return from Moscow, was as follows. To Plauen, where an operational group of the prosecutor general's office was located, they would send Georgy Nikolayevich Alexandrov. As the head of the investigative department of the Soviet delegation, he was allowed much more than the others. The Americans would issue him a permit to leave the American zone and re-enter it. The permit would be issued for him personally and several people accompanying him without specifying their names. This was commonly done, and the Americans usually had no objections.

Rebrov, however, would go to Plauen first with two members of the Soviet staff. One of them would be made to resemble Paulus from a distance. The man would travel there in military uniform, but on the way back he would have the same civilian suit that the witness would also be wearing. In Plauen there was a barber who would make him practically Paulus's doppelganger. Intended as a decoy, they would leave Plauen half an hour earlier than Alexandrov with his people and Paulus. Any possible attack would be directed at them.

In order to direct the attention of any attackers towards the first car, Filin suggested that Rudenko send also his bodyguard, Sgt. Grosman, to Plauen. They knew him well, and if he were in the car, the attackers would see it as a sure sign that something unusual was going on, and they would focus on this particular car.

When Filin told Rudenko all this, the latter shook his head in doubt. "You know that I can't order Sgt. Grosman to do such a thing. It's risky, and the man survived the front, he managed to stay alive through the war…"

Filin was insistent. "That's the thing. Grosman is an experienced soldier, a scout. He would go and grab people behind enemy lines and drag them back to be interrogated. If something happens, he'll be able to act as the situation directs."

"I just can't order him to do such a thing," Rudenko said adamantly.

They agreed that Grosman would be asked to take part in Rebrov's operation, as they had already worked together when they rescued Lidia Korzun.

Notes

It was something of a shock to me to hear the Russian delegation object to our Anglo-American practice as not fair to the defendant … because it does not inform a defendant of the whole evidence against him. Our method, it is said, makes a criminal trial something of a game. This criticism is certainly not irrational.

From the memoirs of Robert H. Jackson,
US chief prosecutor at the Nuremberg trials

PART II. TOWARDS FATE

CHAPTER I. FÜNFHAUSEN

The Soviet rifle division, in the city of Plauen, was based in an old barracks dating back to the Kaiser's era and built from red brick. For some reason, they were called the Tukhachevsky barracks. Nearby there was a green island consisting of five three-story cottages in the midst of an orchard, surrounded by a cast-iron fence with a large gate, checkpoint and stripped barrier. Previously, they had been home to some foreign mission. The Germans called these cottages *"Fünfhausen"*, feared them like the plague, and for some reason compared them to the Gestapo. In fact, this was the home of one of the USSR prosecutor general's operational groups. It served as a waypoint between Moscow and Nuremberg.

The car driven by Grosman came to a stop at the gate. "We're here," said Grosman.

Rebrov, who was seated next to him, said absently, "I see you've been here before, you know it well."

"I've been here a million times!" Grosman answered in a boastful tone, "Guarding comrade general."

The two officers sitting in the back looked out with great interest at the cozy little military facility.

The base's commandant, Maj. Emelin, an awkward man that resembled a member of the reserves who had just been called up, personally met them in the yard and led them to a series of rooms set apart from the others.

Once he was left alone in a small room on the third floor, from which he had a good view of the whole yard, Rebrov opened the window and breathed in the intoxicating fresh air of the orchard that was already awakening from its winter sleep. Then he drew from his briefcase the same volume of Bunin's stories that Peggy had brought from Paris, opened it to the first place he found, and read the last words of a story: "feeling ten years older". What a coincidence. Rebrov himself had felt much older when he returned to Nuremberg from Moscow. It was already clear to him that his rift with Irina was for good. All of those talks they'd had about being young, about how anything could happen, were worth nothing…

He was jarred from his thoughts by a knock at the door. It was Maj. Emelin, he had come to let him know that the plane with their visitor on it would be late due to the weather conditions in Moscow, and that it would probably arrive the next day, in the afternoon. Therefore, they would be spending the night there. Rebrov had nothing against this, he only asked, "Can you help with weapons?"

"No problem," said Emelin. "We've got trophy weapons. What would you like?"

"Let's go to the shooting range tomorrow morning and find something suitable. There you can find weapons for every taste."

"Well, sergeant, show me how you scouts know how to shoot," said Rebrov, egging on the adventurous Grosman, as the latter stood looking at the submachine guns and pistols with relish.

Grosman sniffed resolutely as he chose a German Walther. He emptied the entire clip into the target, and then ran over to check where the bullets had landed. He returned very pleased with himself. "I told you, eight or nine… Scouts don't miss!" Grosman shook his head and then cajoled him, "What about you, Denis Grigoryevich? Are you going to shoot or not? Of course, if you haven't gone shooting in a long time, no reason to feel ashamed. A man has to keep practicing."

Rebrov looked at Grosman's sly face and laughed. Then he took out two pistols and opened fire with both hands. Even from their position, they could see how the bullets had ripped through the center of the paper targets.

Grosman scratched his nose thoughtfully. "I could do that…"

Rebrov put the pistols down. "Maybe we should go with a couple of Schmeissers? Have you ever used one?"

"Have I!" Grosman arched his eyebrows. "We would set off on scouting missions with only them."

"Perhaps," agreed Rebrov. "The main thing is, if the Americans suddenly stop us and begin inspecting the car, tell them that we found them on the way."

When they returned to the base, there was a great commotion. Alexandrov was standing outside the headquarters. Next to him, Maj. Emelin was fidgeting with anticipation. As Rebrov walked up, he could see that Alexandrov was trying to calm the worried Emelin down.

"Don't worry, comrade major, you don't need to do anything else. Everything should be as simple as possible. We'll have a visitor and there will be one German accompanying him. Well, also two of our guys as guards. Is the room ready for them?"

"Yes, sir. We've got an apartment here with a separate entrance, we'll put the visitor there."

"Fantastic. We won't be troubling you for long," said Alexandrov once more to reassure him. "What is our schedule, comrade Rebrov?"

"Rest, dinner, then some healthy but brief sleep. We'll move at dawn. First we'll go, and then about half an hour later, you and the visitor."

Later on, Rebrov, who was lying on the bed still dressed, heard the sound of engines, he went over to the window.

Paulus, in a civilian overcoat, was getting out of a car. The door had been opened, as was the custom, by a smart adjutant in civilian clothes. Paulus calmly looked around. It was already getting dark, so it was difficult for Rebrov to make out his face from the third-floor window. Alexandrov came out of the headquarters building, walked up to Paulus and told him something. Paulus nodded curtly in a military fashion.

About an hour later Rebrov and Alexandrov decided to have a walk through the orchard to share their impressions in peace.

"What do you think about him?" Rebrov asked. "Is he ready to perform?"

"He looks very composed. You can see that the man has made a serious decision and he has an idea of what awaits him. I think he'll be able to hold himself together. Although, in the courtroom, in front of his people… Who knows what effect it might have on him?"

"Ultimately, he ought to realize that a witness can be easily turned into a defendant."

"I think they hinted that to him in Moscow. But who knows what's going on inside his head, what is tearing away at him… After all, he was hesitating for a long time. He was afraid that his testimony might be seen as stabbing Germany in the back…"

After they return to the cottages, they caught sight of Maj. Emelin hurrying to meet them. He was waving his hands and looked confused.

"There's something… I don't really know what I should do…" Emelin moaned.

"What happened?" Alexandrov barked in order to bring him back to his senses.

"Our cook brought him dinner, but he didn't eat."

"Why is that?" Alexandrov was amazed. "Is he afraid that it might have been poisoned? As if they brought him here from Moscow just for that!"

"No," Emelin shook his head. "Just imagine, he said 'I am a soldier and I will only accept food from the hands of a soldier!' Our cook here is a woman! Where can I get a male waiter for him?"

Rebrov and Alexandrov quickly exchanged glances and then burst out laughing.

"That's a German soldier for you! Order and discipline above all," Alexandrov lifted a finger. "When they addressed him as 'colonel general' in Stalingrad, he always corrected them: 'field marshal'. Because that is the right way of doing things!"

"So, what should I do?" Emelin stared at them pitifully. "Who can I send to him? To this field marshal?"

At that moment, a jolly Grosman appeared in the doorway of the cottage with a rag in his hands, aiming to polish his shoes that were already dazzlingly shiny.

"There's a soldier for him," Rebrov smiled. "A real Soviet soldier!" He waved to Grosman and when the latter had flown over like a bird, he hid his smile and said, "You've got a task, sergeant. A very special task! We need you to serve Field Marshal Paulus his dinner."

Grosman was downcast. "I'm not his servant. Why, is there no one else? Why me?"

"Because you're a scout; think of this as a reconnoitering mission. You don't need to capture anyone, just observe how he's behaving. What can we expect from him? Do you understand what I mean? There are no other scouts here. All our hopes are on you."

Grosman shook his head and shrugged: if he had to do it, he had to do it. So, they dressed him in a white jacket and chef's hat and handed him a heavy tray with several bottles on it. The young lady who served as their cook explained to Grosman how to approach Paulus and what things should be set where.

After ten minutes had passed, and Grosman still had not returned, Maj. Emelin was frantic with worry. "What is keeping him there so long?"

"Don't you worry, he's not armed," Rebrov reassured him. "Well, in the worst case he'd be arrested for it, and sent so far away you'd never hear from him again."

Several minutes later, Grosman appeared on the steps of the porch.

"Well, sergeant, what do you have to report?" asked Rebrov. "What have you learned?"

"It was like this: I walk in and he's sitting at the table. I greeted him and he answered. I set everything on the table like I was ordered, and then he thanked me and suddenly asked me to take a seat. Well, I didn't do that, of course, but he suddenly started asking me, 'What is your name? How old are you? Where are you from originally?' I don't know why, but I just said that I was from Siberia…"

Alexandrov was confused. "Why Siberia?"

"I don't know what came over me myself!" Grosman shrugged. "He just shuddered and said, 'Oh, Siberia. *Kalt!*' He said it was cold. And then he suddenly asked, 'Were you at Stalingrad?' I said, 'No.' But he said, 'That's good. The most important thing is that the war is over.' Then he suddenly said, 'How do you feel about the Germans? Do you want to get revenge on them?'

"I told him, 'There are different kinds of Germans. Those who unleashed the war and committed atrocities should face punishment. But not all Germans were like that.' That seemed to please him, because he suddenly said, 'I'd like to give you something as a token of this meeting.' Then he hands me this."

Grosman drew from his large jacket pocket a round ashtray made from brown marble with a gilded rim, with "Field Marshal Friedrich Paulus" engraved on it in black letter.

"I told him that I don't smoke, but he says, 'I don't either. But I have nothing else to give you.' Well, what am I going to do with this now?"

Alexandrov turned the heavy ashtray over in his hands. "Field Marshal Paulus… I suppose this was a gift sent from Berlin for his birthday. The Germans dropped in from a plane over Stalingrad. It might have come from Hitler himself. It's a historical artifact. It was a gift to you, comrade sergeant, you decide."

Notes

By the beginning of the war, the USSR's intelligence-gathering network encompassed around fifty countries. Within them, there were around three hundred legal and illegal residences altogether. Intelligence was very well funded and based on cutting-edge science and technology.

From June 1940, the NKVD's foreign intelligence branch and military intelligence sent Moscow around four hundred and fifty communiques in relation to Germany's preparation for a war of aggression against the USSR.

From declassified archival material.

CHAPTER II.
ENOUGH FORMER SS MEN FOR THAT

The morning fog lay like great white snowdrifts on the grass, which had stayed green throughout the whole Bavarian winter, and was woven amongst the leafless branches in the orchard. It had only just become light, but in the large yard of the military base everything was set in motion. Rebrov was waiting by the car when the newly groomed Captain Stoletov came from the barber. Tall, lean and wearing the same overcoat that Paulus had; Stoletov could indeed pass for the field marshal from a distance. Grosman, who was fidgeting impatiently, whistled in admiration.

Alexandrov, yawning, stepped out of the cottage and cast a scrutinizing glance over the captain. "Well, he does look similar. Maybe we should have him appear at the trials instead, he can testify about everything."

"The only thing I know in German is '*Hände hoch!*' Put your hands up!" Stoletov smiled, embarrassed at all the attention he was getting. "They'd tell I was an impostor right away."

"Well, let's move, then," said Alexandrov, now serious. Shaking Rebrov's hand, "So, we'll start half an hour after you?"

"Just as we agreed," said Rebrov. "If you suddenly hear shooting down the road, you ought to return to base at once."

"But what about you?"

"Don't you worry about us," Rebrov reassures him. "We're ready for whatever comes."

Their car quickly makes its way down the empty road and arrives at the border of the Soviet and American zones. A sleepy American sergeant examines their documents, briefly glancing at the passengers, and raises the barrier. Suddenly he asks, "Are you working at the tribunal in Nuremberg?"

Rebrov nods. "Yes, we're bringing documents. They get delivered there by the truckload."

"You should have shot all those thugs a long time ago," the sergeant spits. "Everyone would have thanked you for it."

Rebrov shrugs. "They wanted everything to be done according to the law."

"There are scum that the law wasn't written for," grumbles the American.

After they have driven off from the checkpoint, Grosman looks at Rebrov admiringly. "You managed to deal with them with English. I'm jealous."

"You've got to learn languages while you're still young and your memory is good."

"But then they'll claim I was a spy. 'Why are you learning foreign languages, dear comrade Grosman? What, you intend to sell military secrets?'"

"You know a lot of them, military secrets!" said the false Paulus laughing from the back seat.

The road was completely deserted, save for an elderly cyclist coming their way, who was pedaling with difficulty. A bundle of sticks lay on the rack of his bicycle. He posed no danger, and Rebrov even thought that they had worried and thought up the whole convoluted operation for nothing.

At that very moment a long series of automatic weapon bursts hit the car. Grosman cries out and grabs his shoulder with one hand as he tries to keep control of the steering wheel with the other. The car was already heading into a ditch.

"Everyone out of the car!" Rebrov roared.

Grosman, cursing vividly, was trying with all his might to brake. The front of the car hit the ground. The false Paulus and the other officer got out of the car. For a second, Rebrov thought that Grosman had lost consciousness, but then suddenly he opened his eyes.

"Sergeant, are you OK?"

"A lot of blood…"

"Alright, but you're still alive!" Rebrov opened both doors. "Should I help you?"

Grosman shook his head.

"Then go ahead," Rebrov nudged him out of the car.

Grosman fell out onto the ground with a thud and then started crawling away from the car. Rebrov fumbled at his feet for the two

Schmeissers and, after he had found them, he calmly followed Grosman out. The silence was so deafening that he could hear Grosman breathing nearby. The false Paulus and the other officer were lying on the ground a few meters away from them.

"Can you shoot?" Rebrov whispered to Grosman.

"With one hand."

"Your wound needs to be bandaged."

"Later. First we need to fight back."

They were in the worst position imaginable: lying in a ditch, unable to see what might be happening above it. If the attackers got any closer, they could finish them off from the road: like shooting fish in a barrel, Rebrov thought. But the question was, would they? Maybe they had already vanished. It depended on what orders they had. However, there was no time to lay there and play guessing games. Alexandrov's car would be passing by soon.

Rebrov gestured to the officers and Grosman that they should stay where they were. He then got up, reached the top of the ditch in two leaps and hits the ground. Then, rising up for a brief second, he looked over at the bushes on the side of the road from which the shots had come. Even though nothing could be seen, he still fired at them with a long burst from his Schmeisser. A sound came from the bushes, as if someone was crying out. If they were still there, Rebrov thought, we need to let them leave, so that they don't try to come this way.

After waiting for a brief moment, Rebrov again fired at the bushes with the second gun. He then quickly ran twenty meters to the side. No sound came from the other side of the road. Judging from everything, the attackers did not intend to turn this into trench warfare. After a few deep breaths, he hunched down and ran across the road. Everything was quiet. The bushes were around thirty meters away, so if there was anyone there, he would have long since given himself away.

As he reached the bushes, he came upon two dead men in ragged uniforms without insignia or buttons. In that instant, the two Soviet officers reached him, holding pistols in their hands, as well as Grosman, who was still clutching at his shoulder.

The false Paulus nodded at the bodies. "What are we going to do with them?"

Rebrov was surprised by the question. "What are we going to do with them? Let them stay here, it's not our zone of occupation. Let the Americans deal with it. Now our guys are coming, they'll pick us up and bring us to Nuremberg. But don't say a word about the attack. No need to worry them. We'll just tell them that the engine died. Well, how are you doing, our Odessan sergeant?" He turned to Grosman. "Are you going to live?"

"Bah," he waves the question away and winces painfully. "I've suffered worse than this!"

"Alright, you just suffer, then. We're just going to get a bandage on you."

General Filin sat listening attentively to Rebrov, who had delivered Paulus to Nuremberg, literally only half an hour earlier. The operation had fortunately proved a success.

"What about this sergeant who serves as Rudenko's bodyguard?" asked Filin. "Did he get hit badly?"

"No, it's nothing too bad, he just lost a lot of blood. But he's a trooper, a real son of Odessa," Rebrov joked tiredly.

"That's good. Otherwise, imagine what Rudenko would do to you and me! What about our guest? What was his reaction to what happened?"

"No reaction, he didn't even notice anything. According to Alexandrov, he kept looking out the side window, at his native fields and meadows. He was carried away by sentimental thoughts."

"That's easy to understand, he hasn't been here for three years. But let me tell you, there are some real intrigues going on here. Hector reports that the British are telling the Americans not to be too hard on Schacht, because they don't consider him a war criminal. Our dear colleague Jackson is regularly receiving anonymous messages that he won't be able to convict a prominent banker like that because he belongs to an untouchable cast. Those British! There's a real quarrel now in the American delegation. Jackson is at odds with Gen. Donovan from the Office of Strategic Services. Donovan spoke with Goering face to face, without any notes being taken of their meeting! He told Schacht that he might go free if he gave the testimony they wanted. That is what is going on here, my friend. Jackson did manage to get Donovan pulled from here though. He's gone now, but he took some important documents with him and said that Jackson would regret getting in his way…"

"I see. I don't envy Jackson. Well, what are my orders with regard to Paulus?"

"You need to stay with Paulus while he's in Nuremberg. Since they didn't manage to get you on the road here, they might strike here. There are enough former SS men for that. A room has been prepared for you in the house where he'll be staying. So, settle in."

"Is it just going to be me and him there?"

"Not at all! Our people also live in the house – investigators, translators, experts. So, it's hard to get in there unnoticed."

Notes

A number of historians claim that in 1946—1947, in spite of the hardships of the war ending, the population in the Soviet zone lived significantly better, overall, than those in the western part of Germany.

Here is how an eyewitness, the famous historian J. P. Nettl, interprets this: "A comparison between Western and Eastern Germany illustrates the relative success of the Russians. The hoarded stocks of consumer goods in Western Germany, which only appeared after the 1948 currency reform, were forced into the market much earlier in the Soviet zone. The general attitude in Eastern Germany in the early part of 1946 was one of economic activity and hope." Similar judgments can be found in works by other British and American scholars.

CHAPTER III. GIVE HIM ROSES!

They showed Paulus to a room on the third floor at the very end of the hall, to the right of the stairs. The guards that had flown with him from Moscow occupied the room opposite, while Rebrov was given the first room to the left of the stairs. Sensing it would be another sleepless night, he wanted to dose off for at least a couple of hours, but then Gavrik suddenly appeared. Gavrik was not a man who looked alarmed, but alarmed he was.

Rebrov did not wait for Gavrik to compose himself, instead he asked him right out, "Has something happened, Gavrik?"

"Something did happen. You know how simultaneous interpretation works?"

"I think so. Everyone in the courtroom had headphones, and by pressing a button they could choose to hear the statements translated into four different languages."

"I don't mean the people in the courtroom," Gavrik let out nervously. "I'm talking about our interpreters. They sit in an office right over the defendants' bench behind a glass partition and they translate German, French or English to Russian, and the three of them only have one microphone. Do you know how hard it is to translate live speech? With different people talking? Legal terminology that has to be translated as precisely as possible? It's extremely stressful. Plus, you can't fall behind the speaker!"

As Rebrov looked at the upset Gavrik, he thought that his friend had already developed quite an understanding of the interpreters' work, and it was mainly because the interpreters included some attractive young ladies.

"So today, when a German lawyer was speaking, our interpreter related his words like this: 'It was when Soviet forces occupied such-and-such German region…' Rudenko literally rushed to the bench and told Lawrence, 'Your honor, I object! Soviet forces did not occupy German lands!' The lawyer immediately said, 'Your honor, I didn't say occupied, *okkupierten*, I said they took, *besetzten*.' Then Lawrence said, 'Clearly, you should have said liberated… It was the interpreter's mistake.'"

"So?"

"You don't understand? Can you imagine what it was like for the interpreter? It was a political mistake! Col. Kosachev could have her arrested for that immediately. The person was just tired, she was exhausted!"

"Well, Kosachev is no longer here with us," Rebrov sought to reassure his agitated friend.

"She grew faint and a little pale, her hands were shaking. Good thing they called a recess just then."

"And her name is…?" Rebrov smiled

"Sonya Ryazhskaya, and you have no idea!"

In fact, the entire Soviet delegation already knew of Gavrik's worship for the slim and boyishly coiffured Sonya Ryazhskaya, who was willing to work for days on end and who never refused to help the document translators who were literally buried under heaps of papers.

"Well, what are you so worried about, Gavrik? She made a mistake, it happens to everyone. No one is going to go after her for such a trifle."

"You really think so?"

"I'm sure of it. Rudenko is an OK guy, I think he'll forget the whole thing."

"But Khasis, the deputy manager of the translation department, he won't forget! He's already wrote a report in Rudenko's name claiming that it wasn't a mere accident or mistake, that it was due to the political views of the interpreter Ryazhskaya, who allows herself to make anti-Soviet claims…"

"What a creep. Where did a guy like that crawl out of? Is he sucking up or something?"

"He's not a creep, Denis, he's just a man who has been completely broken by fear and horror."

"What do you mean?"

"Before the war, he was arrested as a member of some counter-revolutionary organization. He was sentenced to prison, then they let him out. He had to go through a lot of things there. Intense interrogations, you know. Once here in Nuremberg, after he had been drinking, he once said, as if he was talking to himself, 'Did they piss on your head during interrogation?' Sonya happened to be sitting nearby, he realized that she had heard him and he started to hate her for it. It's the fear, you see, that now she knows and can tell others. He's deathly afraid that he'll end up in such a situation again, so he's ready to accuse anyone else, groundlessly, just so that he himself doesn't end up under suspicion. I feel sorry for him, but what does Sonya have to do with it?"

"Well, what do you want me to do?"

"Talk to Filin, could you? Maybe he and Rudenko could stop Khasis somehow, because tomorrow he could be filing a report against someone else: you, me, even Rudenko. Just out of fear, because if some new Kosachev starts going after him…"

Gavrik vanished as unexpectedly as he had appeared. He probably rushed over to Ryazhanskaya's. Left alone, Rebrov, who was saddened, thought that it was a terrible situation no matter what side you looked at it from. He felt sorry, not so much for Sonya Ryazhanskaya, who had done nothing wrong, but for the hapless Khasis, who had been broken by what fate had put him through, and who now became dangerous for others around him. But Rebrov had to talk to Filin nonetheless.

Rebrov was lying in bed, still dressed and holding the volume of Bunin when a noise came from the hallway. He flew out of the room with his pistol in his hand only to find the captain who had been guarding Paulus's room. He looked bewildered.

"What?" Rebrov asked sharply. "What's going on? An attack?"

"He's hysterical," the captain threw up his hands. "He's crying! He's really shaken up!"

"What happened so suddenly? He's been fine this whole time."

"How should I know?"

Dammit, Rebrov thought, tomorrow he has to take the stand and now he does this! Has something got to him? Or someone? What should I do now? Go and reassure him, wipe the tears from his eyes? Or just pour him a drink?

"If you'll allow me, I can try to calm the field marshal down," came the composed voice of a woman from behind him.

Rebrov, startled, turned around. The beautiful Beletskaya was standing before him. He didn't even recognize her at first, for she wasn't wearing her usual working uniform but rather a colorful silk dressing gown that left nothing to the imagination, but rather her indisputably fine figure.

"Who are you?" the captain asked, bewildered by the sudden appearance of such a magnificent woman.

Beletskaya laughed slightly. "My name is Elena Beletskaya, I'm an interpreter for the Soviet delegation. But I'm also a psychologist, and

I'm an expert in calming people down in a crisis. Comrade Rebrov here can back me up."

The captain, dumbfounded, looked at Rebrov, but the latter only shrugged and nodded in agreement. Then he asked quietly, "How did you get in here?"

"It's simple: I live here. In that last room down there on the right. I heard a noise. Well, are we going to calm the field marshal down?"

"How do you know who he is?"

"Field Marshal Paulus? You see, I had to interpret for him a few times when he was being interrogated in Russia. Plus, I've seen his photo in German newspapers so many times, so many newsreels with him, when I was preparing materials on him for my superiors…"

"Does he remember you?"

"I think he does. And that will help calm him down, I can assure you."

"I see. Strange that no one told us about this."

"About what?"

"That fact that you and him are acquainted."

"Well, what kind of acquaintance is that? I just interpreted for him."

The deep hollow of her bosom was visible through the cut of her robe. Rebrov felt a lump in his throat and swallowed. "What, you're going to go to him looking like that?"

"Well, first of all, there's no time to dress into something finer. And secondly, I can assure you that looking like this will have the right effect on him. It will snap him out of the thoughts that are hounding him. So, shall I go in?"

After hesitating for a bit, the officer opened the door to Paulus's room and let Beletskaya in. As she crossed the threshold, she uttered a long sentence in German. The door to the room was left half-open, and Rebrov could hear clearly enough what they were saying inside.

"What is he doing in there?" the captain asked Rebrov impatiently, as he tried to look into the room.

"He's telling her how he remembers how Nuremberg used to be before the war," Rebrov whispered. "It was an old city like something from a fairy tale, covered in roses in bloom and wonderful buildings from the Middle Ages. Now there is no more city, just a complete ruin covered with a horrible smell of bodies…"

"You'd never think he was in Stalingrad," the captain said spitefully. "Give him roses!"

Beletskaya came out of the room around half an hour later. She fixed her hair a little and said, "He's back to his normal self."

"What was wrong with him?" Rebrov asked dryly and business-like.

"Just an ordinary nervous breakdown. He was pretty shaken up by his journey here and he is feeling overwhelmed. The only thing that any man needs in such a situation," Beletskaya smiled bewitchingly, "is a woman next to him. It's the best medicine. Well, I'll be going."

The officer, slack-jawed, watched her go. In her bright dressing gown, Beletskaya looked in the gloomy hallway like some exotic bird.

"I'd also like a woman like that next to me," the officer muttered.

"Maybe if *you* became a field marshal, you could have one," Rebrov laughed.

"Even just being a general would be a fine," the captain smiled. "Well, let's hope that after that visit, our field marshal sleeps like a baby."

Rebrov went to the door of his room, hesitated a bit and then walked further down the hallway. When he got to Beletskaya's door, he again hesitated for a moment but then knocked. The door opened instantly, as if Beletskaya had been standing right behind it.

"I knew it," she laughed.

"What?" Rebrov asked angrily. He realized that the woman was playing some game with him, but it was not that which upset him, but rather the fact that he was participating it in so docilely. "What did you know?"

"That you'd have questions for me. Well, then, maybe you want to come in?" She stepped aside.

"I only have a couple of questions," Rebrov stayed put for some reason, though it was uncomfortable to stand talking like that in the hallway, plus people could have overheard them. "What state is he going to be in tomorrow?"

"I don't know," said Beletskaya, now serious. "He's shaken up. Probably in the prison he was thinking of how he would be visiting the wonderful city of Nuremberg. And now, when he has actually come here and seen it…"

"I see. Will he be able to testify tomorrow?"

"I think so. He is a man of self-control. It's hard to believe he could have experienced a breakdown like that, but with everything that has happened to him recently… But there's something else. He's afraid that he won't get to meet with his wife and son. They did promise him that, though, didn't they?"

"They did."
"Were they lying to him?"
"Why lie to him? It's just that it isn't so easy to arrange that."
"It would come as a terrible blow to him."
"I see. Forgive me for not letting you sleep."
"It's nothing. I'm a night owl, it's the best time for me."

She suddenly put her arms around Rebrov. Her eyes were right next to his, and her scent, the scent of an irresistibly beautiful woman, enveloped him. He ceased to resist the call of this woman and her desire, because it was beyond the power of any human being, and at that moment it was more important than anything else in the world.

Notes

Hunched over her desk,
Lost in a labyrinth of words,
The stenographer writes her chronicle,
For, perhaps, the ages to come…

Boring documents, by the truckload
The prosecutor delivers to court.
He and a pair of hefty assistants
Unload them on the judges' bench.

I won't ask you about the whole trial,
I can't make sense of everything there,
I just want to know: to see them hanged,
How many years must we suffer here?

We're interpreters, we correct the transcripts
But at New Year's Eve you'll see only ladies.
We kindly ask your honor
To remember this and keep it in mind.

A poem collectively written by staff of
the Soviet delegation at the Nuremberg trials

CHAPTER IV.
THE COURT CALLS
FIELD MARSHAL PAULUS

"May it please your honors, it is my task to present the documentary evidence dealing with the aggression against the Union of Soviet Socialist Republics, organized by the fascist war criminals now sitting in the dock. Among the many criminal wars which German fascism, with predatory aim, waged against the freedom-loving nations, the attack on the Union of the Soviet Socialist Republics occupies a place by itself. It can be safely said that the predatory war against the Soviet Union was the keynote of the entire fascist conspiracy against peace…"

Presenting this evidence was Nikolai Zorya, assistant to the USSR chief prosecutor. Still young – not yet forty – he was a handsome man with a shock of dark hair thrown back, wearing a uniform with the rank insignia of a general and a row of decorations. Rudenko sat a bit behind him at the Soviet prosecutors' table and attentively observed the defendants. Goering, who had wrapped his legs in a warm woolen blanket, pretended that he was merely sleeping and had absolutely no interest in what was going on. Recently, he had tried to show in every way that the Russians' opinions did not interest him. When Rudenko was making his opening remarks a few days before, Goering demonstratively took off his headphones and cast them aside. When Rudenko uttered his name, however, Goering could not resist. He slyly glanced aside and put his headphones back on. It doesn't matter, Rudenko thought maliciously, soon you'll be quite awake and you'll realize this isn't a cradle to rock yourself to sleep in, it's a trial of the most unspeakable criminals, and soon it's going to be hotter than the skillet they use to roast sinners in hell…

When Zorya was coming to the testimony that General Walter Warlimont had given Alexandrov during his interrogation in the Nuremberg prison, Lawrence interrupted him. "General Zorya, the Tribunal observes that you are about to read a deposition of Gen. Warlimont… You ought to be prepared to allow Gen. Warlimont to be submitted to the defendants' counsel for cross-examination."

Rudenko grinned and lowered his head towards his papers. We are prepared, your honor, he thought. Prepared like you can't even imagine. We also know perfectly how the defense is going to behave: they will try to put all testimony or documents coming from the Soviet side in doubt, they will demand that all witnesses confirm their testimony here in person, thinking that this won't be possible. Even affidavits, testimony and statements made under oath and legally flawless won't satisfy them. But soon they will have no more desire to doubt in their reliability.

"I think," Zorya said, "that the testimony of a man like Friedrich Paulus, a former field marshal of the German Army, who, as is known, was directly concerned both in the preparations and in the execution of Plan Barbarossa, can provide considerable help in investigating the preparations of this plan. I present the testimony of Friedrich Paulus, dated January 9, 1946, given in a camp for prisoners of war, marked Document Number USSR-156 and request that it be accepted as evidence."

Goering then perked up, wide awake.

Keitel's defense attorney Otto Nelte was already rushing to the microphone. Using the elaborate expressions that everyone had already grown used to hearing, he claimed that Paulus's testimony could not be accepted as evidence: after all, the Soviet prosecution did know about the high court's opinion of such statements and how it had stopped making use of them. Nelte looked around the courtroom triumphantly.

Lord Lawrence affably asked Zorya, "Do you wish to make any answer to what Dr. Nelte has said?"

Zorya glanced aside at Rudenko. Rudenko covered his eyes and nodded as if to say go on, do it just as we agreed…

"Bearing in mind," said Zorya, "that certain witnesses, whose evidence will be presented in a forthcoming session by the Soviet prosecution, are of considerable interest and that it is possible that the defense may wish to cross-examine them, the Soviet prosecution will take all necessary measures to bring some of these witnesses to Nuremberg in order to hear their verbal evidence. Special interest attaches to the deposition of Paulus, extracts from which I propose to quote in my report, and which must be checked no later than this evening, after which Friedrich Paulus will be brought to the courtroom."

At first, total silence filled the courtroom, then it began to buzz. Everyone present started fidgeting and whispering amongst themselves, in the defendants' dock, in the journalists' section, and in the balcony for observers. Lawrence immediately turned on the red lamp that called for order in the court.

"Then I understood from what you said, general, Field Marshal Paulus will be produced as a witness for the defendants' counsel to cross-examine."

"Yes, your honor."

"How long will it take for you to bring your witness here, general?"

"I think that can be done today, very soon," Zorya answered with an expressly business-like tone. "The witness is already here, in the Palace of Justice. He is presently in the lodgings of the Soviet delegation."

At that instant, a bell went off in the corridors, cafeterias and bars to alert the journalists to a huge sensation in the courtroom. Correspondents leapt out of their seats at the bar, munching their sandwiches on the go and wiping beer foam from their lips.

Rudenko calmly watched the defense attorneys rush to speak with their clients. The defendants were whispering in agitation amongst themselves. Well, then, you don't feel like sleeping anymore? Indeed, you would have liked our written testimony a lot more, because in person, Paulus might even say some things that weren't in it…

Lawrence turned to the defense. "That meets your objection, I think, Dr. Nelte."

Nelte, who had been anxiously speaking with Keitel, launched into a rambling and confused explanation, saying how suddenly the defense understood the Soviet prosecution's difficulty with bringing witnesses, and how they weren't too worried about formalities and wanted only evidence in material form…

In the journalists' section, there was a flurry of activity. Some of them were listening, while others had already run out, pushing aside everyone in their path and spreading the news of the sensation.

"The court will call as a witness Friedrich Paulus," Lord Lawrence announced. He then added in a friendly tone with a fair trace of sarcasm, "And now, I think, is the best time to take a recess."

In the corridor it was chaos. Rebrov ran into Peggy, who was rushing for the phones. She looked at him with contempt, shook her head and then her first. "How could you have kept this from me? You're a monster! It's simply inhuman!"

Rebrov began to deny this. "Peggy, I didn't know anything!" Yet his claim turned out rather unconvincing.

"I don't believe you," Peggy snapped. "You're going to regret this!"

This time the courtroom, which in recent days had never been completely full, was packed long before the end of the recess. Finally, the judges arrived. Lord Lawrence, in no hurry, placed his headphones over his shining bald head.

Zorya approached the bench. "Mr. President, in pursuance of the statement made by the Soviet delegation, I will ask for permission to bring before the tribunal for direct examination the field marshal of the former German army, Friedrich Paulus, who will be examined by the chief prosecutor of the USSR, Gen. Rudenko."

Lawrence nodded towards the bailiff. "Very well, the witness may be brought in."

The oak door framed by green marble at the other end of the courtroom opened and Paulus appeared, wearing a civilian suit that fit him well. Photographers' flashes went off, film cameras rolled. Everyone present watched in suspense how Paulus, accompanied by an American soldier, approached the stand. The bailiff then placed the headphones over Paulus's head. His outward appearance was one of complete composure.

In the defendants' dock there was a racket and commotion, like in a bread line. Hess was shouting something angrily at Goering, who had now forgotten about his warm blanket. Keitel and Jodl stared as if petrified at their colleague, who now seemed to be on the other side of the lines.

"Will you please tell me your name?" Lawrence asked politely.

"Friedrich Paulus."

"Will you repeat the oath after me?"

"Of course."

Paulus, looking totally calm, placed his left hand on the Bible and raising two fingers on his right hand, he firmly uttered the solemn oath to tell the truth and only the truth.

Goering roared something in a loud but indistinct voice.

"If you please, general," Lawrence nodded at Rudenko, who had long since taken his place at the stand and was observing coldly everything that was happening.

Notes

I can never forget the commotion that broke out
amongst the defense after Paulus was examined by
the prosecution. Usually the defense attorneys
were quick to cross-examine if it would give
some chances of rebuttal. This time, however,
the defense and the accused were seized by some
kind of paralysis.

> Arkady Poltorak, Soviet appointee
> to the General Secretariat
> of the Nuremberg tribunal

CHAPTER V. HE'S TELLING THE TRUTH

"Your name is Friedrich Paulus?"

"Yes."

"What year were you born?"

"1890."

"You were born in the village of Breitenau, in the district of Kassel, in Germany?"

"Yes."

"By nationality you are a German?"

"Yes."

Paulus sat in front of the microphone in a relaxed posture. The dry sentences that he uttered were precise and resolute. Although he was speaking in German and his words were quite audible across the courtroom, many of the defendants for some reason put their headphones on.

"You are a field marshal of the former German army?"

"Yes."

"Your last official position was Commander-in-Chief of the 6th Army at Stalingrad?"

"Yes."

"Please, tell us, witness, what you know regarding the preparation by the Hitlerite government and the German high command of the armed attack on the Soviet Union."

"From personal experience, I can state the following: On September 3, 1940, I found in my sphere of work, among other things, a still incomplete operational plan dealing with an attack on the Soviet Union. An investigation was to be made as to the possibilities of an attack against the Soviet Union. First, the destruction of those parts of the Russian Army stationed in the west of Russia, to prevent the units which were fit for fighting from escaping deep into Russia… The final aim was the reaching of the Volga-Arkhangelsk line. In conclusion, I confirm the fact that the preparation for this attack on the Soviet Union, which actually took place on June 22, 1941, dated back to the autumn of 1940."

Suddenly one of the defense attorneys shouted, "Field marshal, where are the young German men that Germany entrusted you with?"

Paulus's expression remained calm. Rudenko appealed to Lord Lawrence. "Your honor, I must object to such provocations! Moreover, that attorney is allowing himself to intervene in the questioning of a witness. This is an unacceptable breach of the rules."

"Sustained," Lawrence said. "Gentlemen, please observe the rules."

Paulus continued calmly. "The attack on the Soviet Union was carried out after lengthy preparations and according to a strictly worked-out plan. At the same time, there was no threat that the enemy would try to cross the border."

"How would you define the aims pursued by Germany in attacking Soviet Russia?"

"The aim to reach the Volga line, which was far beyond German strength, is in itself characteristic of Hitler's and the Nazi leadership's boundless policy of conquest."

Goering, furious, whispered something to Hess.

"From a strategic point of view, the achievement of these aims would have meant the destruction of the armed forces of the Soviet Union. By winning the line I have mentioned, the main areas of Soviet Russia with the capital, Moscow, would have been conquered and subjugated, together with the leading political and economic center of the Soviet Union. The objectives given indicate the conquest of the Russian territories for the purpose of colonization with the utilization and spoliation of, and with the resources of which the war in the West was to be brought to a conclusion, with the aim of finally establishing domination over Europe."

"Who amongst the defendants do you consider to be as guilty of the criminal initiation of the war against Soviet Russia?"

Paulus cast a cold and detached gaze over the defendants in the dock. "Of the defendants, as far as I observed them, the top military advisers to Hitler. They are the Chief of the Supreme Command of the Armed Forces, Keitel; Chief of the Operations Branch, Jodl; and Goering, in his capacity as Reich Marshal, as Commander-in-Chief of the Air Forces and as Plenipotentiary for Armament Economy…"

"In concluding the interrogation I shall make a summary. Have I rightly concluded from your testimony that long before June 22 the Hitlerite government and the supreme command of the armed forces were planning an aggressive war against the Soviet Union for the purpose of colonizing the territory of the Soviet Union?"

"That is beyond doubt."

"I have no more questions, your honor," Rudenko concluded.

When Lord Lawrence asked the defense if they would like to ask any questions, Laternser, the counsel for the General Staff, answered for everyone. However, he stated that the defense needed time to prepare, as the witness had appeared completely unexpected and his testimony was extremely important. It was clear that the defense attorneys were confused and needed to gather their thoughts and their strength.

After a noticeable but completely appropriate pause, Rudenko promised that if it pleased the court, the witness would be brought in again the next day.

As he was driving to the baron's house, Olaf was thinking about how he was in for a difficult conversation. The operation involving Paulus had proved a complete fiasco for them and a triumph for the Russians. All the newspapers of the world were trumpeting this. Everything had gone awry in an instant. It was possible to conclude with a high degree of certainty that the Russians had been alerted beforehand about the attempt made on the road to Nuremberg. Judging from how they had prepared an exit plan, had arranged a body double and were carrying a large amount of weapons, they knew that an attack might come. Fortunately, the Russians did not raise any alarm about this, probably because they had already achieved their goal.

The baron was not feeling well and he waited for Olaf in a small office on the second floor. He was wrapped in a robe and looked tired.

"What's wrong, baron?"

The baron waved his hand weakly. "Just the usual spring allergies, my boy. Yesterday I walked through the garden and breathed in this heady spring air and I came across some blooming crocuses, blue and yellow. That's life, let's not let it get us down. So, did Paulus do well during the questioning?"

"Yes, he was calm, composed and he said what the Russians needed him to say."

The baron shrugged. "Considering that he's been their prisoner for so many years, it's no surprise. Especially since he's telling the truth. Yeah, yeah, what are you looking at me surprised for? Is it really not true that Hitler planned an attack on the Soviet Union? That they wanted to break Russia up? And turn the Slavs into slaves whose only right was to work for their brave German masters? It was all part of Hitler's sick imagination and unstable mind. Me, I always preferred the advice from the German chancellor Otto von Bismarck, who had lived in Russia and knew the country. He always warned against war with the Russians!"

The baron shivered and wrapped his robe around himself more tightly. "By the way, soon after the attack on Russia I was at a reception at Goebbels' home. That damn cripple, who looked like a suntanned ape, was raising a toast to celebrating Christmas on Red Square. For some reason, he was sure that a new revolution would break out in Russia. Everyone there applauded. Only one person seemed capable of rebutting him, the actress Olga Chekhova. She said that the Russians would only unite in the face of an outside threat and they would stand together to the very end. She knew Russia and the Russian people a lot better than that ape!"

"There are rumors now that she was Stalin's secret agent."

"Nonsense," the baron waved his claim away. "The Gestapo would have sniffed her out immediately. She was simply a very clever and calculating woman. She understood well then what she could get away with and what she couldn't. Alright, enough with this tabloid gossip. What did our bold defense attorneys do when Paulus was in court? Didn't they manage to shake the field marshal out of his composure?"

"I'm afraid that they would agree with you, baron," Olaf joked.

"What do you mean?" the baron's lips curled in surprise.

"They seem to be convinced that Paulus was telling the truth, so the only thing to do was to resort to ad hominem arguments."

"How's that?"

"They didn't appeal to facts, they criticized the field marshal himself. They asked whether he considers himself a criminal, if the German general staff drew up the plans for a criminal war. They asked him where he's living in Moscow, who is supporting him and whether he is teaching Russian officers in a military academy. It was all quite pitiful. When an American reporter said, "It's silly to ask if he is teaching the Russians to fight! What can a man who got his whole army encircled and who then surrendered, teach anyone?"

"That does make sense."

"All the questions from our defense lawyers immediately evaporated when the Russians started showing footage shot in the towns and cities after our forces left. Or in concentration camps…"

"Sometimes I can really understand them, the Russians. But you and I are Germans, and it is our duty to think of Germany, using our brains.

And my brain is telling me that our efforts should be directed at setting Germany apart from the men sitting there in the dock. Most of them can expect hanging. Schacht might manage to avoid that, his British and American banker friends will see to that. However," the baron insistently lifted a finger, "we have our game to play. We botched the operation with Paulus, so now we need to arrange a new match with our American partners, and we absolutely must win this one. Remember what happened to your friend from the army?"

The baron looked at Olaf with an intense gaze that wasn't at all the gaze of a sick man. His eyes were cold, stern and unbending.

Notes

We drove over to Frankfurt and very quickly saw the branch of the Reichsbank which was located less than a mile from where our headquarters was going to be in the Farben Building. I saw what an excellent building the Reichsbank was for storing the gold and the money and the art treasures. I drove over to General Patton's headquarters and reported to General Patton. Under the Big Three arrangements this part of Germany would be taken over by the Russians. We certainly wanted to get all of this out of here before the Russians get here. I told the generals about the gold, gold bars, gold coins, the boxes containing almost three billion reichsmarks and the valises filled with the loot taken by Germans from the victims in the concentration camps.

> Col. Bernard Bernstein, financial adviser
> to General Dwight D. Eisenhower,
> Supreme Commander of the Allied
> Expeditionary Forces in Europe

CHAPTER VI.
FOR NOTHING IS SECRET, THAT SHALL NOT BE MADE MANIFEST

The forest was full of twittering from unseen birds. The smell of spring was all around, and if it had not been for the smoke from Beletskaya's cigarette, one might have been able to forget about everything. They were sitting in a car which Rebrov had driven as deep as possible into the woods, so far that they risked getting stuck. He put his hands on the steering wheel and looked straight ahead, unsure of how to start the difficult conversation that loomed ahead. Beletskaya smoked her cigarette, occasionally glancing at him; she seemed to guess at something. After the night when Paulus had gone hysterical, they had met a few times. These rendezvous were hurried, risky and uncomfortable. Everything was somehow rushed. Once, Beletskaya joked that she felt like a schoolgirl afraid that her parents would find out. Rebrov nearly burst out that he constantly felt that she was treating him like a mother treats her child and he didn't like that, but thank God he was smart enough to keep his mouth shut.

Now, however, he had to put an end to this strange relationship that had somehow arisen between them. Now, when it hadn't led to a big scene and scandal yet. He had to find the words to explain all of this to her in the right way, so that she would understand. For some reason, this seemed very important.

"Did he manage to see his wife?" she suddenly asked, throwing her cigarette out of the car.

"Who?"

"Paulus?"

"No, I guess not."

"So, we tricked him?"

"Why tricked him? They just couldn't arrange it. They could only bring his son here. Ultimately, this is the American zone, and they decide. They promised him that they would bring his wife to the USSR…"

"And how did he take it?"

"How should he have taken it?" Rebrov felt a slight irritation. Now they had one more thing to talk about! "When it comes down to it, he's a prisoner of war and not an honored guest. He might as well be sitting next to Goering and Keitel and wondering if he is going to be shot or hung."

"You're young," she said pensively. "So very young. That is probably why I feel like I should give you advice and warn you about things as if you were my own son."

"Do you have children?" Rebrov asked, surprised, though he might have asked what there was to be surprised about.

"Yes, two boys. I miss them so much," Beletskaya looked at Rebrov and smiled. Her gaze was again a maternal one, full of love and a desire to warn him about things.

"Do you want to tell me something?"

"You're in intelligence," Beletskaya gently patted him on the head, tousling his hair. "You're supposed to know everything, see everything! Yes, I do want to talk to you about something. About Princess Kurakina…"

This was already a nightmare. She was really talking with him like a mother would talk to her son about a girlfriend that she did not like.

"So, about the princess," she lit another cigarette, "you need to forget about her, my friend. Forget about her once and for all. Because otherwise she is going to destroy you. Yes, destroy you. She's a nice girl, of course, a very nice girl. But you and her are from different worlds. Completely different worlds. The world that Bunin writes about is from a past age, or maybe one that never existed at all. But for her, it is real life, her life. The world that you and I live in, that we belong to, she can't imagine it at all. If you were to be together, one of you would have to completely renounce your world and leave it behind. But that doesn't mean that you would be able to live in a different world, that you would belong there. You won't. You would always feel that you're an outsider."

Rebrov was taken aback and remained silent. He wasn't at all prepared to have a conversation now about Irina. He eventually said with effort, "And why did you decide to tell me that today?"

"Because this is the last time we will meet," Beletskaya smiled.

"Why?" Rebrov asked, stunned.

"Because my husband, Gen. Beletsky, is coming to Nuremberg. What are you looking at me like that for? What, am I so horrible that you don't think I can have a husband?"

"No, of course not. But why?" Rebrov, now completely bewildered, asked helplessly.

"What kind of a question is that!" Beletskaya again patted him on the head. "Haven't you thought that perhaps he misses his wife? And you work in intelligence! Do you want to hear a military secret?"

"What kind of secret?"

"He's coming here on some official duty. And since he is a general, his duty is military. He is being sent here by Moscow. And I, it just so happens, also ended up here. So, it's a strange coincidence. Everyone is going to think that he came to see me, but he'll be busy with some secret business…"

"I just keep thinking, why is Gen. Beletsky coming here?" Such was the question with which Filin greeted Rebrov when the latter had come into his office. It was clear, however, that Filin was not posing this question so much to Rebrov, who had no way of knowing, as to himself. "What is he going to do here? Is it really just to see his wife?"

"He's not coming for that, comrade general," Rebrov reported. "I mean, to see his wife."

Filin stared at him in surprise. "So, it isn't for that! But how do you know that? Come on, out with it!"

"Beletskaya, his wife, told a girlfriend of hers, that the general is being sent by Moscow."

"Moscow?" Filin cut him off. "Beletsky is the political adviser to the head of the Soviet military administration in Germany, and Moscow is sending him from Berlin to Nuremberg, without alerting anyone first, even Rudenko. He's coming under the pretext of seeing his wife, but in fact he has completely different aims. Moscow, Moscow… " Filin, according to his habit, shook his head in either reproach or amazement. "Fine, let's go see Rudenko. As if Beletsky wasn't enough, now we've got Churchill too!"

"What did Churchill do?"

"What did Churchill do?! You really don't know? Are you kidding me? Where have you been that you didn't hear about Churchill? I'd love to head for such a place myself right now."

Along the road, Filin told Rebrov what had happened. Churchill had visited America and gave a speech at Westminster College in Fulton, in the state of Missouri. He was invited there to receive an honorary degree and speak about international relations. He claimed that the coalition of the USA, UK and Soviet Union that had existed since 1941, was in fact no more. Now the brotherhood of Anglo-Saxon nations was to oppose the USSR. The deliberate coarseness of his remarks were noteworthy: "From what I have seen of our Russian friends and Allies during the war, I am convinced that there is nothing they admire so much as strength…"; "Unite to stop Russia!" All the newspapers and radio stations were abuzz. "Sir Winston Churchill is calling for the creation of a single front against Moscow"; "Communism is the greatest danger of our time"; "The West must put a stop to Soviet expansion".

"It's nice that he hasn't called for a crusade yet," Filin shook his head.

"Well, who is he now, this Churchill?" Rebrov shrugged. He couldn't let go after he and Beletskaya had parted and he continued to talk to himself as if explaining things to her. "He's an old man in retirement, he doesn't matter anymore…"

"No, Denis, it is much more serious than that," Filin said gloomily, "and you ought to realize that. First of all, Churchill is a very special figure for the West. Secondly, Churchill had been brought to give his speech by the American president himself, who was present there in the hall and applauded Churchill's words. The president was also completely informed about what Churchill would say. So, I daresay he shares Churchill's views. The Americans aren't ready to make those views officially known yet, but they could be conveniently disclosed through the remarks of a private individual like Churchill. When those words were said, it was like giving the order…"

"And what now?"

"Now there will be a new conflict. The only question is, what form will it take? Of course, one would like to believe that it won't lead to war."

"And what does that mean now for the trials?"

"Let's see how these 'Anglo-Saxon brothers' act. I don't think they will seriously walk away from everything, but… In just a few days, Jackson will begin questioning Goering and then many things will become clear. Jackson can't step away from this, he has bet too much on these trials. If he did walk away, his career would be finished. He feels certain that a battle with Goering would outdo the impression that Paulus's appearance made on everyone. He sees himself as a hero who can reveal the depths of the Nazi evil to the world. He'll triumph over the main evildoer and make him repent before the whole world! The Americans look forward to broadcasting Goering's questioning live to the whole world. America has to establish itself as the supreme moral authority to whom is given the right to judge, punish and at the same time be immune from criticism itself."

"Well, I don't know how it will turn out…"

"Me either. But today the whole group of defendants was like a beehive that someone had put a match to. They looked like people who don't fear anything anymore. Goering put it this way: in the summer of '45 I didn't expect to see the autumn, and now I think I'll be seeing quite a few autumns and winters. So, it won't be easy for Jackson to deal with him. The newspapers are used to depicting him as a miserable loser, a pathetic drug addict, but I think they are in for a disappointment.

Notes

On September 6, 1946, in Stuttgart, American Secretary of State James F. Byrnes gave a speech that marked a sharp turn in the postwar situation around the world. According to his view, the nature of the western Allies' military presence in West Germany had changed: occupation and a regime of control had turned into a "protective shield". Germany had to be protected from the Soviet Union. Due to the initiative of Britain and the USA, who overcame resistance from France, the three occupation zones they controlled were brought together into one economic space, the prototype for the future Federal Republic of Germany.

CHAPTER VII. ONE ON ONE

A crowd of people had come to watch the battle between Jackson and Goering. They packed the courtroom, balcony and bars where the event was to be broadcast. A huge line had formed in advance for the telephones in the press center, so that reporters could relay the hottest developments. Interest in the trials had recently declined across the world as they dragged on for weeks and weeks with no end in sight – the Soviet judge Nikitchenko had even felt it necessary to write a letter to his Western colleagues to express his concern about all sorts of delays and their unfavorable impact on public opinion. Now, in anticipation of the duel between Jackson and Goering, interest again rose.

Rebrov managed to squeeze onto the balcony. As he watched Goering take his seat, where Paulus had sat not long before, he thought that this so-called "number two Nazi" seemed quite calm. In any event, he was trying to stay calm. This was despite the fact that the Americans, as Hector reported, had been doing everything they could to rile him up. For example, they even forbade him from speaking with the other defendants during meals; he now ate alone in a tiny separate room, which made him furious. Plus, it was always cold there and the room received no daylight. In addition, his meetings with his defense attorneys were now always attended by a representative from the American administration, who demonstratively took notes of all that was said.

In the courtroom, Rebrov suddenly spotted Grosman. Usually he only accompanied Rudenko to the doors, but now it seemed that he wanted to watch the trials firsthand and he had a severe mien. Rebrov wondered if he had surrendered his pistol, or if the wily Odessan had managed to bring it with him into the courtroom.

The witness examination immediately took a different direction than Jackson had planned. Goering looked very confident, even defiant. He demonstrated a stunning knowledge of the contents of the captured documents. He cracked jokes, drawing laughter from the people in the spectators' area. The faces of the men sitting behind the tables for the prosecution looked increasingly tense.

Jackson had clearly not expected this behavior from the defendant, who was supposed to collapse before the awesomeness of the American prosecutor. In fact, Jackson was beginning to get nervous. At times he looked angry and confused at the same time. All his hopes and plans had been dashed. However, he did not give up.

"You are perhaps aware that you are the only living man who can expound to us the true purpose of the Nazi Party and the inner workings of its leadership?"

"I am perfectly aware of that," Goering boasted. He was overjoyed at any mention of the significance of his role.

"You, from the very beginning, together with those who were associated with you, intended to overthrow and later did overthrow, the Weimar Republic?"

"That was, as far as I am concerned, my firm intention."

"You, as I understand it, were informed in 1940 of an impending attack by the German army on Soviet Russia?"

"I have explained just how far I was informed of these matters."

"Insofar as you know, the German people were led into the war, attacking Soviet Russia under the belief that you favored it?"

"The German people did not know about the declaration of war against Russia until after the war with Russia had started," Goering laughed. "The German people were not asked; they were told of the fact and of the necessity for it."

"What do you feel is the reason for the end of the German Reich and the collapse of the Nazi state?"

"It was fated to be so. We stumbled in choosing this enemy: we did not know or understand the Russians. They were and still are an enigma for the West. Therefore, even our intelligence, the most advanced in Europe, was unable to grasp the USSR's true military might."

Jackson paused and decided to sharply change the subject towards the period when Hitler and his henchmen were still only planning their actions. He seemed to think that this would give him a better chance of nailing Goering to the wall.

"From this document, published as early as 1935, it follows that you were already planning the rearmament of Germany. Naturally, the rearmament was a secret rearmament!" Jackson exclaimed with a touch of the dramatic.

Goering shook his head reproachfully. "For some reason I can't recall the Joint Chiefs of Staff ever publishing any secret plans of theirs. Do you really think the German staff would do something so silly? That document is an obvious forgery!"

Laughter could be heard from the balcony and Goering cast a triumphant gaze over the courtroom.

Jackson, wounded, suddenly ripped his headphones from his head and threw them down on the table. He appealed to the judges with a childish gesture. "I ask the court to call the defendant to order. I ask that he be obliged to answer questions solely on their merits and not attempt to go off into long and irrelevant tangents!"

Lord Lawrence looked at him with sympathy.

"The report from our agent has already arrived. Jackson is so upset and discouraged that he suggested that the British not even try to examine Goering. Thank God, they told him that this would only be a victory for the Reich Marshal, and a victory not only for him personally but for Nazism in general. They're right. In the POW camps, the German soldiers and officers listened to 'Big Hermann' tangling with the American prosecutor and they responded to every clever retort of his with laughter and approval. The Americans thought that broadcasting the hearing would make them change their minds, but it turned out to have the opposite effect. In one camp, the prisoners shouted 'Heil Hitler!' They had to turn off the radio and the guards were forced to drive the riled-up prisoners back to their barracks. Letters in support of Goering are already being sent to the prison."

After Filin spoke, Rudenko, who was standing at the window of his cottage, turned around. His face showed an expression of unfeigned annoyance. "I didn't expect it from Jackson, this weakness. If Goering is permitted to continue acting like that, others are going to follow his example, because he is an authority figure for them. Then everyone will think that the tribunal doesn't have control of the situation, that it is not in possession of the necessary facts. But there are mountains of documents. Mountains!"

Filin nodded. Jackson's fiasco had come as a surprise to him as well. "They warned Jackson about how best to deal with Goering. After all, he couldn't let him feel that he was some kind of hero. Goering likes to strike poses, but if he adopts one, then he needs to be immediately snapped out of it. I did make one observation, though."

"What's that?"

"I get the impression that Jackson and the judges are quarreling over something..."

"Well, he won't find anything to quarrel about with ours!"

"I mean the Americans and the British. Why did they let Goering behave so brazenly? Why didn't they stop him, put him in his place?"

"Well, that's their problem," Rudenko shrugged. "Soon it'll be my turn to question that pig. We won't hold back."

"We've got to immediately take him by the throat and not let up. Facts, facts, documents and testimony," Filin set out a rigid formula. "And ones that cannot be refuted. Blow after blow. There can be no ambiguity, no different interpretations..."

Rudenko nodded in agreement.

The first person that Rebrov met when he entered Rudenko's cottage was Grosman. He was sitting on the porch and basking in the sun.

"Well now, it's our Odessan scout," Denis waved. "How are you doing?"

"Hello, Denis Grigoryevich," Grosman beamed a smile. "I'm OK. Completely OK. I'm like a dog, I don't stay down and wounded for long. So, if you ever have some business to take care of again, I'm ready. I even had a good time!"

Rebrov laughed. "It's agreed then. I'll let you know right away."

"I was thinking too, that maybe after everything is finished here, you'll take me along?"

Rebrov didn't readily understand. "Where?"

"Well, how would I know? Just take me wherever you need. I'm really a scout by nature. To be honest, I don't even know what I would do in the civilian world. I can fight; I don't know how to do anything else. What would I do there?"

"I'll have to think about it."

Filin appeared on the porch. "Has something happened?"

Rebrov nodded.

"What is it?"

"We've got some interesting information..."

Filin thought for a moment, and then nodded. "Well, come on, let's walk."

When they had gone a fair distance, Filin asked. "Did you get something from Hector?"

"No, I'm talking about Gen. Beletsky..."

"How interesting."

Rebrov tried to ignore Filin's irony. "This is how things are," he said cheerfully. "His wife told…"

"*Very* interesting! Who did she tell? A girlfriend of hers again?" Filin asked suspiciously.

Rebrov remained unflappable. "A girlfriend of hers. She said that the general had unexpectedly been summoned to Moscow given orders from the very top. He was to fly to Nuremberg as if he was meeting his wife, but in fact his mission is to observe the Soviet delegation, because Moscow seems to have received reports that the work is flagging, the trials are being deliberately drawn out, and we're not dealing with the enemy's intrigues properly."

"Again," Filin sighed. What Rebrov had said sounded too close to the truth. "Is that all?"

"More or less. But there is one more detail, a very curious one. Beletsky has not been assigned any particular tasks."

"What do you mean?"

"He hasn't been instructed to find something in particular, to uncover wreckers and saboteurs. His order is simply to observe and send in an objective report."

"And who does he have to report to, I wonder?"

"Comrade Molotov."

Filin stopped, narrowed his eyes and looked at Rebrov. "Well, then. That means it's not Beria behind him. But haven't you thought that maybe this is disinformation? What if Beletskaya said this on her husband's orders?"

"What sense would that make?"

"He *does* have a specific task, and they just want to calm us down."

"I don't think that's it."

"Come on, you don't think? Why don't you think so?"

"She's really on our side."

"Who?"

"Beletskaya. She's on our side."

"What do you mean by that? Is she against her husband?"

"No, it's just that she thinks that we're doing something important here in Nuremberg and she wants to help us. That's all."

"How noble of her. This girlfriend of hers that she told, is she a reliable person. Can we trust her?"

"She has never let us down so far," Rebrov said gloomily.

Notes

The first instruction of the Nazi Party to its members abroad read, "Observe the laws of the country in which you are a visitor." But at the trials, it has now been shown that Hess, in his testimony, left out the second half of this order, "until you become the lords of that country." The mission of Germans abroad was to become the lords of foreign countries.

Sergei Krushinsky in the newspaper *Izvestiya*, March 29, 1946

CHAPTER VIII.
SHOOT HIM WITHOUT
A TRIAL OR CONSEQUENCES!

Muffled voices could be heard coming from a radio in the press bar at the Palace of Justice: the broadcast of Goering's questioning. Rebrov sat alone and drank the rest of his coffee. Most of the journalists were in the courtroom. Everyone knew that a critical moment had come in the trials. The crushed and defeated Goering, it seemed, was allowing himself with complete audacity, as Jackson himself noted, to wrangle with none other than the USA itself! This could lead to Nazi ideology having its prestige restored, he explained to his staff, because Goering was admired by all Nazis, and Germany was still full of them. Furthermore, Goering might drive the other defendants to behave similarly. As it became known, Jackson, feeling wounded, had even thought during the hearing that "it would have made much more sense just to take them all and…" That already implied a nervous breakdown.

Peggy and Kraft now entered the bar. When they saw Rebrov, they waved and headed for his table. Kraft, like always, was grinning and casually elegant, while Peggy this time sported clothes that seemed to belong to a tourist or mountain climber. She wore a thick knitted sweater, sports pants tucked into white stockings and boots with thick soles. Over her shoulder hung a small backpack, the straps of which emphasized her fine chest…

As they reached his table, Peggy threw her backpack down on the floor, flopped down onto a chair and cried out to the bartender, "Can't you make that damned radio quieter? I can't bear any more of that oaf Goering mocking a representative of the United States!"

"I can only make it quieter," the bartender said apologetically, "but I'm not allowed to turn it off."

"Well, at least that's something! I need a drink at once, otherwise I'm just going to burst with indignation! What arrogance, what narcissism! And that prosecutor can't do anything about it!"

Kraft was in a cheerful mood. As he shook Rebrov's hand he said, "Yeah, it seems our friend Jackson had gotten too used to witnesses that don't make clever and biting speeches in court. Still, he's just an ordinary bumpkin from rural America..."

"Plus, he was clearly set up for this," Rebrov remarked.

Kraft did not understand. "What do you mean?"

"Once, when Goering had yet again launched into a lengthy reply and Jackson ordered him to answer certain questions with only 'yes' or 'no', your judge Biddle leaned over to Lawrence and whispered something in his ear. Then, Lawrence told Jackson that the witness could answer questions in whatever way he thought necessary. Goering's face just lit up with joy, as if that was just what he needed. Now he can mock the prosecutor as much as he likes without risking anything. And now the whole world can listen to the lengthy speeches of the great Reich Marshal."

"Yes," Kraft agreed, "old Biddle doesn't much like Jackson. He thinks that his speeches are just highfalutin', sentimental tripe and he doesn't even hide his opinion. You know, he refused to lodge with him in a fine house here, and he said coldly that he wouldn't care for such neighbors."

Denis was amazed. "Why was he like that?"

"Some old feud," Kraft shrugged. "And simple jealously. Biddle considers himself a much more important politician, but Jackson gets so much more: a car, an office, a house. As Biddle says, to get Jackson to listen to anyone other than himself, he needs to get hit, good, over the head. So, that's what he did with Lawrence's help..."

"Dammit, Jackson needs to forget his provincial lawyer ways and remember that he's dealing with an arrogant gangster who scoffs at the whole world," Peggy snapped as she finished her whiskey. "Otherwise he's going to end up a laughingstock."

"Maybe he should just pull a pistol out of his pocket and shoot the bastard." Rebrov laughed. "Remember, just like Marlene Dietrich suggested?"

"That would be better than all his prattle at least," Peggy answered without batting an eye. "Goering thinks he can make fun of him, and that means he is making fun of the victors in general."

"Of course, Lawrence could stop Goering if he just swung his gavel, not at his bunch, but at Goering's head," Kraft said slyly. "But our lord is too old and old-fashioned for that."

Notes

Journalists noted that only a fraction of Germans — political prisoners, opponents of Nazism — saw Germany's defeat in the war as a liberation. For the overwhelming majority it was a crushing blow and a catastrophe. The image of the enemy that Nazi propaganda had instilled, continued to have its effect. There was a great fear of the Red Army. Many people fled west, with German soldiers seeking to surrender to the British and Americans. Even if the Russians had behaved like a heavenly host of angels, as German scholar Erich Kuby put it, it would have hardly changed the views of the German population.

CHAPTER IX. MY LAST FRIEND

It was already dark when Olaf arrived at one of the innumerable houses in downtown Nuremberg of which only the walls remained. The Americans and the new German police did not care for such places, even during the day, and they never poked their noses around there at night.

He made his way down into a basement where Günther Tilowski lay passed out on a filthy sofa, his arm dangling over the floor. He was in fact passed out because, judging from the number of bottles scattered about, he was dead-drunk. Thank God he didn't snore, that would have been completely horrible.

Olaf grabbed the lone chair, brushed it with the gloves he was holding in his hands, and set it a couple of meters away from Günther. It was hard to discern in that face, overgrown with the stubble of many days, any trace of his best friend from childhood. Even if Olaf had had a brother, he would not have felt so close to him.

He had met few soldiers in his life like Günther, but he had had to confront a great many.

Günther suddenly opened his eyes and stared at Olaf. "Oh, my flourishing friend Olaf Holt is here!" he croaked and grinned drunkenly without any surprise. "Sorry that you have to meet me in this shithole. I do have some whiskey, though. You do like whiskey, don't you, Olaf? Have your American friends taught you to like this swill? Maybe you prefer it with soda now?"

Olaf remained quiet as his friend spoke. He realized that Günther had to get all of his anger out and rid himself of the resentment that was weighing on his soul.

Günther lowered his feet to the floor. "You know how I got this whiskey? From Kurt. You remember Kurt, our classmate? Pretty-boy Kurt? Who could throw a knife better than anyone? Now Kurt's a big guy, he's a doorman at a restaurant where Germans aren't allowed to enter. He stands at the entrance in his doorman's uniform and opens it for the American and British. I've seen him at work, our friend Kurt. I've seen the look in his eyes, Olaf? It's like he's not looking anywhere, even into the past. Just nowhere."

"He lost an arm," Olaf said quietly.

"Yes, his right arm. Now he won't be throwing any knives. He keeps the empty sleeve of his wonderful doorman's uniform tucked under his belt. He uses his left hand to open and close the door for our overlords. Just like a rifle: open, close. That's how he earns his pittance. He's been gutted, Olaf! There's nothing left of him!"

"By the way, here," Olaf took a bottle of cognac out of his jacket pocket. "It's French."

Günther scowled. "Well, sure, as we see now, we lost the war to the French, too. They're judging us now, too."

After hesitating for a moment, Günther stretched out his arm and snatched the bottle from Olaf's hands. He pulled the cork stopper out and began to drink greedily. His Adam's apple bobbed up and down, cognac began to leak all over his chin and down his hairy throat onto his chest. Olaf looked away in disgust. When he again turned his eyes on Günther, his friend had a drunken grin on his face.

"What is your plan?" Olaf quickly asked. "Remember, you were talking about taking hostages in the Palace of Justice?"

"Our plan? Why do you care? And what difference does it make? In a few days we're going to storm it!" Günther lifted the bottle up triumphantly.

"You're in no state to do anything serious," Olaf said sternly.

"But it's just the right state to die in."

"Is it worth dying if the war is over?"

"Do you have some other suggestion?"

"Live. And fight on. But in a different way."

"Why did you come, Olaf?" asked Günther, now in a completely sober voice. "You need something. But what do I have to give you besides reminiscences of the way we used to be?"

"I want you to call off the operation."

"It's too late," Günther waved his request away. "But why?"

"Look, Günther, who are you trying to save? Who are you risking your life for? I see these men in the defendants' dock every day and I think, how could we have ever followed these losers? They are already ragged, moth-eaten people, but with the little strength remaining to them they are fighting for their lives. They aren't thinking about anything other than that. Even if you saved a few people, they aren't capable of anything!"

"But you are defending them in the Palace of Justice after all. You are a lawyer!"

"I'm not defending them, I'm defending Germany and the German people. I am trying to distinguish them from Germany and the Germans."

Günther again thoroughly drank from the bottle. To Olaf it suddenly seemed as if he wasn't getting drunk, but rather more clear-witted.

"You think I don't know what kind of men Hess and Kaltenbrunner are?" Günther said, then spat right on the floor. "But I'm not stopping our operation, Olaf."

"Why not?"

"I can't, because the guys that I agreed to help, Giselle and her friends, won't hold back. Giselle was in the Hitler Youth, she was a *blitzmädchen*."

"One of the girls who were specially trained in firing automatic weapons. Usually using live targets…"

"Exactly. So, there's no way I could talk her out of it. She still believes in the Führer. And if I tried to forbid her from doing anything, she would just shoot me. She's got a fire in her eyes, Olaf, just like you and I used to have. They dream of sacrificing themselves and death doesn't scare them. I even think that they simply have a death wish, seeing what is going on all around us. Poor kids!"

Olaf got up and paced about the cellar. He angrily kicked the empty bottle at his feet. "There's another option," he finally said to Günther. "You can save them from a death that serves no one."

"How?"

"Give them up to the Americans."

Günther stared at him in amazement.

"Yeah, yeah, don't you look at me like I'm a traitor. The Americans will just detain them for a while, and their lives will be safe. I think they'll spend a very short time in prison and then be released. They won't be charged with anything. They haven't even done anything yet."

"And what do you have in store for me?" Günther looked at his friend with dead, cold eyes.

"You can also surrender to the Americans. If you don't like that option, you can simply leave Nuremberg and give me a list of the members of your group and where they are located."

"I see. It's still betrayal…"

"It's saving everyone, Günther. Saving young Germans who might die just for some old geezers who are shitting their pants in fear! If you don't do this, these young German men and women are going to get killed, but they could go on living! You said yourself that they are still so young. After all the victims that Germany has suffered, young Germans should live!"

"Do you really believe what you're saying, Olaf?" asked Günther thoughtfully. "Just don't lie to me. Remember all I've done for you and you for me."

"Yes, Günther, I'm telling you the very truth."

"That's good. But you know me, friend. You know I couldn't do it, no matter what you say!"

"Just think about it, Günther. Think about it. It's me, Olaf Todt, telling you this."

"And up there," Günther pointed at the ceiling, "are there already American jeeps waiting?"

"There's no one up there. I came alone. You can go and see for yourself."

"Well, thanks, then."

Günther took a sheet of paper, a pencil and quickly jotted something down. Then, he suddenly drew a pistol from under his pillow. He looked at Olaf with a smile. "We were tough guys, Olaf, weren't we? Strong and brave…"

Olaf, tense and feeling anything might happen, nodded. He was aware that he had no idea what Günther had in mind. Olaf also had a gun, but he knew he wouldn't manage to draw it in time. Günther would shoot him first.

"We just trusted in the wrong people. But there wasn't anyone else. That's where our tragedy lies, Olaf. There wasn't anyone else. There was only Hitler, no one else…"

Olaf swallowed the lump in his throat. "So what have you decided?"

"You shouldn't do what you shouldn't do," Günther shook his head. "Nothing good will come of it. Remember that, Olaf. And just so that don't forget my advice, I'm doing this…"

In an instant, Günther had raised the gun to his temple and pulled the trigger.

Olaf reflexively jumped back, then rushed to his friend and grabbed his limp body. He was dead. Olaf looked down and saw that the piece of paper had fallen to the floor. He picked it up and found written on it several names and addresses.

Two days later, Giselle Zelinsky and Peter Lainz, a young man who had long been hopelessly in love with her, met near the Johannisfriedhof cemetery. In Giselle's bag was the same pistol with which Günther Tilkowski had shot himself. She had found his body in the cellar the night before and ever since she had been taken with a nervous tick that she could not control. When Peter timidly suggested that maybe they should call the operation off, she looked at him with such a fury that he immediately felt uneasy. He realized that she might be capable of anything, not so much from a desire to free the prisoners as out of her love for Günther, something that had long been an open secret in their group and a cause of much suffering for Peter. For him, Günther's death had raised his hopes that Giselle might, with time, respond to his feelings and they would finally be together. Now Peter was afraid for his life and felt that anything might happen.

Giselle suddenly stopped, opened her bag, and stuck her hand into it. "They're on to us," she whispered. "That American jeep back there, it has been following us for a while now. And there's another one up there ahead."

Peter, who had been lost in his own thoughts, turned to look. There was indeed a jeep full of American soldiers behind them.

"Run!" Giselle screamed. Drawing the pistol from her bag, she fired several times at the jeep.

Peter, bewildered, also drew his gun and, without aiming at anything in particular, also began firing as he ran.

The two American jeeps increased their speed and raced directly towards them. They had to hide somewhere. Only a few steps remained until they could reach the cemetery; they managed to dive through its iron gate.

Rebrov, who had just picked up a routine message from Hector, was just getting ready to leave the cemetery when shots began to ring out ahead of him. As he listened carefully and tried to discern what was going on, the shots began to get closer, and they were coming from submachine guns to boot. Several bullets dug into the trunk of the tree that he decided to hide behind just in case.

When Rebrov peeked out for an instant from behind the tree, he saw a girl running directly towards him with a gun in her hand. A young man followed right behind her. A second later, the girl stumbled and fell to the ground.

American soldiers with weapons then appeared on the cemetery's path. They were not sparing their bullets in the least, and Rebrov again hid behind the tree trunk, which fortunately was thick and strong enough to protect him.

When the shooting suddenly ceased, he again looked out.

The girl had crawled towards Dürer's grave with her last strength, attempting to hide behind the massive tombstone rising from the earth, but she could no longer make it. The young man was standing alongside the brick wall with his hands up. He dropped his gun, fell to his knees, and began sobbing and moaning.

The Americans were carefully approaching with their rifles at the ready.

Rebrov again hid behind a tree. It was clear that he was about to be spotted, so he had to surrender himself honestly. He drew his credentials from his pocket, took a deep breath and then cried out in English, "Don't shoot! I'm unarmed! I'm from the Russian delegation!" He came out from behind the tree. "I'm part of the Russian staff at the international tribunal. I've got my credentials here…"

"Walk forward, but slowly!" ordered the sergeant, who had a flamboyant mustache and was clearly of Hispanic background.

Rebrov reached the Americans. One of the soldiers took his credentials and handed them over to the sergeant. Meanwhile, the girl's body seemed so small and childlike next to the massive tombstone that was the German old master's resting place.

The sergeant finally handed Rebrov's identification back to him. "So, you're a Russian?"

"Yes."

"What are you doing here?"

"I was going for walk. I came to look at Dürer's grave…"

"Who?"

"A great German artist, from the 16th century…" Rebrov said. Then he nodded at Giselle's body. "But who is that girl?"

"Hitler Youth," the sergeant scowled. "They were preparing an attack on the prison. They wanted to free all the Nazi leaders. We wanted to arrest them, but they decided to start shooting."

"So young…"

"We didn't want to kill them," the sergeant shrugged. "Just arrest them. But we didn't want to get a bullet in the head from them after the war is already over…"

"I understand," Rebrov sighed.

"We didn't even manage to say anything before they started shooting," the sergeant went on, increasingly agitated. "Idiot teenagers! That Hitler really knew how to brainwash people!"

Notes

Irma Grese was a farmer's daughter from Thuringia and had gone to a Nazi school. The foreign journalists abundantly present at the trial called her "the Beautiful Beast". She was a Gorgon in a Gretchen's disguise, the cruelest of all in the Belsen and Auschwitz camps, where she ran, for a long time, one of the death factories. Unsatisfied with the tried and traditional ways of murdering people, and having an affinity for such things, she came up with new ways of execution. Her eyebrows were furrowed, her lips pressed. Her bulging watery eyes, as if swollen from terrible visions, look for a long time without blinking, like a pointed gun. Children probably fell dead just at the sight of her. When she was led from the courtroom and into a prison van, one of those decent and well-kempt Germans lining the streets called out, "Irma, are you afraid?" She answered through clenched teeth, "No."

Leonid Leonov on the Belsen trial, 1945

CHAPTER X.
THE RUSSIAN PROSECUTOR
WON'T LET GO OF HIM

It was clear to all that the American chief prosecutor had not managed to break Goering. He hadn't nailed him to the wall, he hadn't made him repent and confess to his crimes.

"Jackson had not only made no impression but actually built up the fat boy further. I think I knocked him reasonably off his perch," wrote the British chief prosecutor Sir David Maxwell Fyfe during these days to his wife. Maxwell Fyfe got his turn to examine Goering after Jackson.

Years would go by, but Jackson would continually look back at his fight with Goering and try to figure out what had gone wrong. As one of the judges – and Jackson's detractor – Biddle said, it was all a matter of Jackson not wanting to act like a smart, tough and well-prepared prosecutor. Rather, he acted like the Pope, expecting everyone to bow down to his preaching. Goering didn't need any such sermonizing, Biddle felt, as he was a hardened criminal with his own goals.

Sir Maxwell Fyfe was no fan of such fantasies. He had been born into a humble family and, as an experienced lawyer of the old school, understood clearly that in Goering, he was dealing with a fierce fighter who was completely devoid of scruples and was ashamed of no action with which he might be able to protect himself. He therefore decided to ask Goering only clear and simple questions, questions that Goering could not answer with demagoguery. The first thing he asked about was Goering's relation to the execution of fifty British pilots who disappeared from a German POW camp in 1944. This was, even Jackson recognized, a punch straight in the gut.

And yet, even though the British prosecutor had managed to deal a blow to Goering's confidence and pin him down with his line of questioning, it was clear that the main battle still lay ahead. It would begin when the USSR chief prosecutor stepped forward for his turn, and the outcome remained unclear. Especially if one considered Churchill's speech in Fulton, which had got Goering very excited. There was now a chasm between the Russians and the Anglo-Saxons; Churchill had revealed it and now it was necessary to make it wider and deeper, to prove that its existence had been conditioned by history and would exist forever. Goering believed that it was in this that his best chances lay.

"If I understand you, defendant Goering, you said that all of the basic decisions concerning foreign, political and military matters were taken by Hitler alone? Do I understand you rightly?"

From the start, Rudenko's questioning had been harsh, cold and business-like. He even pronounced the word "defendant" in a clearly enunciated fashion that visibly got on Goering's nerves.

"Yes, certainly. After all, he was the Führer," Goering attempted to crack a joke like he had during Jackson's questioning. However, the Reich Marshal sensed that matters were coming to a decisive moment.

"Will you tell me then, who was the closest collaborator of Hitler?"

"The close collaborators of the Führer were first I, myself. Another close associate was Dr. Goebbels. Towards the end, it was Bormann first and foremost. It was Himmler also, when certain questions were dealt with."

"Could we conclude that any recommendations which Hitler's leading associates might make, would have had any considerable influence on Hitler's final decisions?"

"Their influence was only effective to the extent that their convictions concurred with those of the Fuehrer."

Rudenko continued energetically. "That is clear. Let us now pass to the next set of questions. When exactly did you start the working out of the plan of action for the use of the German Luftwaffe against the Soviet Union in connection with Operation Barbarossa?"

"The deployment of the Luftwaffe for Operation Barbarossa was worked out by my general staff, after the first directive of the Führer's, that is, after the November directive."

"In 1940?"

"In 1940."

"It was in November 1940, when Germany was preparing to attack Russia? Plans were already being prepared for this attack with your participation?"

"At the time a plan for dealing with the political situation and the potential threat from Russia had been worked out..." said Goering trying to speculate on the winds of politics, but Rudenko cut him off.

"I ask you to reply to this question briefly, 'yes' or 'no'. Can you reply to this briefly?"

Goering wasn't willing to give up so easily and began to wriggle. "Yes, but not in the sense in which you are presenting it."

"It seems to me that I have put the question quite clearly, and there is no ambiguity here at all," shrugged Rudenko. "Thus, you admit that the attack on the Soviet Union was planned several months in advance of the attack itself?"

This time Goering readily agreed. "That is right."

"You admit that as chief of the German Air Force and Reich Marshal you participated in preparations for the attack on the Soviet Union?"

"I once more repeat that I prepared for the possibility of an attack..."

Rudenko, as if he hadn't even heard him, continued to hammer in his nails. "But you do not deny that the plan was already prepared in November 1940?"

"Yes."

"Do you admit that the objectives of the war against the Soviet Union consisted of invading and seizing Soviet territory up to the Ural Mountains and joining it to the German Reich, including the Baltic territories, the Crimea, the Caucasus; also the subjugation by Germany of the Ukraine, of Belorussia and of other regions of the Soviet Union?"

Goering bit his lip. "That I certainly do not admit."

"You do not admit that!" Rudenko laughed sarcastically. "Do you not remember that during the conference at Hitler's headquarters on June 16, 1941, at which you were present, as well as Bormann, Keitel, Rosenberg and others, Hitler stated the objectives of the attack against the Soviet Union exactly as I have stated them? This was shown by the document submitted to the Tribunal. Have you forgotten about that?"

"I have a fair recollection of the discussion at the conference..."

"I shall remind you of various parts of the minutes. Page 2, second paragraph, Point 2, about the Crimea: 'The Crimea must be freed of all foreigners and populated by the Germans...' I want to draw your attention to the end of the minutes. It says here: 'The Führer, furthermore, stresses that the Volga region also must become Reich territory, as well as the Baku province, which must become a military colony of the Reich. The Führer will level Leningrad to the ground and give it to the Finns afterwards...' Have you found the place?"

"Yes," Goering muttered submissively.

"The facts bear witness that even before this conference, aims to annex foreign territories had been fixed in accordance with the plan prepared months ago. That is correct, is it not?

"Yes that is correct, but I would like to emphasize… Will you allow me to do so?" Goering suddenly pleaded pathetically.

Rudenko only nodded. Let him ask for permission, he thought, it'll help him understand what position he's in.

"In these minutes I steered away from these endless discussions. If we had won…"

Rudenko just finished the sentence for him: "…then you would have carried all of this out."

Goering said nothing.

The baron, who had been observing the Reich Marshal's questioning from the observers' gallery, now put his head in his hands. It was over, everyone might as well leave. The baron had little love for this fat man who adored white uniforms and countless medals, but he had little desire to watch the Soviet prosecutor beat everything that the Russians needed from Goering. After waiting for a recess to be called, he headed for the exit, where Olaf stood waiting for him.

They left the Palace of Justice and walked along the street, in no particular hurry. The baron's car followed at a close distance.

"Well, then," said the baron, as if continuing a conversation that had already begun. "As one American gentleman said, 'This goose is cooked.' Goering can go on fighting, but the Russian prosecutor has him cornered."

"Yes," agreed Olaf. "He isn't like himself today. When the American prosecutor examined him, he was completely different."

"Yeah, yeah, I heard incredible tales of his battle against the American. Legends in the spirit of the Nibelungs…"

"Maybe he'll still find some strength within himself?"

The baron was amazed. "Do you really want him to?"

"He is a German, after all," answered Olaf. "And it would be nice if he still had some dignity."

"Dignity." The baron grinned and looked at the ruins that surrounded them. At that moment a military truck drove by and American soldiers were frantically shouting something. The two men involuntarily turned to watch them go.

"Dignity," the baron repeated. "In Nuremberg, today, that sounds rather out of place. Even Hjalmar Schacht doesn't look like the embodiment of virtue. At least he has something to hope for though. As far as Goering goes… I think that the Soviet prosecutor isn't going to give him any peace, just like he wouldn't let go of Paulus. But let's go back to our own affairs. We've made quite a good reputation for ourselves by leading the Americans to those poor conspirators, and now I think that with their help it's time to put these Russian comrades in their place. They can't all win at everything! And Mr. Churchill already gave us a clear signal."

"Shall we throw that dead cat that you were talking about?"

"Yes, that's exactly right. We'll see how they handle that."

That evening Rudenko, wearing the same tunic he had worn at the trial, fell asleep in his armchair without even touching his supper. The cat lay dozing on his lap. His wife Maria looked at him with pity and tiptoed out to the kitchen, where Grosman was enjoying some pastries.

"He's tired," sighed Maria. "Let him sleep, we'll take off his boots later."

"The comrade general really put the screws on that creep Goering today!" Grosman shook his clenched fist. "He had him right against the wall and Goering couldn't find anything to say! You know how our guys are. Goering can mess with the Americans, but not with us! Goering kept flailing about, 'That's not how it was', 'That's not the right translation', 'That's not what was written'. And the comrade general just kept thrashing him. What about this? Or that? There you go! You're lying, you creep, you can't get out of this!"

Maria Fyodorovna just listened with a quiet pride in her husband.

Notes

The justification that the financier Hjalmar Schacht offers can only be interpreted as meaning that the Nazi industrialists and men of finance, who financially supported the Nazi Party and created the economic foundation without which Hitler would have been powerless, do not share any culpability in the aggression and crimes against humanity… The true meaning of Schacht's justification becomes clear if

one sees it as only part of the entire policy
that the United States and Britain maintained
regarding Germany.

Secretary of the US National Lawyers Guild

CHAPTER XI. NIBELUNG LOYALTY

This time Rebrov was heading to the Palace of Justice with Gavrik in a car driven by a German driver. When they reached the Palace, the German suddenly asked, "May I ask you gentlemen a question?"

Gavrik nodded. "Go ahead, Wolfgang." He had already rode with this driver many times.

"Is it true that at the trial Gen. Rudenko took out a pistol and shot Goering?"

Denis and Gavrik exchanged glances.

The driver was amazed. "You really haven't heard about it? All of Nuremberg is talking about it today."

"That's not possible!" Gavrik laughed. "Just some crazy rumors. Someone's playing a joke on you, Wolfgang."

"Everyone is saying that it was written about in an American newspaper. I don't have anything against it. Goering has always disgusted me."

Gavrik turned to Rebrov. "Do you understand any of this?"

Rebrov merely shrugged.

Inside the Palace, they looked for the latest issue of the American newspaper *Stars and Stripes*. In it was a passage that had been crossed out with a blue pencil, which Rebrov translated for Gavrik:

Tragic events at the Nuremberg trials: Soviet prosecutor shoots Hermann Goering. Unable to withstand the defendant's defiant and offensive behavior, the Soviet chief prosecutor, Gen. Rudenko, drew his pistol in the middle of his examination and shot at the former Reich Marshal.

"There's no signature. Let's go to the press bar, they can probably tell us everything there."

At the press bar they were met by laughter and shouts.

A British journalist waved a newspaper. "There's an English saying: 'Never approach a bull from the front, a horse from the rear, or an American reporter from any direction!'"

Rebrov finally located Peggy, who was modestly perched at the bar. He caught her eye and shook his head reproachfully, but Peggy only flashed an innocent smile. Then she came over to Rebrov, took his arm, and standing on her tiptoes whispered into his ears, "Just don't give me away!"

Rebrov gave her a baleful look. "Peggy, you're terrible! You didn't just make this up, you stole the idea from Marlene Dietrich!"

"So what? Neither Marlene nor your general will lose anything from it. And you're to blame for the whole thing anyway, you should have told me something juicy. Then I wouldn't have had to make something up!" She looked at him with shining eyes that were completely shameless.

Rudenko, who had laughed heartily at the silly sensational article, now continued his examination of Goering, who was visibly struggling. Goering was constantly wavering between assurances of his "Nibelung loyalty" to Hitler and a desire to absolve himself of personal responsibility for any specific crimes. Albert Speer, who was sitting not far away from him on the defendants' bench, noted caustically that as soon as they slightly pressed on him, he would immediately begin to insist that he was actually plotting against Hitler, that he didn't know anything, and if he had known, he would have never agreed to it. Yet, before that, he had boasted that he had been Hitler's most devoted servant.

"Defendant, do you admit that as the delegate for the Four Year Plan you were in full charge of the working out of the plans for the economic exploitation of all the occupied territories, as well as the realization of these plans?" asked Rudenko.

"I have already admitted that I assumed responsibility for the economic policy in the occupied territories."

"On August 6, 1942, there was a conference of commissioners of the occupied regions and of the representatives of the military command. You spoke at this conference, and I would like to remind you of some of the things you said."

"May I have a look at these minutes?"

"Certainly. I will ask you to look only at page 111 of this stenographic record. You said the following: 'You certainly are not sent there to work for the welfare of the population.' And later: 'It used to be called plundering. It was up to the party in question to carry off what had been conquered. But today things have become more humane. In spite of that, I intend to plunder and to do it thoroughly.' Have you found the sentence?"

"Yes, I have found it."

"Did you say that?"

"I certainly assume that I did say it, yes," muttered Goering.

"You did say that," Rudenko looked over the courtroom with a smile. "Very well. Let us go to the next question. Do you admit that you directed the deportation to forced labor of millions of citizens from the occupied territories?"

"To the extent that I was informed, I will take my part of the responsibility…" Goering began to explain in a confused manner.

"But you do not deny the underlying meaning that you were speaking of here, of millions of people who were carried off forcibly to Germany for slave labor? You do not deny that this was forced labor, slavery?"

"Slavery; that I deny. Forced labor did of course partly come into it."

"You heard, defendant Goering, that a series of German documents have been read which make it clear that these people from the occupied territories were sent forcibly to Germany. They were rounded up and sent to Germany under military guard. If they refused to go to Germany or tried to evade mobilization, the peaceful inhabitants were shot and submitted to tortures of various nature. Is that not so?"

"Not to slavery; they were sent to Germany to work," said Goering, although he knew himself how helpless it all sounded.

"Well, what do you think, Sergei Ivanovich?" said Rudenko, who was taking tea in his office and waiting for the end of the lunch break. He looked completely soldierly, but spoke in a merry manner. "It looks like the operation was a success, wasn't it? We struck the enemy on his own territory!"

Filin, who had just received Hector's latest message and was reading over it, smiled to see the chief prosecutor in such a fighting mood. "You've got to beat this enemy, Roman Andreyevich. You've got to fight without mercy to the very end."

"Today, the reporters kept asking me about the defendants' hope that the Allies would start squabbling amongst themselves and whether the trials might be called off…"

"Well, they must have all read Churchill's speech in Fulton. What did you tell them?"

"I gave them a philosophical answer. History may sometimes take an unexpected turn, but judging by how the trials are proceeding now, we don't foresee anything like that happening. I said that all of the parties are working together faithfully and everything is founded on mutual respect, that we are united in our aim to see the truth come out. They also asked me if the trials were proceeding too slowly. After all, enough has already come out to find them all guilty, along with Bormann who is still missing. I explained that this is the first international trial, isn't it? There are no historical precedents for it, no experience. We have had to start from scratch. Am I right?"

"Well, we can't drag things out either, Roman Andreyevich. Interest in the trials in the West is flagging, and soon it will stop being front-page news. Now, there might have been a flash of excitement about Paulus and Goering, but then things will fall back into a routine, and…"

"Well, Sergei Ivanovich, I'm a lawyer, not an actor," said Rudenko throwing up his hands. "We are dealing with a court, a tribunal, not a theatre performance."

"I realize that, but…"

"Alright, Sergei Ivanovich, you agree," laughed Rudenko. "I think that we'll finish with Goering today."

"He's going to fight to the end though, like a chained animal that is prepared to bite its own paw off in order to get free. Do you know what he told an American after he had to watch a newsreel about what the Nazis did on our territory?"

"What?"

"He said that you could make a film against anyone about what 'evil monsters' they are: all you have to do is exhume some corpses, then show a bulldozer pushing them all into a common grave. And that he knew perfectly well that the Russians could have killed a few hundred German prisoners and dressed them in Soviet uniforms in order to shoot this film."

"What a creep. Goddamn fascist!" Filin and Rudenko turned in surprise to see Grosman standing in the doorway with a package in his hand. He was unusually emotional. "Comrade general, I've got an urgent parcel for you," he said excitedly. "Sorry, comrade general, I can't listen to things like that. I saw with my own eyes how they… in the camps…"

Rudenko walked up to him and laid a hand on his shoulder. "It's OK, comrade sergeant, it's OK. He'll get what's coming to him, I can assure you. He knows the Russians. Well, no, he doesn't *really* know us."

After Grosman left, Filin waited for Rudenko to examine his parcel and then he continued their conversation. "Roman Andreyevich, Goering isn't just attacking us. According to recent reports from our agent, the other defendants have sharply increased their attacks on the

Soviet Union and the Russians. Here's what they're saying about us. Goering said, and I quote, 'The Russians are primitive folk. Bolshevism is against private property, and I am all in favor of private property. The delusion that all men are equal is ridiculous… How ironic it is that crude Russian peasants who wear the uniforms of generals now sit in judgment against me…'" Filin's face took on a very disgusted and stern look, then he now looked up at Rudenko.

Rudenko however chuckled maliciously. "Well, I am from the peasantry. Roman, the farmer's son. So, he doesn't like it! Well, he shouldn't worry, he won't have to suffer much longer."

"Here's what Kaltenbrunner said: 'Hitler always remarked that if America really fought for democracy, then America could have done away with the antidemocratic system in the Soviet Union.' And now Frank: 'There is only one power in the world now that can overcome Russia: America. We were not strong enough.' Grand Admiral Dönitz: 'Russia is the greatest criminal nation in the world,' against which the only alternative would be 'a commonwealth of nations of Europe to band together and balance Russia in the east.' And Field Marshal Kesselring: 'Europe has only one enemy: Russia.'"

"Did they say that amongst themselves?"

"No, they openly said it to an American psychologist that was assigned to monitor them."

"What for? Are they burning with rage? Bursting with anger?"

"I don't think so. They know perfectly well that all of their statements are immediately passed on to American intelligence and further along. They are deliberately trying to make the Americans scared of us and instead see them as their allies."

"And thus be merciful."

"Indeed."

Rudenko stood up and looked at Filin with mischief in his eyes. "Well, I'm going to go deal with the Reich Marshal in my own way, the peasant way."

"Defendant Goering, in 1941 the German high command drew up a series of instructions and orders with regard to the conduct of the troops in the East and how they were to treat the Soviet population. According to these instructions, the German officers had the right to shoot any person suspected of having a hostile attitude towards the Germans, without bringing that person to court. This directive also stated that the German soldiers could not be punished for crimes which they committed against the local population."

"Actually this document did not go straight to me. Actually, as far as my troops were concerned, I issued very severe disciplinary orders."

"I draw your attention once more to the date in the right-hand corner. It states there, Führer headquarters, May 13, 1941. Therefore, it means that this was a month before the German attack on the Soviet Union? Already, directives were formulated about military jurisdiction within the regions covered by Case Barbarossa. And the officers were given the right to shoot civilians without bringing them to trial… The second document is dated September 16, 1941. It states that 'as a general rule the death of one German soldier must be paid for by the lives of fifty to one hundred Communists.' Was this document also unknown to you?"

"It was not directed to me. It was sometime during the war that I heard that…"

"Fifty to one hundred people for one German?"

"The number was originally five to ten and the Fuehrer personally added on a zero."

"How generous. Do you know anything about the directives of the OKW with regard to the treatment of Soviet prisoners of war?"

"I shall have to see them…"

"Please. Here it is said that prisoners of war who are trying to escape should be shot without warning."

"I did not know of this document."

Rudenko's tone became even harsher. "The majority of these criminal orders and directives of the high command, were they not issued even before the beginning of the war against the Soviet Union and as part of the preparations for that war? Does this not show that the German government and the high command already had a prepared plan for exterminating the Soviet population?"

"It only shows that we considered a struggle with the Soviet Union which would be an extremely bitter one, and that it would be conducted according to other rules as there were no conventions…"

"Defendant Goering, do you know about Himmler's directives given in 1941 about the extermination of thirty million Slavs?"

"Yes. But it was not an order but a speech."

"It is known to you that there was an order by the high command regarding the branding of Soviet prisoners of war?"

"No representative of the air force was present at this preliminary discussion as I have ascertained here from the records."

"Defendant, I am interested as to whether you knew about this or not. The orders are quite clear."

"No."

"Do you know that the German high command ordered that Soviet war prisoners and Soviet citizens had to be used for clearing mine fields and transporting bombs that had not exploded?"

"I know that Russian prisoners of war who were engineers had to clear the mines which they had laid. To what extent the civilian population was employed for that purpose I do not know."

"Do you know about an order regarding the destruction of the towns of Leningrad, Moscow and other towns of the Soviet Union?"

"Of the destruction of Moscow I know nothing at all."

"I have a few concluding questions to put to you, defendant. I should like to put to you only one question in this connection and I should like you to reply directly to it. Were you in accord with this principle of the master race and education of the German people in the spirit of it?"

"I have never expressed my agreement with the theory that one race should be considered as a master race, superior to the others, but I have emphasized the difference between races."

"Do you recognize that, as the second man in Germany, you are responsible for the organizing on a national scale, of murders of millions of innocent people, independently of whether you knew about those facts or not? Tell me briefly, 'yes' or 'no'."

"No, because I did not know anything about them and did not cause them."

"You were the second person in the government, it was your duty to know about these facts! Millions of Germans knew about the crimes which were being perpetrated, and you did not know about them… You stated to the tribunal that Hitler's government brought great prosperity to Germany. Are you still sure that that is so?"

"The collapse was due only to the war's being lost."

"So up to that point, everything was done correctly?" Without waiting for Goering's answer, Rudenko added, "Defendant Goering, you and your colleagues brought Germany to military and political destruction." He then turned to the judges and said in a perfectly calm tone, "Your honors, I have no more questions."

Notes

In recent months the German people have experienced such terrible hardships and hunger, news of Hitler's suicide, by which the man had avoided trial, posed almost no interest and wasn't even a topic of conversation. In those days, the people were in a state of apathy and fatigue, and they had only one passionate desire left: that all this finally end and forever.

However, many Germans (and not even remotely the worst of my compatriots) had to undergo another trial. This trial was the cruel discovery that all of the tremendous sacrifices and selfless devotion of German troops had been in vain, that millions of valiant men risked their lives for a cause that was, and became clear, evil.

Lt. Gen. Siegfried Westphal, 1946

CHAPTER XII.
SPEAKING GENERAL TO GENERAL

After the epic battles with Paulus and Goering, which had drawn the attention of the whole world, the tribunal decided to catch its breath for a bit and settle back into its routine. It was clear to everyone that Churchill's Fulton speech posed no threat to the international tribunal and it was firmly bent on seeing the trials through to the end. Ribbentrop's upcoming appearance in court awoke no sensational interest, as it was known to all that Ribbentrop was now quite a miserable sight, and if he were capable of anything, it would just be endless, meaningless lies that he wouldn't even try to endow with some facade of plausibility.

However, Gen. Filin had some serious doubts about that. Ribbentrop was scared, of course, and he was only capable of wriggling and proving that he wasn't involved with anything. But, according to reports from Hector, Goering was putting pressure on his fellow Nazi, demanding that Ribbentrop make the so-called secret protocol to the non-aggression pact signed with Molotov the central point of his defense. Goering had initially been knocked down by Maxwell Fyfe and Rudenko's punches, but now he had grown angry and keen on striking back through Ribbentrop. He dreamed of getting revenge on the Russians. Furthermore, the other defendants were now lending him support. Ribbentrop wasn't sure, he only mumbled that the non-aggression pact would get some attention, but nobody knew how things would actually proceed. Especially if the lawyers got heavily involved; due to Lord Lawrence's overly gentlemanly hand on the rudder, they might dare to do who knows what.

After Filin had finished discussing the present situation with Rudenko, the prosecutor declared that he would stay on his guard, but the court had already refused to admit some documents in this regard, so it was unlikely to reverse itself now. Plus, no one needed this.

Rebrov also had his own worries. He continued to feel uneasy, for some reason, about that young assistant to the defense, Olaf Todt, who had the manners and build of an authentic Nordic warrior. He should have been worked over by investigators, but what could you do here in the American zone, where the trans-Atlantic masters kept a tight watch over everything and weren't sharing any of their secrets, even with the British. It was not especially surprising in itself that Todt had a military bearing, as all young German men had gone through special training. Still, there was something suspicious about him, he gave off a sense of danger. Rebrov even wondered if it was worth sharing his feelings with Filin. Could Hector find out something about this Todt? But Rebrov thought it would be foolish to trouble Filin with suspicions that he wasn't even sure about himself. He had to take some steps of his own first…

However, Rebrov did not manage to do anything at that time, as Filin called to say that they would be flying to Moscow at once, and that he would expect to see Rebrov at the airport.

On arrival he found a gloomy Filin already standing next to the plane bound for Berlin. The pilot was smoking a few steps away.

"What are we waiting for, captain?" Filin asked the pilot.

"They asked us to take one more passenger," explained the pilot. "It must be an important person if they asked me to wait here."

At that same moment a huge German car painted in black drove up to the plane. An imposing military man with general's stripes got out. He was followed by Beletskaya wearing a light coat and a white beret.

The general took Beletskaya by the arm and walked up to Filin. "Good evening, Sergei Ivanovich. I'm the reason you're being held up. Forgive me, it's just so hard for me to say goodbye to my wife here. I've really missed her."

"Are you also bound for Moscow?" Filin asked.

"No, Berlin. There's nothing for me to do here, I'm no expert on jurisprudence like all of you. I've now got my own work cut out for me: I'll be personally overseeing land redistribution in the Soviet zone with an emphasis on collective farming."

"Sounds interesting," said Filin politely.

"It sure is!"

Beletsky embraced his wife. "Lena, darling, maybe we should forget all about Nuremberg, huh? Aren't you tired of these fascists already? Maybe you want to come with me? I'll settle everything with Moscow."

Beletskaya, who was trying all this time not to look at Rebrov, laughed. "As our American allies say, I've got to serve my contract to the end."

"Well, you see, then," the general sighed. He was clearly already tired of talking about this subject.

After Rebrov had gone up into the plane, he looked for a long time at a beautiful woman in a white coat who was waving to someone…

After the plane picked up speed, Beletsky sat down alongside Filin. He smelled of cognac and was generally easygoing and relaxed after the several days spent with his wife. "Listen, Sergei Ivanovich, I want to tell you something. I don't have anything to do with you being summoned to Moscow. I'm telling you that as a frontline soldier. To be honest, I don't even know why they sent me here."

"It happens."

"Well, of course I know," Beletsky corrected himself. "They said to me, you'll be an outsider there, an objective witness, so go and see how our people in Nuremberg are doing…"

"They just called you and told you that?" Filin asked bluntly.

"Well, it's just… I understood there were signs that you people here were almost dragging out the trials. Or at least not preventing it from being dragged out, not making an effort against the enemy's intrigues. And that maybe you had become too comfortable here amongst the Americans. Well, you understand how it is, what I'm telling you."

"I understand."

"As for who feels that way, well, you can imagine yourself. At the very top they decided to go and see what you are doing over here. So, I came and had a look. You seem to be working hard here. I don't even know how you can stomach spending all this time with Goering and Hess, those bastards! So, that's how it is, general. I'm on your side. But when it comes to who exactly is after you, sorry, I'm not in the loop."

Beletsky blissfully closed his eyes for a moment, as if remembering something. He then gestured towards Rebrov. "Why is your officer there looking so glum? He looks like he's wracked with grief. I bet he's in love with someone, am I right? And he didn't want to be apart from her?"

"Maybe," said Filin, who decided not to argue.

"He's a good-looking guy. Girls would line up for a guy like that. Our girls, though, or a foreign one?"

"He's keeping it a secret."

"Well, then, he's doing the smart thing."

Notes

Then there was the pressing question of what to wear to Nuremberg.

Besides my overcoat, I had no clothes at all. Right before departure, they gave me a cut of fabric for a dress, shoes and a horrible beret. I thought I would be the most fashionable woman there, but it turned out that the Americans and British were better dressed. However, in exchange for food rations and American cigarettes (Camel) we quickly bartered with the Germans for a number of chic dresses.

They based us on the outskirts of the city in some cottages that had remained intact after the Allied bombing. My husband and I lived with a banker's family. Groceries were supplied by the Americans, but Germans served us at the table. We got various juices, fruit and chocolate, but towards the end of the trials the Americans stopped supplying us, allegedly due to budgetary limitations. For three days we were starving, as there was nowhere to buy food. However, they soon began delivering us rations from the Soviet zone.

In the evenings we would go to the Grand Hotel restaurant, where one could have dinner and drink sherry for German marks. Women were not allowed inside without stockings. So, we learned from the French women to draw the chic black-seamed stockings of the time on our legs with a pencil.

From the memoirs of Era Bogdanovich,
secretary in the Soviet delegation

CHAPTER XIII.
A CAT DRIVEN INTO A CORNER

Alfred Seidl, Hess's defense attorney, was young and had an unassuming appearance. He was short, thin and fidgety. Nor did have good manners: he spoke hurriedly and excitedly. He excessively displayed a sardonic smile, although this smile resembled a cramp or a nervous tick. However, he was an ambitious man. He understood that taking part in the trials would grant him a solid footing in the legal profession, plus, he was as fierce as a wild animal that, when cornered, could strike out at anyone. But it was his own ambition and vain aspirations that made him a cornered man. That's why Olaf chose him.

"Do you really think that the court will agree to admit this document?" said Seidl, rubbing the tip of this long nose, when Olaf had presented him with his suggestion. There was no one else besides them in this room of the Palace of Justice where the defense attorneys poured over their documents, so they could speak freely. "You yourself have said that at a secret meeting, the prosecutors' committee decided to not let the defense have its way and to not discuss any documents relating to the foreign policy of the victor countries."

"Yes, but a lot has changed since then. New circumstances have arisen. I trust you have heard about Churchill's speech in Fulton?"

"Sure, it was a brilliant and inspiring speech."

"It won't be without political consequences, as you can imagine."

"Of course. But not during these trials."

"It might seem that way superficially. But under the surface, things are moving completely differently, there are different forces at work. And my offer confirms this. You must understand that behind him are people who hold the power, today, in our occupation zone."

Seidl resumed scratching his nose. "Well, Herr Todt, there is something else here. Judge Lawrence might be an old man, but he'll remember that the court has already refused to admit this document.

Judges really don't like it when they are presented with a document that has already been rejected."

"Let's not decide for Lawrence, Herr Seidl," said Olaf coldly. He was thinking that it would be easy enough to just stretch out his arm and lightly squeeze the lawyer's throat, and Seidl wouldn't be raising any more objections. Nonetheless… "Your task is simple. You need to find a chance to show the whole world the secret protocol to the Molotov-Ribbentrop pact."

"They are uncertified photocopies, Herr Todt! We can't find any originals, and no one has even seen such a thing. We would be dealing with something that completely lacks signatures or seals."

Olaf cut him off. "I know how things are. That's why we need to do this when a defendant or a witness is being examined, so we can get the secret protocol included in the official record of the tribunal. Ribbentrop's examination would be a very convenient time for this."

"Maybe, although, between you and me, with the state that Ribbentrop's in…"

"I don't care what state he's in! I don't care what he has to say about this. What is important here is showing the whole world."

"I understand. But they will immediately ask how I got my hands on the document. What should I answer?"

"Tell them that it was anonymously given to you by an American intelligence officer."

Seidl looked at Olaf in bewilderment. "An American intelligence officer?"

"I can assure you, it's the absolute truth."

"Except that they weren't given to me personally, so it's completely untrue."

"I don't see a difference," snapped Olaf. He now stretched his arm out towards Seidl, but his fingers gripped not the lawyer's throat but his scrawny shoulder. Olaf squeezed in a light, almost friendly way and Seidl winced from pain.

"What difference does it make who got them first?" said Olaf, looking the man right in the eyes. "The important thing is that they are in our hands!"

"Yes, of course," said Seidl shuddering under his gaze. "And I've got a suggestion."

"What?"

"Let's try going the more or less official route first."

"What do you mean?"

"Let's turn to Maxwell Fyfe from the British prosecution. It is his duty to check the authenticity of any documents submitted to the tribunal. He has photocopies of any originals from the German Ministry of Foreign Affairs that are presently available. We'll ask him to certify that these documents are authentic, and we'll see what he says."

"Judging from how he's leading the questioning, he won't have anything good to say. He's one of those people who thinks Germany should be forced down on its knees forever."

"Still, it's worth a try," said Seidl. "Then we can always say that we went the official route. For a lawyer that is very important."

"Fine, let's try," agreed Olaf. He placed his hand on Seidl's shoulder and told him that whatever the British prosecutor answered, the photocopies must be presented in court.

Seidl nodded obediently.

Seidl sat outside the office of Sir David Maxwell Fyfe, the deputy to the main British prosecutor but who in practice is responsible for all duties. Olaf sat with Seidl, intent on seeing for himself that everything was done properly.

Maxwell Fyfe was a stocky, red-faced man with coarse manners. After listening to Seidl's request to verify the authenticity of their photocopies, he looked the two men over with anger and even with a bit of slight disgust. Everyone had known for a long time that Sir David preferred to express himself figuratively, and with relish, and to resort to legal equivocation and casuistry only when absolutely necessary.

"Look, my esteemed attorney, here is what I'll tell you," Maxwell Fyfe muttered, his lower jaw bulldog-like. "We are sitting here in a bombed-out city where the streets were full of dead bodies not long ago and we're looking into the monstrous crimes that your clients committed. Scoundrels' like that brazen fat man Goering or that pathological case Kaltenbrunner. After what I have seen and discovered, an ordinary man would lose the will to go on living. My sole wish is to get away from Nuremberg, from Germany, and from the German people who are now pretending that they knew nothing about what was done under their own noses and with their full approval."

Maxwell Fyfe snorted angrily and went on, "But when I see the piles of clothing from the infants killed in Auschwitz and the heaps of gold teeth pulled from those killed in the gas chambers, I think it is worth giving up a year of my life to document the shock and horror that mankind has experienced at the hands of your clients. To document it and to bring it to judgment, so that nothing like this ever happens again!"

Seidl was shocked by Maxwell Fyfe's vehemence and frankness. "But Sir David…"

The British prosecutor paid no attention to Seidl's objection. He continued, "You are coming to me with some photocopies given to you by God knows whom, and you want me to actively help you knock the trials off course and drag them out further. Why the hell should I help you?! I think that by doing this, you only want to drag things out and set us quarreling with the Russians. Now you want us to fight with your criminal brothers in white gloves! No, the Nazis must be destroyed at any cost. That is the only way! So, I do not intend to verify anything for you." He brusquely pushed the photocopies away.

Seidl began to fold them and place them into his enormous briefcase. Maxwell Fyfe suddenly permitted himself a brief grin. "I can only give you one bit of advice: go to Gen. Rudenko and let him verify the authenticity of these papers." He grinned again, imagining what Gen. Rudenko would have to say to Seidl and where he might tell him to go.

Yet, one had to give Seidl credit. He didn't just throw up his hands in resignation. He was driven by the same bravery of a cornered wild animal that Olaf saw in him. Though his hands shook, he slammed his briefcase shut and headed towards that part of the Palace of Justice where the Soviet delegation worked. Olaf even followed him with some curiosity. Really, something had happened inside Seidl!

At Rudenko's office they were met by the secretary, a uniformed young man with the kind face of a village teacher, neatly-parted hair and round spectacles.

"Allow me to introduce myself. I am Seidl, a defense attorney. My clients, as you probably know, are Rudolf Hess and Hans Frank. My assistant and I would like to see Gen. Rudenko for a very important matter relating to the trials."

The secretary looked at them with a detailed scrutiny they hadn't expected and then politely said, "Gen. Rudenko is not presently in the city. However, if your matter is really important for the tribunal, then his assistant Gen. Zorya might deal with it."

Zorya showed no pleasure at this unexpected visit. On the contrary, he let it show that he was very busy and the sooner the visitors left his office, the better.

Seidl spoke quickly and enthusiastically. "General, I have at my disposal photocopies of two 'secret annexes', signed on August 23 and September 28 after the signing of the non-aggression pact by the Reich Ministry of Foreign Affairs and your Foreign Commissariat…"

Zorya cut him off. "As I understand, neither of those so-called documents are certified copies of any original. Furthermore, the court has already refused to consider them as evidence."

"Nonetheless," Seidl blurted out, "we suggest that the Soviet delegation should be convinced, itself, of this material's authenticity and confirm it."

Zorya looked at him with total astonishment. This was an utter impertinence. If Olaf were in Zorya's shoes, he would have immediately kicked Seidl out of the office, but for some reason the Russian general did not do so. Meaning they could work on him further.

"Sir Maxwell Fyfe, the representative of the British delegation, has already confirmed their authenticity," lied Olaf with total composure.

Zorya thought the matter over. Clearly, this has come as a completely unexpected surprise for him, and he had no idea what to do. He was probably very curious to have a look at the papers, but did not want to grab them and thus reveal his interest.

"I know who Sir Maxwell Fyfe is," Zorya finally said. "But I don't know what he told you. I'll say it again, the court has already made its decision on this matter. I think it makes no sense to talk about it further. If that is all, then I kindly ask you to leave my office."

The Russian general said this in a very resolute tone, but Olaf noted the confusion brewing within him.

Notes

Life at the Villa Contradty is completely spoiling me. For instance, last night for dinner we had a most excellent cauliflower soup, cold trout with mayonnaise, stewed veal, fresh peas, a delicious salad and gooseberry tarts. On the other side, Dry Martinis Cliquot and some Martel brandy…

From a 1946 letter written by Francis Biddle, American judge at Nuremberg

CHAPTER XIV.
SOMEONE IS STANDING BEHIND HIM!

The next day, Seidl was cross-examining the witness Ernst von Weizsä-cker, the former state secretary at Germany's Ministry of Foreign Affairs when it was led by Ribbentrop.

"Witness, I'd like to direct your attention here," said Seidl hurriedly, as if he was afraid that he would immediately be prevented from speaking. "I want to ask you a question regarding the secret documents signed in 1939 during the…"

Rudenko resolutely stood up from behind the Soviet prosecutors' table and angrily said, "Your honors, I would like to object! The question which is being put to him at this moment by the defense counsel Seidl has no connection with the examination of the case in hand!"

The judges stopped to confer with one another. It was clear that a serious dispute had arisen between them and the Soviet judges were arguing with the American and British judges and the court president Lawrence. Finally, Lord Lawrence announced, "The court will allow the defense to continue questioning the witness."

Seidl beamed and hurried on. "Witness, I will now present you with a document, the authenticity of which had been confirmed by other staff of the German Ministry of Foreign Affairs…"

Rudenko glanced savagely at the lawyer, then turned his gaze to Lawrence and quickly rose to his feet. "Your honors, the document which defense counsel Seidl is attempting to put to the witness has been rejected by the tribunal. This can only be seen as a provocation and contempt of court."

Lord Lawrence, as if suddenly being jarred awake, asked, "Defense, what is this document that you are presenting to the witness? There is a document which you have already presented to the tribunal and which has been ruled out. Is that the same document?"

Seidl coughed.

"So, is that the same document?" Lawrence insisted.

"It is the document," Seidl admitted. "But I should, your honor, like to read this text in order to stimulate the memory of the witness."

Rudenko, who was still on his feet, angrily snapped, "I would like to remind the court that we are examining the matter of the crimes of the major German war criminals. We are not investigating the foreign policies of other states. I say it again: this supposed document has been rejected by the tribunal! His actions can only be seen as an utter contempt of court. Contempt and deliberate provocation!"

Thomas Dodd, assistant to the American prosecution, unexpectedly rose. "I certainly join Gen. Rudenko in objecting to the use of this document. Plus, the defense is avoiding answering the question of how this document came into his hands."

"The only thing I can say," Seidl muttered, "is that I received this document from a man on the Allied side who appeared absolutely reliable."

"Who exactly?" Dodd insisted.

"I cannot disclose that," Seidl pursed his lips. "I received it only on condition that I would not divulge its origin."

"The court will recess for a brief deliberation," Lawrence announced. He clearly understood that this matter needed to be urgently rectified.

There was a nervous conversation at the Soviet prosecutors' table during the recess. Rudenko, drumming his fingers on the table, whispered, "Someone is clearly standing behind him. He's being used by someone. Who? The Americans? Damn, and it's our luck that Filin isn't here. What did he have to go back to Moscow for?"

After the court resumed, Lord Lawrence was hardly recognizable. He looked angry and determined, as few had ever seen him before.

"The court has decided," he stated, with a stern glance at Seidl. "In view of the fact that the origin of the document cannot be established, the tribunal has decided not to put the document to the witness. Continue your cross-examination, defense, but do not think of returning to this matter again."

Seidl squinted at the defense bench and found Olaf there. Olaf gave a slight, barely noticeable nod of approval: it had been done.

Notes

As Winston Churchill, British prime minister in 1940–1945, wrote in his memoirs, the fact that such an agreement between Berlin and Moscow could be reached, attested to the failure of British and French diplomacy: they had managed to neither direct the Nazi aggression towards the USSR nor make the USSR their ally before World War II. Nonetheless, the USSR cannot be called a clear beneficiary of the pact either, although the country secured an additional two years of peacetime and a significant amount of additional territory at its western borders.

As a result of the pact, Germany in 1939–1944 avoided a war on two fronts after decisively defeating Poland, France and the small countries of Europe, and it also received an army with two years of fighting experience for its attack on the USSR in 1941. Thus, according to many historians, Nazi Germany can be considered the main beneficiary of the pact.

From *Sovetskaya istoriografiya* (Soviet Historiography, published by RGGU, 1992)

CHAPTER XV. A DUCK DECOY

At this time, General Filin found himself in Moscow in a very tense and dangerous situation. Stalin had always placed great importance on the tribunal in Nuremberg, but after Churchill's speech in Fulton he gave increased attention to the trials.

Stalin was clearly exasperated by Churchill. Stalin even gave an interview to the newspaper *Pravda* to voice his concerns, an action he rarely took. Filin remembered well the words of the great leader when he said he viewed Mr. Churchill's speech in the USA as a dangerous action meant to sow the seeds of discord amongst the Allies and prevent them from working together. Stalin went on in a severe tone: "As a matter of fact, Mr. Churchill now takes the stand of the warmongers, and in this Mr. Churchill is not alone. He has friends not only in Britain but in the United States of America as well."

As far as Nuremberg was concerned, there was only one goal: to ensure that the trial was brought to a successful end. The tasks assigned to the Soviet delegation must absolutely be achieved.

Thus, when Stalin received word that a German agent was active in Moscow and his mission concerned Nuremberg specifically, he erupted into a great fury. "Either you plug this breach," he said, "or your foolishness and failure to act will be seen as a betrayal of the people's interest." This meant, first of all, Filin's friend Gen. Gres.

For this reason, their conversation in Moscow was an unhappy one from the very beginning.

"You have been summoned here in connection with the same mole that we've got crawling around here and can't identify," said Gres, not even trying to paint a happy picture of the situation.

"Paulus might not have even made it to Nuremberg. They were waiting for him there," said Filin, not to aggravate the situation but to simply show that he understood why Gres was anxious and shared that feeling.

"I know. If something had happened, then you and me… After all, the idea to use Paulus came down from the very top." Gres points a finger at the ceiling, referring to Stalin. "But Spitz is a very well cloaked agent. If he spent the whole war here and never got caught… An idea has come to us, one that is connected to you personally, by the way, Sergei Ivanovich."

Filin straightened. "How interesting. And what is that?"

"I'll tell you what…" Gres's hands were now placed on the table, and he now exaggeratedly spread out his fingers as if to pat someone on the head. "If we suspect correctly that he is working somewhere in our department, and if he has been assigned a mission dealing with the trials, then there is no better candidate for attracting his attention than you. You've just been brought here from Nuremberg, and a person can go into all kinds of speculations why."

Filin didn't follow. "So what should I do?"

"Nothing," laughed Gres.

"Nothing?"

"You will be our duck decoy. You just have to swim around in circles and quack as loud as possible." Gres smiled at Filin and shrugged as if to say sorry, brother, nothing else can be done.

"What a role." Filin was not offended by the general's unusual proposition, but rather he simply didn't understand what Gres had in mind.

"Don't get upset, Sergei Ivanovich. Here's the plan: we'll spread rumors that comrade Filin has come from Nuremberg with a top-secret file containing a plan we have that will make the Americans agree with everything in the Soviet delegation. This file will be completely secret and based on discovered archival materials, documents known to no one, but which will prove completely devastating."

"And what might those documents be?"

"What difference does it make?! That the Americans and Gestapo collaborated during the war and after, or that the Germans handed over the Nazi gold in exchange for the defendants' lives and a guarantee there will be no further trials like Nuremberg. It doesn't really matter. It's just important to put a fog around it, and the thicker the better. Of course, Spitz will report on this to his side, and he will be tasked with either getting a hold of the file or determining its contents. So, that is what he will try to do, and as he does that we will have to ferret him out."

Filin smiled. "What if he decides to simply kill me?"

Gres remained serious. "What good would that get him? No, he will need the documents themselves to find out what we possess."

Filin sat in his office, trying to imagine himself swimming around in circles and quacking with all his might, when Rebrov rushed in without even knocking. He had a disheveled look.

"Sergei Ivanovich, Gen. Zorya shot himself! In Nuremberg…"

Filin stood up and let out a deep breath. He walked to the coat hanger and took his coat. "I know, Denis. Let's go have a walk. It's fine weather today."

Filin had known since that morning that Zorya had been found dead in his room, with a pistol lying next to him. He was also aware of the newspaper headlines in the West: "Accident or suicide?", "Was the general killed by his own secret agents?" Judging from the way that Rebrov looked, he too was already aware of the version going around in the West.

A quiet Moscow lane behind the massive ministry building led them to the boulevards. The streets were utterly deserted and pretty, as they were in springtime when the greenery was still bright and seemed almost lacquered with sunlight.

"I just can't imagine Zorya shooting himself!" said Rebrov, stunned. "He wasn't the kind of man to do that."

"The official version is that he was handling his weapon carelessly," Filin gently corrected him. "He was cleaning his pistol and forgot that there was a bullet in the chamber. Those things can happen."

"Do you believe that, Sergei Ivanovich? Do you know what the Western newspapers are saying?"

"I know what Western reporters are saying. I know what kind of things they can come up with, like how Rudenko supposedly shot Goering during questioning. But what do you and I know about what they think here in Moscow? If we were still in Nuremberg… Do you know what has been going on there in the last few days? What the situation at the trials is like? The defense attorneys are demanding that copies of some supposed secret protocol to the non-aggression pact be admitted. They openly declared that they had received the copies from American intelligence, that is, they knowingly and intentionally handed these documents over to the defense. And that in spite of the prosecutors of all countries agreeing not to allow the defendants and their attorneys to refer to the politics of other countries. So, this is what is happening. And remember what Churchill said in Fulton! And what Stalin said in response."

"I remember. He said that other countries had been presented with an ultimatum, 'Accept our rule voluntarily, and then all will be well; otherwise war is inevitable.' We will never accept their rule."

Filin sighed and gazed up at the clear blue sky. "So those are the conditions that we have to work under. And Zorya... He was kind to you and me, but now his death is not just a personal tragedy but also a political event. They will try to use it to attack the whole tribunal. And let's not forget what I told you in the very beginning: for you and me, the war is still going on, and the fighting is even fiercer. Wherever there is war, there are victims, including accidental victims."

Filin was quiet for some time, but then went on. "Maybe Zorya simply couldn't handle the stress. After all, he did work for the Polish Committee of National Liberation during the Warsaw uprising, which Hitler's men crushed. Many Poles still malign us for not helping them, though they didn't think it necessary to discuss things with us first before they started their uprising. We didn't even have any ability to help them except at the cost of our soldiers' lives. Countless men would have perished. The Poles play their own games..."

A boy on a bicycle came flying towards them, frantically pedaling and ringing his bell heartily. Filin stepped aside to let him pass, then spent a long time watching him go.

"Zorya couldn't handle it then. He suffered such a severe shock that he resigned his post. He spent a year out of work, just recovering, coming back to his senses. When they sent him to Nuremberg, they thought he was already over everything. After all, he was still a young guy, not even forty. But who knows what Nuremberg did to his mental state? He was a conscientious man, he ended up in a difficult situation, and he might have decided to end it all. And then who knows..."

Again a bicycle bell rang behind them. The mop-headed rider came racing back past them with the same happy smile.

Notes

A point to be noted is that in this respect Mr. Churchill and his friends bear a striking resemblance to Hitler and his friends. Hitler began his work of unleashing war by proclaiming a race theory, declaring that only German-speaking people constituted a superior nation. Mr. Churchill sets out to unleash war with a race theory, asserting that only English-speaking nations are superior nations, who are called upon to decide the destinies of the entire world. The German race theory led Hitler and his friends to the conclusion that the Germans, as the only superior nation, should rule over other nations. The English race theory leads Mr. Churchill and his friends to the conclusion that the English-speaking nations, as the only superior nations, should rule over the rest of the nations of the world.

Actually, Mr. Churchill, and his friends in Britain and the United States, present to the non-English speaking nations something in the nature of an ultimatum: "Accept our rule voluntarily, and then all will be well; otherwise war is inevitable."

But the nations shed their blood in the course of five years' fierce war for the sake of the liberty and independence of their countries, and not in order to exchange the domination of the Hitlers for the domination of the Churchills. It is quite probable, accordingly, that the non-English-speaking nations, which constitute the vast majority of the population of the world, will not agree to submit to a new slavery.

From an interview with Joseph Stalin
published in *Pravda* in 1946

CHAPTER XVI. THE ATOMIC PROJECT

"What are we going to do about that damned Spitz?" said Gres, pacing nervously around his office. His puffy face was flushed with consternation. "The worm is hiding, he's not doing anything. He won't take our bait! We did everything to spread word of your file except for broadcasting it over the radio, but he still hasn't popped up. He's a cunning creature."

Filin knew Gres well and could see that he was being pushed to his limits. The pressure on him coming from the very top must have been terrible. "I think he only acts when he gets specific orders to, so he won't show any initiative on his own," said Filin soberly, hoping to lower the tension a little. "All signs suggest that his orders are coming from Nuremberg, and that means we need to ensure they order him to get his hands on the file."

"And how are we going to do that?" Gres grunted.

"We can involve Hector. Let him get that information out there. There is that American reporter Peggy Butcher, she's very popular. It was with her help that we got the Americans to act tougher on those SS prisoners. Let Hector throw her some tidbits about secret documents that are being worked on in Moscow... Our friend Peggy can't keep quiet."

"'Our friend Peggy'?" Gres suddenly squinted in a sly manner. "Everything's so complicated there with you! I suppose your Maj. Rebrov is working with this Peggy? Alright, then, do it. Time is of the essence."

Several days later, some sensational reporting hit the front pages of several Western newspapers: "At Nuremberg trials, Russians may speak of Hitler–American business cooperation", "How American industrialists built Hitler's army", "Who armed Hitler?", "What are American teams searching for in German mines?", "Russians believe West aims to save defendant Schacht."

Peggy, like always, added some details of her own pure invention to the information that Hector tossed her.

One night, the door to Filin's empty office opened and someone silently crept inside. The beam of a flashlight swept across the office and stopped on a safe. The owner of the flashlight moved to the safe, took a set of keys from his pocket, and began to try them one by one in the safe's lock. He worked calmly and unhurriedly.

However, an instant later, someone leapt on him from behind and knocked him to the ground. The ring of skeleton keys rang loudly on the wooden floor and the flashlight rolled into the corner.

Two officers rushed into the office with their pistols drawn and turned the lights on.

A man was lying on the floor with Rebrov atop of him holding his hands against his back.

When Gres and Filin came into the office, Rebrov quickly searched the man. "He doesn't appear to have any weapons."

The man lay there with his face down and said nothing.

"Lift him up," Gres ordered the officers.

The officers lifted the man up by his arms and set him in front of the generals. He was a middle-aged man in a worker's uniform. He stood with his eyes closed, expressionless, his utterly proletarian face showing nothing.

"Who are you," Gres asked him keenly.

The man's face continued to show no expression.

Rebrov reached for the man's breast pocket and drew out his papers. "He's Matvei Semyonovich Ugarov. A telephone operator…"

"A telephone operator," Gres repeated. "Just a telephone operator. Well, now, Spitz, have you been telephoning your people for a long time now?"

Ugarov lifted his head as if he was about to say something, but suddenly he grimaced and ground his teeth so strongly that his jaws flared out. He immediately went into convulsions and hung limply in the officers' arms.

"Dammit, he's poisoned himself!" Filin shouted. "Doctor! Quickly, a doctor!"

In Gres's office over a bottle of cognac, the generals went over the results of this restless night.

"Judging by the poison capsule hidden in his tooth, it's German work," said Gres placidly. "That's their style, the Germans. Dammit! A mere telephone operator! He's been sitting here for twelve years among us and listening to every conversation. He could get into any office by just pretending to repair the line. How did we miss him all this time?"

"And we were wasting our time searching among the initiated few!" Filin smiles. He was truly happy for his friend, though he thought of how many years Spitz had taken from his life with his reports. "We investigated high-ranking people who have access to great secrets. And here is a mere telephone operator, a common worker. He would sit in the basement somewhere, no one would see him, no one knew about him. And yet he could listen in on everyone and find out everything. At night he would check the telephone lines and help himself to the safes at the same time. Well, I did my job, it's time to head back to Nuremberg."

Gres snorted. He said nothing in answer and merely turned his glass over.

"Well, then," Filin stretched. "Do I understand correctly that I haven't done everything yet. Have the higher-ups thought up more ideas?"

"That's what the higher-ups are for, to think," Gres wagged a finger severely.

"And it's for others to suffer."

"I don't follow."

"As Pushkin said, 'I want to live – to think and suffer...' Alright, then, forget about it, the joke didn't work."

"No, it didn't," said Gres, suddenly serious. "I've had to go through so much suffering that..."

Filin again thought about how Gres had really been worn down by recent events if he reacted to simple jokes like that.

Gres, however, had already regained his composure. He was, after all, a tough and tenacious general. "Nuremberg can wait," waving the matter away. "You're being put to work on the atomic bomb project. You yourself can imagine how important this is. An enormous amount of men and resources have been dedicated to it, even as the country is in ruins and people have nothing. But if we can quickly come up with an atomic weapon, at any cost, then... The Americans have already drawn up plans for the atomic bombing of our cities. Anyway, it's always like that with us, but come hell or high water, we have to do it!"

"But why me? I'm not a physicist..."

"Don't be silly! I know you're not a physicist! But I need you not as a physicist, but as an intelligence professional. Basically, your task is like this. In the USA there are a few of our agents working on the atomic bomb. They are very promising people, but they are working on their own. Many of them don't know the specifics of the case and are behaving very carelessly, they could easily be discovered… That's why we've decided to send a dedicated sleeper agent there for the atomic bomb. He'll direct the whole network, establish a network with them and with the center. We need to think about how to set up a path towards making him legal in America. Who should he pretend to be? What background should we give him? How are we going to get him there? Well, why am I explaining all this to you, you know more about these things than I do." Gres yawned wearily. Outside, the early dawn of May had already come. "You ready that sleeper agent, and then head back to Nuremberg. Everything will be finished there by the autumn, all the games around the sentencing will start, and then you'll return here."

"What about Rebrov?"

"He'll remain here with you. I think he could really use a break from Nuremberg."

"Are you hinting at something?"

"I'm hinting," said Gres, "at the fact that he has too much success with the ladies."

"I see. And who told you that?"

"Take a guess."

"Kosachev. After all, he's working here now with you…"

"He is," said Gres coldly. "The leadership made the decision. Don't forget that that man went through the war, and he also has his merits. Anyone can succumb to foolishness when it comes to women."

"That I know. By the way, concerning Rebrov… For someone working in intelligence, enjoying success with the ladies can come in very handy."

"I didn't say it was a bad thing. I said it was *too much* success. Do you see the difference?"

Rebrov spent all summer in Moscow carrying out an endless series of tasks that Filin had given him. Only a couple of times did he actually catch a glimpse of the sleeper agent they were readying. It was the task of others to work with him directly, while Rebrov was only charged with analyzing the case and preparing materials, a task that required working through a huge amount of information, including that from the press. He remained very aware of what was going on in Nuremberg. The trials were coming, with a high degree of methodicalness and conscientiousness, to an end. In July, Gavrik flew over for a couple of days and told Rebrov, in detail, of what was happening.

That summer in Bavaria had turned out to be a hot one. Suddenly there were many lilacs in bloom and poplar down swept through the streets like a snowstorm. One wanted more than anything else to laze in the sun and not think about anything. Many reporters, already weary of everything, simply fell asleep in the courtroom. For Rebrov this came as no news. Only the day before, he had been leafing through an American illustrated magazine with a whole series of shots from Nuremberg. The headline of the spread was "The trials already past the six-month mark". There were whole rows of photos of sleeping reporters. Even Peggy was among them. Gavrik recounted, laughing, how the Soviet reporters had even held a meeting to set down that no beer should be drank at lunch, and should anyone be struck by the misfortune of falling asleep, his neighbors should immediately wake him up, but without drawing attention and by tugging for a while at his headphones.

Gavrik laughed for a bit, but then became serious and sighed. Nuremberg was a joyless place. The heat, the clouds of dust and grime blowing from the ruins. Those who had spent the winter and spring in cellars and in public lavatories under street level now came outside, built ramshackle huts or tents from burnt plywood and twisted iron and immediately started cooking something or washing clothes… Speculation had reached epic proportions; for a packet of rations, Americans could buy anything, even Dürer's engravings. Elsewhere, in the completely unscathed neighborhoods of aristocratic villas, life went on merrily, where one would encounter dashing policemen in high helmets and white armlets, advertisements posted with alluring beauties, and even ladies with little dogs…

"Beletskaya – you remember, the beauty married to a general – has left. Her husband suddenly fell gravely ill."

"I see," Rebrov responded lamely. "Listen, there was one assistant to the defense there. He was like, you know, the Aryans in propaganda posters, a blond beast. Is he still around at the trials?"

"I suppose so. Why are you interested in him?"

"I just remembered him…"

"That's all?"

"For now. The rest we'll see."

Notes

A mere twelve days after the first American atomic
bomb was produced, blueprints and instructions
for how to realize them were delivered from
New York and Washington to Moscow. Then,
Moscow obtained photographs of the factories
in Oak Ridge, the secret portion of the report
to the American administration and Congress,
information on the individual components of the
bomb and the logs of the first test detonations
in the Alamogordo desert.

The information on atomic weapons obtained from
the United States began to be complemented,
starting from the late 1940s, with information
obtained by Soviet intelligence in Western
Europe, where many of the European scientists
who had participated in the Manhattan Project
returned after the war.

CHAPTER XVII.
MONA FROM PITTSBURGH

Two young American soldiers serving as security were wandering along the hot streets of Nuremberg in August, unsure of what to do with themselves. One, wearing round spectacles, resembled a high school student who was still only dreaming of losing his virginity but unsure of how to go about it. The other, older and rather impudent, was clearly already troubled by other issues.

"We can take any girl we want, Dick," said the older soldier, grinning and then spat on the sidewalk. "Have you heard the joke? For a pair of American stockings, even that fat-assed, big-titted sculpture at the Palace of Justice would move from her pedestal! And ordinary German girls…" He spat again, considering it to be a fashionable habit to have. "You just listen to Patrick Kelly here."

Two German girls in light summer dresses were walking towards them. They were clearly strolling with a particular aim in mind, as they swung their handbags invitingly. One even seemed shy, but the other, an aggressive brunette, was rapaciously turning her eyes here and there. They walked straight towards the soldiers and made it obvious that they didn't want to move aside. Two steps away from them, the brunette winked at the soldiers enticingly, and Kelly immediately rushed at them. "*Bier… Strumpf…*" he said with a wink.

"You can speak English," said the brunette gaily as she grabbed him by the arm. "Mona and I understand our American friends very well."

"Great," Patrick stuck his thumb up. "I don't have to bust my mouth with your crazy words that are impossible to pronounce!"

The brunette began to introduce herself. "My name is Inga."

"I'm Patrick Kelly. This is my friend Dick Sturridge. He's a little shy, so you girls be gentle. Agreed? Let's go drink a beer to start with." He then pointed towards the door of a nearby bar.

"That sounds great," giggled Inga. "And what are we going to have with the beer?"

"Whatever you'd like!"

"May I?" asked Mona, shyly, as she took Dick by the arm. The latter blushed and nodded in embarrassment.

In the smoke-filled bar, Kelly immediately began to paw at Inga, who only responded with rather coarse laughter. Kelly took out a pack of cigarettes and placed it on the table, then another one on top of it, and then a third… Inga swept the cigarette packs into her handbag and whispered something into Kelly's ear.

Kelly stood up. After drinking beer with schnapps, he was noticeably staggering. "Dick, I've got to go for a walk with this nice German girl. She's got a room close by here. I'm going first, then it'll be your turn," he nodded towards Mona. "So, get ready!"

Mona smoked her cigarette indifferently, as if she hadn't heard a thing, while Dick looked at his friend with frightened eyes. After Kelly and Inga had left, a long silence settled on them. Finally, Dick dared to ask, "Excuse me, but where did you learn such good English?"

"I can say I'm American," said Mona, waving her cigarette.

"An American?" Dick's eyes widened.

"Yes. I was born in America, but after several years my parents – Germans – came back to their native country…"

"They left America?" said Dick incredulously.

"Yes, they came into an inheritance. Alas, it was quite a small one, and now there is nothing left of it. How would they know what was going to happen here? They died in a concentration camp…" Mona took a sip of her beer and then had a long drag of her cigarette. "I don't have anyone left here now except Inga. I'd love to go back to Pittsburgh with you, but how?"

Dick was even more surprised. "Pittsburgh?"

"Yes, that's where we lived."

"Pittsburgh? I'm from there, too!" said Dick in amazement.

"Get out of here!" said Mona, not believing him.

"It's impossible! Lord, meeting like this, a girl from Pittsburgh!" Dick couldn't get a hold of himself. "Nobody would believe it!"

"Maybe we should get out of here? There's so many drunk people." She frowned in disgust.

"What about Kelly?" Dick reminded her.

"Oh, I can assure you, he won't be back anytime soon. Trust me, I know Inga."

Dick and Mona slowly strolled along the street. Dick was utterly happy and rambled on endlessly.

"So, you're guarding the men on trial?" asked Mona. "I would have never have thought that you're a guard."

"Why not?"

"You're too sweet for something like that. All guards, in my opinion, are cruel and terrible. Or they should be, at any rate. Just imagine the people you are guarding!"

"Generally we just accompany them from the prison to the courtroom," explained Dick. "And they aren't so scary-looking at all."

"And you see them as close-up as we are now? No, I can't believe it!"

"I could even reach out and touch them if I wanted to," laughed Dick. "And we're even allowed to say a few words to them now…"

"I've never seen any of them in real life," said Mona. "Only in newsreels. For me, they're something so… Goering was number two after Hitler. Almost God himself!"

"I've got his autograph!" boasted Dick.

"Really?"

"Yes. Want me to show it to you? I think with time it'll be worth a whole lot of money!"

"I guess so. How do they look?"

"Who?"

"Well, them. Goering, Ribbentrop…"

"Well, you know, now they are all quiet and brooding. Very polite. I could have never imagined that these men could have done everything they talk about in the courtroom. Goering is generally a really nice guy. He speaks English pretty well. Sometimes I even chat with him."

"No way," said Mona shaking her head in disbelief. "What do you talk about?"

"Sports, airplanes. He was a famous pilot, after all, and when I was a kid I dreamt of becoming a pilot. Just like Lindbergh!"

"I heard that he's very sick," said Mona suddenly.

Dick was surprised to hear this. "Sick? Well, I don't know, he seems in a jolly mood. It's just that he lost a lot of weight. Well, in prison it's hard to get fit. No, he's holding on OK. He makes a lot of jokes. As I said, he's a normal guy."

Mona took him by the arm. "What else did you dream about when you were a kid?"

Dick hesitated a little. "You won't laugh?"

"I promise."

"Of getting a good violin," he sighed. "I learned to play, but I never had a good instrument. A really good one."

An hour later Mona was standing in a city square next to what remained of a fountain. She looked around nervously. She now looked completely different; her shyness was gone, and she could clearly repulse any man if she wanted too.

Finally, a car stopped next to her and, after briefly looking around again, Mona dived into it. The car immediately resumed its motion.

"Well, how is that four-eyes from Pittsburgh?" said Olaf Todt, who was seated at the wheel, looking inquiringly at Mona.

"He's very sweet," she snorted. "If you ask me, he's still a virgin."

"Like we all were once. Is it worth using him?"

"I think so. Goering is even nice to him, he signed his autograph for him. They talked about planes, pilots, sports…"

"He ought to have talked with the Reich Marshal about the Jews," laughed Olaf. "Although, if you listen to the Reich Marshal these days, there was never a better friend of the Jews…"

"What's funny is that our American virgin doesn't like Jews either. As a child he dreamt of having a nice violin like the Jewish boy next door, but his parents said it was too expensive."

"So, he's the dreaming sort?"

"Yes, and he doesn't even know what he wants anymore, a nice violin or a nice woman."

"Well, if a person has dreams, then you can use him…"

Notes

In France in 1944—45, five thousand French women were executed for sexual relations with enemy soldiers. Twenty thousand were shaved bald and sentenced to one year in prison and loss of French citizenship.

Argumenty i Fakty, issue 28, June 13—19, 2010

CHAPTER XVIII. NUREMBERG AGAIN

When Rebrov discovered that he was to return to Nuremberg, he wanted to beg Filin to let him stay in the USSR, to send him to any godforsaken place, just so that he wouldn't have to go back to a city where everything reminded him of Irina.

Rebrov had only recently thought that the pain of parting from her had passed, or at least been dulled. If it hadn't left entirely, then it had at least retreated into the depths of his mind and ceased to torment him. But as soon as he heard that he had to go back, this time in the role of a journalist – they even supplied him with accreditation as a newspaper reporter – his longing arose afresh and struck him like a blow. Not only was it a painful feeling, but he now realized that everything that had happened between them was an unimaginable happiness that could never be repeated, therefore, the loss could never be amended and would remain with him for the rest of his life. At the same time, he had nothing to blame himself for; there was nothing he could do. Or was there? What could he do if fate hung over him and Irina?

The closer their plane got to Nuremberg, the more they talked about the trials, which were reaching their end. The prosecutors and the defense had already given their final speeches, the defendants had had the last word and the judges were conferring to decide on the verdicts, which were expected any day now. Filin said that the judges were having serious arguments over the phrasing of the verdicts and the specific punishment to be handed out to each of the defendants. These disagreements had already gone on for a month, since late August. According to the agreement, these discussions were to be kept strictly confidential and should not be disclosed to others under any circumstances.

Rebrov listened, but he was thinking to himself, how, in just a few hours, he would again be in the place where he had seen her, where it had all happened…

September in Nuremberg was warm like a summer day, but from time to time strong gusts of wind blew. In the city center the wind lifted up clouds of dust and sand from the ruins, carrying through the streets a strange smell that many said was the stench of dead bodies…

Mona jumped out of bed, went to the window and slammed it shut. She was completely naked; Dick Sturridge watched her from the bed with eyes mad from joy and delight. The apartment in which he had become a real man, thanks to Mona, was tiny and rather run-down, but Dick didn't notice: he had eyes only for Mona.

With a feline motion Mona stretched, threw on a light robe and went into the miserable little kitchen, tousling Dick's hair on the way out. He tried to pull her back into bed, but she easily broke free of his grasp.

"Get up. My cousin is going to be here soon."

With a goofy smile, Dick began to reluctantly get dressed.

Later, when they were drinking the coffee that Dick had brought along, he constantly tried to brush against Mona, as if by accident.

The doorbell suddenly rang. Mona got up.

"That's my cousin. Get ready, he's got a surprise for you."

Her cousin turned out to be none other than Olaf. He wore a wig and a glued-on mustache and held a bundle in his hands. "Hello, Mr. Sturridge," he said ceremoniously. "I'm happy to meet an American soldier, one of those who freed us from Nazism."

"Well now," said Dick, embarrassed, "I'm not exactly General Eisenhower."

"Still. You can't imagine what we've lived through. Mona's parents died in the camps. I was chased by the Gestapo because I didn't want to fight against American soldiers like you. So, for us you are a true liberator, Mr. Sturridge. So, when Mona told me about your dream, I was quite happy, because I could help make it true. Here, look." Olaf handed Dick the bundle.

Dick turned it over and saw it was a violin case. He looked at Olaf in bafflement.

"Open it," said Olaf solemnly.

Dick opened the case and found a violin inside. He immediately noticed that it was an old and valuable instrument.

"Take it out, Mr. Sturridge," said Olaf, again in the same solemn tone. "You'll see that this is an instrument from a great maker."

Dick lifted the violin up with trembling hands and stared at it in ecstasy.

"Sure, it's not a Stradivarius," said Olaf. "But it's a very, very good instrument."

"What do you want for it?" asked Dick, barely able to get the words out. "Dollars? Food? Clothes?"

"No, Mr. Sturridge, I'm just doing what Mona asked of me. She wanted to make you happy, because she likes you very much and you're both, as I understand, from the same town."

"Yes, I'm from Pittsburgh too."

"So you see. I just want to ask one condition."

"One condition?" asked Dick, without taking his eyes off the violin.

"Yes. Mona mentioned in passing that you're guarding Hermann Goering…"

"Yes, I walk him and the others to the courtroom. But what? What does Goering have to do with anything?"

"You see, I ran into his wife and little girl. She is extremely worried about him. She says that he is in serious pain…"

"Well, yeah, prison is no day at the beach."

"And that's the thing. Couldn't you hand him a little package from his wife and daughter?"

Dick lifted his eyes from the violin and grew tense. "A package? That's strictly forbidden."

"Oh, maybe I didn't say it right," Olaf corrected himself. "Not a package! It's just a pen. His wife asked if you could give him a pen." Then he showed Dick a disarming smile.

"A pen? Why does he need a pen?"

"It's not just a pen, Mr. Sturridge. It's a pen from his wife. His favorite pen, that his wife says he used to love to write with. Imagine how happy he'll be when he finds out that she found his old pen, and that he can write letters to his wife with it. Especially now, when he's awaiting his sentence, which is sure to be a very grave one."

"Yes, he often says that there is nothing dearer to him than his wife and daughter. He's got a photo of them in his cell."

"You see? I think he would be very happy to get something like that from his wife and daughter, and then write her some heartfelt words with it…"

Mona walked up behind Dick and put her arms around him. Her hair fell over his shoulders.

Dick gave in once he was hit by the fragrance of this woman who drove him crazy. "Sure, I could do it. I've always said that he's an ordinary and polite guy."

"Well, then I'll be off," Olaf quickly said and left the pen on the table. "I'm sure the sound of that violin will really impress you."

Dick once again stared in fascination at this dream instrument. While Olaf and Mona exchanged quick glances in understanding.

Notes

My only sweetheart,

Upon mature consideration and after profound prayers to my God, I have decided to take my own life and thus not allow my enemies to execute me. But the Reich Marshal of Germany, the great, cannot allow himself to be hanged. Moreover, the killings were to be carried out like a spectacle with the press and film cameras there (I assume for the newsreel pictures). Sensation is all that matters.

I however want to die quietly and out of the public eye. My life came to an end the moment I said my last farewell to you.

Your Hermann
From Hermann Goering's
last letter to his wife
before his death

CHAPTER XIX.
THE DAY OF JUDGMENT HAS COME

On the day that the court's verdict was to be announced, September 30, 1946, the courtroom and the Palace of Justice were packed, just like during the first days of the tribunal, although only specially authorized people were admitted. The balcony where observers were designated to sit, looked like it was about to collapse. In the press room it was impossible to find a seat due to the enormous crowd of reporters from every corner of the earth.

Col. Andrus, who had enjoyed a vacation during the court's long recess, had come back full of strength and energy. In the days before the sentencing was announced, he led secret meetings with his officers and vowed not to let any unforeseen circumstances disrupt this important ceremony. There were to be no terrorist strikes, no suicides, no worries, no attacks! Carrying anything into the courtroom was strictly forbidden. An order was given to limit, as much as possible, the number of Germans in the Palace of Justice. Even the lawyers for the defense were searched. The area around the Palace was cordoned off and checkpoints were posted on all roads leading into Nuremberg. While chatting with Rebrov, some American reporters laughed goodheartedly and said that the colonel wasn't so much worried about security as demonstrating his zeal. Were tanks necessary? Why were the wives of the defendants ordered to leave Nuremberg?

This time the defendants were not brought into the courtroom in one long line but rather one by one, with a long interval between them. They sat down in their accustomed places and tried not to look at one another, because they were already divided into those who would go on living and those who could expect death soon.

Such silence hung over the courtroom that one could hear the technicians in the radio room testing their equipment. Then the voice of the bailiff shattered this silence.

"All rise, the court is in session!"

Lord Lawrence held in his hands a folder with the verdicts. As it had been announced, each judge would read from it in turn, with the whole proceeding taking less than an hour.

The journalists who had not managed to get into the courtroom crowded in the press room and listened to the broadcast, trying to guess what the sentences would be. Hanging? Death by firing squad? Life imprisonment? Acquittal? Bets were being taken at the bar. Of course, none of the Soviet reporters who were present took part in the betting.

At the center of the big circle was Peggy, who was dressed completely in black and wearing a black hat with a veil. Rebrov, who had been loitering in the corridor, saw her and waved, but Peggy seemed to not notice him. She was too busy basking in everyone's attention.

"Attention, gentlemen!" Peggy raised her hand, which was clad in a black lace glove. "Whoever can tell me exact details of the verdicts, I'm prepared to spend the night with him! No joke!"

The men burst out cheering, while the few women present pursed their lips.

"What a shame, I don't see any worthy men here!" a disappointed Peggy announced a minute later, casting her gaze over those gathered.

She walked out, the men parting to let her pass and headed straight for Rebrov. "Dammit, Denis, where have you been? I might have used every opportunity to get out of this godforsaken town, but at least I came back! You just disappeared without saying anything! I thought I'd never see you again. I heard rumors you had been sent to Siberia for some kind of transgression. I hope none of that was true."

"It wasn't." Rebrov smiled. It was a pleasure to see Peggy again. "We're colleagues now. I've become a journalist too."

"Well, I don't know if I should congratulate you," said Peggy. "I liked you a lot more as a secret source. Now you'll be just another one of any of these people who'd sell their own mother for a sensation."

Rebrov laughed heartily. "Peggy, just a minute ago you were like Cleopatra, offering her bed for information on the sentencing!"

"What do you think I should do? Spend some time in a reporter's shoes and you'll understand what this job entails!"

"By the way, as far as your horrible proposition goes…"

Peggy perked up. "Do you have something to tell me about the sentences? Don't torment me!"

"Alas, Peggy," Rebrov threw up his hands, "I just wanted to tell you that your making your attractive offer to the wrong people. How would reporters know? You should have addressed people working at the court."

Peggy wrinkled her nose. "I made such an offer to one knowledgeable person there. He did after all seem to be interested in me for a long time."

"And?"

"He was a real pig! He said he would be at my service the day after tomorrow. What do I need him for then, when the whole world will already know about the verdicts?"

"By the way, where is our friend Kraft?" asked Rebrov.

"Around here somewhere. He's a very busy man – he bought up so many memoirs rights that he doesn't know how to get a good price for them. Well, it doesn't matter. Alex is the last person I'd be worried about!"

The world learned the verdicts the next day. First, the acquittals were announced, three of them: Schacht, Papen and Fritzsche. They were set free in the courtroom and during the recess they gave interviews and held a press conference.

Then the last court session began. The defendants' dock was empty. The men came out of the door one by one, accompanied by guards in white helmets, to each of them the court's president Lord Lawrence read the sentence.

Goering was brought in first.

"Defendant Hermann Wilhelm Goering, the International Military Tribunal sentences you to death by hanging…"

Notes

It so happened that I was to conduct the last witness examination at the Nuremberg trials. The witness was Walter Schreiber, a professor at the German military's medical school and an expert in hygiene and bacteriology. He spoke about the German high command's plans for bacterial warfare with the use of plague agents and tests on living subjects.

Georgy Alexandrov,
head of the Investigative Group
for the USSR Chief Prosecutor at Nuremberg

CHAPTER XX.
WHEN EVERYTHING WAS OVER

The baron and Olaf were dining together, like they used to in the good days of yore. The table was elaborately decorated: a snow-white tablecloth, starched napkins, old china and silver, fine wine, and exquisite dishes brought by an old and well-trained servant.

"So, eleven of them sentenced to death by hanging," said the baron coldly as he set his newspaper aside.

"And for the rest, life imprisonment or twelve years behind bars," Olaf filled in.

"Yes, I am aware of that." The baron idly turned his heavy fork in his hand.

"The men sentenced to hanging appealed to the Allied Control Council and asked that death by hanging be changed to death by firing squad. But Goering didn't join them in doing that."

"I think he simply sees how pointless it would be."

"His lawyer did it for him though."

"It's pointless, my boy, just pointless. The case is closed. I've received word from London. The Labour government has held an extraordinary meeting to discuss the situation in Nuremberg."

"And?"

"A member of the Control Council, Douglas – he's the Marshal of the Royal Air Force – received a secret telegram to not agree to any petitions and to not make any changes to the sentencing. The British do not intend to forgive Goering for 'coventrizing.'"

"Coventrizing?"

"Well, you remember how Goering's Luftwaffe bombed the city of Coventry to hell? After that, Goering's men were quite fond of the term 'coventrizing'. They thought it was very funny. I don't know what they think of it now."

"But then came Dresden, when the British wiped out a city that, unlike Coventry, didn't even have wartime factories," Olaf pointed out.

"Yes," agreed the baron, "there was no one living there then except refugees. But we Germans should remember that, while the British are thinking about Coventry."

"The Russians are also unconvinced."

"Of course. There's something else that worries me. We've stopped getting information from Moscow. I fear that our agent there has been discovered. One way or another, everything is settled with Goering's sentence: he'll be hanged. But it's another matter if we can help the Reich Marshal escape the shame of the noose."

"The American guy that we're using said that he already gave Goering the pen."

"Can you trust him?"

"He's so in love with that slut that he'd do anything. But I can't give a one-hundred-percent guarantee of success."

"So, we'll only find out if everything worked after the sentences are carried out. Let the Reich Marshal pray and hope for the best. The best thing for him now would be to avoid the shame of hanging. It's the only thing that he, one of the leaders of the Thousand-Year Reich, has left." Adjusting his snow-white napkin, he went on, "You and me should eat our dinner. We'll need strength if we are going to work to Germany's benefit. A lot of strength."

The baron raised his glass, admired the deep ruby color of the wine, breathed in the aroma of the grapes with its memory of sunshine and the salutary earth. It was the smell of life that would go on, a life in which he had not yet said his last. And most important of all, he had Olaf, young and strong, who he could trust to carry on the fight.

Notes

General plan Ost went even further than the Holocaust of the Jews. This plan included coldblooded, mathematical calculations for an Eastern Europe free of Slavs. It was to be a Holocaust not of the Jews but now of the Slavs! The idea of wiping out the subject people through slave labor was filled out by calculations of new

methods to preserve a labor force of a million
slaves for a limited period of time, but still
preventing them from reproducing.

Thus, there was soon a requirement for the forced
sterilization of large numbers of people.

From *If Hitler Had Won* by Ralph Giordano,
German writer and publicist

CHAPTER XXI.
THIRTEEN STEPS TO HELL

"The Quadripartite Commission for the Detention of Major War Criminals has authorized forty officers and generals from the Allies to attend the executions. There are to be two journalists each from the USA, USSR, Britain and France. There will also be a separate group of twenty-four American officers. Two Germans have been allowed to be present, representatives of the Bavarian authorities…"

Filin set the report aside and turned towards Rebrov with a thoughtful look. "One of those journalists will be you, Denis. We've got to be sure that we know everything that happens there."

On October 16, at eight o'clock in the evening Berlin time, the reporters – four of which would write dispatches while the other four took photos – arrived at the Palace of Justice, which was now frightfully empty and dark.

Colonel Andrus met them at the entrance, tapping his staff against the side of his boot. "Gentlemen, you will now be lodged in the rooms where the defendants usually met with their lawyers. Each of you is obliged to stay within the prison building and the place assigned to you until the Quadripartite Commission specially tells you otherwise. You are not to communicate with anyone until you are told to do so. Now you will be given the opportunity to tour the prison and see the prisoners, on the condition that you maintain complete silence."

"Colonel, have the defendants already been informed that their petitions for clemency have been rejected?" asked an American reporter standing next to Rebrov.

"No."

"And do they know that their sentences will be immediately carried out?"

"No. Follow me, please, gentlemen. Now you'll see everything with your own eyes."

The journalists walked down a narrow metal staircase and through a tunnel into the prison.

Darkness reigned in the hallway on the first floor. Only by eleven doors were bright electric bulbs set, the light from which was cast by reflectors into the cells. A guard stood at each door, closely observing the behavior of the prisoner.

The journalists kept silent and one by one they approached, almost on tiptoe, each of the cells to look through the peephole.

Keitel, for some reason, was making his bed in a soldierly way, ensuring there were no creases…

Ribbentrop was talking with a pastor…

Jodl was sitting at the table with his back to the door and writing something…

Goering was lying in bed with his eyes closed…

Frick, covered with a blanket, was reading a book…

Kaltenbrunner was also reading…

Streicher, it seemed, was sleeping…

Saucker nervously paced around his cell…

Frank, seated at the table, smoked a cigarette…

Rosenberg was lying in bed, keeping his hands on top of the blanket as he had become accustomed to…

Seyss-Inquart brushed his teeth…

As they looked at these elderly, obviously sickly men engaged in such ordinary, simple pursuits, it was hard to imagine that they had been responsible for the unspeakable evil that had befallen humanity. Rebrov suddenly thought that he didn't at all feel that sense of revenge that had gripped him during the war.

Time would pass and he would learn of what the Russian writer Ivan Bunin had put down in his diary the day before: "I keep thinking what a terrible day it will be the day after tomorrow in Nuremberg. Monstrous crimes, the deserved gallows – and yet my soul cannot accept what will be done the day after tomorrow by human beings. It is completely impossible to imagine how all these men, who the day after tomorrow will be strangled like dogs, can await this hour, how they can eat, drink, take care of their bodily needs or sleep through these last nights on the earth."

After reading these words, Rebrov thought that while the great writer could not imagine this, it had all in fact happened, quite simply. These monstrous criminals calmly attended to their own needs, thinking only of how suddenly everything might be avoided and they would be allowed to live…

"It looks like they don't realize that they're screwed. They're still hoping for something," a Soviet photojournalist whispered hotly in Rebrov's ear. He was an ordinary low-ranking soldier, who had passed through every front during the war and seen so much that there was no longer room in his soul for subtle emotions.

At twenty-one hours and thirty minutes the deathly silence in the prison was broken by the sound of a gong.

"That's the signal for sleep," explained Andrus. "All of the prisoners should now lie down and sleep. I will now take you gentlemen to the place where the sentences will be carried out."

They walked across the prison courtyard to a one-story stone building at the end of the garden. There, Rebrov knew, was a small gym.

Now, three scaffolds stood facing the door in the empty room. They were painted a dark-green, blackish color. The base of the scaffolds, over two meters high, was covered with a tarpaulin. Wooden stairs led up them. "Thirteen," the photojournalist whispered in Rebrov's ear. "Thirteen steps, I counted them." From cast-iron blocks, thick ropes ending in a noose fell towards the gallows. The two hangmen wore black caps…

"Hoods will be thrown over the prisoners' heads at the last minute," explained Andrus. "The sentence will be carried out by two executioners. The third is a backup, just in case. Those are manila ropes, they can easily support up to four hundred pounds. Under each of the gallows is a trapdoor with two flaps that are opened using a lever. The prisoner will fall down to a depth of two meters, sixty-five centimeters. A doctor will ensure that he is dead. The sentence will be carried out by Sergeant Woods."

Andrus pointed with his staff towards a stocky man with a long nose and a double chin, who was busily inspecting his kingdom. There was no need for Andrus to point him out, as the sergeant had become a real celebrity in recent days. He had volunteered beforehand to carry out the executions, and when his request was approved, he started giving his autograph and speaking to journalists, willingly posing for their cameras with a smile.

"Colonel, why is that corner covered up with a tarpaulin?" asked one of the British reporters.

"That's where the bodies of the executed will be taken, so they don't just fall on top of one another," answered the colonel. "The tables set in front of the scaffolds are for representatives of the four victor countries.

Behind them is a bench for the interpreters. For you gentlemen from the press there are special tables, those four over there. And now you will have to return to the rooms assigned to you and wait for everything to begin."

"I've been waiting so many years for this moment," the photojournalist said to Rebrov in the room they had been assigned, as he smoked yet another cigarette. "If you had told me in Stalingrad that I'd be in Nuremberg witnessing their execution… It's just a shame that Hitler isn't among them."

Suddenly there was a rumble of footsteps in the corridor outside and tense voices.

"Sounds like a big screw-up," said the photojournalist. "Did someone escape or something?"

Rebrov rushed to the door.

In the hallway, the journalists who were pouring out of their rooms were met by Col. Andrus, who was hitting his staff against his boot much more vehemently than usual. His face was burning with anger.

"Gentlemen, I am forced to announce…" hesitated Andrus, then went on, "The prisoner Goering is dead, the result of suicide. He took poison." After a moment of silence, Andrus looked across everyone present and dejectedly added, "He was supposed to be the first to hang."

The colonel looked rather pitiful. Rebrov thought that this must come as a terrible blow to his pride and his career. They would never forgive him for letting Goering commit suicide. Andrus could try his best to justify himself or shift the blame elsewhere, but nothing could help him now.

"What now, colonel?" asked an American journalist. "Is everything being called off?"

"Not at all. The plan remains in force. They'll be calling you in soon."

Around an hour later they were sitting at a distance of three or four meters from the scaffold.

Then members of the Quadripartite Commission appeared, officers of the American guard.

The executioner Sgt. Wood and a military interpreter took their places on the gallows, in a bright circle of unnaturally white light.

And then, the first condemned prisoner appeared in the doorway, accompanied by two soldiers…

At four o'clock in the morning, the coffins with the bodies of the executed men were loaded onto two covered trucks belonging to the US Army. These trucks, accompanied by an American military police jeep with a machine gun mounted on it, drove from the prison gates.

They were immediately followed by several civilian cars that had been waiting nearby. These cars were packed with journalists from around the world. Peggy Butcher's flame-red mane could be seen in the first of them. This peculiar convoy remained together until the town of Erlangen, but then the jeep sharply turned to block the way for the journalists. The soldier at the machine gun threateningly looked at them. The journalists began to loudly protest and curse.

An American officer leapt out of the jeep, lifted his hand and loudly said, "Ladies and gentlemen, I must inform you that trying to follow the convoy any further might be hazardous to your lives. The military police have been ordered to shoot if these rules are violated."

When the trucks and the jeep had disappeared into the darkness, Peggy burst out with the filthiest curses that she knew.

Notes

What struck me most during the trials was that the defendants lacked even a hint of remorse — late as it might come — or compassion for the millions of people killed and tortured at their orders… Nevertheless, retribution was not our goal. By underscoring the horrors that the world went through because of them, we dreamed of creating a new, more humane life for all mankind.

Ben Ferencz, American prosecutor
during the subsequent Nuremberg trials
of lower-ranking Nazi commanders

CHAPTER XXII.
ON A PURE MONDAY

Hector reported that the coffins were transported to the Dachau concentration camp and burned in the crematorium there. Then, the ashes were put into tin cans, taken to the Marienklausen bridge that spanned a canal near Munich, and scattered over the water…

Gen. Filin was listening to Rebrov's report on the events of the preceding night in silence. Photographs from the site of the executions lay in front of him on his desk. "When did Goering's body appear?" he asked.

"They brought him in on a stretcher after everything was already over and set him down among the executed men, so that everyone could be sure that Goering was dead and hadn't escaped…"

"How did he manage to keep that poison hidden for so long? They did search them, all of them. It really botched everything up…"

"An investigation has been launched. A commission was founded and they'll set up questioning. Andrus has already pointed to some German workers in the prison as the main suspects, but I think that's just to draw attention away from his own men."

"I see. Well, frankly I couldn't care less how Goering left this world." Filin threw the photo aside. "The main thing is that he did leave it."

"You know what the hottest item on the market is now?" laughed Denis. "The ropes used to hang them! Sgt. Wood asked Andrus for the ropes as a reward for his services and then he started hawking them. He's selling them in different lengths from long to short depending on how much people are willing to pay."

"It wouldn't surprise me if someone starts selling their ashes. And by weight. Alright then, Denis, you and I can consider our work in Nuremberg done. It's time to say goodbye to the city."

Half an hour later Rebrov was sitting at a corner table in the press bar, which was now nearly deserted. The world's reporters had left in a hurry. He was about to leave when a jolly band of people swept in, at the center of which was Peggy. Standing next to her was Kraft, who flashed his eternal American smile.

"God, Denis, why are you such a sourpuss?" Peggy shouted, thumping Rebrov on the shoulder. "Everything's over! Thank God I won't have to see their stupid mugs any more, or listen to their scrawny little voices saying that they didn't know anything! No, you won't lure me back to Germany again for a long time!"

Kraft shook Rebrov's hand and interrupted her. "Peggy, babe, didn't you have something important to tell our Russian friend?"

"Something important? I can't remember... Those damned executions have destroyed my brain!"

"Come on, Peggy, try to remember! You know, Paris..."

"God, I'm such a dummy!" Peggy slapped her forehead. "Denis, I was in Paris to do an interview with Marlene Dietrich. It was on a Monday, and I saw... Irina."

Rebrov felt that an enormous void had suddenly formed within him where his heart had been.

"Yes, our dear princess. I told her that I might see you again and I asked her if there was anything she wanted me to tell you? She said that she had just two words: 'pure Monday'. Yes, that was all, 'pure Monday'. I don't know what that means! I understand that for Russians there is some special meaning hidden in this?"

"Peggy, of course you wouldn't understand," said Kraft condescendingly. "Pure Monday is the first day of the Lenten fast in the Russian Orthodox Church. It's a day when the faithful try to fight against their sinful passion, to make themselves pure."

"Geez, Alex, how do you know that?"

"I lived next door to a Russian family for a few years, they taught me everything."

"But that's not all! There was a translator here, Baron Rosen. Do you remember that guy? Pavel Rosen? In the French delegation? He hung himself!" Peggy shrugged in amazement. "Yes, hung himself. They told me it was out of remorse for something. He had done something terrible and his Russian friends stopped talking to him because of it. Those crazy Russians, hanging themselves after the war when everyone is having fun and dancing!"

Rebrov, whose sole wish now was to be alone, stood up. "I've got to go, friends. It's a shame that we might not see each other again."

Peggy, cleverly grasping the situation, only hugged him. Rebrov shook hands and walked out. He had to get out of this dark building that had shattered his life forever.

Denis was walking down the empty, half-lit corridor when a man suddenly appeared walking towards him. Rebrov recognized him at once: it was the same young assistant to the German defense attorneys who looked too much like a stereotypical Aryan from Nazi propaganda.

They came towards each other and looked one another right in the eye. It was clearly the look of enemies, merciless, implacable. Enemies forever.

Notes

The eminent German philosopher, psychologist and psychiatrist Karl Jaspers called on the Germans to "change within themselves", but they did not wish to heed his urging.

When the Nuremberg trials were being prepared and when they were under way, talk of Nazism and the problem of guilt went on, but after, under the conditions of the Cold War and the division of Germany, these discussions essentially ended. The Germans did not want to look back on the recent past and answer any such "damned questions" as:

Was the Nazi dictatorship the natural product of German history or the embodiment of a rift with the traditions of the past, some kind of unusual development?

Could the installment of the Nazi regime in Germany have been prevented?

Who bears responsibility for the installment of
the regime and its crimes?

How was it possible for the Germans to support
this criminal state in their masses?

EPILOGUE

In the spring of 1959 in East Berlin, a meeting was held at the Stasi building for representatives of the Communist bloc's intelligence services. They spoke about the battle with the Nazi underground, which was being fought in many countries across different continents.

In a dark auditorium, photographs were projected, one after another, of those who had been sought for many years. Photographs from the war years were followed by more recent ones, and a voice delivered a commentary. "The Third Reich's most famous special-operations officer was SS-Obersturmbannführer Otto Skorzeny. He was arrested by the Americans on May 15, 1945. After many hours of official interrogation and secret talks, the American military tribunal acquitted him. Clearly this was in exchange for the information he provided them. Then Skorzeny was arrested as part of the denazification process and sent to an internment camp in Darmstadt. He managed to escape from the camp under mysterious circumstances… According to some reports, Skorzeny's escape was aided by a former member of his team, Olaf Todt…"

The screen showed photographs of Olaf from various years, including during the Nuremberg trials.

"During the trials in Nuremberg, Todt worked as an assistant to one of the German defense attorneys, but he was playing a double game. He had tight connections with American intelligence whilst at the same time he was helping his former comrades escape responsibility. For example, there are reasons to believe that he aided Hermann Goering's suicide, which helped that Nazi leader avoid hanging…"

Denis Rebrov, seated in the first row, looked pensively at Olaf Todt as he was photographed during the Nuremberg trials.

"After Nuremberg, Todt began working with West German intelligence. At the same time, according to the Simon Wiesenthal Center in Israel, he was assisting the Skorzeny-led groups Der Bruderschaft, ODESSA and Die Spinne. Thanks to these organizations, hundreds of former Nazis managed to get away and avoid responsibility."

A young Soviet officer squeezed through the door of the auditorium and discreetly walked down to Rebrov. "Comrade general, you are wanted on the phone. The call is for you personally, it's urgent."

Rebrov nodded. At the entrance to the auditorium a young German officer handed him the phone.

"Gen. Rebrov here."

"Hello Denis, its Gen. Svistun. We got a call from a checkpoint on the Berlin autobahn. A man there is claiming that he's a Soviet intelligence officer. Maybe you should send someone to have a look…"

"He didn't give his name?"

"No. He asks to meet with representatives of Soviet intelligence."

"Alright, I'll go down there myself."

At the checkpoint, on the line with West Berlin, Rebrov was met by a German border guard.

"I'm Gen. Rebrov from the KGB," Rebrov introduced himself as he got out of the car. "Where's the man you called about?"

"He's having breakfast. Please, this way…"

Rebrov threw open the door he was shown to. In the small room, a man with stubble was seated at the table and eagerly drinking coffee and eating a sandwich. Rebrov recognized him at once, and it was not hard, for in the last thirteen years he had hardly changed.

"Good lord, it's you, Kraft!" shouted Denis with joy. "At long last! We had completely lost track of you!"

"Denis? Rebrov! How did you get here?" Kraft jumped up. "I would have never imagined. Did you come here just to meet me?"

"No, I just happened to be here in Berlin on business. I'm flying out already this evening. What a coincidence!"

"I guess I'm lucky," laughed Kraft.

Rebrov turned to the border guard. "We'll take him from here." The guard answered with a salute.

In the car Rebrov besieged Kraft with questions. "What happened to you? Where did you disappear to? We didn't know what to think!"

"A couple of months ago I suddenly realized that they were on to me and getting close. They were following my every move. They didn't have any proof, but it was clear that things were looking bad for me. Sooner or later, they'd get me all the same. I ran to Europe, but they tracked me down, even here."

"You couldn't give us a heads-up?"

"Sadly, no. I realized that I had to completely get away, and the easiest place to do this was Berlin. I flew to West Berlin on a British passport. Then I wandered into a checkpoint like the prodigal son."

"God, you can't imagine how shocked I was when I came back to Moscow after the trials and found out that the cocky American businessman Kraft was actually our agent Hector. They were one and the same! In Nuremberg I had been completely convinced that you were really working for the American intelligence and trying to get some information out of me. When Gen. Filin was leaving his position and handing things over to me, he told me this and I couldn't believe my ears. He laughed as he saw me sitting there slack-jawed!"

"How is he doing, by the way?"

"Sergei Ivanovich died. He had a bad heart…"

That year the first ever Moscow Film Festival took place; it was an extraordinary event. Throngs of people besieged the cinemas where the festival's films were screened. All of Moscow was bedecked with posters for *Fate of a Man*, where Sergei Bondarchuk played a prisoner in a Nazi concentration camp.

As they walked unhurriedly down a busy Moscow street, Rebrov and Kraft paused at one of these posters.

"Do you ever look back at Nuremberg?" asked Kraft.

"Quite often. Especially Peggy," laughed Rebrov. "Could you ever forget something like that?"

"Peggy's not with us any more, Denis."

Stunned, Rebrov stopped. "I can't believe it. Peggy… What happened?"

"A year ago she found out that there was a whole town in the mountains of Bolivia where Nazis who fled Germany had settled. She felt it was her duty, her duty as a human being who had seen Nuremberg firsthand, to go there and write what was going on there. I saw her before she left, I warned her that it might be dangerous. But you know how Peggy was, it's impossible to stop her from doing something. She went there anyway, and then… She never came back."

"Was she killed?"

"Nobody knows. She simply never came back."

They walked together for a moment in silence.

"Do you remember Princess Kurakina?" Kraft suddenly asked in a rather enigmatic tone. "The one you had a thing for? Come on, don't be ashamed! By the way, back then in Nuremberg I didn't understand what she meant with those two words she asked Peggy to tell you, 'pure Monday.'"

"She meant the short story by Bunin. The woman in the story sacrifices her love and retreats to a nunnery."

"So that was it," said Kraft. After they had taken a few steps he stopped, turned to Rebrov, and softly but insistently said, "Life's not a short story, Denis."

"What do you mean?"

"I mean what I said. Life isn't a short story with a definite ending. It's a long novel where victory can turn into defeat and a catastrophe might become a great triumph."

"What are you talking about?"

"I saw Princess Kurakina in Paris when I was traveling around Europe."

"When?"

"Six months ago. She lectures in the history of Russian culture at the Sorbonne."

"So, she…"

"No, she didn't retreat to a nunnery. She was a novice, preparing to take vows, but then realized that she wasn't ready to make such a choice. She's still a princess, by the way, as she never married. Do you know why I'm telling you all this?"

"Agent Hector is used to reporting any secret developments," Rebrov awkwardly tried to joke the tension away.

"Well, maybe. But now agent Hector is reporting that a delegation of French film people will arrive in Moscow today on a visit, and amongst them, as an interpreter, is Irina Kurakina…"

The press conference of the dazzling French film stars was buzzing and lively. Princess Kurakina and another interpreter struggled to keep up with the rapid exchange of questions and answers.

Suddenly, Irina felt someone looking at her. She turned and saw Rebrov. He looked at her with a persistent gaze, and at that moment she admitted what she had been afraid to admit earlier: she had come to Moscow only for this encounter, the consequences of which she could not imagine and did not even try to.

Notes

How everything was going to end, I did not know
and tried not to think about. All of this kept
me in an endless, unresolved tension, a painful
anticipation, and yet, at the same time, I was
happy beyond words…

Ivan Bunin, "Pure Monday"

The Flying Dutchman

by Anatoly Kudryavitsky

Some time in the 1970s, Konstantin Alpheyev, a well-known Russian musicologist, finds himself in trouble with the KGB, the Russian secret police, after the death of his girlfriend, for which one of their officers may have been responsible. He has to flee from the city and to go into hiding. He rents an old house located on the bank of a big Russian river, and lives there like a recluse observing nature and working on his new book about Wagner. The house, a part of an old barge, undergoes strange metamorphoses rebuilding itself as a medieval schooner, and Alpheyev begins to identify himself with the Flying Dutchman. Meanwhile, the police locate his new whereabouts and put him under surveillance. A chain of strange events in the nearby village makes the police officer contact the KGB, and the latter figure out who the new tenant of the old house actually is.

Buy it > www.glagoslav.com

Nikolai Gumilev's Africa

Gumilev holds a unique position in the history of Russian poetry as a result of his profound involvement with Africa. He extensively wrote both poetry and prose on the culture of the continent in general and on Ethiopia (Abyssinia, as it was called in Gumilev's time) in particular. During his abbreviated lifetime Gumilev made four trips to Northern and Eastern Africa, the most extensive of which was a 1913 expedition to Abyssinia undertaken on assignment from the St. Petersburg Imperial Museum of Anthropology and Ethnography. During that trip Gumilev collected Ethiopian folklore and ethnographic objects, which, upon his return to St. Petersburg, he deposited at the Museum. He and his assistant Nikolai Sverchkov also made more than 200 photographs that offer a unique picture of the African country in the early part of the century.

This volume collects all of Gumilev's poetry and prose written about Africa for the first time as well as a number of the photographs that he and Nikolai Sverchkov took during their trip that give a fascinating view of that part of the world in the early twentieth century.

A Brown Man in Russia
Lessons Learned on the Trans-Siberian
by Vijay Menon

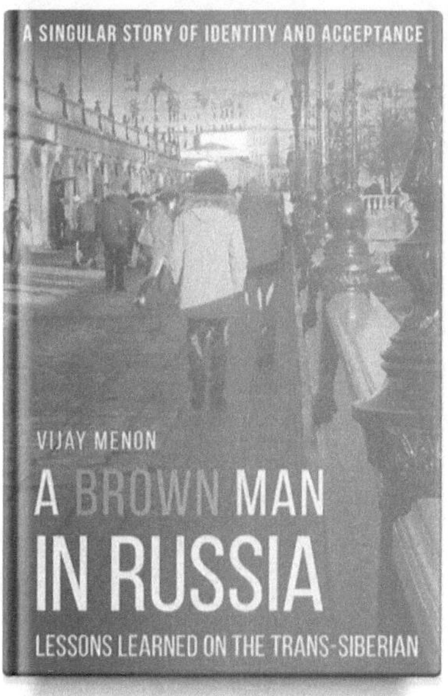

A Brown Man in Russia describes the fantastical travels of a young, colored American traveler as he backpacks across Russia in the middle of winter via the Trans-Siberian. The book is a hybrid between the curmudgeonly travelogues of Paul Theroux and the philosophical works of Robert Pirsig. Styled in the vein of Hofstadter, the author lays out a series of absurd, but true stories followed by a deeper rumination on what they mean and why they matter. Each chapter presents a vivid anecdote from the perspective of the fumbling traveler and concludes with a deeper lesson to be gleaned. For those who recognize the discordant nature of our world in a time ripe for demagoguery and for those who want to make it better, the book is an all too welcome antidote. It explores the current global climate of despair over differences and outputs a very different message – one of hope and shared understanding. At times surreal, at times inappropriate, at times hilarious, and at times deeply human, *A Brown Man in Russia* is a reminder to those who feel marginalized, hopeless, or endlessly divided that harmony is achievable even in the most unlikely of places.

Buy it > www.glagoslav.com

Glagoslav Publications Catalogue

- *The Time of Women* by Elena Chizhova
- *Andrei Tarkovsky: The Collector of Dreams* by Layla Alexander-Garrett
- *Andrei Tarkovsky - A Life on the Cross* by Lyudmila Boyadzhieva
- *Sin* by Zakhar Prilepin
- *Hardly Ever Otherwise* by Maria Matios
- *Khatyn* by Ales Adamovich
- *The Lost Button* by Irene Rozdobudko
- *Christened with Crosses* by Eduard Kochergin
- *The Vital Needs of the Dead* by Igor Sakhnovsky
- *The Sarabande of Sara's Band* by Larysa Denysenko
- *A Poet and Bin Laden* by Hamid Ismailov
- *Watching The Russians (Dutch Edition)* by Maria Konyukova
- *Kobzar* by Taras Shevchenko
- *The Stone Bridge* by Alexander Terekhov
- *Moryak* by Lee Mandel
- *King Stakh's Wild Hunt* by Uladzimir Karatkevich
- *The Hawks of Peace* by Dmitry Rogozin
- *Harlequin's Costume* by Leonid Yuzefovich
- *Depeche Mode* by Serhii Zhadan
- *The Grand Slam and other stories (Dutch Edition)*
  by Leonid Andreev
- *METRO 2033 (Dutch Edition)* by Dmitry Glukhovsky
- *METRO 2034 (Dutch Edition)* by Dmitry Glukhovsky
- *A Russian Story* by Eugenia Kononenko
- *Herstories, An Anthology of New Ukrainian Women Prose Writers*
- *The Battle of the Sexes Russian Style* by Nadezhda Ptushkina
- *A Book Without Photographs* by Sergey Shargunov
- *Down Among The Fishes* by Natalka Babina
- *disUNITY* by Anatoly Kudryavitsky
- *Sankya* by Zakhar Prilepin
- *Wolf Messing* by Tatiana Lungin
- *Good Stalin* by Victor Erofeyev
- *Solar Plexus* by Rustam Ibragimbekov

- *Don't Call me a Victim!* by Dina Yafasova
- *Poetin (Dutch Edition)* by Chris Hutchins and Alexander Korobko
- *A History of Belarus* by Lubov Bazan
- *Children's Fashion of the Russian Empire* by Alexander Vasiliev
- *Empire of Corruption - The Russian National Pastime* by Vladimir Soloviev
- *Heroes of the 90s: People and Money. The Modern History of Russian Capitalism*
- *Fifty Highlights from the Russian Literature (Dutch Edition)* by Maarten Tengbergen
- *Bajesvolk (Dutch Edition)* by Mikhail Khodorkovsky
- *Tsarina Alexandra's Diary (Dutch Edition)*
- *Myths about Russia* by Vladimir Medinskiy
- *Boris Yeltsin: The Decade that Shook the World* by Boris Minaev
- *A Man Of Change: A study of the political life of Boris Yeltsin*
- *Sberbank: The Rebirth of Russia's Financial Giant* by Evgeny Karasyuk
- *To Get Ukraine* by Oleksandr Shyshko
- *Asystole* by Oleg Pavlov
- *Gnedich* by Maria Rybakova
- *Marina Tsvetaeva: The Essential Poetry*
- *Multiple Personalities* by Tatyana Shcherbina
- *The Investigator* by Margarita Khemlin
- *The Exile* by Zinaida Tulub
- *Leo Tolstoy: Flight from paradise* by Pavel Basinsky
- *Moscow in the 1930* by Natalia Gromova
- *Laurus (Dutch edition)* by Evgenij Vodolazkin
- *Prisoner* by Anna Nemzer
- *The Crime of Chernobyl: The Nuclear Goulag* by Wladimir Tchertkoff
- *Alpine Ballad* by Vasil Bykau
- *The Complete Correspondence of Hryhory Skovoroda*
- *The Tale of Aypi* by Ak Welsapar
- *Selected Poems* by Lydia Grigorieva
- *The Fantastic Worlds of Yuri Vynnychuk*

- *The Garden of Divine Songs and Collected Poetry of Hryhory Skovoroda*
- *Adventures in the Slavic Kitchen: A Book of Essays with Recipes*
- *Seven Signs of the Lion* by Michael M. Naydan
- *Forefathers' Eve* by Adam Mickiewicz
- *One-Two* by Igor Eliseev
- *Girls, be Good* by Bojan Babić
- *Time of the Octopus* by Anatoly Kucherena
- *The Grand Harmony* by Bohdan Ihor Antonych
- *The Selected Lyric Poetry Of Maksym Rylsky*
- *The Shining Light* by Galymkair Mutanov
- *The Frontier: 28 Contemporary Ukrainian Poets - An Anthology*
- *Acropolis: The Wawel Plays* by Stanisław Wyspiański
- *Contours of the City* by Attyla Mohylny
- *Conversations Before Silence: The Selected Poetry of Oles Ilchenko*
- *The Secret History of my Sojourn in Russia* by Jaroslav Hašek
- *Mirror Sand: An Anthology of Russian Short Poems in English Translation* (A Bilingual Edition)
- *Maybe We're Leaving* by Jan Balaban
- *Death of the Snake Catcher* by Ak Welsapar
- *A Brown Man in Russia: Perambulations Through A Siberian Winter* by Vijay Menon
- *Hard Times* by Ostap Vyshnia
- *The Flying Dutchman* by Anatoly Kudryavitsky
- *Nikolai Gumilev's Africa* by Nikolai Gumilev
- *Combustions* by Srđan Srdić
- *The Sonnets* by Adam Mickiewicz
- *Dramatic Works* by Zygmunt Krasiński
- *Four Plays* by Juliusz Słowacki
- *Little Zinnobers* by Elena Chizhova
- *Duel* by Borys Antonenko-Davydovych
- *The Hemingway Game* by Evgeni Grishkovets
- *Mikhail Bulgakov: The Life and Times* by Marietta Chudakova

More coming soon...

- *Don't Call me a Victim!* by Dina Yafasova
- *Poetin (Dutch Edition)* by Chris Hutchins and Alexander Korobko
- *A History of Belarus* by Lubov Bazan
- *Children's Fashion of the Russian Empire* by Alexander Vasiliev
- *Empire of Corruption - The Russian National Pastime* by Vladimir Soloviev
- *Heroes of the 90s: People and Money. The Modern History of Russian Capitalism*
- *Fifty Highlights from the Russian Literature (Dutch Edition)* by Maarten Tengbergen
- *Bajesvolk (Dutch Edition)* by Mikhail Khodorkovsky
- *Tsarina Alexandra's Diary (Dutch Edition)*
- *Myths about Russia* by Vladimir Medinskiy
- *Boris Yeltsin: The Decade that Shook the World* by Boris Minaev
- *A Man Of Change: A study of the political life of Boris Yeltsin*
- *Sberbank: The Rebirth of Russia's Financial Giant* by Evgeny Karasyuk
- *To Get Ukraine* by Oleksandr Shyshko
- *Asystole* by Oleg Pavlov
- *Gnedich* by Maria Rybakova
- *Marina Tsvetaeva: The Essential Poetry*
- *Multiple Personalities* by Tatyana Shcherbina
- *The Investigator* by Margarita Khemlin
- *The Exile* by Zinaida Tulub
- *Leo Tolstoy: Flight from paradise* by Pavel Basinsky
- *Moscow in the 1930* by Natalia Gromova
- *Laurus (Dutch edition)* by Evgenij Vodolazkin
- *Prisoner* by Anna Nemzer
- *The Crime of Chernobyl: The Nuclear Goulag* by Wladimir Tchertkoff
- *Alpine Ballad* by Vasil Bykau
- *The Complete Correspondence of Hryhory Skovoroda*
- *The Tale of Aypi* by Ak Welsapar
- *Selected Poems* by Lydia Grigorieva
- *The Fantastic Worlds of Yuri Vynnychuk*

- *The Garden of Divine Songs and Collected Poetry of Hryhory Skovoroda*
- *Adventures in the Slavic Kitchen: A Book of Essays with Recipes*
- *Seven Signs of the Lion* by Michael M. Naydan
- *Forefathers' Eve* by Adam Mickiewicz
- *One-Two* by Igor Eliseev
- *Girls, be Good* by Bojan Babić
- *Time of the Octopus* by Anatoly Kucherena
- *The Grand Harmony* by Bohdan Ihor Antonych
- *The Selected Lyric Poetry Of Maksym Rylsky*
- *The Shining Light* by Galymkair Mutanov
- *The Frontier: 28 Contemporary Ukrainian Poets - An Anthology*
- *Acropolis: The Wawel Plays* by Stanisław Wyspiański
- *Contours of the City* by Attyla Mohylny
- *Conversations Before Silence: The Selected Poetry of Oles Ilchenko*
- *The Secret History of my Sojourn in Russia* by Jaroslav Hašek
- *Mirror Sand: An Anthology of Russian Short Poems in English Translation* (A Bilingual Edition)
- *Maybe We're Leaving* by Jan Balaban
- *Death of the Snake Catcher* by Ak Welsapar
- *A Brown Man in Russia: Perambulations Through A Siberian Winter* by Vijay Menon
- *Hard Times* by Ostap Vyshnia
- *The Flying Dutchman* by Anatoly Kudryavitsky
- *Nikolai Gumilev's Africa* by Nikolai Gumilev
- *Combustions* by Srđan Srdić
- *The Sonnets* by Adam Mickiewicz
- *Dramatic Works* by Zygmunt Krasiński
- *Four Plays* by Juliusz Słowacki
- *Little Zinnobers* by Elena Chizhova
- *Duel* by Borys Antonenko-Davydovych
- *The Hemingway Game* by Evgeni Grishkovets
- *Mikhail Bulgakov: The Life and Times* by Marietta Chudakova

More coming soon...